HOME . . .TO

Before a cold purple dusk, Marie Therese beheld a village ahead, the lodges glowing from the fires within, each an amber cone against an indigo sky, the sight so beautiful and welcoming that her soul soared like an eagle. A full moon painted the village in pastels, and she could see the darkness of the horse herd, the silver of smoke drifting from the vents, the poles of countless lodges pricking the early stars, and beyond the somber black ridge of the Rockies.

And even as she stood on the ridge absorbing a sight so sweet she could not fathom her own feelings, she saw horsemen approach at a trot, and knew the village police, the Mad Dog Society, had seen her. She awaited them calmly, joyous that her journey was coming to an end and that she was safe. Maybe this was her mother's band!

They reined in their ponies around her and stared, their hands not far from their war clubs and lances. They didn't look at all friendly and suddenly Marie Therese feared for her life. . . .

Rivers West
Ask your bookseller for the books you have missed.

Book 1 — THE YELLOWSTONE by Win Blevins
Book 2 — THE SMOKY HILL by Don Coldsmith
Book 3 — THE COLORADO by Gary McCarthy
Book 4 — THE POWDER RIVER by Win Blevins
Book 5 — THE RUSSIAN RIVER by Gary McCarthy
Book 6 — THE ARKANSAS RIVER by Jory Sherman
Book 7 — THE AMERICAN RIVER by Gary McCarthy
Book 8 — THE SNAKE RIVER by Win Blevins

RIVERS WEST
Book 9

THE TWO MEDICINE RIVER

Richard S. Wheeler

DOMAIN™

BANTAM BOOKS

NEW YORK • TORONTO • LONDON • SYDNEY • AUCKLAND

THE TWO MEDICINE RIVER

A Bantam Domain Book / May 1993

ISBN 0-553-29771-6

Published simultaneously in the United States and Canada

Bantam Books are published by Bantam Books, a division of Bantam Doubleday Dell Publishing Group, Inc. Its trademark, consisting of the words "Bantam Books" and the portrayal of a rooster, is Registered in U.S. Patent and Trademark Office and in other countries. Marca Registrada. Bantam Books, 1540 Broadway, New York, New York 10036.

PRINTED IN THE UNITED STATES OF AMERICA

RAD 0 9 8 7 6 5 4 3 2 1

For Jon Tuska and Vicki Piekarski,
with admiration

"I only know the names of three savages upon the Plains—Colonel Baker, General Custer, and at the head of all, General Sheridan."

—WENDELL PHILLIPS

Women and babes shrieking awoke
To perish 'mid the battle smoke,
Murdered or turned out there to die
Beneath the stern, gray, wintry sky.

Both quoted in *The Reformers and the American Indian* by Robert Winston Mardock

Author's Note

The Two Medicine River rises in the eastern slope of the Rocky Mountains not far south of the Canadian border. It drains lovely alpine lakes in what is now Glacier Park and flows easterly through mountains and rough foothills; through deep canyons and out upon the great plains, which are ridged and broken in that area. The Two Medicine debouches into the Marias River, which flows east and then south, discharging its waters into the Missouri, a little east of Fort Benton. These two rivers lie in the heart of the Blackfoot country, and were favorite hunting and camping haunts of the Blackfoot tribe. Together, they form the locale of this story.

There are at least two variations of its name. James Willard Schultz, who lived among the Blackfeet during the latter part of the nineteenth century, calls it the Two Medicine Lodges River, Matoki Okas. But Walter McClintock, who lived for a while with the Blackfeet around the turn of the century, was told that the river acquired its name from two connected piskuns, or buffalo jumps, places of great medicine for a people wanting meat. Whether the river was named after medicine lodges or buffalo jumps, it is a mythic and important river to the Piegan and Blood Blackfeet who lived along its banks.

Part One

THE RIVER

Chapter One

She felt his gaze again, and turned her back to him. A nun's back, she supposed, black broadcloth and a knit shawl, though she wasn't a nun. Her blue-tinted jet hair told him that.

Beneath her she felt the sinister throb of the *St. Ange,* the steam demons slowly churning the paddle wheel at the rear, pushing the packet into the chocolate water of the Missouri. She clutched the rail and watched St. Louis diminish in morning fog, dark buildings on long bluffs under a cast-iron sky, and with it, a part of her life.

She had grown used to the stares of men, even at age fifteen and even as a convent girl. It had started two or three years earlier among the brothers of her classmates, and their fathers, and sometimes their beaux. The sisters had noticed too, and had alternately delighted at the attentions men paid to Marie Therese, and scolded and warned. But mostly, she thought, they had delighted in it. How the Sisters of the Sacred Heart loved to encourage good Catholic marriages!

But it puzzled her even so. Just as the unwavering gaze she felt upon her back puzzled her now, when she wished to be alone with the image of St. Louis growing dim on the gray horizon. It must be that he noticed her height, she thought. She towered above the other girls; above many men. It didn't embarrass her as it might some girls. Her father's blood hadn't made her tall, but her mother's Piegan blood, the blood of Meadowlark, had fashioned her. The thought of her mother awakened some sort of emotion she couldn't identify. She hadn't seen Meadowlark for eight years.

An amulet of agate shaped into a tiny buffalo dangled between her breasts, suspended by a cord of rawhide. It was Meadowlark's gift to the seven-year-old girl about to go down the river to be schooled. Marie Therese had swiftly hidden it back then, when she learned such things were idols and forbidden. But now she wore it. Meadowlark's gift was a powerful totem of the Piegan people, with good medicine in it; but above, resting on the loose bodice of her dress, dangled a silver crucifix suspended from a necklace of turquoise-colored beads.

She watched the wooded shores roll by, and heard the slap and gurgle of water hammering on the hull. Smoke from the twin chimneys of the *St. Ange* sometimes whirled down on her, leaving grit and ash in her nostrils. And still the boy behind her gawked.

Perhaps, she thought, she should turn and face him; let him see her blood. Let him see her brown flesh and her heavy cheekbones. She had never understood why Indians had been called redskins. Hers was golden brown, and so was the flesh of all of her mother's people, the Pikuni the whites called Piegan, the Kainah they called Bloods, and the Siksika they called Blackfeet. Let him see her flesh and that would stop the staring. It often did. No matter how welcome mountain children had been in St. Louis, she had found that barrier everywhere, unspoken. Sometimes even among the sisters.

She had to turn and face him anyway. She felt trapped at the rail, with no place to go but overboard into the murky river. Her few things had been stowed by a porter back in the women's cabin over the thundering paddle wheel, beneath one of the six bunks in that common room. She'd go there, where men were forbidden, now that the city had been ripped from her vision and the monotonous shores offered nothing.

She turned to face the boy, some reserve in her face, and met his gaze coldly. He surprised her a little. His face looked as dark as her own, a little redder perhaps, and the features of two races melded in him as it did in her. Skinny, she thought. Hair oddly red on an Indian face. Dressed in a gray suit jacket and baggy britches.

"I didn't know you had gray eyes," he said.

"Please stop staring at me," she replied. Her gray eyes had been one of the gifts from her father, Charles Pierre Jacques Eduard de Paris. They didn't fit in her Pikuni face; they didn't belong, and they always startled people.

From him she had those eyes and a thin nose and sharp chinline and small bones and a knowledge of French and English and maybe even some of his peculiar arrogance. Yes, she thought, she especially had that. He'd always somehow seemed above the American Fur Company's other engagés, and even looked different from them, slim and patrician, while they were burly and rough and hearty.

"I think I know you," the boy said.

She'd been pushing past him, but paused.

"I think you're Marie Therese de Paris. I remember when you went away."

He'd surprised her. She stared back, dredging memories from her childhood. She wasn't sure at first. Could he be that boy?

"You are Peter Kipp."

He grinned triumphantly. "I've been to school here, same as you," he said. "Only we aren't Catholic."

She stared uncertainly. He'd been such a quiet boy. Now he seemed different, bold, almost insolent, with a wide grin that mocked her. "You kept looking at me," she said, to put him off balance.

"I couldn't help it. You're beautiful, Marie Therese. Now that I'm grown-up, I see things—"

"Neither of us are grown-up."

"I'm seventeen."

People had joked that Peter Kipp's father was the American Fur Company. In 1840, when he was about five, a Salish woman had come to Fort McKenzie and handed the half-breed boy to the factor there, Alec Culbertson. "The child is yours," she had said. "His name is Peter." And she'd left without revealing anything more. Peter. They'd all studied the boy's face and red hair and guessed at the father. Young James Kipp, even then a veteran American Fur Company trader, took the boy in and raised him, or rather, his lovely Mandan wife Ipasha, or Good Eagle Tail, had. No one ever supposed Kipp had sired the child.

"I must go to my cabin now," Marie Therese said.

"Why do that? We have a whole steamboat to see. Don't you want to see it? We can go anywhere, I guess."

"I don't like the boat."

"Why?" he asked, intensely curious.

"The underwater spirits are bad."

"Bad medicine!" He laughed. "Bad medicine! Do you still believe that stuff?"

She refused to reply. Meadowlark had told her long ago that the things under the water were dark spirits, like the things under the earth. The *St. Ange* crawled with them. She felt the packet shudder with dark spirits, felt the steam from dark fires make the boat go upstream against the current.

"I see you do," he said a little scornfully. "This isn't magic. It's the machinery of white men, harnessing the powers of nature. The fires make steam and the steam pushes two big pistons connected to pitman rods which are connected to the paddle wheel. It is all perfectly sensible to rational minds. It is all science. Didn't they teach you that Indian religion is all superstition?"

"Yes," she said reluctantly. The sisters had told her that all the spirits the Pikuni respected were idols and evil. Marie Therese had tried to believe them; tried to believe that the only God was the invisible one above and the visible one on the cross. It troubled her.

"Then you should forget all those silly myths. Just because our mothers had them doesn't mean they're right."

She was suddenly aware of the amulet under the

bodice of her dress. It troubled her. Everything that divided her mother's beliefs from her father's beliefs troubled her.

"Let's go looking around," he said. "Since the fur company chartered the *St. Ange*, it's like we own it, almost."

She didn't reply, but didn't resist. She hadn't intended to explore the evil fireboat because of the bad spirits she felt everywhere. She meant to cloister herself in the cabin. But Peter's enthusiasm tugged at her.

She followed the boy past cords of firewood destined to make steam, past deck passengers making camp as comfortably as they could. Peter headed for the companionway that would take them up to the boiler deck, where the cabins and staterooms were, as well as the segregated men's and women's lounges fore and aft. But he didn't pause there. He tackled the next companionway, while she tagged behind, her heart racing with the sudden exertion. This one took them to the top deck, the texas deck, a dizzy height above the river. The pilothouse perched here, and just behind it the texas, or officers' quarters.

"See!" he cried. "Feel the power of it! Don't you see?"

She felt the power, the throb of the engines. Just above her the twin chimneys belched black smoke and ash. White men had harnessed the power of fire and water to make the *St. Ange* run against the Big River. That was the Pikuni name for the Missouri—the Big River. In the pilothouse she saw a steersman and another in blue uniform, Joseph La Barge, the ship's master, pilot, and owner. No man, they said, knew the river better. Before her, rising from the main deck, were wooden booms and spars, and beyond them, the shimmering flood that would take her home . . . home to a place she'd never seen and a father she barely remembered.

Dizzily she peered down at the river far below, feeling the power of the white men. Near the prow she saw two priests. She knew the name of one of them. Any Blackfoot would. She cried out, feeling the water demons convulse the packet, and ran for the companionway.

"Where are you going, Marie Therese?" Peter cried.

"I'm afraid," she said, descending the stair as fast as

her skirts would let her. She reached the boiler deck and raced down the corridor dividing the staterooms, reaching the women's lounge, a tiny cubicle actually, and then the women's cabin behind it. Just beyond it the wooden paddle wheel splashed and rumbled and sprayed her fear back upon her.

They stood at the bow of the boat on a sultry afternoon watching sweating deckhands hoist lengths of ash and oak aboard to feed the hungry firebox. Eighteen cords a day, and whenever wood wasn't available from the wood yards along the banks, Captain La Barge sent his crew and passengers to the forested flats along the river to cut fuel.

She wore her cream dimity with the frills about the neck, but in the oppressive heat of the river snaking by, it seemed as heavy as her black woolen dress. From the time she'd arrived in St. Louis and the lower river, she'd hated summers and hungered for the dry air of her homeland far, far away. Her underthings stuck to her, and her body felt greased and dirty, as if the moist air would not let her flesh breathe.

Peter didn't seem to mind. The ebullient boy didn't mind anything, including her cold stares and reluctant companionship. In truth, she'd become fond of him. He made her laugh. His shining eyes were seeing the universe in ways her own eyes hadn't, and slowly she'd come to enjoy that, and him.

"Marie Therese," he said solemnly, "would you listen carefully, and even if you oppose what I ask, would you take me seriously?"

He peered earnestly at her, his face glistening with sweat, his eyes searching her own and then traveling longingly to her breast, whose contours were visible under the light dimity.

"Yes, Peter," she replied, sensing his earnestness.

"Would you marry me? I love you."

"Peter!"

But she saw such longing in his face, she didn't laugh, though the question was ridiculous. Behind him she watched sweat-blackened deckhands carry the logs up a gangplank and pile them neatly near the firebox.

"Marie Therese, I know you're young. Fifteen's young to marry. I know I'm just starting. I'm going to rise in the fur company. I'm going to the top. I'm going to become a chief trader at one of the posts. Maybe even a partner of old Chouteau, like Alec Culbertson. I'm going to do it, Marie Therese. . . ."

She smiled at Peter, knowing what her answer would have to be. But still she enjoyed this. No one had ever proposed to her before. The sisters had talked about it all the time. Say yes to a good Catholic man, they had said, but don't let him touch you until after the nuptials. Now here was a boy, not a man, and a Protestant too. But that didn't matter.

"Marie Therese, we're mixed-bloods, you and me. You know how it is, what they think of half-breeds. Some of them call us bastards, or mountain children, because there are no priests and ministers up the river. You know how it is. But if we marry, if we stay together . . . Don't you see? The fur company's a safe place for us, don't you see? What does it matter, what they think down here? We'll be us there, where it's cool and good. I can make us a good living with the company, don't you see? I know all the things of the whites. We can take these to our mothers' people—the Pikuni, the Salish, and give them—"

"Peter," she said, "I don't like the world of the whites. What they do. What they think. How they treat me. How they treat my mother's people . . ."

"You haven't answered me."

"I can't. Not now. Maybe not ever, Peter."

"I'll ask you tomorrow," he replied. "And the next day and the next. I will ask you every day to Fort Benton, and then I'll ask you every day when we get there. I love you, Marie Therese."

She smiled. "You are a Protestant." She meant to say, You are a Christian, but didn't. She could not say what she was; only that other spirits tugged her soul.

He fell silent and together they watched from the rail

as the *St. Ange* built up steam until it throbbed from the escapement pipe and oily clouds of smoke belched toward ivory skies. She'd scarcely seen here a blue sky of the sort she had grown up with, on the high Missouri.

The sun dazzled off the water so viciously she wished she'd worn her one hat with its broad brim which shaded the eyes. She felt the prick of oily sweat collect around the amulet between her breasts. She could not marry Peter. Something else tugged at her. Something dim and strange had been forming in her soul—she liked that white man's word, soul—that would lead her along strange paths. Beautiful paths.

"I am Pikuni," she murmured to him, but he didn't notice. He paid rapt attention to everything on board, and now he watched the deckhands drag the gangplank aboard.

She felt the steam demons again, the hissing power of the *St. Ange* as it shuddered free of the levee and out upon the copper river. Far above, on the enameled texas deck, she saw Mrs. La Barge, Pelagie, who had come along with the captain this trip. And their children. They had two staterooms just behind the men's lounge far forward.

She saw the priests, still in their black cassocks, and wondered how they endured the steamy heat. One of them, the Jesuit Pierre-Jean DeSmet, had become a legend among her people. The other was new to her. Christopher Hoecken, she'd learned on the second day of the voyage. She'd learned the names of other passengers too, such as Dr. John Evans, a geologist. A man who examined the bones of mother earth. Somehow, he disturbed her. His irreverence for the earth mother disturbed her. Would he not let the spirits rest?

Around her on the burning deck a motley crowd of American Fur Company people, French Canadians, Scots, Missourians, Assiniboin, Sioux, Crow, and breeds like herself, all rank with oozing sweat, found shade against the murderous sun and waited for twilight. She thought of the shade of the women's cabin. But its fetid air and closed society deterred her. The few white women on board, bound for St. Joseph or Leavenworth mostly, had studied her dark skin coldly, unable to prevent such contact as they had, but not yielding an inch to her. Later, above Leavenworth, virtually everyone remaining on board would be connected in some way with the company. But until then she had no place to call her own.

An easterly tailwind pushed the packet, carrying on its hot breath the smell of the water closets perched aft on the main deck and projecting out from the coaming so that wastes dropped into the brown river—unless they streaked first along the stained hull just ahead of the wheelhouse. Couldn't these white people ever be clean? Why didn't they take sweats and wash each day in the river, as her mother's people did?

She found shade under the boiler deck, and relief from the nauseating odors around the stern. Peter followed her, as he always did, almost a shadow, wanting to squander every second on board this bad-medicine ship with her. She didn't mind. His blood was something like her own, Salish and perhaps Scottish Canadian, but at least mixed. And that made him precious to her. And he had become her protector too, fending off stinking men in buckskins and greasy calicos, whose stringy hair hadn't seen soap in months. Men with lidded eyes and something hungry in their gaze that always paused at her breasts and thighs.

Beside her a man with a wild mop of brown hair sketched deftly on a pad, catching a dozing mountain man slumped against cordwood. She peered at the sketch and marveled.

"You like it, yes? I am Rudolph Freidrich Kurz of Berne, Switzerland," he said in heavily accented English. "You are a daughter of the mountains, yes?"

She nodded warily. That could mean anything.

"I will sketch you next. What tribe do I see in your face, mademoiselle?"

"Pikuni—ah, Piegan. Ah, Blackfeet."

"Ah! You are from far above! That's where I am going, far west and north where the air is cool and this—this steam doesn't . . ." His voice faded off. "You have free will. I see it in you, free will. I will catch your inner spirit, your freedom!" Something in that excited her. Could this artist catch the thing inside of her, the Pikuni spirit, the medicine that separated her from whites, that separated her even from her father?

"I would like that!"

"Sketch me too," said Peter. "My mother is Salish."

Forward, near the booms, amidst a welter of crates mounded on the grubby deck, a crowd gathered around a writhing young man of the mountains who lay groaning and gasping air through his honey-colored beard.

The growing crowd caught her eye and chilled her. Kurz, still sketching, scarcely noticed. Peter glanced forward uneasily and then turned away. But she watched.

Slowly the man's writhing subsided, and then he lay quiet except for irregular gulps. He looked blue beneath the brown stain of outdoorsman's flesh. She stared at this bad medicine, seeing the Under-Earth Spirits dance about him, mesmerized by something evil that she had known would come, she had felt in this *St. Ange* ever since she stepped aboard and felt its chill.

And then the hot deck echoed with a terrible wail that rent the June afternoon, a word she had heard too often that year of 1851 and the previous years as well.

"Cholera, cholera . . ."

Chapter Two

Death . . . a plague packet.

It seemed to Peter that cholera perched atop the pilothouse far above, pointing now here, now there, striking men at random, with no respect for virtue or sin. The *St. Ange* plowed grimly up the white river while news of its cargo raced ahead by fast horse, faster by far than its slow passage up the twisting flood.

They docked at deserted woodlots whose proprietors had fled, and loaded the lengths of cordwood, carefully measured by the mate, under a broiling sun. At each site Captain La Barge left a receipt in a bottle, payable upon the ship's return or negotiable at St. Louis.

On board, people shrank from one another, ceased talking, stared bitterly into space, sweated in the heavy air, ignored the ash that cascaded from the chimneys onto them. Cabin passengers took to their bunks, dreading the burning deck.

A few died swiftly, as the first man had. Most died slowly, over two days or three, dehydrated by the convulsions of their bowels, unable to keep down any liquid. It struck some so swiftly they had no time to race to the cabinets aft. They could only drop their britches and spew the waste of their spasming bellies over the side, where it smeared its way down the white hull and into the murky river. Some couldn't wait at all, and the filth soaked their dungarees and oozed out upon the worn planks of the deck. Others, in the oppressive heat of their cabins, filled foul chamber pots so fast the cabin boys couldn't empty them. Cabin and stateroom passengers had only the enameled pots whose lids failed to contain the stench within.

Marie Therese had angrily retreated to her women's quarters, and Peter hadn't seen her in days, and wondered if she'd been stricken. Bad medicine! she'd cried. White men's evil! Until the white men came up the river, bearing their evils, her mother's people had scarcely known disease. But in 1837 the pox had come, wrapped in a foul blanket aboard the *St. Peter*—why did they name their evil ships after saints?—and slew a third of the Pikuni, and almost all the Mandans, and the Arikara and Assiniboin. . . . Did white men slay everyone? she'd asked, and then turned away, in tears. Peter hadn't seen her for three days.

Peter trudged the ship as if it were a hot frying pan, afraid to touch anything, peering at handrails with black suspicion, detouring around the few other passengers who walked, refusing to eat the poisoned food, terrified to put his lips to river water.

Death was everywhere, lurking, waiting to pounce. Just that hot morning he had watched a man who seemed well enough standing beside the rail amidships.

"Oh, no," the man had said quietly, walking stiffly rearward toward the closets. He'd emerged flushed and fevered. Wobbling forward to the foredeck, he settled down, his back to cordwood, and clutched his convulsing torso . . . doomed. Father Hoecken had spotted him and taken the man's cold hand into his own.

"Our good Lord awaits you on the other side, in Paradise," the priest had whispered.

"I don't want . . ." the man muttered.

"No one wants to die. But we go when we are called. What may I do for you? Are you baptized? Have you anything to confess?"

"Not Catholic."

The priest had nodded quietly. "Are there messages? Have you loved ones? Do you want to make a will?"

The man vomited, the treacly stuff sliding green across the hot deck.

"Yes," he'd whispered. "Tell my wife . . ."

Peter had watched, transfixed, as the bearded man in butternut homespun coughed out names and messages, while the Jesuit quietly penciled words on foolscap.

The man didn't die. He lay gasping and blue-fleshed as the pearly sun fried him through the afternoon. No one dared drag him to shade. But Father Hoecken brought him a tumbler of water with a little whiskey in it. The man gulped the liquid, and then vomited it out, wheezing. Peter stared frequently, morbidly curious about the moment when breath left the man; curious about what would happen. What would that man feel when it happened? Peter wondered whether he would see God and angels just beforehand, or demons . . . or nothing at all. What would it be like? He could scarcely imagine it.

Not me! he thought. Not me! I'm too young!

But he knew he wasn't too young. Terror drove him forward to the prow. That put death behind him, not ahead. Death back there, not up here! He closed his eyes, concentrating on his stomach. Was that quiver a first sign? He wiped his heated brow. Had he fevered? His forehead burned!

He felt a new throb in the hammering engines, felt them slow. He peered high up to the pilothouse, and made out the captain gesturing to the wheelsman, shouting down the speaking tube to the engineers on the main deck. The silent ship settled slightly in the coiling current and then slid north toward a wooded shore with a meadowed hill rising above it. Not a woodlot in sight, and it puzzled him. Slowly the silent packet eased toward the bank until the paddles ceased splashing and the boat glided almost to land.

Then he understood. Six crewmen with spades stood ready. And at their feet lay two bodies wrapped in ship's canvas. And above them stood the Jesuit Pierre-Jean DeSmet, florid and beefy-faced, a missal in hand, an ivory stole threaded with gold over his neck. Captain La Barge had stopped for a burying.

Something in Peter cried out to walk down the plank they were sliding out, to flee the packet while he could. The plank didn't quite reach land, disappearing into muddy water three feet from shore. He could run! Run! Deckhands splashed to the bank and made the boat fast, fore and aft, to brush.

"Who are they? Who died?" Peter asked a weathered man beside him, the geologist John Evans.

"Fur company men. Cadotte and Rambeau. Deck passengers. It seems to affect the deck passengers worse."

Peter knew Eduard Rambeau—he'd labored for years at Fort McKenzie. "I don't want to die!" he exclaimed.

Together they watched crewmen trudge up the hill and begin digging under a chalky sky, sweating in the glare of the river. Captain La Barge watched silently from the texas deck.

"Who are you, lad?" asked the geologist.

"Peter Kipp."

"James Kipp's son?"

"Sort of," Peter said shortly. "I live with them. I've been at school for seven years."

Something abrupt in his tone evoked a caution in the older man. "There's a way to fight the cholera, Peter. I've seen it work. Use a little spirits in everything; soak your food in spirits, dip bread in it. Never drink plain water, but mix some spirits in."

"How do you know that works?"

"I've seen it work. I'm out a lot—out beyond the cities, on the California Trail, and the Santa Fe. And I've been on the boats. Out where the claws of cholera stretch to rake us. Peter, lad, do as I ask, eh?"

"I don't drink spirits. I'm too young."

"Spirits are dangerous and you're wise, Peter. But use a little now. A little in everything you eat. Or at least wine with every meal. I've been telling that to a lot of people on board. Some follow it; most don't."

"Is it scientific?" Peter asked. Science impressed him

more than anything he'd learned in St. Paul's School for Boys, run by the Anglicans.

"I'm afraid not. We know no cause and effect. But if science observes and records results, then I'd say yes, it's scientific. So use spirits. Table wine. Or a little whiskey."

Peter had scarcely eaten since the packet had been stricken with disease. Meals were served on folding tables set up in the men's and women's lounges, mostly meats and vegetables cooked in a galley aft on the main deck and brought up to the boiler deck.

"I'm not hungry," Peter mumbled.

"You look starved. Eat, lad. But only as I say."

"Have you told the women? There's a friend of mine—Marie Therese de Paris. Would you tell her?"

"I have. The young lady refuses. She seems quite angry."

The deckhands were lowering the limp cylinders of canvas into the red clay on the hill above, and Peter watched silently, a safe distance from death. A breeze caught the robes of the two priests and flapped them as they read something. Peter caught a Latin word or phrase on the moist air, but could scarcely hear. Far upstream in a cooler and dryer land, two mountain widows would learn of this. Except for the distant murmur of priests, a suffocating quietness gripped the *St. Ange.*

They watched the burial party return down the emerald slope and board silently.

"I believe in science," Peter said. "It is power. Perhaps even power over death. My mother's people . . . she's Salish. Flathead. They believe in hoodoo—totems, earth spirits. Some became Catholics because that one"—he pointed at the ruddy, short priest, DeSmet—"that one came to them."

"He's a splendid man."

"Maybe he preaches white men's hoodoo."

Steam popped idly from the escapement, and only a thin smear of smoke lifted from the chimneys. From above, Captain La Barge snapped commands through a speaking horn, and the mate set the hands to doing something new.

They plucked buckets of silty water from the river, mixed it with quicklime, and splashed the decks, swirling away vomit and the offal of corrupted bowels, flooding the boat stem to stern, splashing odor and filth overboard—except where the bearded man gasped out his last hours next to the stack of cordwood. No one dared clean the foul deck under him.

"It's scarcely begun. And we haven't made Independence yet," Evans muttered.

Dawn. Walls. Outside the porthole a bronze mist. She could not bear this choking. The Under-Earth Spirits clamped her throat. Her heart raced. She threw the sheet off and bounded up, feeling the cling of her damp chemise. The two white women slept uneasily. The fetid air stuck in her throat, rejected by her lungs.

She hastened into her begrimed dress, wishing she might clean herself. Did these people never wash? She peered dourly at the enameled pot on the floor with its leaky lid, and scorned it. Let them have their pots and their stink. She would crouch on the deck. Spirits clawed at her, brushed by her, laughed silently. She ignored them and hooked her shoes tight, shoes that bit her feet and made her yearn for the high moccasins of her mother's people, and slid quietly through brown light to the door. It creaked.

More walls. Did white people have nothing but walls? The sisters hid behind walls, confined her within walls. And here on this packet there were walls everywhere, walls separating men from women so they could not even eat together. Walls. Cubicles, cells, prisons. She hastened across the silent women's lounge, feeling the scorn of the males who designed and built this little jail for women. She eased open the frosted-glass door into the corridor. More walls, but heading toward space, toward freedom. It was dark, with only the brown haze of dawn glowing at either end. But her heart slowed.

She found her way to the boiler-deck walk surrounding the cabins. Honey-colored light filtered through the cool haze. Honey light and violet shadow where dawn failed to pierce. Even the white enamel of the packet had been stained to copper by the sun shouldering over the horizon.

She sucked the bad air into her lungs and watched. Below, firemen were building the fire, stinging the steam demons. No one else stirred. Deck passengers lay in dark lumps surrounded by their gear. Some dead, she thought. Some would not rise this dawn because of the cholera stalking and laughing and telling evil people they must pay for their sins.

She padded down the companionway to the main deck, sliding past prone people, still deep in night fog. Aft, ever aft, toward the cabinets, toward the great paddle wheel resting in its casing until the steam demons maddened it. The odors choked her, and her heart started rambling again, but she stilled herself. She glared around, defying these people to stop her, and then squatted on the coaming, lifting her grimy skirts, and made water, waiting for the noise to stir someone, But nothing happened. She adjusted her skirts defiantly and padded up again.

She'd forgotten her hat, so she slipped back to the women's cabin, hating the way it choked off her air. She slid through two creaking doors and plucked the hat from her bunk. The fatter woman lay awake, staring. Silent. The pair of them had said nothing to the breed girl. Walls. The women talked as if Marie Therese didn't exist.

Walls and Underwater Spirits clawed at her. She bolted out and felt calm again as she swung up the companionway to the texas deck, the one that some called the hurricane. She saw two men in the pilothouse, but the texas itself, the officers' cabins, lay dark in the russet fog. One of the men was Captain La Barge, but he didn't see her because he leaned over something, charts perhaps.

She thought to head aft on the texas deck, as far aft as she could, but then spotted a ladder, slim dowels marching up to the top of the texas, to a gently curved roof there—the highest place. The roof of the pilothouse. Nimbly she sprang up the ladder and stepped out on the small rectangular deck, a dizzy distance from the main deck below.

She skidded on the dew-moist wood and feared she'd awaken the mate or someone else. But nothing happened. She settled down, feeling the dew soak through her dimity and linen, feeling the coldness wet her hand. There were no walls here. Her spirit quieted and she felt at home. This was her place. Everything had turned to brass now. The river mist shone the color of bugles, and the trees the color of cymbals and horns, and the river gleamed sulfurously below.

Perhaps they would drive her off, but for now she would stay, free at last from Underwater Spirits and walls. A thin stream of brown smoke boiled from the chimneys and lowered down on her, but she didn't mind. No steam yet; the escapement pipe didn't hiss and pop. Here she would stay, and when the sun pierced high, she'd wear her wide-brimmed hat. She didn't burn the way whites did. The honey brown of her flesh only deepened a little under the summer sun, turning her golden and making her gray eyes almost white.

Pale blue began to stain the sky and color seeped into the world. Below, people stirred and shouted, and all she heard was cholera and fear. Nothing would happen to her. Some medicine spirit, maybe sent by her mother, whispered to her not to be afraid of this white man's disease. The totem lying cool between her breasts reminded her. Far below, a cabin boy began dumping the contents of chamber pots over the side and then dipping the pots into the river to rinse them. What strange and fearsome people were these. They possessed the magic of fireboats and guns and blankets and the powder that flashes and bullet metals. Great medicine balanced by terrible diseases like pox, cholera, dysentery . . . and by walls. Walls between man and woman, between white people and hers, between those who could read and those who couldn't. Walls enclosing the virgins in the convent. Walls that turned their dwellings into caves.

The sun caught her and she blinked at its glare. Below, the deckhands noticed her and pointed. One trotted up the companionways carrying word of her to the mate. What law prevented her from being here, so high and free, away from walls and cholera? They would find one or invent one.

She heard muffled talk in the speaking tube of the pilothouse, and moments later Captain La Barge trotted back along the texas deck and peered upward. He was a blocky man in a rumpled suit, with lively eyes taking in her defiant stare.

"I rather like that place up there myself," he said. "King on the mountain. But no rails to hold you and a deck that curves."

"I would like to stay."

"I've never seen a lady there. But it seems a fine place for a young lady."

"I don't like walls."

"You don't like the cholera either, I imagine."

"The cholera won't touch me."

His eyes flicked briefly to the crucifix on her bodice. "Perhaps you're right, our Lord willing."

"My medicine," she retorted.

This time he studied her closer, absorbing the Indian in her. "Medicine, then," he agreed. He smiled. "We need whatever help may be granted to us. You are?"

"Marie Therese de Paris."

"Charles Pierre's daughter. I know him well. A fine Creole and an asset to AFC."

"I wouldn't know," she snapped.

"You've been in school? Perhaps Sacred Heart?"

"Yes."

"A mademoiselle grows tired of walls, eh?"

"I want the plains where my people are, where there is no wall and no fence and we go freely where we will and do what we will, all according to our good medicine, and live and die as we will after many winters. . . ."

"Ah! I've seen the magic of such places!"

"Then you won't mind my staying here?"

"It pleases me, Mademoiselle Marie Therese. But it'll become infernally hot soon."

"I have a hat."

"And we'll make Independence today. I'm expecting difficulty."

"The cholera?"

He nodded. "We have coffee and lemonade—we've a crate of New Orleans lemons aboard—and rolls in our little galley here. Shall I have the boy bring—"

"I can't eat—thank you. The wet air takes my hunger away. I won't eat until we reach the grasslands and the air become sweet and dry."

"That's a long way, a long way. You'd starve before then."

"Coffee with lots of sugar," she said.

He nodded and started forward. Then turned back. "If trouble comes, I'd like you to come down and protect yourself—behind walls. Sometimes people get hysterical about cholera."

Chapter Three

Under a brass sky the *St. Ange* drifted toward the levee, barely under power. A silent mob waited and watched. Deckhands threw lines to shore, but nobody caught them or made the packet fast.

Some of them carried arms, Peter noticed. Rifles and fowling pieces. All of them scowled at the crowd lining the main-deck rail of the packet.

"La Barge," said an older man in a dark frock coat. "You have cholera aboard?"

"I do," said the captain. Peter could see him standing quietly just outside the pilothouse, far above.

"Well, you're not stopping here, then."

"I have ten passengers for Independence. All healthy."

"No," the man said. Apparently he was the law here, though Peter saw no star or badge of office. "Anyone leaving that boat gets shot."

"I doubt that you'd murder," the captain replied quietly. He nodded at the mate, who barked a command. Deckmen retrieved the lines.

"You heard me. Get that boat out of here."

"We'll load firewood."

"I see a cord there; enough to get you and your plague boat away from Independence."

La Barge nodded and did nothing, letting the untethered packet slip slowly downstream.

"You want your mail?" the captain asked.

"You can throw it down here."

"Mail comes off with the passengers," La Barge replied.

"You can't refuse to deliver the St. Louis mail."

Near Peter the debarking passengers waited dourly, wanting to get to their destinations. Two women, eight men. At La Barge's command the wheel splashed and the boat drifted forward slowly, edging back to the levee.

"How many dead?" yelled the lawman.

"Nine, and one sick," replied La Barge.

Men on shore backed away at the news, shoved by some invisible hand.

"We'll unload upstream, above Independence," La Barge said.

"No you don't! We're following you."

"If you want your mail, make the ship fast."

This time men on shore reluctantly caught the thrown lines and snubbed them to posts. Deckhands dropped the gangplank while La Barge himself clambered down the companionways to the main deck and picked up a light canvas mail pouch.

"I warned you La Barge—first person to walk down that plank gets shot."

The captain ignored him, hoisted the pouch to his shoulder and walked. The bores of a dozen pieces swung toward him. Above, on the boiler deck, Pelagie La Barge moaned.

Peter gaped, scared that the captain would fall under a fusillade. Except for steam chuffing from the escapement pipe far above, a stretching silence settled over the levee.

The lawman pulled his frock coat back, exposing a brocaded ivory vest, and drew a Dragoon Colt.

"You heard me," he rasped.

La Barge kept walking.

The lawman shot, splintering plank a few feet ahead of the ship's master. Powder smoke hung blue in the morning air. La Barge stopped. The bores of a dozen rifles pointed at him now, in the hands of itchy-fingered men.

The lawman lifted the Colt until it aimed at La Barge's chest. "One more step, La Barge. It'd be a pleasure."

"Come back!" cried Peter. He couldn't bear what he had been witnessing.

"All right, then," La Barge said quietly, and retraced his steps.

"Leave the mail," the lawman yelled.

"It goes off when the passengers go off." The captain regained the ship without further trouble. "Are we taking on any new passengers?" he asked.

The mob glowered back, saying nothing.

"Very well, then," said La Barge. At his nod, deck-hands pulled in the gangplank.

"Don't let them off above town. We'll be following you," snapped the lawman. "Anyone sets foot on the Missouri shore, he gets shot."

La Barge ignored him and climbed slowly up the companionways. The firemen leapt to work, and steam soon snarled from the escapement pipe while the chimneys belched oily smoke into the morning skies.

The men of Independence were as good as their word. A posse of a dozen rode the bluffs above the river, following the boat upstream.

"I thought they'd kill him," Peter ventured to Dr. Evans.

"I confess, I did too. La Barge was fearless. Men with courage do amazing things, eh, Peter?"

"We're prisoners on this cholera boat," Peter said. "Everyone's afraid of dying. You could see it in them on the levee. I guess I am too. I wish I could get off this packet. I can't stand it anymore."

"Amazing," Evans muttered.

At Fort Leavenworth things went a bit easier. The army had dealt with cholera and plagues before, and would again. The sight of the post stretching up the slope from the glinting river stirred something in Peter. From here, the United States Army ruled the world, stretched its power clear out upon the prairies, even to Fort Union and Fort Benton, the jewels of American Fur Company.

Everything dazzled in the long light of early evening. Far up on the top of the bluff, white wood and brick. Stone and even log buildings neatly arrayed. Order and power under the penetrating, low sun. Shining brass, black cannon, and everywhere the genius of white men imposing sense upon chaos. But on the shadowed levee below him, Peter saw only one officer, a trim captain with sweat staining the armpits of his tunic, and several blue-shirted men.

"We won't search the packet, sir," the captain said to La Barge. "But we'll take your sworn word. Is this cargo manifest correct?"

"It is," said La Barge from high above.

"Have you spirits aboard?"

"Normal ship's stores, sir."

"How many dead?"

"Ah, ten now. No new cases at the moment. No, I take that back. The priest, Father Hoecken, tells me he's unwell. We have Father DeSmet with us also."

The army captain nodded. "We'll take your passengers, then. They'll be quarantined a few days, I'm afraid."

Peter felt dismayed. Father Hoecken? Who'd soothed dying souls, listened to dying men weep, taken messages, held clammy hands, sung solemn requiems on grassy hilltops, comforted men and women of all faiths . . . Father Hoecken ill?

Three weary women, all of them deck passengers, stumbled down to the shore and were marched off . . . laundresses . . . wives of noncoms. Then an auburn-haired woman who had been destined to land at Independence. Then others—gentlemen in rumpled frock coats; a few Independence-bound frontiersmen in butternut and calico and buckskins. And after that, their small possessions followed. The Independence mail pouch went last. Down on the levee the soldiers quietly circled around them, at a respectful quarantining distance. Brown twilight settled over the bottoms, and a breath of cooler air.

"We can't have you staying here tonight, Mr. La Barge. For obvious reasons," the army officer said.

"We'll go up a few miles," La Barge replied. "We need wood."

"Not from the military reservation," the captain replied.

Peter watched the debarked passengers being herded like prisoners toward their fate, their freedom taken from them for a few days. It made him oddly angry, as if the army were stealing a few days of their lives. He glanced toward the texas, seeking the small figure perched above, on the roof of the officers' quarters. She sat there in her wide-brimmed bonnet, staring at the departing column, the prisoners of cholera and the army.

Twice he'd tried to join Marie Therese up there, even during the heat of midday, and twice she'd angrily refused his company. He wanted hers more than anything. All through the sultry day, Captain La Barge had brought her things in cups and plates, and that angered him too—special treatment.

In the long June twilight, La Barge anchored on a wooded shore that lay indigo in the fading light. "All men off for a woodcutting detail," he announced.

Deckhands thrust axes and saws into the hands of reluctant male passengers and they all radiated out into a forest to harvest dead limbs and trees. Peter helped drag the long lengths of wood toward the riverbanks, where other sweat-washed crew members loaded it in the hot night air.

These packets ate so much wood, they'd soon strip the banks of the Missouri bare, he thought. That's how white people lived, using nature better than Indians did. When at last the task was done, the soaked men clambered back aboard. Peter glanced upward toward the stars above the texas deck. Marie Therese still sat there, a dark figure against the hollow night sky. Turning Piegan day by day, he realized, as if those sisters had never taught her a thing.

If anything, matters worsened above Fort Leavenworth. Vigilante gangs harassed the ship from both banks, shooting whenever it approached a woodlot. Missourians vigiled against it from the left bank; while over in the Indian Territory a similar mob of possemen stalked the plague packet. One barrage had drilled three holes in the chimneys, and now these spewed tiny horizontal streams of smoke up above Marie Therese. Once when the *St. Ange* approached a woodlot, a dozen rifles raked it, and one sent a ball through the thin wood of the pilothouse, barely missing the steersman.

"The imbeciles!" La Barge raged. But he pulled the packet into the main channel as fast as its splashing paddles permitted. He would not risk passengers' lives for that.

Marie Therese refused to budge from her perch on the texas.

"It's dangerous, mam'selle," La Barge snapped. "You come down. You're the most obvious target on the ship. They can't tell man from woman—especially not those human wolves. They think nothing of murder to keep cholera away."

"I'll come down if there's trouble," Marie Therese replied, but she never did, and the captain grumbled at her, threatening to remove her bodily. But he never did either. In any case, she could see them from her perch better than anyone; her Indian eyes caught glimpses of them on either bank, hunkered in ambush, and a word of warning from her sometimes kept the packet out of rifle shot.

So the plague ship churned north through a funnel of fear, stopping at islands for wood and anchoring at islands by night. It turned out to be not a bad thing. The fierce river had piled banks of driftwood about the upstream heads of many islands, sometimes into a ten- or fifteen-foot mountain of bleached dry wood that burned hotly. Some islands lay in shallows and could be reached only by splashing through knee-high water and muck. Passengers and crew alike toiled to cart the sandy wood out to the packet. Brutal toil, all of it, but the salvation of the *St. Ange*.

Two days later Jesuit father Christopher Hoecken died, after lingering on his shadowed bunk.

Posses were still potshooting at the packet when the Jesuit died, and the body of the priest lay hour after hour wrapped in canvas while worried passengers stared at it and

Father DeSmet peered grimly at distant green shores. But that lavender evening the channel curved sharply toward a high island and La Barge steered for its shore, relying on the soundings of deckmen at the prow. They made fast in a quiet hour sweetened by the chirp of crickets.

"We'll bury Father Hoecken here. Surely you'll join us, mam'selle. We owe our good priest that and more."

She agreed.

They buried Father Hoecken in apricot twilight on the knoll of a river island a day's journey above Fort Leavenworth. Buried the priest quietly and with tears, while Father DeSmet read a solemn prayer, his ruddy face alternately gaunt with grief and radiant with joy that so good a priest had come to the embrace of God. Marie Therese felt the familiar Latin roll over her, felt the mystery of death and the passage of a soul, saw the medicine of it hovering over the heads of the solemn assemblage of fur company engagés, river men, and a few Protestants. She felt the familiar tugging in two directions, the tugging of this sacred belief of the whites, and the tugging of the spirits known to the Pikuni and others of her tribes. They tossed the sandy river soil over Father Hoecken and fashioned a wooden cross to mark the place, and she walked slowly back to the packet, enjoying the land under her feet.

St. Joseph welcomed the packet with rifle shots and horsemen brandishing weapons. The rude town sprawling up hills around the site of the old Robidoux trading post, and now a jumping-off point for the great California Trail, had turned out for the plague packet armed and ready to kill. La Barge took note, and so did the dozen passengers scheduled to debark there.

"Take your safety, gentlemen," he called down. Some did, slipping behind cordwood or the boilers.

"Mam'selle," he said sternly, "at least take refuge on the lee side of the texas."

But she didn't. And in the end it didn't matter. The *St. Ange* never slowed, and the ominous mob didn't shoot. The packet slid past St. Joseph under a herringbone heaven and continued on up the glassy river in moist air. That cast-iron afternoon, three more took sick, two deck passengers and one deckhand.

North of St. Joseph settlement thinned. She rarely saw the riders along the riverbanks, and the packet churned ahead unmolested. Far below her men lay dying. She'd seen so much of it, she no longer recoiled the way she did at first. From her perch it seemed distant and abstract. The perch seemed a good place, above death, above the blinding glare of the river, above the heat of the sunbaked vessel, above the fetid women's cabin she'd abandoned. Nights, she rolled up in a blanket on the texas deck, alone and unmolested, free to watch the heavens rotate around Polaris, the North Star. While the world slept she slipped down to the main deck to the island shores and there scrubbed herself and took care of her simple needs. A time or two she'd caught Peter staring up at her from his post at the prow, wanting to talk. Such a puppy dog! she'd thought. He was two years older but she felt like she was the elder. She discouraged his attentions.

Some subtle change had come. The air remained hot, but less steamy, and faintly suggested the sweet winds of the high plains. How she yearned for that! Not even eight years in St. Louis had erased the memory of the dry winds from her soul. The land changed too, and the distant river bluffs were grassy now rather than forested. And beyond she caught glimpses of open prairie, rolling flat country that raced to far horizons, and such sights made her spirit run. When she peered down upon the *St. Ange* she no longer saw the underwater demons crawling over the vessel, dancing and mocking among the passengers. The cholera hadn't stopped but it would soon. It struck mostly deck passengers now. Apparently the cabin passengers followed the advice of the geologist and drank wine and kept themselves cleaner. One person she hadn't seen at all was the artist, Kurz. He'd disappeared into his stateroom when the cholera raged and hadn't emerged.

Captain La Barge continued to anchor at islands at night for safety's sake, even though they slipped deeper each day into unsettled lands and saw no one except a few woodhawks along the banks. The islands themselves changed, from muddy places crowded with dense forest, to open and sandy spits of land, lightly forested with trees that rang bells in her soul, the western cottonwoods. The moon progressed from new to half to almost full, and one clear, warm night she slipped quietly below, down the plank to land, and walked the moon-dappled island to its far shore, well-screened from the slumbering packet. She peered about sharply and then unhooked her bedraggled dress, slid it off, and scrubbed it briskly in the cool water, wishing for soap. She slid from her chemise and petticoat and scrubbed them next, hanging them over driftwood to dry, feeling night air upon her goose-bumped flesh. The Big River glinted inky and silver and lemon, and she waded cautiously into it, feeling its relentless tug around her ankles and thighs. She swam, as she had swum as a child but never since in the cloistered world of the sisters, scrubbing flesh with handfuls of sand until her body tingled.

She turned for shore and saw Peter, standing stupidly on the sandy bank beside her drying things.

"You've been watching me, Peter Kipp!" she snapped, ducking low in the water until it flowed over her breasts.

"I—I didn't know. I couldn't help it. I just . . ."

The boy seemed so pathetic. It didn't matter. Almost every dawn except in extreme weather, her mother's people walked to whatever stream was at hand and bathed. Men and women and children. What difference did it make?

"Peter, it doesn't matter. The whites worry about it more than I do."

"I saw you leave the packet. I just wanted to talk. To walk in the moonlight with you, Marie Therese. I didn't—"

"You've become a white man," she accused.

"No I haven't—yes I have!"

"I'm coming out."

"I'll turn my back. I'll leave for a minute. Please let me stay, Marie Therese."

"I don't care if you do or don't."

But he turned his back. She had no towel, only the blanket she'd plucked from her bunk days before. She wrapped it about her and settled on the sand in the snowy moonlight.

"We can talk now," she said.

He settled beside her, almost fearfully, staring. "What is that?" he asked, pointing at her buffalo amulet, suspended on a wet thong.

"It is medicine my mother gave me before I was taken to St. Louis. A buffalo. It keeps me safe. The horns stab evil. One of our words for the buffalo is *ni-ai* and it means, 'My shelter and protection.' "

"Do you believe that stuff?"

"Do you believe in Christ on a cross?"

"I don't know. I think I believe in science."

She snorted. "I see many things you don't see," she said quietly. "I see the things my mother showed me. I sometimes see a person's medicine. I see a lot of things, Peter."

"Would you tell me about them?"

He peered at her so earnestly in the chalky light that she laughed. A shooting star streaked green across the sky. A sign, she thought. So she told him of all the mysteries of the universe, right from the beginning when the People were made; of Sun, who traversed the heavens each day and retired to his lodge at night; of Moon, his pale wife, and of Morning Star, son of Sun and Moon. . . .

But she knew he didn't believe a word of it.

Chapter Four

Above Council Bluffs the *St. Ange* slid to a halt at the west bank to bury four more men, two deckhands and two passengers, both fur company employees. Pierre DeSmet himself lay feverish in his bunk, so it fell to Captain La Barge to say some words.

Death riveted Peter. He'd seen so much of it this trip, and yet he never got used to it. He'd see a healthy man one day, see him cold, blue, and dehydrated the next, and sometime after that, usually another day or so, he'd see the man waxen and still, his spirit gone; his songs, prayers, and hopes lost, his self vanished forever. It seemed an aching mystery. Where had the man gone? And why? The faces of some had bloomed into peace when their spirits left; others froze into grotesque and horrifying anguish, mouths gaping, terror stamped in their open, sightless eyes. One by one. Coming closer and closer.

When it came to him, how would he feel? He felt his brow for heat; his heart leapt with terror at every quiver of his bowels. And yet—so far—he had eluded death. Too young to die! Just starting life! Who would weep for him? His foster parents? Here on the river no one wept, at least not visibly. For these were lone men of the frontier. The deckhands had been recruited from the hard precincts along the wharfs of St. Louis. The fur men, half of them, had escaped something dark back east, and lived out their lives alone, looking over their shoulder from time to time. Lone men dying, with no one to care for them except the two priests, one dead and the other feverish. Perhaps that made it easier, Peter thought. If Captain La Barge himself took sick and died, who on board would bear the weeping of Pelagie and their children? There'd been too much death for tears. Later, perhaps. Later, in the cool air of Fort Benton, he might look back on all this and weep. If cholera didn't smite him first.

Beyond the bluffs the prairies stretched desolate in all directions like an unlived life, seas of tawny grass waving softly in the copper sun of the July evening. They'd never buried four in one day before, and these brought the total to thirty. The *St. Ange* had been a true death ship. Deckhands hefted the four bodies, each wrapped in a brown ship's blanket bound with cord. Others carried spades; one, an ax for roots. Captain La Barge followed behind, his blue uniform freshly brushed, a King James bible in his hand, though he was Creole Catholic. After La Barge, a few passengers trudged along, including Peter.

They reached the crest of the bluff and stared westward upon an ocean of shimmering grass. Behind and below, in the shadow of the bluff, Peter saw the fated packet, and the tiny figure of Marie Therese sitting quietly at her station atop the texas, as she always did. He'd visited her there from time to time—she welcomed him now—but the heat and glare had always driven him back to the main deck after a while.

Spades bit the caliche and bounced from it, the hardpan resisting the bodies that awaited it. They hacked the cast-iron earth with the ax, and scarcely chipped anything loose. La Barge nodded and the procession wound back down to the flood plain and the alluvial soils there. The spades plunged into yellow soil, and gradually the breast of the earth was laid open, a surgical wound to receive the dead.

Were their souls here, watching this? Peter wondered. Or were they far gone someplace? Or no place at all, as extinct as any dead animal? The more he concentrated on death, the less he could imagine it. It came to nothing, and he couldn't conceive of nothing in his mind, a time when even his own awareness had vanished. Death didn't seem so frightening, but *dying* did. The pain . . . he'd seen them convulse on the burning deck; watched them writhe in nausea and pain beyond his imagining. Watched them sweat and fever, gasp, watched their pulses explode, watched them puke and soak their britches and die.

The breeze here felt dry and pleasant, but the backs of the diggers blackened with sweat. It came to half a grave, two feet deep and just wide enough to cram in four blanketed bodies. The bitter earth resisted these treasures.

Captain La Barge looked as if he scarcely knew what to do. His business was owning and piloting river packets for profit, not burying men. "In the name of the Father, Son, and Holy Ghost," he began, touching his breast at the points of the cross.

He named the dead, and commended them to God and God's mercy. He urged those who stood at graveside to think on Paradise and the life to come. Grave diggers stood, still panting, faces as expressionless and distant as temple idols. Deckhands waited for it to be over, and no matter that the deceased had broken bread with the living hours before. And then he led them uneasily in the Lord's Prayer. A few said "forgive us our debts," and the rest said "forgive us our trespasses." A few mumbled the gloria that the Protestants had included, "For thine is the Kingdom . . ." while the Catholics and heathen stood mute.

The shoveling went fast, and soon only coarse earth marked the spot. They found no wood about to fashion a cross, but some gray rock with lichen in its cracks sufficed. Peter didn't want to be buried like that, unremembered, unloved, far from anyone dear, in an anonymous grave in a desolate and lonely place, the site unmarked in an unmapped land and soon forgotten.

If nothing else, this trip up the river had started him thinking how he wanted to die. If death might be something he could control a little, he hoped he could do better. There seemed to be good ways to die and bad. One might die in bed with loved ones at hand, or one might have life ripped away in a wilderness by a disease that disemboweled its victims and left them stinking, alone, and crushed.

They all trudged quietly to the packet in the amber light of a cloudless sunset. La Barge steamed ahead another mile or two; no one wanted to tie up for the night where they'd buried so many others. And anyway, they'd have to find wood because no wood hawks had appeared in the area. Dolorously the steamboat churned up the green river into a fresh night breeze. The sky darkened to amethyst and then cobalt and finally a transparent indigo, pierced by stars. They anchored beside a cottonwood-choked island.

The ship seemed mournful. Passengers and crew had thinned. The numerous St. Joseph passengers had eventually debarked furtively upriver and made their way down to their destination. Those who remained aboard now would—if they lived—go all the way to Fort Union, so far away Peter could scarcely imagine it; a place not far from British Canada.

He heard the dinner bell gong but ignored it. He couldn't eat. Instead he left his silent companion, Dr. Evans, and worked up the companionways, out upon the texas deck, and up the dizzy ladder to the roof of the texas.

"This is the last of the cholera," Marie Therese said. "Don't you feel it?"

"How do you know?"

Marie Therese shrugged. "I just know. The air or something. I see the Above Spirits here, not the Below Spirits. Don't you see them?"

"We'll see," he muttered. "Marie Therese, sometimes I think you're crazy. Or full of old superstitions."

She laughed. He'd hardly ever heard her laugh.

"Aren't you afraid of death? I am."

"My mother told me the Sand Hills are clean and cool and sweet and every day is fine."

"That's where Piegan souls go?"

"All my people—except for a few who are witches. They wander homeless, like people with no name."

"Why do you call them your people? Your father's a white man."

She didn't reply, but smoothed her wrinkled dimity.

"It's your father's people that make steamboats like this, and guns and powder, and have glass windows and carriages with wheels instead of travois. They're the future. Our mothers are the past."

"You are right, Peter," she said softly, and wouldn't talk with him for a while.

"When do you ever eat?" he asked.

"The captain brings things. They have a little galley here. The mate does too. I like them. I can see something in Mr. La Barge's soul."

"Don't they laugh at you?"

"Never."

"One man—a deck passenger—said it's a scandal. You visit them at night."

She didn't reply, and he itched to know what her thoughts were. "Have you thought any more about when you get to Fort Benton? Whether you care about me? Whether—you know—whether we could marry? No one bothers mixed-bloods there. We could—"

"Peter," she said softly, reaching for his hand in the darkness. "Peter, I can't think about such things now. Something draws me in another direction. I think I will never be with a man. But I'm glad you care about me. I like you. We are alone together. Could we just be friends?"

"No! No! Not just friends. Yes, I mean. You're my best friend. But—"

"I won't say no, Peter. I'll say I don't know my future and I must learn it. Maybe sometime . . ." She squeezed his hand and held it, and he felt the earnest warmth of her in the pressure of her fingers. "I do love you, Peter, in a way. . . ."

He had never heard words more beautiful.

Joseph La Barge loved to wrestle the river. Each year the restless Missouri transformed itself, chewing new channels, caving banks, shortcutting old oxbows, abrading away islands, piling mountains of driftwood in dams right across a channel. A Missouri pilot could memorize nothing because of the tricks of the river. A Mississippi pilot might master every bend and bar, but never a Missouri pilot, for bars grew where there'd been none, and channels swept the left bank one year and the right bank the next, and sometimes only a crewman sounding the water up at the stem could tell him where safety lay.

This trip had been a somber one, and he wished he hadn't brought dear Pelagie, she of the lustrous black hair, and their three imps, Josephine, Annette, and Eduard. But he had, and so far, thank God, cholera had not felled them. But they'd all cowered in their stateroom next to his own quarters, sensing that safety lay in isolation. La Barge wasn't sure of that: Who knew where cholera came from? He'd started something recently that seemed to help. Each morning now, crewmen swabbed down the main deck with buckets of river water, washing the filth and debris of the mob there into the river. The deck passengers didn't like that a bit: It meant moving their gear and bedrolls and tents each day for the relentless deckhands and their wet brooms. The firemen didn't like it either, because the water soaked the bottom layers of cordwood.

La Barge had done more too. Just below the hamlet of Sioux Falls, he'd started fumigating with sulfur. The hold first, and then crew's quarters forward, and then the galley. A slow business, but proceeding step by step.

Let them complain, he thought. In fact, they'd gone three days now with no new cases. Better air, they said, and that seemed true enough. The prairie winds here seemed dryer and cooler. They whipped away the fetid odors that had oppressed the *St. Ange*.

He peered up the sunny channel, whose restless waters glinted blue and aqua under a cobalt sky. The next half mile looked good—no shoals or wind reefs, no sawyers hulking like alligators, ready to pierce a hull. AFC had been slow to wharf all its trade goods this year, and they'd started late. But the river ran high, dumping ever east and south its incredible load of water still cold from the shining mountains.

He glanced down toward the stem, noting the familiar sight of that lad there, his young frame pressed into the rails as if to pull the packet along behind him. An eager one and a good one, La Barge thought. And who was that with him? Could it be? Indeed! Father Pierre-Jean DeSmet, up and ruddy after wrestling with death, some magical delight etched on his face. Captain La Barge slipped out of the pilothouse.

"Come up for tea, Father, if you can."

Far below, the priest waved and smiled. La Barge watched him tackle the first companionway slowly—the man had not yet recovered his strength—and make his way upward. If ever a man had gladness written on him, DeSmet was the one. His square frame and face exuded some robust joy that pleased those who knew him.

La Barge met him at the last stair.

"A long way for a man just up from the sickbed, Father."

"Oh, I'll manage," he replied, puffing. "And what is this? A beautiful statue above us?"

La Barge caught the direction of his upward gaze and smiled. "Father, I would like you to meet Marie Therese de Paris, who's en route to Fort Benton where her father is a senior man for American Fur."

Above them, from the roof of the texas, Marie Therese nodded.

"Now, that's a place to be. Safe from cholera there, is that it, Marie Therese?"

"No, safe from walls."

"Walls?"

"Mam'selle has just emerged from seven years of schooling at the Convent of the Sacred Heart in St. Louis," La Barge said mischievously.

"Walls! Ah! Walls!" exclaimed Pierre DeSmet. "Ah!" he said, chuckling. "Ah!"

Above them, Marie Therese smiled.

"I don't like walls either. What magic this land, eh? No fences. Just grass and a place each evening to watch a sunset."

"Those things must appeal to you now, Father. The things you thought you'd never see again," La Barge said softly.

The merriment seeped from the Jesuit's face, but not the happiness in it. "I will tell you how it was, Captain. Yes, it came, the dark hand, gutting me like hanging meat. That's how it is, Captain. Cholera slices down your gut and tears your innards out while you live.

"I prepared myself to die. Hoecken gone, and I'd be next. Sick, oh, I'll not tell you how that felt. I knew it couldn't be far off. Minutes, hours. My heart thumping desperately, my lungs refusing to draw. For a moment I regretted going. Oh, how sweet the good earth is, the breath of life, yes. I was going, a small helpless bit of will in a raging black tide. But how to go, how to go? Afraid? Oh, yes. In pain, yes. But I lay on my back and grasped my crucifix, this one here, and held it and focused my mind on what was to come, for it would not do for a priest to leave the world with any feeling other than joy. So I thought of joy, and the life to come, not death, and eventually a hand, a soft hand, touched me, stilled the anguish, stopped even the pain. . . . Ah, Mr. La Barge, the hand of our Lord." He peered upward. "Yes, mam'selle, the hand. I felt the hand. . . ."

Above, Marie Therese stared, a hand unconsciously fingering the silver crucifix that still dangled on the bodice of her dress.

"You inspire us, Father," said La Barge.

"Not I, not I," the priest replied. "But I sense it's about over, eh? I hear we've no new cases."

"Let us hope," muttered La Barge. He summoned a boy to fetch tea, and briefly instructed the steersman in the pilothouse before returning to Father DeSmet on the texas deck.

"What brings you up the river again, Father?"

"Mitchell. David Mitchell. He asked for my help in gathering the tribes at Fort Laramie for a council in August."

"Mitchell? The old fur man?"

"Heads the Indian Bureau now. He thought my good offices—my many friends among the northern tribes trust me—my good offices would help. And we'd—I'd be safer. . . ."

"August? But that's so close!"

The priest sighed. "I know, I know. I'll abandon the boat at Fort Pierre and head west, catching the Assiniboin, Sioux, Crow . . . maybe the Cheyenne if I can."

"The Blackfeet too?" asked Marie Therese from the roof of the texas above.

The priest looked startled a moment, registering the voice above him. "Why, they're invited. Mitchell wanted them."

"I hope they don't come," she snapped.

La Barge found himself peering up at the girl, wanting more from her, but she said nothing.

Pierre-Jean DeSmet gazed toward the bluffs and the endless prairie beyond, seeing distant things. "Our Lord willing, perhaps I can protect my brothers in the tribes. Speak for them . . . help them understand the terms of the treaties. They are my flock—I must protect them."

"I don't want my mother's people to be fenced in. I don't want everything taken from them."

"Oh, mam'selle, that won't happen, surely," La Barge said, feeling a little uncertain about it. "Perhaps you shouldn't be addressing Father DeSmet in such a way."

"No, no, it's perfectly proper. I understand, Marie Therese, and I share your worry. Your people are fine, and I have a great affection for them."

"If you do, Father, let them alone. For as long as the buffalo last and they have freedom, they will get along."

"I see you care about them very much. Have you similar feelings toward your father's people? It is good to love all, without favor."

She drew into herself, and the captain sensed that the girl's heart lay with the Piegan mother and her band.

At last she addressed the priest. "If you love my people, and the people of the other tribes, why do you do the bidding of the Indian Bureau? The treaties are made only to take things away. Our land first, and then our food."

DeSmet answered gravely in the midday quiet. "As the Europeans fill the land there will come great changes. Such things are beyond my control, I'm afraid. But, please God, I might bring peace and—transformation. Bring the Blackfeet to my Lord, and the sacraments . . . bring them less warlike ways. It's true, you know, that these peoples spend most every day—except the bitterest cold ones—warring on one another, stealing horses and taking captives. The old life, Marie Therese—will vanish, about as fast as the buffalo will vanish. And then, if my mission pleases God, I may have prepared these tribes for the better things."

"Prepare them for starvation."

Both Captain La Barge and the Jesuit stared into her unblinking gray eyes.

"On this trip I've learned what I will be," she said. "You would not approve."

Chapter Five

When she saw the sacred buffalo, she knew her people would not be far away. From her perch on the texas she spotted them before the rest. Indian eyes, they said. But she knew that eyes that seek the sacred see farther than eyes that don't, see around and through, to the beyond. And so she saw the pair of them watering at twilight, holy in a lavender shadow. In their short summer hair they looked bronze in the horizontal light of sunset, the hair over their backs faintly bleached by summer sun.

She stared transfixed at the sight of this holy thing, as sacred to her as the communion wafer. Two old bulls, actually, with great manes about their throats, and weak eyes and lordly disdain for the wolves waiting for them to die. These two they would not shoot. When they found some tender cows, with delicious tongue and hump meat, the passengers on the *St. Ange* would feast, and so would she. But her feast would also be a Piegan communion, a reunion with her world.

"Do you see them?" she called down to Captain La Barge, standing on the deck below.

"There you go, seeing around corners," he replied. In truth the ship paddled slowly around a great bend of the Missouri, in a wide valley hemmed by the distant grassy bluffs of Dakota.

"Old bulls," she said. "Don't shoot them. They've come to welcome us to the land beyond."

La Barge laughed. "Not much worth eating in an old bull. I imagine tomorrow we'll feast, though."

She suddenly longed for the sweet flesh of the sacred animal on her tongue, the meat that sustained her people and made them strong and hardy. The sweet firm meat that gave its power, the buffalo power, to the Blackfeet, unlike the soft weak flesh of white men's cattle.

She'd seen antelope a few days earlier, white-rumped and watchful, and knew the buffalo would not be far. For weeks the *St. Ange* had plowed into a new land of high prairie and sweeping vistas, green with the rains of early summer. Mist had vanished from the air and now from her high point she could see to far horizons. The dry air seemed bluer and intense, lowering over receding prairies like a cobalt dome. It was the land of her mothers, if not her fathers. A land where these white people scarcely belonged. She peered sourly at them down below on the main deck. They milled down there, wanting to shoot the old bulls, but La Barge said no; he didn't want to stop. Tomorrow they'd find good meat.

The cholera had vanished, and all that remained was bad memory and uneasy fear that it would rise from its ashes and pounce upon them. She'd wandered the ship again, but never for long, always returning to her place atop the texas, where she shunned the company of all the white people below, except for Peter. The crowds had thinned anyway, and nearly all aboard were fur company engagés.

The *St. Ange* made good time, finding wood plentiful at the woodlots in cottonwood flats and sold eagerly by rough-looking wood hawks who either hadn't heard of the plague ship or didn't care. Eighteen cords a day it took to fuel this ship up to Fort Union, and a lesser amount going downstream. That whole business fascinated Peter, but she scarcely noticed it.

The buffalo bulls snorted and lumbered into the cottonwood brush as the riverboat approached. She watched them go, and composed a song to them.

Buffalo spirits, do not go away.
Stay with my people always.
If you go away, strong buffalo,
My people will perish from the world.

She could barely remember her mother's tongue, though once she spoke it as a child, so she sang it in English. Four times she sang it because four was the sacred number, and when she'd finished, she felt glad that Peter hadn't heard her. He would have laughed.

Each day as the *St. Ange* plowed ever north and west, he'd come to be with her. Each day he asked her to marry him, and she enjoyed being asked. But she always said no. Usually the sun and glare of her high perch drove him off in an hour or so. She liked him and was glad of his visits, but she resisted all his entreaties to go down to the prow with him.

One day they rounded a grassy bend and came upon a great camp of Yanktonai along the river. Three hundred lodges, a forest of cones pointing into the skies. But not very many people in sight, as if the whole camp lay asleep. The Dakota people were enemies of her Pikuni mother, and yet she stared out upon the village with its barking dogs and smoldering cookfires, and medicine tripods decked with scalps and feathers and skulls next to the yellow cowhide lodges, and felt kinship—and something more.

Some of the engagés shouted back and forth with Yanktonais on the bank in a tongue she didn't know, but she could read a few of the signs made by deft fingers and flying hands.

"Cap'in, don't stop. This here village got the pox," one engagé shouted to La Barge, above.

Smallpox. Now she understood why the great village lay quiet and solemn in the late afternoon. Why did white men bring terrible diseases with them? The pox had destroyed the Mandans and Hidatsi, killed two thirds of her mother's Piegan people, and scythed its way through villages everywhere. The medicine men had prayed and sacrificed, and declared that whole villages were being punished by the Above Ones for great evil. And still they died, from 1837 onward, in waves of disease insidiously creeping up the Missouri, pox and cholera, measles and typhoid and evils unnamed.

From the deck Father DeSmet called upward. "Captain, will you be stopping ahead a bit for the night? I'd like to minister to these people."

"Island up about two miles. I don't want the pox on board. Not after all we've been through."

"Put me off, then," said the priest. "I'll catch up during the night sometime."

Captain La Barge sighed, stared at the priest, nodded and signaled his crew. She watched them lower a flatboat and help the priest clamber in.

"Wait!" she cried, scrambling down the ladder to the texas deck and then whirling down the companionways.

"Miss de Paris!" La Barge shouted, but she ignored him. Suddenly, with some unfathomable yearning tugging her, she had to go to the Yanktonai.

"Marie Therese! It's dangerous!" cried Peter from the main deck.

"Don't go, then," she retorted. She landed smartly in the flatboat, along with a crewman and Father DeSmet who stared at her sharply.

"I don't suppose I can discourage you either," he said.

"I must go to them."

He stared, saying nothing. The burly crewman dug into the water with his oars, and the boat skidded toward shore, where Yanktonais stood silently.

"Why?" asked DeSmet. "These aren't your people. In fact, they're enemies."

She couldn't think of an answer, and fingered the small crucifix on the bodice of her tattered dimity.

"I think I know," he said softly as the boat slid to the bank. He helped her out of the leaky, wobbling boat, and then the crewman rowed powerfully toward the *St. Ange*.

"DeSmet," said a headman. They knew him. All the villages knew him. Yanktonai people stood quietly, not milling around. Not even dogs barked.

She watched black smoke boil from the chimneys and the ivory *St. Ange* shudder its way forward on the purple water, and found herself alone: a convent girl, a priest, and a pox-stricken village of her mother's enemies. The priest spoke a few words of broken Sioux, supplementing with his fingers and hands.

"Marie Therese de Paris," she heard him say aloud, and they stared at her, at her modest convent clothes. "Let's go, Marie Therese. We will pray for the sick and anoint them. Baptize them if some wish it. You will be a great help to me."

Bewildered, not knowing why she'd come, she followed behind him, past bronze people in plain skin clothes stripped of all ornament, except for one gray wiry man, naked but for a breechclout and a wolf-claw necklace and red-trimmed moccasins. That one carried two coppery gourd rattles and a hoop adorned with olive and gray rattlesnake heads—a medicine man, eyeing them with ill-concealed rage.

A strange, silent village, she thought, wending between lodges so thick she could scarcely see the distant dun bluffs. She smelled leather and boiled meat and dog offal and something else, sinister and faintly sweet. She smelled death.

"This headman, Curved Buffalo Horns, says their chief lies ill, with his whole family. We'll start there, Marie Therese."

She found herself entering a spacious lodge, behind the black cassock of Father DeSmet. Within, she was smacked by the odor of mortification. In the dim light she counted seven people on their pallets, Chief Old Wolf, his sits-beside-him wife Sees the Moon, two other women and several children. All feverish, bright-eyed with the heat of burning flesh, and hollow-cheeked. But as her eyes grew accustomed, she saw the horror of smallpox, white scabs, blisters and boils and inflamed ruby holes pitting their whole flesh. They lay naked, unable to bear the touch of cloth or leather.

Father DeSmet glanced at her. "Marie Therese, I'm sorry, I—"

"I grew up Pikuni," she retorted.

He nodded and knelt beside the middle-aged leader of this Yanktonai village. Behind her she sensed others entering the lodge, village headmen and elders, who spread themselves silently and politely in the places of lowest honor.

"Pray with me, Marie Therese. Our Lord says that whenever two or more are gathered in His name—"

"I know," she replied shortly, some pain welling through her, unfathomable anger rising from sources she didn't know.

He placed his hand on the pale brow of the fevered chief, who stared back indifferently, and prayed in sonorous Latin, whose meaning she barely understood. What was she doing here, praying to this God of the whites? It amazed her and troubled her heart. She'd come to nurture these brown people of the earth, as a rebuke against the invaders who came to destroy, and kill black buffalo, and herd them all into land prisons they called reserves, where they would all starve slowly, invisibly.

Father DeSmet anointed the man, spreading his holy oil in the sign of the cross, and then moved to the next one, the chief's wife, whose face and limbs oozed pus and yellow fluids from a hundred suppurating eruptions. Even the flesh between her old breasts oozed, pearl and lemon pus, along with the rest of her. Marie Therese felt desperate for air, wanting fresh air, wanting to escape this terror before it struck her. She'd received Jenner's vaccine long ago, like most mountain children, although she didn't trust it. But she took courage from the stocky priest, who prayed tenderly over each one while these Dakota people watched.

She prayed along with him, remembering her amens and the sign of the cross, and begging this God of DeSmet's to bless each of these souls. Then he was done, and they were led to the next lodge, a dark and silent one. But here death slapped her. They slid into a preternatural quiet, and she saw the Underwater Spirits here occupying this umber place. Death. Five in this lodge, inert. Two men in their prime, two women, and an infant.

"They're gone," he muttered. He stood in the lodge and blessed it, and they slid out into the russet twilight to the next one. She wondered where Dakota spirits went. Not to the happy place her mother's Pikuni people called the Sand Hills. Some other place, where their Wakan Tanka took them, she supposed. Unless they were all witches. She'd never met a Dakota witch.

Outside, the Yanktonai watched DeSmet intently, silently—a white medicine man who'd stepped off a fire-ship to allay white man's disease. She felt the curious, complex things they felt—anger, hope, bitterness, wonder, sorrow, grief, despair—a village mortifying, flesh rotting, and those few who recovered pocked and blistered until they looked like creatures from the Under-Earth places, with evil stamped upon their ruined flesh. She wondered how she'd look if her smooth young skin were pitted and twisted into the grotesque ugliness she saw here.

From lodge to lodge they trudged through afternoon and dusk, and she wondered how they'd anoint all of these sick and still hike the two or three miles upstream to the island where the *St. Ange* lay over. But Father DeSmet didn't seem to notice. His soul hovered outside of himself—she could see that—and he seemed to have all the time in the world, pouring love out upon each lodge, the quick and the dead. Purple night lowered, and she found herself entering lodges in which she could see nothing: No one within was well enough to cook a meal or maintain even a tiny fire for light. And still he prayed, this stocky, fair man in black, somehow finding each sick one with Indian eyes, taking all the time in the world.

A gibbous moon rose, slanting orange light down across the bluffs, lighting the silent village, poking under the rolled-up lodge skirts to illumine those within, death-glow. She shuddered. The moon climbed and bleached itself white, and still they wandered, guided to each lodge by Curved Buffalo Horns, who watched impassively. She followed the priest's lead by rote now, muttering her part, saying her amens, wondering if all this Latin halted disease. Did this God hear only Latin? Did he ever perform a miracle on an Indian? Did he care about anyone who wasn't Catholic? Did she dare add her own medicine prayers to his? Talk to the Above Spirits, even while he talked with his God? It confused her.

She wearied, and her bones creaked from kneeling and rising, and her eyes refused to look at suppuration, death, and fever anymore. Then suddenly he finished praying in the last dark lodge. A hundred of them were vessels of disease. They crawled out of the door and stood in the ghostly light, where elders and medicine men awaited them solemnly. It was then that she saw the future of all the Indian people. Dark lodges . . . this had been a foretaste of all to come. It made her heart burst with grief—dark lodges. Did he see it? Did he understand?

She peered at him. He seemed as fresh and ruddy as when they'd entered the first lodge in the afternoon, but she saw his spirit had returned to him and no longer hovered over the sick and dying. He seemed a great man of the whites, and she felt a pang of guilt to have doubted his faith and powers. His very spirit tugged at her, slipped into her soul, drawing her to his faith, which she knew intimately from her years in the convent. Not among her mother's people had she met a man like this, with a healing power in his hands and in his very faith. He tore her to pieces, especially when he caught her eye and smiled. In all of this he had never forgotten her, and walking from one lodge to the next he had found a kind word for her, for her courage and caring.

"But you don't understand! I do it because I don't like whites!" she'd cried once, and he'd smiled at her.

"I know," he had said. "But God loves all people."

Now they stood in the silent village, surrounded by curved moonlit cones, while Father DeSmet spoke his few guttural Siouan words, accompanied by his sign talk. She understood it. Separate the sick from the well, he was saying. Not both in the same lodge. Bury the dead now; don't wait. And trust in the One Above, whom I serve.

He blessed them and told them he'd leave now for the fireboat up the river. Curved Buffalo Horns muttered something, and a woman appeared with a long pouch of the soft leather of unborn calf, decorated with intricate quill work. Curved Buffalo Horns gently withdrew a medicine pipe from within, a fine long pipe with a carmine pipestone bowl and a stem of polished wood. He handed it to DeSmet, saying things she didn't understand.

Father DeSmet exclaimed and accepted the gift. Minutes later she found herself trudging wearily up the moonlit riverbank away from the dark lodges, along a worn trace that seemed to have been carved by countless men and animals. A night breeze drove the stink of mortification from her clothes.

"The pipe was his most prized possession," DeSmet said to her. "A Cree pipe once, given or captured, I don't know."

"He honored you. I hope your prayers work."

"My prayers, Marie Therese?"

She slid into silence.

"Perhaps yours were to your Above Spirits."

"You whites bring diseases and death; you kill the buffalo. You drive the people into the small corners of the earth! Some of you shoot the Pikuni, and any Indians, as if they were dogs!"

"All that you say is true, Marie Therese."

They plunged into a forest of cottonwoods, thick along the river, and found something more. Ghostly in the moonlight above them lay silent scaffolds laced together with rawhide, each burdened with a Yanktonai who'd recently lived and breathed as part of the village. Sometimes two, husband and wife. Mother and child. She shrank away, knowing that places of death are cursed, and lost spirits and witch spirits roam them in the night.

"Hurry," she said tautly. She could barely fathom the dark burdens lying on the crude scaffolds above, but she knew each Yanktonai was probably wrapped in a blanket, with a few possessions, a bow and arrow and quiver, to help that one reach the spirit world. She approved. She thought the departed ones should be given to the sun, not the cold clammy earth. The night danced. The wind wailed. And the dark lodge of heaven vaulted upward.

"So many gone," he replied, his eyes scanning the endless scaffolds occupying every cottonwood limb as far as they could see. He caught her fear, and paused. "No harm will come to us here, Mam'selle de Paris."

"You won't let them into your Christian heaven. The sisters and the priests told me—no Paradise . . . no happiness. No joy for these people. It's so cruel. What've they done to deserve Hell? If they didn't even know about your—about our Lord, then how can you condemn—"

"Lost, not condemned, Marie Therese. Hell is reserved for the disobedient."

"Lost!" she cried. "What have they done to be lost forever in the next life, never seeing goodness? All my people—except for the witches—go to the Sand Hills, and are happier there."

An animal bolted, a wolf or coyote, frightening her. A spirit animal, burdened with ghosts. She resisted turning back to the village.

"The boat is not far ahead," he said kindly.

She caught up with him where the trail widened, and walked silently, drawing strength from him. No one of Pikuni blood belonged here, especially at night.

"We can pray for the lost. It's why I'm here, why I'm a priest," he continued peacefully. "Maybe the whites, including your father, bring these people the gift of eternal life, eh?"

"Death," she retorted.

"You could help the Piegan find a new life."

"Not the way you'd want me to, Father."

He sighed. "I know. I know you, Marie Therese."

She was curious. "What do you know?"

"I wish it were not so. But you're a child of destiny, set for the fall of nations and peoples. The things the good sisters taught you seem to disappear in you day by day—I've watched that. And yet, they don't entirely disappear. You could not really pray beside me back there, but neither did you deny. You're baptized and not lost to us, but I think your heart will take you far away, far away from us. To your mother's people. Am I right?"

"I'm not good at confession," she said.

He smiled gently in the moonlight.

Chapter Six

Captain La Barge stopped the packet twice a day to gather wood for his insatiable boilers. This deep into the Dakota country of Nebraska Territory, the wood hawks had vanished. Life on the lonely prairies, hacking down trees in the infrequent cottonwood groves along the river, was too isolated and precarious even for the wildest spirits out beyond the frontier. Too many had died at the hands of sudden unwanted company, their skeletons and molding clothing found months later, with arrowheads and shafts quilling them.

On these wood-gathering pauses, all able-bodied men were recruited, including Peter, who found an ax or saw thrust in his hand, and the expectation that he would use it along with crewmen and the burly engagés of the fur company. Even the scientist, Dr. Evans, was dragooned into that all-important task.

The exception was the Swiss artist Rudolph Kurz, who explained that the rough work would lacerate his hands, the tools of his trade. Moreover, he insisted he was exempt as a paying passenger. So La Barge gave him another task. Wherever he sent the men out to cut timber, he sent Kurz armed with a carbine and spyglass up to the nearest bluff to keep a sharp eye out for hostile tribesmen. That delighted the artist.

At these lengthy pauses, Marie Therese took to joining

Kurz, and Peter often watched enviously as she walked lithely beside the Swiss, until they became small specks on distant, sun-swept promontories. That was exactly what he wished to do with her each day, he thought. For when she stepped onto land, something about her was transformed. It was as if a caged bird had been set free and soared above them all, wheeling on the wind, wild as an eagle.

Peter hacked viciously at a shaggy cottonwood limb, finally dropping it to earth with a crash. Then he hacked it into eight-foot lengths that could be carried back to the packet. He liked to be considered a man, doing a man's work twice a day, but he resented it too. He wanted to be with her. Each day as the boat pushed north into a wild, free land, she'd turned more beautiful: tall and willowy, her wavy jet hair loose over her shoulders, and the sharp Indian cheekbones of her face accenting her bold gray eyes. He'd never known such haunting beauty, rising from some spiritual fire blazing in her soul.

Why Kurz? Why not him?

He liked the artist well enough. After the cholera had vanished, the intense, voluble Swiss had emerged from his cabin, taken the air, commandeered the whole packet as his own, and had started sketching again. Some of the drawings had shocked Peter. Indian women with naked breasts. Sketches of Marie Therese, her form plain on the paper, and barely covered by her dresses. She had very little clothing, he knew. The black convent girl's dress; a tan dimity, bulky and peculiar, and the other outfit he loved most: a long gray skirt and a loose, high-necked white blouse. It seemed to cling, then let go of her slender figure and high breasts with her every movement, until he trembled at the image of her, cool and fiery in his heart.

He felt his own sweat river down his sides under his armpits as he hauled the cordwood up the wobbling plank and dropped it near the firebox. He always stank at the end of these wood-gathering episodes, and couldn't do anything about it. He had only one change of clothing, and he could barely keep clean. It galled him that the Swiss could always look splendid, washed, and cultivated, wooing the girl he wanted to marry.

A pistol shot from La Barge's pilothouse summoned Marie Therese and Kurz back. Peter watched them stand and stretch, the prairie zephyrs playing with her skirts, molding them around her form, and something in him sank toward desperation. He dragged the last of the wood aboard and followed the other dripping men onto the main deck, anger and longing building to some unbearable crescendo in him.

The firemen jammed long cottonwood limbs into the firebox, building steam. Soon the escapement above hissed and popped with the fierce pressure that stroked two giant pistons cranking the fifteen-foot wheel at the rear of the packet. He gulped cool river water from a jug the crewmen passed around, watching Kurz climb toward his cabin and Marie Therese continue upward, ever upward, to her strange perch high in the blue sky.

Steam hissed and the roar of the firebox echoed off the distant bluffs, and hot smoke belched from black chimneys, spraying ash over the aquamarine river. He felt the pent-up animal force of the packet, matching the force in himself. He plunged up the companionway to the boiler deck, around the bend and up to the hurricane deck, and then up the ladder of the texas.

She sat serenely there on a blanket, gazing out upon a breathtaking view of the upper Missouri and its distant tan banks spreading in all directions. He stared, his head just over the level of the roof of the texas.

"Peter!"

"I suppose you don't want to see me."

She smiled. "Why do you think that? Of course I do!"

"Because I stink. And I'm not fancy and a grown man like that artist. And I do a man's work cutting wood instead of making drawings of you and flattering you and drawing your form as if he can see right through—"

"Peter!"

But he wasn't done. Something drove him, heated him, melted and teased him until his belly hurt. "I guess

I'm just some fur company breed, and all you want is some dandy from Europe who can have his way with you and has soft hands and knows how to speak two or three tongues and sees me and all of us as curiosities—something to gossip about when he gets back across the ocean, and sit over there drinking coffee and being superior and laughing at all the barbarians in America, meaning me, and how he had an easy conquest—"

She slugged him. He careened backward, almost losing his footing on the ladder, and then hopped forward out upon the deck.

"I hate him," he yelled.

Her gray eyes held him, transfixing him. "You owe me something."

He glowered at her, knowing, unwilling.

"Rudolph has never touched me and never will." She said no more, waiting.

"It looks like he does!" he retorted hotly.

She smiled. "You don't owe me anything, Peter. Forget it."

Her forgiveness bewildered him more than her request for an apology after he'd sullied her.

"Come talk," she added softly. "You never seem to stay long up here."

"That's because I can't stand it." He felt miserable still, in spite of her gentleness. He wanted only to hold her hand, or slip his arms about her, but he couldn't. Not up here, where everyone below could see. They were like ensigns flying here.

"Next time we stop for wood, come walk with me. They can't make me cut wood. I'm not their engagé. We'll go to the hilltop and watch, and talk, just ourselves, and that artist with his soft hands can cut wood."

"I'd like that. You don't talk to me much anymore."

"That's because you never come down. You're stuck on that artist. He's twice your age too."

"Peter . . ." Her hand found his. "If there ever is anyone—anyone for me—it's you." She peered unblinkingly at him. "But I don't think there will be. There's something calling me. You know the sisters in St. Louis. Something called them. Instead of marrying and—having babies—they gave themselves. Something's calling me, but not that. Not being a sister. Peter, I don't belong to any man—especially any white man. I like Father DeSmet. He understands me and—doesn't force me to believe . . ." She paused. "And Captain La Barge too. He lets me stay here, and he comes with a laugh and kindness. But Peter . . . something's calling me."

He sighed, feeling his rage and envy subside. He felt he'd been an awkward boy, resenting Kurz. But even as the pressure subsided in the boilers of his heart, his sadness increased. For she slipped further from him, before his very eyes, into some world of her own, pure Pikuni and filled with spirits from under the earth and up in the heavens, Napi and Sun and Morning Star.

"We're children of this land," she said. "You and I, Peter. We'll share that. Always, we'll have that."

It didn't console him, and yet he felt her reaching toward him with promises in her soft, intent gaze.

"What do you think it'll be like when we get there?" she asked.

"I want to see what my father's like."

"I do too. I was eight years old when he sent me."

They'd talked of this before. Neither had ever seen this Fort Benton where their fathers labored. Peter's foster father, James Kipp, had become second in command, and ran everything when Alec Culbertson was away, which was often. And her father—she scarcely knew him. He'd rarely written. An annual note in French, sent down on the annual packet. He might have written more, with letters coming downriver on every mackinaw.

It left them both uneasy, returning to fathers and strangers. Men to command them, to tell them what to do and what not to do. Were they kind or cruel? Fair or unfair? Would they exploit them as handmaiden and cook and servant and woodcutter, or perhaps care, and see to their future? Men who might or might not love.

Peter's wasn't even his true father. He supposed he

was really a bastard, a child spawned by some trapper with a Salish woman he didn't know either. Some red-haired trapper. Suddenly his sense of aloneness engulfed him again, the darkness he fought by making himself a white man and readying himself to climb high, high, to the pinnacle of Pratte, Chouteau and Company.

She was waiting for his answer, what he thought it would be like when they met their fathers in that new log and adobe place, but he didn't reply because he had no vision.

At the big bend of the Missouri, Captain La Barge sent most of the men ashore with axes and saws. The bend formed a giant horseshoe that took ten or eleven hours to steam around, while walkers could cut across its neck in an hour and a half and spend the remaining time cutting and stacking wood. Peter found himself hiking up a steep bluff to the grassy plateau above, in the company of a polyglot mixture of engagés, mostly French, German, and Swiss, boatmen except for the fire crew, many of them blacks, and also Dr. Evans, Father DeSmet, the artist Rudolph Kurz, and Marie Therese, who never missed a chance to go by land.

When they reached the top of the bluff, they paused, seeing the tiny packet probe its way around a bend and out of sight. Peter felt overwhelmed by the sudden silent vastness of the land, which stretched beyond the eye. It subdued him. But Marie walked gaily, filled with some unfathomable joy to be strolling out upon the high plains, the brisk wind whipping her soft dark hair about her shoulders. La Barge had frowned when she'd skipped down the gangplank, and nodded to his second mate, who grabbed an extra breech-loading carbine for the protection of this large but helpless party, and the young lady with it.

Every facet of the trip absorbed Peter, whose mind funneled in the details of modern travel and forgot nothing. If he were ever to be the head man of the Chouteau company's Upper Missouri Outfit, he'd need to know everything. He wanted to master the miracles of modern ingenuity, the genius of the Europeans settling this continent.

Day after day he'd watched sweating firemen begin to build steam as early as four in the morning. It took three shifts of them to fuel the packet all day, because heaving giant logs into the roaring fire exhausted and blistered them, and sometimes sickened them when they padded between the roaring furnaces and the damp, cold woodpiles on a foggy day. He didn't envy them, and wanted no part of a life like that, so he learned obsessively, feeling that knowledge would usher him into something better.

The day never seemed to end for crewmen and engagés. At the end of each day, they let the fires burn down to ash, and then the first and second engineers opened the mud valves to drain the giant boilers because the Missouri's water was so thick with dissolved minerals that it deposited scale inside the boilers, which had to be chipped out after each day. "The river's fit to drink if you have other water to wash it down with," they joked. The rest of the time they hovered about the steam engines, oiling and cleaning, and repacking the giant cylinder to make it more efficient. Peter studied them, learned the trade just by watching.

He learned about the way woods burned, and how the crew made do with what they could scrounge. Dry driftwood, which the crew prized, burned well, but wet driftwood required handfuls of rosin or knots to make it blaze. Cottonwood and the river willows growing on the islands burned well but lacked heat, so the packet often had to struggle against current and wind. Sometimes La Barge shouted down the tube for more steam, and then the firemen poured on the rosin.

On the lower river the cook and steward bought meat and produce directly from farmers along the riverbanks, negotiating for milk, chicken, eggs, and even live hogs whenever the packet stopped for loads of wood. Now that they'd reached antelope and buffalo country, the meat supply grew, and Peter noticed several carcasses hanging near the galley at the rear of the packet, just ahead of the great wheelhouse that enclosed part of the thundering paddle wheel. They'd started to encounter buffalo and elk along the banks, and the engagés banged away at them with their old mountain rifles, many of them percussion locks made by Hawken. Sometimes La Barge sent a yawl out to fetch a floating carcass. Crewmen towed the meat to the packet and then winched it aboard, where it eventually became a plentiful feast. The cookstoves required wood too, Peter noticed, and at every wood stop the cooks commandeered smaller limbs and kindling.

The river had dropped noticeably now that the mountain runoff had declined, and crewmen talked knowingly of sandbars and snags ahead. So far La Barge had escaped grounding, although several times the packet had scraped across something solid, and once a giant sawyer had caromed off the hull, almost piercing it. Above all else, the sawyers, tumbling trees or logs, somersaulting down the river, endangered them, threatening the precious cargo of trade goods destined for the trading windows of the upper river forts. Without the annual resupply, the posts would have nothing to offer for tanned buffalo robes brought in by tribesmen.

Marie Therese chose his company, which delighted Peter. He glanced furtively at her, wanting her, sensing her joy as she traversed the wild open land with all its duns and lavenders and salmons and spare silvery greens. Even her stride seemed somehow Indian to him, a lithe padding that looked effortless and fluid compared to the heavy tread of the white men in their boots. Her gray eyes gazed serenely at the shortgrass growing in bunches, so different from the lush, tall thick grass of St. Louis, and then she seemed to embrace the whole vast heaven, drinking it in, serene with the Wind Maker and Sky Chief, following his daily journey from east to west. *Her land* . . . not quite, but almost. And it transformed her in a way that mystified him. He'd come from the same country and yet felt nothing of whatever percolated through her soul now.

"What are you thinking of?" he asked.

She smiled, fixing him in her gray gaze. "Of last

night's dream. Nitsokan came—the Dream Maker. He's the child of Early Riser, morning star, and he showed me my mother, Meadowlark. She is happy."

"Didn't you dream of your father? I'm always thinking of James Kipp. I hope—he welcomes me."

"You think he might not, Peter? I think he will. You'll please him."

"What of your father, Marie Therese?"

"I don't know my father."

She turned inward, and he kept quiet. He'd learned she would not talk in those times, as if her mind had fastened onto a distant place beyond the horizon of time. Still, he felt content just to have her at his side. Somehow he'd won out over that artist, and she had been closer to him for days. It lifted his spirits. Soon he'd win her heart; soon he'd propose again, but maybe it'd take a year and a regular fur company income and position before she'd say yes. It didn't matter what they said. He and Marie were old enough. Lots of people got married at seventeen. Anyway, she'd be sixteen soon.

The party wound into a coulee and then, rounding a bend, the river appeared to them, a silver and blue ribbon coiling between immense dun bluffs below. And at the foot of their trail was a small cottonwood flat, half stripped of its wood by passing crews.

The afternoon turned hot as they toiled down a long narrow trail into the bottoms, and below the bluffs the dry air barely stirred. Ahead of them DeSmet and Evans discussed fossils and natural history. The scientist intended to hunt for fossil bones in the badlands of Dakota, west of Fort Pierre, and do it alone too, which startled Peter. He heard Evans arguing that the world might be a million years old or more, while Father DeSmet demurred and insisted it could not be. Peter thought he'd like to join that conversation, but not at the price of abandoning Marie Therese. He glanced at her covertly, as he often did. She wore his favorite today, the long severe skirt and puffed white blouse that concealed and yet revealed the lithe figure that transfixed him. She exuded joy, like some freed creature just discovering her liberty, and her happiness kindled his own.

Below, the half-pillaged cottonwood grove spread like a green sea along the turquoise river. Then, ahead, they heard shouting. Crewmen and engagés both were peering and pointing. Peter stared and saw what had drawn their attention. A dozen horsemen astride ponies standing quietly in the dappled shade. Bronze and naked, some in breechclouts, others wearing only a quiver over their backs and one or two eagle feathers in their braided jet hair.

All about him trappers slipped caps over the nipples of their mountain rifles, and the two crewmen carrying breech-loading carbines checked their loads.

Marie Therese's joy vanished in an instant. "They're not painted," she said sharply, in a voice intended to carry below to the advancing crewmen. "They're just curious. Maybe they want to trade! You don't even know who they are!"

Father DeSmet took up her plea. "I'll talk with them," he called to those ahead. "They know me—most do. And they know my badges of office." He hurried forward, intending to prevent an incident.

"Them Injuns are all trouble. Best shoot a few and scare them off," yelled a pockmarked crewman, one with a breech-loading carbine in hand.

"You will not!" she cried.

"No damn breed girl's going to stop me."

"You'd best wait for Father DeSmet," said John Evans with an edge in his voice.

"You keep out of it," the crewman snapped.

"You got something against breeds?" yelled Peter, white heat racing through him.

"What's it to you, breed?" The man glared at Peter, radiating a contempt reserved for dogs and coyotes, and swung his carbine around, lifting it toward the headman a hundred yards below, who sat his paint pony, waiting quietly.

That's when Peter landed on the larger man, knocking him sideways just as the carbine roared.

Chapter Seven

Peter's blow ruined the crewman's shot. He snarled, swung a huge fist that landed in Peter's gut. Peter gasped. The giant crewman grabbed him and shook him like a puppy and threw him off. Then he opened the breech and jammed another paper cartridge in. Peter sprawled on the slope, gasping and sobbing.

Down below, the headman touched moccasins to his pony and lurched toward cover in the cottonwoods. The other Indians vanished in the trees. Marie stood on the grassy slope, horrified. Then just ahead, other ship's crewmen began firing their carbines. Father DeSmet yelled at them. Just as the headman reached the edge of the cottonwoods, something struck him wickedly, jamming him forward over his pony's withers and then heavily to earth. Blood bloomed on his chest. From within the woods she heard howls and rage.

She peered about frantically. They all stood exposed on the grassy slope, without an iota of cover.

"Stop!" cried Father DeSmet. "In the name of God, stop!"

The crewmen didn't. The fur company engagés, trappers, and hands at the fort hadn't fired. They knew better and had dealt with Indians all their lives in the western wilderness.

"Rees!" cried one.

Arikara. Their villages lay up the river a piece, permanent walled fortifications surrounded by fields of Indian corn. They'd been troublesome years ago. Enemies of her mother's Pikuni, she thought.

The pocked giant sighted and fired again, hitting the body of the downed headman, poking a bloody hole through his neck.

"You heard Father!" she snapped. She knew him now, Scruggs, the second mate, a villainous man plucked up off the sinister wharves of St. Louis. White trash.

He laughed and loaded. "Good Injuns are dead Injuns, breed girl."

She threw herself at him, spoiling his aim again as his carbine belched fire.

He roared, grabbed her slim body, his great paw cupping a breast, and threw her to earth. Then he leapt at her, lifted her by the bodice of her torn blouse and began slapping her, his giant dirty hands smacking hard until she felt blood in her mouth and nose.

"Filthy breed. Sitting up there like some Injun queen all day. Think we 'uns don't see it? Smiling at all them officers and such? Getting to be La Barge's pet? Just wait, breed. We'll make a pet of you one of these days, and you'll like it. Oh, you'll like it!"

He threw her to the ground just as Father DeSmet leapt to pull him off. One hard smack of the second mate's fist caromed the priest into Marie Therese and sent him rolling downslope. That's when three giant engagés jumped Scruggs and flattened him.

She wept, feeling the sting of those blows, feeling the sting of this white man's contempt for Indians.

"Are you all right, Marie Therese?" asked Evans.

She hated whites so much at that instant she refused to reply. She glared at him, feeling tears still welling in her eyes.

"I'll help you up," he said, but she shook her head violently.

"You—Scruggs—I'm making a full report to Captain La Barge, including what you did to this girl. And shooting at Indians who wanted only to parley or trade."

"You say a word, Evans, and you'll end up overboard in the night, arms tied," Scruggs muttered.

"I'll tell him," snapped Marie Therese.

Scruggs grinned at the engagés who were watching him coldly, and said, "Breed squaws ain't missed either."

Robidoux, one of the fur company trappers, swung his Hawken until it pointed at Scruggs's chest, and grinned. "It gets told, all of it. The shoot. The trouble maybe you cause *capitaine* now. How you treat this *fille,* this daughter of my ami de Paris, yes?"

Scruggs seemed to recover confidence as he stood up and balled his fists. "Never saw an Injun worth spit. Goes double for breeds, spawn of white men on red sluts."

She ignored him, wearied suddenly by the exploding violence. The rest of the party edged cautiously downslope, fearing a volley from the umber shade of the trees, but it never came. Beside a shaggy gray cottonwood trunk, the body of the Arikara sprawled silently.

She tucked her torn and grass-stained white blouse into her skirt and trudged after the others. Peter had slid away from Scruggs and hastened to distance himself. The engagés and the rest recovered axes and saws and trotted swiftly into the bottoms, congregating silently around the dead Arikara.

"Rees always was trouble," muttered one of the deckhands. "Used to be, they'd hit anything going past their villages—mackinaws, keelboats, canoes—it didn't matter. Bloody bastards. He got what he deserved."

"He deserved death for standing there peacefully?" she shot back.

The deckhand laughed. "You see it from the Injun side, girl. I see it from white."

"All right, start cutting wood. We got no time to waste on dead Injuns," Scruggs said.

The trappers and engagés stared at him and drifted into the woods, eyeing likely deadwood for the insatiable furnaces.

"Get going, priest," said Scruggs. "You too," he shot at Dr. Evans. "You, breed bitch, start carrying."

"I'm going to bury this man," said Father DeSmet quietly.

"Hell you are. Hunks of red meat don't need burying."

DeSmet ignored him. "Peter, Marie Therese, perhaps you'll help me. We'll build a scaffold and pay our respects."

Father DeSmet knelt beside the dead Arikara and seemed to shut the rest of the world out of his consciousness. Until Scruggs roared and yanked DeSmet up by the collar of his black suitcoat, pitching him into the grass.

"You heard me."

DeSmet rolled up from the ground. "I will bury this man," he said wearily. He stood, his hands balled into big fists.

"You'll cut wood." The bore of Scruggs's carbine swung toward the priest, and then toward John Evans, and settled at last on Peter. He grinned. "Ain't any of them trappers around to protect you now, breed."

"No, sir," said Peter. "Filthy Injun isn't worth burying."

She gaped as Peter trotted off, ax over his shoulder, heading for the woods. Sadness and anger filled her, but then she excused him. He'd been terrified by Scruggs.

"Get going now. We need all the wood we can get. Place up the river with no trees, so we got to get two days' worth now."

Father DeSmet stood wearily, doing nothing until Scruggs prodded him and Evans along with his carbine, Scruggs laughing to himself.

"Come along, breed."

She refused to budge, and settled into the grass beside the dead Arikara.

He paused, and she saw him weighing things, eyeing the two whites and her. Then he shrugged.

"Have your Injun funeral, then, girly. Crew and me, we'll have a little party with you one of these days."

She watched them vanish into the shadows. From within the dense bottom brush she heard the ring of axes and bite of saws, and the drift of male voices. She sat beside the man, feeling warm sun heat her dark skirt. The green-bellied flies had found the Arikara, and crawled into his nostrils and drank at the two terrible holes in him, one erupting from his chest above the heart, and one right through the base of his neck.

She stared at him for the first time. A handsome man, sinewy, with a sharp aquiline nose and wide prominent cheekbones a little like hers. His flesh tone was yellower than hers. His blue-black straight hair had been parted into two braids, and tucked into his hair were two eagle feathers, white and black-tipped, ensigns of success in battle. His eyes, oddly yellow, remained open, staring, but no spirit lay behind them. She wondered where his spirit had gone, where Arikara spirits go after death. A good place, she hoped. He hadn't died bravely in battle, but innocently looking for trade, or maybe hoping to beg a little tobacco or a few bullets and powder.

She closed her eyes, feeling something kindred about him, this victim of white men. This man had been shot casually like a dog, like a coyote, just because he was there to shoot. Some bitterness crept over her, staining this moment of empathy. Bitterness toward all whites. Hatred of that part of her. Bewilderment that these people who brought with them the miracles of civilization, pots and kettles and guns and powder and blankets, brought death and disease too.

She wept, the sunny afternoon turning blurry and choked as tears slid down her cheeks. She didn't know who to pray to for this one's soul. She couldn't pray to Father DeSmet's god. Napi, Old Man, might care a little about this one. Sky Chief, Sun, the blessing of her mother's Pikuni, saw this. Oh, Sky Chief, carry this one to the good place beyond the edge of the world, where you spend your nights, she begged. Take him where white men don't shoot the peoples of the plains; where there will always be buffalo on the horizon, or at the river drinking sweet, cool water; where the Cold Maker never comes. Take him there . . .

Then an odd impulse possessed her. She blessed herself, her hand flying from forehead to breastbone to left and right, ending over her heart. "In the name of the Father, Son, and Holy Ghost," she added, bewildered with herself and yet fulfilled.

A magpie exploded near her and she peered around sharply, seeing nothing. From deep within the flats axes thumped. A bee hovered about her, settling on a yellow daisy beside the Arikara's twisted head. She wanted to protect this man from the white men, from coyote and wolf and crow. Maybe his people would come back for him once the packet left.

She pondered the whiteness within her. Was her father like the others, like second mate Scruggs, a murderer who killed red men just for the pleasure of killing them? She hoped not. This had been the work of boat crewmen and not fur company men. But that could change. Whites were whites.

She didn't grieve long, not for this silent one she didn't know, not even of her mother's people. She wondered if she might build a scaffold for him. But she had nothing for the cutting of wood and no rawhide to bind it together. And no way to lift him up and give him to Sun, forever. And if she cut wood, Scruggs would steal it anyway.

Bury him, then. She stood, dusting off her skirts, hunting for rock. Plenty of it lay about, deteriorated strata of sandstone, tumbling dun and cracked-in slabs with gray lichen spotting them. That would have to do, she thought. She found some loose rock and lifted it, fearful of rattlesnakes, and carried it to the Arikara. Heavy, hurting her arms. His limbs were akimbo, so she paused to straighten them and collect his old Norwester fusil, a pathetic flintlock smoothbore, and place it beside him for his spirit journey. Maybe it'd help him to reach wherever Arikara people went.

For an hour she tugged and sweated and dragged stone to the dead man, slowly building a rock coffin up his legs and onto his torso. Then, as she tugged another gritty slab toward him, the young brown man materialized out of nowhere, muscular and hard-eyed. One of them. He eyed her, and her work, and studied her face, seeing her blood.

His hands flashed. "Who are you, sister?"

She glanced uneasily into the cottonwoods, waiting for trouble to explode, but the muffled noises there came from close along the river now.

"Marie Therese de Paris," she said. And her hands told him the rest, remembering the sign language.

We will take Black Bear to our people, his hands said. And you.

No, I am going to my father now, her hands replied. She glared at him, afraid.

He eyed her sharply, and nodded. Swiftly, he undid her work and carried the fallen headman off, downstream. She watched him go, full of emptiness. She belonged to no one, and not even the sun-warmed loam under her, the earth mother, was hers to rest upon. She'd seen death this long trip, and for a moment she yearned for it because it was a Place.

Peter sweated through the endless afternoon, driving his young body to its limits. The great lengths of rough wood were too much for one person to carry, and he teamed with others to heft the logs to the shoreline where previous woodcutters had fashioned a crude levee. The bark bit his hands and scraped threads out of his shirt.

He'd do better than these whites! He'd show them he was no worthless Injun hanging around, refusing to labor because that was squaw's work. Squaws cut and hoed and dragged and drudged. Men hunted and warred. But not white men! These burly whites around him sweated until they stank. Some had doffed their shirts—the engagés, especially, whose buckskins grew hot and clammy in the summer heat.

"Stinking redskins," he muttered to one of the fur men. "All they do is cause trouble."

"Ah! Monsieur, was it not trouble from the Rees, yes?"

"They came begging!"

The trapper shrugged. Together they lifted a long thin willow limb, still green. It wouldn't burn well, but the firemen could mix it with dryer wood.

They trudged and careened toward the riverbank, stumbling over deadfall, passing close to Scruggs, who watched him, amused.

"Breeds can't do a day's work," the second mate muttered.

"I'm a white man!" Peter cried. "My name's Kipp!"

Scruggs's ax handle slid outward insidiously, tangling Peter's feet. He toppled into underbrush, and the willow log landed on him, hurting his right thigh.

"Wuthless," said Scruggs.

"My father's second in command at American Fur! And I'll run it some day!"

But Scruggs had turned back to the tree he was cutting, his cotton shirt blackened by sweat. Peter picked himself up, and then the willow log.

"I think maybe we make a little detour next time, yes?" said his partner.

"I won't. I'm a better man than Scruggs. He's just bigger, is all. I can read and cipher and he can't."

"He can kill, *garçon.*"

They dropped the log onto a growing pile of them beside the river, and Peter stopped to dash the turbid water over his face. He felt like quitting, but sheer pride prohibited it. He'd carry logs until he dropped, if that would make him equal to them.

Purple shadows from the opposite shore lengthened across the restless water and crept over the wooded bottoms, cooling them instantly. Peter toiled on, every muscle in him shrieking now, protesting. And still he labored, bloody from a hundred small cuts where rough wood lacerated his hands and arms. And still no sign of the *St. Ange.*

The priest and the geologist emerged from the lavender woods, long-faced and grim, settling themselves beside the river. Peter wondered where Marie Therese was. He realized he'd seen nothing of her for hours. Why she dithered about that dirty Ree he couldn't understand. Just a beggar wanting a twist of tobacco. All beggars, taking what they could get away with, stealing it if they couldn't beg it. Scruggs had been right. Drive them off. Drive them out. Drive them beyond the end of the earth.

Scruggs emerged from the cottonwoods, carrying his carbine and his ax. He spotted DeSmet and Evans beside the river.

"All worn out, are ye? Well, now ye know how the other half lives, by sweat and toil from dawn to dusk. You're as lazy as those Injuns."

"I must say, you've taught me something, sir," said Father DeSmet gently.

Scruggs hawked and spat. "It ain't over, mate. We got to load it all when she arrives. After that you can go tattle to the master. If ye've got the guts."

Twilight thickened. The grassy bluffs above glowed apricot and amber in the long light. Daylight up there, but blue night crawling along in the bottoms. Worried, Peter slipped away and began to hunt for Marie Therese, threading through dark clawing woods and brush toward the place where the Arikara had died.

What was the matter with her? Mooning like that over some primitive savage bent on theft? Far off he heard the ship's whistle echoing eerily down the valley that channeled the great river. Summoning them all, telling them to finish up, gather at the bank, ready to load. A half mile off, maybe. He plunged out of the far side of the woods, where the slope invaded it and denied water to the hungry trees. He found the spot. A number of small slab rocks had been gathered there, gray in the dull light. The Injun had vanished. And he found no trace of her.

"Marie?" he cried. "Marie Therese?"

"I'm here, Peter."

Her soft voice drifted to him from the slope and when he studied the grassy hill, he found her partway up, lying quietly.

"Marie Therese! What are you doing there? The boat's coming!"

"I heard."

"We'll be late!"

"They'll spend the night here, Peter. They have wood to load. I'm not ready to go to the boat."

"But he won't stay here! Not with Ree injuns around. He'll go to an island after they load."

She said nothing, and he forced his weary legs to scale the path upward, until he could sit beside her. The boat's whistle howled, much closer now. And he could hear the thump of the great pistons as it rounded the last bend.

"Where's that Ree? You bury him somewhere?"

"They took him."

"You mean they came back while we were cutting wood?"

"One did. A brave young one. Not much older than me. He did a brave thing."

"Endangered you! Lucky he didn't kill you or take you! We'd better get back to safety."

"We're safe. And the one who came is my friend."

He peered at her closely, seeing her dirty, torn blouse and the grass stains. "That Injun do that to you?"

"The second mate. He put his hand on my breast."

"Don't talk like that! You shouldn't say anything, anything."

"It happened. And he's threatening worse. So maybe I'll stay here and not go with the boat."

He had nothing to say to that, but someone else did.

"Forgive him, Marie Theresc. Forgive us all." It was Father DeSmet's gentle voice rising to them from the forest edge. "Come along, you two. The wood will be loaded by the time we get there, and you and Dr. Evans and I'll have a talk with Captain La Barge. I assure you, little one, things will be better for you. It won't just be the captain. Every engagé, every trapper, every person with the House of Chouteau, is pledged now to see to your safety. Marie Therese, you've brightened their days, flying on top of the texas like a flag of honor."

He laughed gently, and she rose. Peter did too, escorting her down the long treacherous slope.

Chapter Eight

For Pierre-Jean DeSmet the episode at the great bend had been particularly distressing. The Arikara were among the tribes that the Indian commissioner, David Mitchell, wanted to gather at a peace council at Fort Laramie later in the summer. They lived in permanent villages upriver, and the priest hoped to start their chief, Iron Bear, westward for the conference.

Now he doubted the *St. Ange* could even dock there, and quite likely would be fired upon as it steamed up the Missouri.

For what seemed to be no reason at all, Joseph La Barge had cut back the power and let the packet drift toward the west bank in the middle of the morning. The Jesuit puzzled about it. No woodlot was visible, and plenty of cordwood still lay stacked on the deck.

Deckhands made fast to the shore while La Barge trotted down the companionways in his trim blue suit, until at last he stood on the main deck face-to-face with second mate Scruggs. The master was smaller than the pockmarked second mate.

Deckhands and engagés sensed some sort of confrontation and gathered around. Above, Pelagie La Barge watched her husband fearfully, her hand to her mouth.

"Mr. Scruggs," said the master. "Here is where we part company."

The surly mate eyed him narrowly.

"Gather your things—or rather, you, Mr. Picotte, fetch them. Mr. Scruggs, I am putting you off."

"I signed on for the trip. You can't do that."

"I am doing it."

"You're shorthanded."

"I am. Eight to cholera and you'll be ninth."

"How am I to survive, La Barge?"

"You should have thought of that earlier. I have it from numerous witnesses that you conducted yourself in a manner that requires my attention. Against the strenuous opposition of fur company engagés and others, you shot and struck an Arikara headman whose intent was plainly peaceful. Others of this crew shot too, and some say your shot was not the killing one. I've taken that into consideration. With that reckless act, you've endangered this packet. You've endangered Father DeSmet's peace mission.

"But that's not all, Scruggs. You've abused a woman passenger, slapped her viciously, engaged in insults to her person and threatened much more. Threatened death upon the priest himself, and Dr. Evans. Engaged in a melee with these passengers. You took liberties with Miss de Paris—"

"Just a breed, La Barge."

"An honorable woman, Scruggs."

"You're just a bunch of Injun-lovers."

"Call it what you will, Scruggs. We voyage peaceably through their lands. But they are fully capable of destroying this vessel and everyone on it. The fur company that has chartered this packet has friendly dealings with all of them. Its engagés are experienced when it comes to discerning peaceful or hostile intent. You knew that perfectly well. Many of their Indian wives and children are on this packet. You ignored them and my own wishes."

Picotte returned with the second mate's small possessions, clothing mostly, and a knife.

"You can't put me out there without food and arms, La Barge."

"I am doing it. The alternative is to lock you in one of our staterooms clear to Fort Union and then down to St.

Louis, and turn you over to authorities. I haven't a brig on this vessel, so I have chosen this."

"Maybe I won't go. Maybe you're afraid to put me off."

"I suspect I'm sparing you from death, Scruggs. If not from some of the engagés who have come to me, then from the Arikaras we will be meeting soon."

Father DeSmet thought to mitigate the punishment. "Perhaps, Mr. La Barge, some line and fishhooks . . ."

La Barge nodded curtly, and at a glance, a deckhand scurried off to fetch them from ship's stores.

"Fish!" snarled Scruggs, clenching his fists. Without warning, he plunged into La Barge, swinging roundhouse punches. The blocky master had expected it, and met the flailing arms with fists of his own, as hard as butcher blocks. Around him fur company men stood poised to handle any others of the deckhands, but the fight was between La Barge and the second mate. Above, Pelagie moaned. Farther above, the priest glimpsed Marie Therese, watching intently from her perch on the texas.

La Barge's tactics were simple: He bulled forward, driving Scruggs back until he reached the ship's rail. Then La Barge shoved the second mate over the rail and into shallow water a few feet from the bank. The splash startled DeSmet. The mate sputtered and stood, water draining from his grimy shirt and blue britches, into the murky river flowing past his knees.

"I'll kill you, La Barge. And every fur company man I ever see. And every stinking Injun."

La Barge nodded. Picotte lifted the man's possessions and pitched them toward the bank. Some landed in water. Scruggs snatched at the clothing before it vanished. His knife glinted in the mud.

"Anyone else?" roared La Barge, glaring around at his crew.

The deckhands stood frozen.

He nodded, and crewmen freed the lines. The *St. Ange* drifted downstream for a moment while the helmsman let it slip into deeper waters, and then the tremor of the two pistons signaled that the ship was under power.

The master turned to the fur company men who'd watched it and quietly sided with him. "I'm in need of hands. Anyone who'd like the return of half his passage in exchange for crew work the rest of the trip, see me."

Two mountain men looked as if they might.

The packet gained the azure channel and fought its way up the river again. On the far bank the rigid figure of Scruggs grew smaller and smaller, until they rounded a bight and he disappeared.

Pierre-Jean DeSmet sighed, wondering how it would go for the big second mate. A harsh thing. Not as harsh as ocean discipline, though. The man had clothing, summer weather, a knife, some personal effects to trade, and could probably walk out—if he didn't insult every tribesman he encountered. He might end up as a wood hawk. That's how many a wood hawk started in business.

Father DeSmet followed the master up the companionways and into the pilothouse, wanting to talk.

La Barge glared at him. "If you've come to rebuke me—"

DeSmet grinned. "Not at all."

But La Barge wasn't done. "I recruit them off the St. Louis levee, sometimes out of the roughest dives you've ever seen. Some from there, some up from New Orleans. I try to sort them out—have a good eye for it, I think. I want them strong and hard. Mates especially. They've got to knock heads sometimes. I had my doubts about this one. You can tell, you know. A man wears his soul on his face, eh? But you can't always be choosy. Other masters snatch the better ones from you. We got started late, AFC slow to wharf its trade goods. The river's dropping now, and we'll start hitting bars any time too. . . ." He turned to the priest. "I do what I must for the safety and well-being of the packet."

DeSmet saw fire in the man's eye. "You're not hearing objection from me, Joseph. I was wondering, really, if the man poses any more danger. I suppose a determined man could catch up with us with a lot of night-walking while we lie-to. If he traded for a horse, he'd do it easily. I fear he might make an attempt on you or your family. I worry about the young lady up there. She slips out nights to bathe."

"I'll think on it. There's no one in the women's lounge now—all the women are deck passengers, mostly bound for Fort Pierre with their men. I never asked, but always figured she'd run into trouble there—being a breed."

"Mind if I talk with her?"

La Barge smiled at the priest and returned to his piloting. Reef patterns showed ahead.

Father DeSmet found his way to the ladder to the top of the texas and climbed it, feeling the fierce heat of midday on the plains.

She watched him clamber out upon the roof.

"I've never been here before. Quite a view, Marie Therese! Why, you can even see prairies we can't see down at the water."

"They put the man off because of me," she said. "I wish they'd put him off for another reason."

"Several reasons, I think. He assaulted passengers, killed a friendly Indian."

"No one cared about him—the Indian that was killed. All they worry about is whether the incident might stir up the Arikaras and endanger the rest of us." She glared at him.

"I cared about him."

"Not very much."

"Do you know that beyond a doubt, Marie Therese?"

"No whites care about Indians, except to get something from them, like robes and land."

"Perhaps you are judging too harshly. In 1840 I went west into their lands, seeking neither robes nor land. And in 1841 others came with me to give rather than receive."

"Maybe you collect souls."

He smiled. "I've been coming into the western wilderness for a decade now, and everywhere I turn I find white men and Indian women living happily together. I've married many. Surely your French father cares about your Piegan mother."

"She left him when I was a little girl."

"Isn't divorce common among the Blackfeet and other tribes? And as simple as piling a spouse's goods outside of the lodge?"

She averted her eyes.

"Captain La Barge says there's no one in the women's cabin now, and he thought you might like to use it. I believe the last one got off at Bellevue or somewhere near there."

"I'm happy where I am."

"A man who wants revenge or murder could trade for a horse and might overtake us. We make about fifty miles a day."

"Are you going to lock me in?" she retorted. Then a softness came over her. "I'm sorry, Father. I shouldn't talk to you like this. I can look after myself."

"It might be wise to take care of your needs in that cabin."

She smiled suddenly. "I appreciate your concern. But Father, we anchor at many islands."

He felt defeated, not a customary feeling in a Jesuit counseling a young woman. An authority he'd long taken for granted had deserted him. "I'll remember you in my prayers," he muttered. "Perhaps you would find merit in the sacrament of reconciliation before evening Mass. If I've offended, Marie Therese, please forgive me."

She grinned at him. He clambered down the ladder, feeling her soul slip further from him with every mile they probed into the Indian lands.

Peter signed on as cabin boy. He wrestled with temptation for a day after Captain La Barge offered to hire fur company men. Why should he drudge a living when his stepfather was second in command of the Upper Missouri Outfit? But the thought of profit consumed him. He'd earn half of his cabin fare of $150, and he thought James Kipp would let him keep it. Seventy-five dollars was as much as some engagés earned in half a year, and it would be all his.

What's more, he'd learn things. He wanted to learn everything. He wanted to rise to the top, doing everything, making a fortune. Marie Therese could scarcely resist a fortune or an ambitious, hardworking husband. The refund of half a fare might be his beginning, cash enough to buy some trade goods and do his own bargaining for buffalo robes. He'd never been indolent. At school he'd been driven by some sort of inner demons that put him at the head of his classes, ahead of all the boys who had no Indian blood in them. He was bright and quick, and some of them resented it, or declared that mastering reading and arithmetic was for the clerk class, not for gentlemen. That never bothered him a bit . . . nor did it now.

He made his way to La Barge in the pilothouse, made his offer, and found himself under the supervision of the steward, Monsieur Picotte, scion of a famous St. Louis family, also making his own way. At six in the morning of the next day, his indolent liberty ended. Picotte directed him first to carry meals from the galley on the main deck up to the texas, where the officers would breakfast. In the small common room there he was to set table, serve, and bring back the dirtied dishes to the galley. Then he was to prepare breakfast for the cabin passengers. This meant setting up folding tables in the men's lounge and again hauling quantities of food up to the boiler deck from the galley.

"Look who's serving us today," said Rudolph Kurz.

Peter nodded, too busy to worry about what others thought. He served John Evans, Father DeSmet, Mrs. La Barge and her children, and others, racing from lounge to the galley below until he felt ready to collapse. And the day had barely begun. He cleared away the dishes, folded the tables, and then trundled the detritus of the meal back to the galley, where he was told to wash dishes. With his hands in dirty, lukewarm water he wondered whether he'd been a fool. He could always quit, he thought; but some stubborn quality in him refused to consider it further.

After that it was time to clean the cabins and haul the

chamber pots down to the main deck and dump their redolent contents into the murky green river. That proved to be the most disgusting of his tasks. He knocked on rooms, which were usually empty, collected the pots two at a time, and carried them down the companionway. Using a gaff, he lowered each into the river and let the great Missouri flood away the contents, whatever they were. The other cabin boy, who ranked Peter, had the easier task of straightening the bedclothes on the bunks and tidying each cabin and stateroom.

His discovered at once that his new duties didn't exempt him from firewood duty. When Joseph La Barge eased the spoon-billed packet close to a cottonwooded bank, ship's bells summoned all hands to collect fuel. And now he couldn't refuse if he didn't feel like cutting wood. The first mate handed him a redheaded ax and told him to cut. So Peter stumbled into the woods, located old limbs and deadfall, and began hacking it into long lengths with never a pause for rest.

By noon Peter thought he'd put in two or three days, and yet his own was scarcely half over. Picotte sent him down aft to the engine room with pots of tea for the engineers and ship's carpenter. He'd never been in that deafening place. Two black iron cylinders huffed and vibrated as steam drove the great pistons within them back and forth. Long hardwood pitman rods cranked giant flywheels that thundered in their bearings.

Peter set his tray on the carpenter's workbench and watched, fascinated by the raw power that vibrated through the soles of his feet, making the packet a living thing. Above he saw the other end of the speaking tube leading to the pilothouse, and wondered how the engineers could hear anything the captain shouted. The two engineers scarcely noticed him as they hovered over bearings, lubricating them constantly, slaves of the monsters they tended. He paused, studying all this, putting names to things: feed pump, escapement pipe, cam rods, throttle, bilge pump. Each of the pistons ran independent of the other, so the packet could proceed on a single cylinder while the other underwent repairs. He spotted the coupling that could disengage the engines from the thundering paddle wheel just aft. He needed to master it all, every bolt and screw, until he could run one of these giants himself. But even as he watched, he heard himself being summoned, the voice in the speaking tube hollow and strange.

He stumbled up to the galley and found Monsieur Picotte waiting with a tray. "To Kurz," he said. "Cabin eight."

The small tray contained a pitcher of fragrant heavy coffee, sugar, and a white, vitreous mug.

He stumbled sullenly up the companionway, suddenly aware that he'd be serving his rival the rest of the journey. He'd been so frantic all day, he'd scarcely thought of Marie Therese, and suddenly he envied her the freedom she had to watch the river slide by from her high sunny perch. He pushed through the men's lounge and down the central corridor to eight, and knocked.

"Ah! It is the right thing for a sleepy afternoon, yes?"

Peter nodded and set the tray down on the small table beside the bunk.

"I am impressed that you would do this thing when you don't need to," Kurz said amiably.

"I'm going to get ahead."

"Sit a moment, young man. I have a cup here and I'll pour for you too, yes? Sit and I will show you something."

Peter sagged into the bentwood hard-bottomed chair, glad to steal a moment, even if it had to be with the Swiss artist.

"You know," said Kurz, "of all the people on this *St. Ange*, I like most to sketch the young lady, Mam'selle de Paris."

Peter glowered while the artist leafed through a large portfolio, finally extracting a dozen sketches. He propped them up along the wall behind the bunk, and Peter gaped, seeing not just beauty, but something magic, something beyond comprehension.

"Do you like them?"

Peter nodded reluctantly.

"Mam'selle's the most interesting subject on the packet. No one else is like her. I try to see beneath the flesh, beyond expression, pierce to the essence—yes, the soul, the will. Do you see her in these?"

"Why are you so interested in her?"

The artist grinned. "Not for the reasons you suppose, young man. You love her. I see it in your face, every hour, every day. Your young heart brims with her. Ah, how can a mortal hide what's in his soul from any artist? I love her too—"

Peter growled in anger.

"—as a subject. Not as an affair of the heart, Mr. Kipp. Truly, I've never seen a woman with such mysteries in her, fires of soul, lanterns of eyes, two sides, angry and tender, all at war within her. Such will! Has any woman in all Europe such will! I say to you, young Mr. Kipp, she's destined for something great, something our feeble imaginations can't even imagine, but I fear it won't include you."

Pain lanced Peter. "Why are you showing me these drawings? Saying these things to me?"

"Ah, I see you, young friend, daggers in your eyes. I'm telling you my interests are different. I'm not stealing her from you. She inspires my sketching hand, makes my pencil fly over the paper. . . . Every artist dreams of a model like her. Do you see?"

Peter felt himself a boy again, and sensed that the manhood he sought eluded him. "I guess so," he muttered.

"Pick one, my young friend."

"For me?"

Kurz nodded.

A few minutes later Peter left, clutching a fine sketch of Marie Therese, sitting in a grassy meadow. He couldn't keep his eyes off of it, couldn't stop wanting to possess her.

Chapter Nine

Though Marie Therese scarcely realized it, the journey had become a voyage of the soul. As the *St. Ange* churned deeper into the Indian lands, so did her heart. She grew alive to the world around her, while her years with the sisters in St. Louis faded into paleness. From her perch upon the texas she watched the things of her childhood reappear; the bunchgrass, the arid high plains, the white-rumped antelope, the mule deer, and at last, the monarchs of the plains, the shaggy buffalo. Love fevered her. Still, not until she saw again the sawtooth peaks of the faraway mountains would she feel she had returned to the homeland of her Pikuni mother.

She knew English and French better than she knew the tongue of her mother, Meadowlark, O-toch-koki. It gladdened her that her mother had been named for the yellow-breast. Yellow was the sacred color of the little buffalo totem that dangled from her neck under her dimity dress, safe from the eyes of Father DeSmet, whom the Pikuni called Innu-e-kinni, or Long Teeth. She loved yellow, the color of the sacred Yellow Buffalo Lodge, which she had seen as a little girl.

One hot afternoon she spotted a great herd of the giants standing belly deep in water to escape biting flies. Out of the mists of her girlhood she remembered a Blackfoot name for the great creatures: black horns, or ee-nau-ah. Ee-nau-ah! A herd of the life-givers there in the water! Her spirit leapt in her breast.

"Noks-sto-mo-au!" she cried. You are my relative!

And then she wondered where the words had come from, and how long they had been buried under the snows of the convent.

But even as the *St. Ange* drew abreast, the white men on the grimy deck far below began shooting at them, their heavy mountain rifles booming and snarling and spitting death. A bull's head bloomed red, and the lord of the plains slowly slid into the water, staining it. A stricken cow bucked and humped as blood leaked from her jaws, and then shivered into death, even as the relentless river rolled her dying body away.

"They're my brothers!" she cried, but not one heard her.

She saw Peter and another crewman launch the yawl, row swiftly toward the floating cow and catch it with a gaff hook. Then Peter rowed back toward the idling packet while the other one towed the buffalo. Tonight they'd all enjoy the succulent buffalo cow. But she grieved anyway; grieved for the cow that surrendered her spirit without being asked, and for the six or seven dead or wounded buffalo, ee-nau-ah, bobbing lifelessly down the great river. "Save us from them," they said to her. "We are sacred to your people."

"I will!" she cried.

"You'll what?"

Startled, she peered down upon Father DeSmet, Long Teeth. "Nothing," she said.

"May I join you, Marie Therese? For a bit, anyway? It gets hot up there."

She nodded, and he ascended the ladder and settled himself beside her, eyeing her quizzically.

"Soon you'll be home."

"Fort Benton? I've never seen it."

"Your father's there. That's home enough, I imagine."

She didn't reply to that. She could barely remember her father.

"Ah, Marie Therese, how you've changed. Each mile of the river changes you. The convent girl vanishes day by day. But what is replacing her, eh? Mam'selle, even your face! Now you are a Piegan; a month ago you were French!"

"I didn't know that."

"I see it. Trust an old priest to see the spirit of a person. I worry about you, Marie Therese. Do you miss your mother—and her people?"

"I don't really remember her."

"Is she well?"

"I've not heard otherwise."

"Is she among the Piegans?"

"The Pikuni? Yes. I want to find her. I want to be named. I have no Pikuni name."

"I'll make inquiries, Marie Therese. Perhaps I can find her for you. I've many friends among your people."

That surprised her. "You would help me? You?"

"Ah, Miss de Paris, you are a soul destined by God for great tasks."

She bridled at that.

He laughed softly. "Sometimes, young lady, even a napikwan priest might have a spiritual insight or two."

He had used the Siksika name for white man, napikwan. She listened intently.

"I've watched these wild lands reclaim you. I've watched you talk to the animals on the river banks. I've watched everything of your father's civilization—and mine—slide away from you, while the Pikuni blooms. It's Destiny—the will of God."

She started to protest, but he held up an authoritative Jesuit hand.

"Ah, trust me. I believe in free will. But some of us are captives of God, and those have no control over their Destinies or the tasks given to them. You are such a one."

"My mother's people worship the Mystery of the Sun, giver of all good things and life. And Napi, the Old Man." She said it defiantly.

"Mark my words, Miss de Paris. You're destined to

help your mother's people. You'll suffer more than you can imagine. You'll grieve the dead and comfort the dying. You'll wrestle with hatred and bitterness—and triumph over them. You'll witness terrible injustice. You'll see one race destroyed by another. You'll see starvation—people so poor they eat rodents and grass. You'll see the buffalo disappear and nothing to replace them. You'll share your wisdom—but you won't always be heard, even by your own. You'll use what you've learned of us—the napikwan—to help the Blackfeet, but some won't understand you, and others will scorn you. And it's all the terrible gift of God."

She wanted to laugh at him, but he had spoken earnestly and with great gentleness. "I am simply going to Fort Benton and my father," she said at last.

"You are at that," he said agreeably. "Please send him my regards."

"But Father—"

Pierre-Jean DeSmet had already lumbered to his feet.

"—how do you know?"

"How does any prophet know?"

"I don't believe you."

He looked as if he were about to lecture her, discuss her obligations to the Holy Faith, lament her drift toward the heathen beliefs of the Siksika—but he simply smiled. "We are both priests and messengers," he said, an odd, wry kindness in his face.

A great tenderness infused her, and she met his gaze. His words confused her—calling her a priest and messenger—and yet they contained something terribly and urgently true. "I don't know what I am or what I want. I'm a mixed-blood, and we don't belong anywhere. You see how Peter and I are condemned by the whites."

"Miss de Paris—you're closer to the core of life than Peter is. Bless him, he's devoured science and mechanics. He wishes to render himself a white man, but I sigh for him. See him down there, bright and busy and eager, driven by his hurts. He loves you, you know. You're a mixed-blood like him, and that pierces his soul. The work he does—and the half fare he's earning for it—is a gift to you,

you know. He's saying he's a person of substance, fit to make a good husband for you."

"He's very dear—but it can't be, Father."

"Ah! I know how that is! When we're called, we follow!"

"No one has called me."

"I think when you reach Fort Benton you'll hear yourself being called. That's in the heart of the Blackfoot country, and we're not there yet. These naked prairies"—he waved a hand toward a blurred horizon—"are Assiniboin and Cree and Sioux. But ah, Fort Benton!"

"Can I see the Rocky Mountains there?"

"No, only the Highwoods."

"Sitosis Tuksi—Middle Mountains," she blurted, wondering again where the Siksika words came from.

"There. You see?" He paused, hesitant. "I have only one small favor to ask of you, Miss de Paris."

She nodded, waiting.

"You'll see all manner of evil done by white men. But don't blame the Holy Faith that tells them not to do it."

She nodded. She would not blame the faith, strange as it was to her. She remembered the sisters, most of them sweet and kind, some distant, and others sour and even cruel, lording over a little breed girl as if she were nothing.

"Well, then, Captain La Barge tells me we'll make Fort Union tomorrow afternoon. I'll be leaving you tomorrow—the Indian superintendent, David Mitchell, wants me to gather up the leaders of the northwestern tribes for some treaty-making. Use my good offices, as he put it!" DeSmet laughed. "I'll do so. Alec Culbertson and I've been drafted, you might say. I'll be there, if only to protect the tribes from the clerks."

"You care for us."

He peered intently into her eyes. "More than I can put into words. Care and fear for you. I came up here, really, to say good-bye—there won't be time in the hubbub tomorrow. We shall be messengers of God together, you and I."

That disturbed her, and she didn't know what to make of it.

* * *

Fort Union! Peter Kipp pressed against the rail, watching the distant dot on the north bank of the Missouri grow into a stockaded post, its silvery cottonwood walls jutting high into the azure sky. Fort Union! He'd grown up there, the seat of empire for the American Fur Company, while his stepfather ran the post. Fort Union! It was an arrogant island of white men's civilization rooted a few miles above the confluence of the Yellowstone and Missouri, commanding the rivers and all that passed along them in that yellow, arid land of rough bluffs and sparse grasses.

This was Assiniboin country, but the post's clients also included the Sioux and Pawnee, the Cree and Crow, the Blackfeet and even other tribesmen who came great distances. Usually these ancient enemies observed the neutrality of the post, camped side by side while trading, only to butcher each other away from the white men.

Fort Union! Smoke erupted from the near bastion, followed instantly by a concussion—the welcoming cannon. Above, Peter heard the joyous shrill of the steam whistle in response. The *St. Ange* slowed, its paddles turning languorously and its thunder dimming as the boat slid toward the levee at the foot of a steep bank below the post. Even as he watched, throngs of tribesmen raced toward the riverbank to gawk at the fireboat—white men's magic—and study the mountains of trade goods that would soon erupt from the belly of the boat.

Tomorrow the trading season would begin. The post's factor, Edwin Denig, would dress in his best black suit, along with the clerks, and there'd be a windy-worded ceremony before the front gates and trading window. Then whiskey-nosed Denig would lavish gifts on the assembled chiefs, there'd be some flag-raising and more speeches, and the trading would begin. Peter had seen it all as a boy, and relished the chance to see it again.

But it was not to be. "Kipp, what ye be doin', wasting company time? Git ye down in thar." The mate pointed at the dark hold. Peter remembered that he was an employee, and hastened toward the great hatches in the foredeck that had been swung open by deckmen. Others were swinging a boom around and lowering a cargo net into the shallow hold, where a mountain of trade goods and supplies awaited.

Peter clambered into the low belly of the riverboat and couldn't stand upright in the five feet of headroom. No light other than what bled down from the hatch illumined his way. The darkness matched his spirits. He'd scarcely even see Fort Union, or people he knew! They directed him aft, where he joined a sweating crew that was wrestling barrels and bales onto a little handcart that ran on a circular track from the hatch rearward.

"Tons o' junk for the redskins," muttered a big bull of a man as he hefted a cask of awls onto the handcart. "An' after that, tons o' robes and pelts for old Chouteau in his mansion down upon St. Louie."

"An' after dat, more firewood," said another, who was hefting bales of Witney trade blankets identical to those used by Hudson's Bay Company.

Peter choked down his disappointment. He'd spend every minute down in this black hold. But he plunged in fiercely, lifting a long crate of Leman trade rifles and a bale of bolts of flannel trade cloth in rainbow colors until the handcart could hold no more.

"Take 'er, Petey," said one.

Peter pushed the heavy cart along its rails to the hold while the deckmen behind him rested. They were going to let him unload it all into the waiting cargo net at the hatch! Anger brimmed up in him and receded. He'd earn his seventy-five dollars; he'd show them all that a mixed-blood was just as good as they were.

Furiously he unloaded blankets and kegs of gunpowder and crates of rifles into the cargo net. He heaped baled blankets and bolts of cloth onto them, and added pasteboard boxes of ribbons and hanks of red, blue, green, and white trade beads. He rolled a cask of ax heads, lifted a crate of hatchets, and kegs of Wilson knives. He wrestled heavy pigs of bullet lead, and sacks of sugar and coffee beans, sweating in the square of light under the hatch, his soul yearning to be out in the blue sky above.

"What's the damned trouble down there?" bellowed the mate above. The man peered down, barked a command, and several deckhands clattered down to help.

"I can do it!" Peter muttered.

"Lazy breed," one retorted.

In moments they cleaned off the handcart and sent Peter into the gloom while men above drew the load out of the hatch and swung it to shore, where fur company engagés unloaded it all into waiting wagons.

All that afternoon Peter slaved in the belly of the *St. Ange*, while most of his shipmates, including Father DeSmet and the artist, Kurz, abandoned the ship. Peter ached; he didn't have time to eat or even for a sip of water. But by late afternoon he and the crew had unloaded a mountain of bright gewgaws for the surrounding tribes: ribbons, round hand mirrors, hawk bells, needles and thread, brass kettles, iron skillets, tin pots, brass wire, cubes of Oriental vermilion wrapped in waxy paper, shawls, ready-made blue shirts, beaver-felt hats, hoop iron, ready-made arrow points, cotton sacks of sugar—a favorite of all the tribes—burlap-bagged corn and rice, bed ticking; traders' supplies—including ledgers, steel nibs, and paper—cooking utensils, lamp oil, vinegar, and a hundred things more that were so precious fifteen hundred miles from civilization.

Then, when everything except the goods destined for Fort Benton had been wrestled out, the robes started coming in. Now it was all reversed: heavy, hundred-pound bales, usually with ten winter robes and sometimes an eleventh summer robe, were lowered into the gloomy hold, and Peter wearily hoisted them onto the hand truck and delivered them to the crew aft, where they were settled on boards well above the bilge. The boat had vomited one form of treasure only to swallow a greater one in robes and peltries. This year, according to the crewmen's gossip, the packet would take twenty thousand robes and two thousand other pelts—the entire previous year's harvest—down the mighty river to the Chouteau warehouse on the St. Louis levee. Eventually they'd become greatcoats, belts to run machinery in eastern factories, carriage and sleigh robes, and leather clothing.

Then, well after the supper hour, Peter felt the power of the *St. Ange* as it built steam. He heard shouts and commands above, the rumble of the steam pistons, the mighty splash of the paddles, and the river packet thundered into the evening, still westbound. Peter sat on a bale of robes, dejected. He'd not even gotten off the boat.

As last they let him out upon the deck, into a summer evening that lifted his spirits. He could see Marie Therese high above at her usual station on the texas. She waved, and he rejoiced. They were going to Fort Benton together! He was earning money—money to show her he could support her; even a mixed-blood could be worthy of her, a good husband and father!

The *St. Ange* made one more stop that evening, on the south bank ten miles west of the fort, for firewood. But Peter had had all he could endure, and clambered swiftly up companionways and out upon the texas, out of sight of the mates.

She smiled. "You work hard, Peter."

He rejoiced. A word from Marie was all it took to lift his spirits. "I didn't even get a chance to say good-bye to Father DeSmet and Rudolph Kurz. I didn't even get off the boat. But I did more than anyone else. And them all older than me too. I showed them I could do it. I showed them I'm worth something."

"Peter—we'll always be breeds to them."

"Yes—but I'll show them I'm just as good! I'm earning half my fare back! Soon I'll start my own business!"

"What will that be?"

"I don't know yet. But I think I'll be a freighter. I'm going to get a wagon and a team. I can earn a good living that way. I can help open up the country for settlement—take things to settlements."

Something clouded passed across her face. He studied her in the lavender twilight, and loved her more than ever.

"You want the settlers to come," she said. It wasn't a question.

"Of course I do! Soon there'll be farms and cattle plantations, and brick cities and good carriages and houses with comfortable parlors with stoves in them, and—"

"Peter, don't."

He held himself in. They'd been through this many times before. "Are you glad to be back? I mean, when we get to Fort Benton?"

"Yes, Peter."

"Will you be glad to see your father? I sure will!"

"I think so. But I was just a little girl. . . ." Her voice trailed off, and he sensed her uncertainty.

"I'm glad we're both on the boat. We'll both be on the keelboat. We'll both live at Fort Benton."

"I wonder about Fort Benton, Peter. It might not—"

"It's better than Union. That's what I hear. All new and comfortable and doing more trading than any other post—with the Blackfeet."

"Maybe my mother will come," she said. "Meadowlark. I don't know what band she's with. Maybe the Grease Melters. Oh, Peter . . ."

"I don't have a mother. Some Salish woman I've never seen. I wouldn't want to see her. Some savage woman, dumb as a stump."

"Peter."

The tone of her voice upset him. "Look, Marie—when we get there, we've got to look ahead. We've got to let go of the past—let go of the dumb Indian stuff. I will, and you just have to! You must! They're all so—primitive. Dying away because a better people are coming along. Our fathers' people!"

Marie Therese didn't answer. Instead she dug into the bodice of her cream dimity and pulled out an amulet. He saw a little buffalo honed from yellow agate, suspended from a thong around her neck. He never knew she wore the thong or the amulet under her dress, beneath the small silver cross on its silver chain, which had always lain over her heart.

"I'm a buffalo woman," she said, and Peter intuitively knew. And grieved.

Chapter Ten

Peter admired the cautious way that the master of the *St. Ange* probed through uncharted and unknown waters above Fort Union. The captain had agreed to rendezvous with the Fort Benton keelboat at the confluence of the Poplar River, miles above Fort Union, water levels permitting. Without the contribution of the Yellowstone, the Missouri had shrunk dramatically, but the lightened steamer was drawing only twenty-eight inches instead of nearly four feet. With almost all the passengers off, Peter's work had lessened, and La Barge had stationed him at the duckbill prow with a long, marked pole to take soundings and shout them up to the pilothouse. He found the work pleasant compared to the brutal toil of the previous weeks. The *St. Ange* coiled around giant oxbows, so that in the space of any hour the sun swung down at him from every imaginable angle and shadows bobbed across the deck.

They pierced through a gloomy trench that sliced an arid, featureless land. Occasional copses of cottonwoods along the banks provided the wood for the hungry firebox. Peter toiled gladly. If white men wouldn't accept his mixed blood, perhaps they would accept his work.

They found the keelboat tied to the north bank just above the Poplar. The Creoles aboard it cheered, and the *St. Ange* whistled its pleasure. The burly French would drag, pole, and row the keelboat to Benton, with an occasional assist from any wind that would fill the square-rigged sail. No other river people had the strength or courage or will to perform the Herculean task.

Swiftly Peter, deckmen, and the Creoles unloaded the last twenty-five tons of cargo and stowed it in the hold of the sturdy keelboat. This Pittsburgh-made craft measured seventy feet and had an eighteen-foot beam. A small cabin rose at the middle, with foot passage on the deck to either side. Its mast rose just forward of the cabin. A sandbox on the forward deck, with a small cookstove upon it, comprised the galley. Forward and aft of the central cargo box were storage areas for the crew and supplies. Peter marveled that such a large boat could be wrestled up the swift Missouri by nothing more than human toil.

He raced back to the women's cabin of the *St. Ange* and gathered Marie Therese's trunk, which he stowed in the cramped cabin of the keelboat. It would be her exclusive domain, shielding her from male stares. She watched solemnly, but with excitement shining in her eyes. Then she stepped down the cleated stage to the keelboat while the voyageurs watched wordlessly. They rarely had a female passenger. Their frank, assessing gazes irked Peter, but he couldn't do a thing about it.

Then, at last, he raced up the companionways to the texas deck, where La Barge awaited him.

"Well, Mr. Kipp. You've done a commendable job, and I've taken the liberty of drafting a letter of recommendation that might help you with the company. Give my regards to your father, eh?"

"Where's my pay?" Peter blurted.

"Why—I thought to post it in your father's accounts in St. Louis."

"I earned it!" Peter cried, wild anxiety crowded him.

La Barge seemed taken aback. "Why, Mr. Kipp, so you did. I imagine you've the right to it. Perhaps you'll want to settle with your father."

"I just want the money. I worked hard."

"Yes, you did. Well? How'll we do it? A letter of

credit you can use at the post? Open an account in St. Louis with Chouteau, the way many engagés do?"

"I'll take your letter of credit, sir."

Captain La Barge drafted the note, blotted it, and handed it to the young man. "Ah, mon ami, you're a one to do work. You'll go far!"

Peter folded the precious document and raced to the waiting keelboat, where Marie had already settled herself atop the low cabin. Moments later the *St. Ange* swung around while the voyageurs uncoiled the thousand-foot cordelle, the line anchored to the mast that they would use to drag the boat up the Missouri. Without being asked, Peter joined them.

"Ah, my frien' Kipp—take this, eh?" said one of the voyageurs. The man handed Peter an ax and a hatchet. "Cut a path."

Peter was puzzled.

"You'll see. For the cordelliers, cut the path. I'm the capitaine, La Roux, eh?"

Peter did see. When at last the long line had been stretched out, a gang of voyageurs shouldered it and began to tug. A single man, La Roux, stayed on the keelboat to handle the sweep rudder and hoist the square-rigged sail whenever a following breeze came along. Peter was to scythe a path through the rough brush along the bank where the cordelliers would come.

In most places thick brush, rosebushes and bullberries, crowded the banks, the thorny brush sometimes rising ten or twelve feet. It would be up to Peter to cut through it, somehow staying ahead of the gang, upslope and down, never ceasing. He chopped and hacked ruthlessly, wearying himself in minutes, barely opening a path for the sweating cordelliers. They never seemed to pause, tugging through blazing July sun, mosquitoes, biting black flies, rattlers, swamps, rapids, log snags, collapsed trees, rocky precipices; slowly dragging the lumbering keelboat through the swift green water. Here the river ran clean, having not yet picked up the load of silt that turned it into café-au-lait a thousand river miles to the south and east.

Just about the time when Peter could swing his ax no more, they reached a sheer bank that stopped the cordelling. At once the cheerful Creoles wound up the line and jumped aboard. They plucked up long poles with a round knob at one end and aligned themselves on either side of the keelboat.

"La bas les perches," bawled La Roux, and in unison the voyageurs drove their poles into the river bottom, then walked aft, passing to either side of the cabin on the narrow walks as they did, propelling the boat forward.

"Levez les perches," bellowed La Roux, and at once the boatmen lifted their poles and raced forward to begin the process again before the boat lost momentum.

Swiftly Peter got the hang of it. The knob at the end of the pole fit comfortably into his armpit and he could lean into the pole as he walked rearward, feeling the heavy boat yield under his tread. If anything, the poling exhausted him more than the path-cutting, but there were moments of rest. At last the boatmen put to shore for a break where some cottonwoods grew. Most of the voyageurs filled their pipes with tabac and smoked quietly through the midday heat. But not for long—soon La Roux summoned them to the next ordeal.

Peter either hacked brush or poled until he could endure no more, and stumbled along, sobbing, his body rebelling and hurting beyond any pain he'd ever known, while the voyageurs grinned knowingly. In a perverse way, they enjoyed Peter's suffering, which affirmed their own toughness.

But late in the afternoon they swept into an oxbow that bestowed a following wind. Gratefully, Peter scrambled aboard and collapsed, even as the square sail bulged out and dragged the lumbering boat into the swift current.

"Are you well, Peter? You're terribly red."

He found Marie peering down at him from the roof of the little cabin. He didn't answer. Even talking was work. She slid down beside him and wiped his face with cool river water while he struggled for breath. The river glare hurt his eyes.

"You don't have to, you know. We're passengers."

"I have to."

"Why, Peter?"

"You know why."

She nodded, and wiped his fevered face with a handkerchief.

The afternoon breeze held, and after a half-hour doze, Peter sat up, needing the company of the tender girl he would someday claim as his own. She sat solemnly beside him, waiting for his company. To gaze upon her was to love her.

"We're in Blackfeet country, Marie Therese. Are you happy?"

"No. I'm thinking about my père—my father."

"I am too. I haven't seen Mr. Kipp since—a long time I guess."

She nodded. "I'm afraid. What if I don't like him? What if he doesn't like me?"

"You're his flesh and blood!" It reminded Peter that he had no flesh and blood—an unknown Salish woman who might not still be alive; and a stepfather who'd raised him because he was an abandoned breed boy. He had a stepmother he didn't remember, Ipasha, or Good Eagle Tail, a daughter of the Mandan chief Matotopa. And stepbrothers and sisters he'd never met. But none of them were his flesh and blood. Maybe he wasn't going home to anything.

"He might like me. He might make me—you know." She faltered.

"No, I don't."

"He might not know what to do with me. Maybe he'll promise me to some engagé. Maybe someone higher up. I can read and write and do figures and play the harp and—all that." She sounded dejected. "Peter—don't you tell a soul. Don't you tell anyone I'm afraid. I don't think I'm going to like him."

"But Marie Therese, you've got to give him a chance! Anyway, he's different."

She acknowledged that with a nod. Her father, with

hair of brass, slight build, slim patrician nose, and something else—an air, a subtle something—that didn't resemble anything she'd seen in the rough Creoles or French Canadians in the fur trade. No one knew his past but everyone knew from his clipped, sonorous way of speaking French that de Paris had been born in France.

"Peter—if I don't like him . . . would you help me?" An urgency filled her voice.

"Help you?"

"Yes! I'll need your help."

"What are you going to do?"

She stared at him silently, ideas and words and dreams flowing through her face, her gray eyes alive. Even though she said nothing, he knew. She might ask him to do what would break his heart into bits.

The new Fort Benton seemed even more bleak to Marie than Fort Union. It rose close to the river on the north bank, in a barren flat hemmed by dreary bluffs. An incomplete adobe bastion was rising at a rear corner—protection against her mother's people. An opposition post, Fort Campbell, had been built a few hundred yards upstream. Not a tree grew on the entire flat; they'd all been felled to make the post or supply its firewood. The bleakness perfectly matched the dread in her heart of meeting a father she barely knew, whose world she didn't like. Would this be her future? Would she spin out all of her narrow life here? An anguish built within her as she thought of it.

Even as she watched, the log and adobe post seemed to grow as the boat approached, while the crowds on the riverbank howled with delight. Rifle shots cracked; engagés and traders erupted from the yawning double gates and hastened to the nearby river; tribesmen—no doubt Blackfeet—raced from their lodges surrounding the fort to witness this important moment—the arrival of the annual resupply. Where was her father? Surely his brass hair would stand out in a dark throng like that. On board, the sweating voyageurs, poling now, redoubled their efforts, their frenzy driving the lumbering keelboat toward the levee, their catcalls announcing their own joy.

Peter was poling too, but she saw him peering anxiously toward the bank, as uncertain of his fate as she was of hers. Then she saw her father, a pool of calm in the mad throng, patrician and quiet, standing back a way near the towering plank doors. Charles Pierre Jacques Eduard de Paris; a man strangely out of place among the dark, rough Creoles.

An odd anxiety seized her, and she tugged at her cream dimity until its folds fell properly. But not properly enough. She could never wear a white woman's dress well. The Blackfeet crowded to the bank, toes to the water, and her heart leapt. Her mother's people! They looked just as she remembered them—tall and proud and joyous. The Blackfeet were the tallest tribe in North America, she'd once been told. Marie herself stood an awkward five feet ten, taller than her French father.

Would Meadowlark be here? She studied the women anxiously, her heart tripping, a new kind of dread assaulting her. They all wore their festival finery. Some women wore blue trade-cloth dresses, elaborately decorated with blue and white beads. Blue had always been a favorite color of the Blackfeet. Other women wore soft doe- or antelope-skin dresses, tanned to white, velvety beauty, decorated with beads or quillwork across the bodices and hems or down the arms. And the men! There they stood in their fringed leggins and shirts, their medicine blazoning from them, their pride displayed in otterskin pendants, eagle feathers, bear-claw necklaces, all in riotous colors and geometric designs.

She didn't see her mother, and oddly, that relieved her. She could cope with only so much. Long ago her Pikuni mother had divorced her father, an act as simple as putting his things out the door. Her mother had fled to her people carrying Marie, a babe in arms. Marie had grown up in the Grease Melters band surrounded by doting grandparents, uncles and aunts, and flocks of children, until her father had retrieved her and sent her to St. Louis when she was seven.

The image of Meadowlark's face as it had been eight years ago floated in Marie's mind. Maybe she'd remarried and joined some other band. Maybe she was dead! She saw no one like her mother on the bank as the keelboat slid to shore amidst an uproar.

Moments later she found herself on the riverbank, peering shyly at the man who'd sired her.

"Chérie?"

"I'm here, Father."

"Parlez-vous—"

She stared, suddenly shocked because she couldn't communicate with him.

"You prefer the anglais?"

"I don't know much French—except a little the sisters taught."

He nodded. "Ah . . . We'll talk in English. I am so—so happy you are here! *Vous êtes belle, Marie*—ah! I must remember. You are a beautiful woman, Marie. All grown up."

He steered her through the throngs, oblivious of them, toward the gates. She wanted to go with him but she wanted to see everyone and everything too, especially the strong, handsome Blackfeet crowding the levee. But she let him guide her toward the post and some private place within.

He seemed so different—older and sadder than what she vaguely remembered when she was just a little girl. His temples had grayed, but the sharp lines of his face remained, and the probing kindness of his gaze.

"Father, what about my trunk?"

"It will be brought, chère Marie."

They passed through the yawning gates into a hushed yard, redolent with the aromas of robes and pelts, kitchen smells, smoke and sweat. Fur posts were much alike, and she understood this one at once, spotting the trading room adjacent to the massive gates, the robe warehouse, the robe press in the yard, the factor's handsome home and offices, guest quarters, apartments for senior employees, traders and translators and clerks—a kitchen, dining room, and barracks for the single engagés, and some rooms for the married ones, all jammed under the high stockades of adobe and cottonwood posts.

He steered her toward a door near the factor's home, and she entered a clean, spartan room of squared cottonwood logs lit by a tiny window of scraped and oiled rawhide that supplied a grudging light. A blanket screened a pallet in an alcove that she knew would be hers. Home.

"Father—"

"Would you like tea? I'll have some sent! Coffee? Are you hungry?"

"No." She found herself studying this little nest, not wanting to stare at him. By fur trade standards it was luxurious. They had space enough, furniture of rawhide, tables of hewn and adzed cottonwood, an iron stove that had come up the river, a puncheon floor, scarlet trade blankets and exquisitely tanned robes heaped everywhere, all of it clean and shining and tight, with a certain wild, sweet aroma penetrating the air.

"Ah, chère Marie! Do you like it? I've waited so long, so long for this!"

"Yes, Papa." The word seemed strange on her lips. Now, suddenly, she was thrown in with her father, and on the most intimate terms. It alarmed her. How was one to behave toward a strange man?

"I want you to be happy, chérie. Anything, anything at all that you wish—it shall be my command!"

She met his gaze at last, and found a yearning in his face, and some sort of joy exuding from him. Truly he had waited for this, and wanted to befriend the daughter he didn't know. How handsome he was! So unlike the rough engagés she'd met. He smiled, and she did also.

"Come, let us sit—*la bas*." He waved toward two chairs of rawhide hung upon frames.

"Shouldn't we be out helping unload, Papa? Don't they need us?"

"Ah! Oui, they need us! *Mais*—But I wanted to have this petite moment, this little treasure for the two of us, this—first tenderness, oui?"

"First tenderness?"

"Oui, you are the only daughter I have. You are the only family I have."

She wanted to say no! You and Meadowlark! But you couldn't keep her! She smiled tentatively.

"I see you are wearing a totem of the Pieds Noirs—the little yellow buffalo. How beautiful! Is it something you got at Fort Union?"

She chose not to conceal what she had hidden for eight years from the sisters. "No. My mother gave it to me when she brought me to you. She said it would protect me, that I would always have . . . buffalo medicine. And I do." She said the last boldly, even a little defiantly.

But he chuckled amiably. He was not like the sisters. For that, suddenly, she liked him a lot. He had passed some sort of test she had imposed on him without quite realizing it.

"Would you do me a great favor, chérie? Would you talk in French? Learn it? You must remember some, and the good nuns must have taught you more. It is—hard for me to make English. And you're my chérie."

"I want to work on my Blackfeet first—but if you want me to . . . "

"Oui! I do. You have no need for the Blackfeet."

"I want to see my mother. Is she here—out there?"

"Non, she—her band didn't come in to trade. I don't see her. Not even when they come."

"Which band, Papa?"

"Who knows? They wander from one to another, you know. Marry and unmarry."

She didn't like that too casual response. Something subtle drifted between them. Perhaps it was only his fears that she might, with her mixed blood, choose to return to her mother's people. His fear was well-founded, and she knew she would not hide her wishes.

"She's my mother and I'd like to see her."

He frowned, noticing the fragile disharmony. "Ah, chérie, when your mother comes, you'll see her. But she'll seem different to you now—after those years in St. Louis. So different."

She knew what he was saying, and something welled up within her. "You're telling me she'll seem to be a savage."

His amiable gaze faltered. "No, chérie. But she'll be different, not the woman you remember from when you were seven years old. Now! Let's find your trunk and get you settled. Over there is your little nest. We've so much to talk about—your future and mine. I've many years with the company now, and I'm a senior trader, and soon we can go to St. Louis. It is safe for me to go to St. Louis now."

"What do you mean?"

He shrugged. "The revolution in France is over. No one is looking for my family anymore."

She waited for more, but he simply smiled.

"Someday would you tell me? It's my birthright."

He nodded. "You have good blood. Someday I will tell you about it."

"Yours," she said darkly, wondering if he'd catch her meaning.

"Noble blood on both sides, chérie. Your mother lives with the Pikuni, but she's the daughter of a Kainah chief. She and Mrs. Culbertson—who's here with the major—they're distant relatives.

"Natawista?"

"Oui. You'll be seeing her shortly. She's always in red, always dazzling everyone. She'll tell you about your mother."

Natawista Culbertson, the Blood wife of the head of Pierre Chouteau's Upper Missouri Outfit, was the subject of endless gossip in St. Louis; gossip that penetrated the cloisters. The major's lady reigned right here as queen of the High Missouri. Alec Culbertson had built this very post to expand trade with Natawista's people and wean them from Hudson's Bay Company. She had taken joyously to white civilization, enjoyed her role, and had done much to encourage trade between her Blackfeet and the fur company.

Mrs. Culbertson knew English and French, but rarely spoke it, preferring instead to chatter in her own Blackfoot tongue. Marie Therese knew at once that she'd seek out the Blood woman, learn about her mother and her mother's people, and master the tongue she had forgotten.

"Let's go watch the unloading, chérie. I just wanted this one tender moment with you. And to show you our comforts. And to start you thinking about your future."

Delight lit his face, but she wasn't sure she felt his joy.

Chapter Eleven

Peter saw at once that James Kipp had aged. White hair at the temples had changed that hawkish face, and after unabated weathering his stepfather seemed as dark and creased as an old Indian. But for a man almost fifty, Kipp seemed to be in good condition, and didn't have the tiredness of the old in his eyes. Kipp, a Montrealer, had been in the fur trading business since his early twenties and now was one of Pierre Chouteau's partners, owning one of the six shares of the company that Chouteau had distributed to his senior men. No man at Fort Benton had more experience or had survived the brutal trade longer than Peter's stepfather. And that had stamped Kipp's eyes with a hard, penetrating gaze that always frightened Petcr.

"Well, Peter. You're a man! I sent away a boy!" Delight lit his face and an iron hand clasped Peter's. "Welcome back! You've had a safe passage and we rejoice."

"Yes, sir. You're looking fine yourself." He turned shyly toward Ipasha, who stood serenely beside his stepfather. His stepmother had aged too, and her black hair fell in braids shot with white. She rarely spoke English, but knew it well enough.

"I'm pleased to be here, ma'am," he said. He had never known how to address her.

She nodded and smiled. Peter collected his duffel and they walked awkwardly toward the gates, through mobs of staring Blackfeet, clerks, sweating engagés, voyageurs, and racing dogs. Already engagés were toting trade goods into the trading room, where clerks were shelving them. In the morning Fort Benton's new season would begin, just as it had at Fort Union.

"Ye'll tell us what they taught you, and what you're fit to do," Kipp said. Peter's father was making conversation. He'd been to St. Louis several times and had always stopped at the Anglican school for a brief, if painful, visit, unlike Marie Therese's father. James Kipp knew what Peter had learned.

"I'm fit to do anything, sir. I can cipher, read and write, keep ledgers, speak Spanish and read German."

"How was the trip, Peter?"

He never said son. From the beginning, it had been Peter.

"Plagued by the cholera, sir. We lost thirty. And more were deathly sick. Passengers and crew. It frightened us all out of our wits. When we got to the Platte, it stopped. Captain La Barge had the boat fumigated with sulfur and scrubbed with quicklime."

"Cholera! They bring it up the river. It's a blessing we're so far away from the cesspools. You've had a bad time, then—fear of death upon ye."

Kipp steered him into the post, and Peter beheld a fort very like the others he'd seen. But this one was newer, made mostly of adobe, and incomplete. Kipp headed straight toward one of the adobe apartments for senior men. "That two-story one there is Alec Culbertson's home. But he's not going to be here for a while. Malcolm Clarke's the factor, and I'm second for the time being. Culbertson's off rounding up chiefs for a peace meeting that David Mitchell wants."

"Yes, sir. He and Father DeSmet were on the boat."

Peter beheld a fine parlor, with rose settees and chairs brought clear up the river, damask drapes, cut glass and silver glinting on a sideboard, a glow of civilization gleaming in the dusky, barbaric light. His stepfather's home.

"Are you hungry or thirsty, Peter?"

"Thirsty, sir. A glass of water."

Kipp grinned slightly. "You wouldn't admit to any sampling?"

"No, sir. You always said that breeds and pure-bloods are vulnerable to spirits."

Silently Ipasha vanished into a pantry to the rear, returning with a tumbler of water.

"How do you like her? Benton, I mean?"

"I can see it's a fine post, sir. Rather bleak setting, though. Not a tree in sight. Where do you fetch wood?"

"We cut it on the Teton River flats and haul it."

James Kipp probed Peter genially about school, about the trip, about people he'd met, about Marie Therese.

"Did she weather it? A convent girl like that—hard for her to plunge into a world like this. I imagine de Paris'll find a husband for her. Not much else for her here."

"I hope not! That's for her to decide!"

"Ah, Peter, in a fur post you need to find something for everyone to do. . . ."

"I think she should work for the company!"

Kipp smiled. "Well, it might be possible—for her board. We need a laundress, and we're always shy a cook or two."

"But—" Peter wanted to tell him that Marie Therese shouldn't do such menial things, that Marie Therese could do figures, keep books, keep the post log.

"And what of you, Peter?"

"Why, sir. I've saved seventy-five dollars. I want to go into business."

"Seventy-five, you say?"

"Yes, sir. After the cholera struck, Captain La Barge needed crewmen. He offered half fare to anyone willing to work. I volunteered, sir. I worked hard, and now I have a letter of credit."

Kipp frowned, his lips pursing. "Half the fare I laid out for you. Don't ye think you owe it?"

"Why—sir—I worked hard. I cleaned cabins. I cut wood, I—"

"That's not what I asked you. I asked, don't you think

you owe it? I took a body in, I sent you down the river and schooled you and brought you back fit to work."

"Mr. Kipp, sir. I'm grateful—I really am. I just—I worked hard. I'd like—"

"Ah, you don't know what was done for ye, then."

"I do, sir." A misery flooded through Peter.

Painfully he extracted La Barge's note from his duffel and handed it to James Kipp.

"I don't feel you know what was done for you. The passage up the river alone was a year's wage for an engagé."

"I know," Peter whispered. "I—I was selfish, sir."

"Now, now, let's not eat crow. I've some plans for you, Peter. The company'll put you in service, the usual three-year contract, for a hundred fifty a year and an outfit of clothes. Ye'll be put to various things until you find what suits ye. I'll have you cut and haul firewood, mix adobes for the bastions, press and bale robes, care for the horses, grade pelts, stock shelves, carpenter, maybe do some smithing and shoeing. Find out what suits ye. In the second or third year you can try clerking, if you learnt figures. I can't make you a trader unless you learn the tongues. But you'll go as far as you can. This is a good, profitable post. We shipped over twenty-one thousand robes last year; we'll do better this year. Plus the tongues and other peltries. Ye can't do better than enlist here and climb the ladder."

"That's what I hoped, sir."

"I'm not holding you to anything. You're seventeen, a man, free to walk through the gates. Try another post if you wish."

"I want to stay here, sir."

"Ah, I was hoping for that. I can't promise you any special treatment—the engagés'd be some put out. But I'll be overseeing ye. Now today, stay for supper, and we'll have a talk."

"Stay for supper?"

"Before you settle in the barracks."

Peter stared dumbly at his father, suddenly aware that this would not be his home. He sat here by invitation rather than right. A terrible loneliness washed through him. Except for Marie Therese, no one in the world cared.

"I can go over there and unpack, sir."

"As you wish."

"I can eat there, sir."

"That's fine, Peter. They bell the supper, and you'll find a place in the dining hall. Do you want to engage for three years first? The office's just by."

"Sir—may I think on it tonight?"

"Tonight only. I can afford ye that."

"Thank you, sir."

"Ah, Peter, lad. You did a man's work coming up the river, and you'll do fine here if you give as much. La Barge scratched a recommendation right on this bill. He's a man to know good character. I'm proud of ye. As proud as I am of my own lads."

Peter nodded his head up and down, nodded crazily because nodding was all he could manage.

He plucked up his canvas satchel, which contained all his worldly possessions: two changes of clothes and a knife and a book and fire steel.

"Have Picotte issue you a pair of blankets and a tick and all. You'll find him in the robe warehouse."

"Yes, sir."

Peter fled into the blinding sun of the yard. The engagés' barrack would be directly opposite, so he steered across the endless yard, raising dust with each step. It was a hundred feet in all, but it might as well have been a hundred miles. Each step widened the gulf between the orphan breed boy and his white benefactor—a gulf that yawned into a chasm within Peter's heart.

He found an empty pallet, nothing but ripsawn plank, and made a nest of it, getting the provisions from Picotte. He found straw in the stable and stuffed his tick. He hung up his spare britches and shirt. He slid the sheathed Green River knife and his Testament, given him by his teachers, under the prickly tick. It reminded him of school, actually. There he possessed nothing but a small space, surrounded by others coughing and snoring in the night, his world compassed by the designs of every other boy. Here he had no more than that. But this dark place reeked of man-things: tobacco and sweat, stale and rank.

The engagés' small possessions hung from wooden pegs in the log walls. Few owned anything more than clothing. He would be the humblest of mortals on the lowest rung of the company ladder, mixing with comic and brutal Creoles, and reprobate whites fleeing civilization and law. And he, the mixed-breed, would be lowest of all.

The thought lit a wild flame in his heart that scorched his soul. He would show them.

Few Blackfoot bands came to Fort Benton in the summer. The real trading season would begin after cold weather had haired out the buffalo and the pelts were prime. Most of the summer trade was to small bands of warriors, horse-stealing parties, war parties, off to collect Crow ponies or Salish scalps. They would trade light summer robes for powder and lead and knives, and ride away upon their mischief.

Marie Therese watched them come and go, and sometimes slid a shawl over her dress and wandered among them, seeking someone she might know; someone who might recognize the girl who had lived with them over seven winters ago. But none did. Pikuni warriors squinted at her, absorbing her unusual height, her straight jet hair in two braids, her Indian flesh, her broad cheekbones and slender nose, but also her gray eyes and white woman's clothes and shoes. She wanted news of Meadowlark and found none. She couldn't remember enough of the Siksika tongue she'd spoken the first few years of her life to identify her mother, though with each restless turn around the post, listening to the warriors speak, a little more of her mother's tongue returned to her.

But she didn't venture to speak it, at least not until a headman with two notched eagle feathers tucked into a knot of hair at the nape of his neck said something to her in the tongue of her mother.

"I am called Sis-ta-wan," he said, and she understood. His name meant Bird Rattle. "You are of the Siksika?"

She nodded, still not daring to try out the strange words.

"A two-blood," he said. "Your father is a trader."

She understood that too, and nodded. "I am looking for my mother—O-toch-koki . . . Yellow Breast . . . Meadowlark."

He seemed puzzled.

"Of the Grease Melters, the Ich-poch-semo."

"Ah. We are Don't Laughs."

"You don't know her."

"No, but I will ask. Who are you?"

"Marie Therese de Paris."

"Ah, the Real Old Man People."

She remembered the Siksika called the French the real white men because the French had come first. Faltering, plucking at strange words, she told him the simple outline of her life: that she had lived her first months—she was too young to remember how many—in a fur post; how her mother had taken her away when she was still a babe in arms; how at eight her mother had brought her to her father, and he had sent her down the river to a great city of the whites. And now she wanted to find Meadowlark.

"If O-toch-koki was at the dance of the giving to the sun, in the Moon when Berries are Ripe, someone will remember," he said.

"The Sun dance!" She remembered a little of it. It came deep in the summer, late July or early August. At that time all the Siksika gathered at an appointed place for their highest holy days.

"Where was it?"

"It was at Two Medicine River. This year Poi-o-pa-ta-mach-ka, Comes Running, wife of O-mis-tai-po-kah, White Calf, was the sacred woman. They are of the Black Patched Moccasins band."

"Would you tell me when you find out anything?"

He stared levelly at her. "The sacred dance is over—

and now the bands wander and youths go to war against the Absaroka. I am going to steal Absaroka ponies."

"But—I want to meet her!" Her hand caught her yellow buffalo amulet and she showed it to him.

He thought a moment. "If the medicine men say it is good, I will send word."

That summery afternoon, when she walked back through the yawning gates of the post, she felt she was leaving her world and entering an alien white man's one. Now she would live for word from Sis-ta-wan.

Not that the summer had been unpleasant. She couldn't explain to herself why she yearned so to be with her mother and among the Pikuni. It had grown in her, a hunger that raged out of control, leaving her famished for something she couldn't even fathom, except that it was sacred. Her father had been loving and kind, forcing himself to speak English so they could share their days. He seemed a stranger still, but one she had become fond of. Her duties amounted to nothing: keep the apartment; mend and darn their clothing. She didn't cook or do the dishes because they ate in the communal dining hall. He hadn't pressured her to work for the company. All he had done was tease a little about the way she turned the eyes of the clerks in the trading room. She knew it was his way of playing Cupid. A clerk, midway up the company ladder, could offer a good and comfortable life for a mixed-breed girl. But she was not yet sixteen and in no hurry. Neither was her father, whose grave kindness and occasional gifts and sudden offerings of family history made her new life amiable.

One lavender September twilight he told her about the thing she ached to know. He hadn't divorced Meadowlark. She had left him. Marie's mother had grown more and more restless around the several posts, Mackenzie and Union mostly, sinking into an unhappy silence while she cared for the infant Marie Therese. And then she had disappeared, taking Marie with her.

Her father sighed. "Chérie, I wasn't a good husband for an Indian woman. I didn't talk to her in Siksika, and I didn't pay much attention. She had no friends at the posts, except Natawista Culbertson and Kakokima, Malcolm Clarke's wife, now and then. She left—a divorce *façon à pays,* after the fashion of the country. Poor woman. I loved her, you know. We weren't—married—in the Faith."

She thought to herself she was not only a breed, but a bastard child.

"I found out which band—she'd gone to live among the Lone Eaters, but stayed often with her parents in the Grease Melters. She came in with them sometimes, and we talked, and I got a chance to see you, bright as a button in your little doeskin skirts. When you were older, I asked Meadowlark whether she would like for you to receive the medicine wisdom of the whites. The next summer she handed you to me."

"And I went down the river to the sisters."

He nodded, his gaze settling upon the heat-hazed horizon.

She treasured the memory of that night, when she had learned about her past.

She rarely lacked company, even though no other girls her age lived in the post. In his spare moments Peter visited, or caught her in the yard, or took her for a walk along the restless river. He'd plunged into everything with a strange ferocity, a paragon of labor, which at first amused the other engagés and finally annoyed them because he made them all seem lazy. But the demon-driven young man cut firewood furiously, scythed prairie hay on the flats above the Benton bottoms, shelved trade goods, pressed graded robes into bales of ten, and then stacked the heavy bales in the warehouse. Often when she passed by, he was sweating at something, his shirt soaked, his freckled, brown face shining with the grease of his pores. Then he'd pause, and the look in his eyes that frightened her would come, and he'd smile at her intimately, as if to say, I am doing all this for you, Marie Therese, and some day when I am better off, I'll claim you!

Oh, Peter, mad and driven boy!

The callers came to the de Paris apartment; the young and watchful clerks, most of them with names like Baptiste

Picotte, Pierre Gratiot, and Jean La Plante, often with prairie nosegays. Her father entertained them genially with tea and talk, and the clerks all made bright conversation with her in French, supposing she knew the tongue. She rarely smiled when she should, when the rest chuckled. Soon she must choose.

One breathless October day when no air stirred and the sun blistered Fort Benton unseasonably, a day when engagés dozed and clerks hid, a lone Blackfoot headman rode up on a sweated pony, and at the trading window asked to see the young woman Marie. Uneasily, the clerk who had taken the message, Gratiot, contemplated the headman and asked his business.

"To tell her of her mother, O-toch-koki."

Gratiot sought the assistant trader, de Paris, but the man had vanished somewhere in the heat. He hurried himself toward the de Paris apartment and found Marie there, hiding from the burning sun.

"Mademoiselle, a Pieds Noirs headman at the trading window ask for you," he said. "Shall I send him away?"

Marie undid an apron and hastened across the yard. "Is there a name?"

"I didn't ask."

"I'm seeking word of my mother."

"Ah, he said he has news of her."

"It's Sis-ta-wan! Monsieur Gratiot, I need a gift . . . tobacco."

"Mademoiselle, perhaps I'd better find your papa—"

"Put it on his account!"

She swept into the trading room and snatched up a hard brown twist of tobacco, and then hastened through the yawning gates of the sleepy post. The Blackfoot headman stood beside his glossy brown pony, wearing only a breechcloth and moccasins.

"Oh, Sis-ta-wan!"

He looked her up and down, and she felt his odd scrutiny pierce into her soul. "Your mother, O-toch-koki, is with the Lone Eaters, under Chief Siyeh, Mad Wolf."

"Is she—well?"

"Yes. She has a new man, Sinopah, Kit Fox."

"Where, where?"

"They will be at the fall hunt. This time it will be on Birch Creek. The herd is between Two Medicine River and Birch Creek."

"I want to see her! Am I permitted?"

"Do you honor Sun, and Napi, Old Man?"

"Oh yes!"

"Be at the Birch, near the mountains."

"I don't know where that is."

"It is many long walks."

"Would you take me?"

"I have no pony for you. And if I took you, maybe the traders would come after me." She saw a question in his face.

"Oh! You're right. But will you tell me how?"

"Yes. Walk up the Ikinitskatah, Teton River, almost to the mountains. Then go north across many creeks for many days until you see many travois tracks, and follow them."

She stared doubtfully, and knew he could not explain it any better. There was no guide, and no map.

"Take this!" She thrust the twist of tobacco at him. He accepted it gravely.

"You'll go. It's in your face. Do you have a Siksika name?"

She must have, but she didn't remember it, and peered at him blankly.

"I will say that a mixed-blood wearing ee-nau-ah, Black Horns, on her breast is coming to the hunt," he said. With that he rode off into the strange heat.

Chapter Twelve

Marie Therese couldn't find Peter, but she learned he had taken a cart to the Teton valley to cut firewood. She rushed across the Benton flat, clambered up a stock trail up the bluff, and found herself upon an endless broken plain. She raced north toward the Croquant du Nez, the ridge dividing the Teton from the Missouri, and there she found him returning to the post, his creaking Red River cart loaded with long chunks of cottonwood and alder, which the Pikuni people called bad smoke, or stinkwood.

"Oh, Peter!"

He halted his mule and stared. "Marie! What're you doing here? This isn't safe for you!" He saw her smiling. "Now we'll walk back together. I've a rifle." Joy etched his face.

"I've found my mother. I need your help."

The joy drained away and he turned solemn. "Marie Therese, I'll do what I can for you. But . . . " His thoughts drifted away.

"She's with the Lone Eaters, and she has a husband, Kit Fox. They're going to be at the fall hunt. I need to go."

"Marie—wait for her here. She'll come in. After the robes are prime, all the bands come in to trade. It'll be soon."

"I must go."

"Where?" Something in his voice seemed truculent.

"The herds are between Badger Creek and Two Medicine River."

Peter whistled. "No, you're not going. That's a long way."

"I will."

He stopped, and the mule beside him stopped. "Marie Therese—don't talk like that. The weather's about to break. That's how it is here. We get snow in September sometimes. You can't just start walking a hundred and fifty miles."

"I will. I hoped you'd help me."

He seemed so solemn that she pressed her hand into his. "Oh, Peter, I know how you feel. I can't help being what I am."

"Yes, you can, Marie. You're the educated daughter of a Frenchman some people think has noble blood. That's who you are. All I want in life is you. I want to give you everything I can—" He choked up under the flood of his feelings.

She sighed, unable to answer him. They walked together, holding hands, leading the mule that dragged the cart. She didn't know what to say. If Peter wouldn't help, she'd start out alone without help. She had nothing at all; not a cent for provisions or simple things, such as a fire steel and flint.

"You're going to go," he said. "No matter what."

She couldn't answer that either.

"Will you promise to come back?"

"No."

His mood changed suddenly. "Well, go! Stay with your mother awhile. Taste the life of the savages, the cold and dirt and lice and starvation. You'll be back. When they come in, you'll stay and be glad of it. I suppose you haven't told your father you're going. He'd forbid it."

"No I haven't."

He sighed. "I'll be blamed."

"Peter—I think my father knows. I've asked him about my mother. He won't blame you." They walked across the plains toward the Missouri valley, following a deepening coulee. "Peter, just tell me what I'll need, and I'll get them in the trading room and ask them to put it on my father's account."

"No, you asked me to help and I'm going to help. I'll get you everything in the morning. The trading room'll be closed by the time we get in."

"What'll I need?"

"Oh, fire steel, an awl, needle and thread, hatchet, parched corn or something like that, jerked meat, a little tin pot, a good knife, maybe tea or coffee, and warm stuff—a cap, mittens, blanket capote, shoe leather or spare moccasins, canvas poncho."

"How can I carry all that?"

"The mountain men used to wear a lot, hang stuff from their belts, and hang a bundle from their rifle, which they carried over their shoulder. You could carry the bundle on a stick."

"Oh, Peter, thank you. Now I can see Meadowlark!"

"Marie Therese—she won't be what you remembered."

"I know that. And she'll be with a man I don't know. And maybe with children, sisters and brothers, I don't know."

"I can't stop you," he said.

As they walked silently back to the post, she held his hand, knowing it might be a small solace for him. Even before they reached the bottoms, the sun dropped from the sky and a chill rose around them.

They met in the cool morning outside of the post, under the east stockade. She had spent a restless night, not because she had any doubts, but because she didn't know what to say to Charles de Paris, the father who had dug deep into his slim purse to give her a schooling and the best chance that the world had to offer. She had held her buffalo medicine in her hand and pondered it in the blackness, knowing at last that she had nothing to say that could excuse herself. In the morning she had penciled a simple note: *Thank you for your love and your gifts to me. I am going to my mother*. At first she was going to write *visit* my mother, but truthfulness overtook her and she did not use that word.

"Here," Peter said. He thrust a duck-cloth bundle tied to a long stick toward her. "It has everything you'll need."

She undid the thong that drew the cloth tight and beheld the metal things and a sea of blue. She pulled out the blue four-point blanket, made by Witney in England. Its azure flared like winter sky, and its thickness folded soft and warm in her hands. Black bands compassed the ends, as they did the Hudson's Bay variety.

"Oh, Peter," she breathed, humbled by so great a gift.

"You'll need it. And the rest. The wind's shifted and it'll get cold. You can make a capote."

"Peter—" She didn't know how to thank him for a kit that had cost him half a year's labor. Mutely, her feelings sliding beyond the adequacy of words, she clutched him and wept. He held her softly, as if afraid to hold her tight.

"It's the best I could do," he whispered to her. "I love you, Marie Therese. Never forget. Never forget!"

Each word lanced her soul, and she struggled with herself, something in her wanting to abandon this and nestle in the safety of these loving brown arms.

"I won't forget. I adore you, dear Peter."

The words seemed a benediction to him, and he released her as if releasing a falcon, to soar and wheel and glide the blue heaven, a wild thing.

She retied her bundle and walked north across the Benton bottoms in the slanting light of the young sun, unable to look back because she feared her resolve would melt away. When she reached the windswept top of the bluffs, she did look back, and beheld the two tiny posts far below, the white man's vulnerable island in a great sea of grass and loneliness. But that was deceptive: She'd been to St. Louis and she knew, she *knew*.

Up on that blustery prairie, where grasses whirled and dodged, she dug out her blanket and wrapped it around herself, loving the bold blue, the warmth of it, and Peter for giving it. Then she set out in earnest, heading for the Teton and whatever well-worn Indian trails there would take her west. She peered behind her fearfully, looking not only for horsemen from the fur post come to imprison her in a white man's cage, but for the enemies of her people who roamed freely through here—enemies beyond counting, Sioux, Assiniboin, Cree, River Crow, Snakes, Flatheads, and maybe even the Rees or Kootenai. But she saw only dancing brown grass and scudding clouds plowing the sky, hurrying south like the geese.

She reached the Teton bottoms and found warmth there, as well as a trail along the south bank that took her through thick timber. Now she would have to be even more careful, because she couldn't see far ahead. Cottonwoods, chokecherry brush, headlands, and thickets of juniper blocked her view. She eyed the slow river thoughtfully, realizing that she would have to cross it sooner or later. She knew nothing of fords, but she supposed that animal trails, horse or buffalo trails, would give her clues.

The sky clouded up until only patches of blue remained, and the wind increased, whipping the melancholy cottonwoods above her. They hadn't yet turned yellow, though here and there a few golden branches heralded the coming cold. By late afternoon she felt hunger, but resolved not to stop as long as she had a shred of light to open her path. Dusk lowered swiftly, plunging the valley into lavender and then a gray mist, and she knew she must find a sheltered spot. She wished she were on the north side, where she could huddle under a bluff. In the last of the light, she located a thicket of juniper not far from the river, and settled into a protected bower. Some animal skittered away, frightening her. She dreaded a bear most of all, but feared wolves and catamounts as well.

She felt a moment of dread. She scarcely remembered how to build a fire using the steel. There'd been plenty of sulfur matches around the post. She gathered squaw wood, the dead sticks poking from the lower trunks of trees, and found a dead cottonwood log with some bark on it. She pulled the bark off and gathered the fibers of the underbark for her tinder. She labored as if in a dream, knowing what to do without thinking about it, and she supposed the images of her girlhood in the Pikuni camps were guiding her, or perhaps the spirit of the buffalo she wore at her breast.

She slid her fingers into the curved, C-shaped fire steel until the striking edge projected outward from her knuckles, and then dashed it across the flint she found in her sack. A fine burst of orange sparks dropped like meteors into the little nest of tinder. She struck again and again until the tinder glowed in several places. Then she blew lightly, making the orange dots bloom and eat the fiber. Then, suddenly, one erupted into tiny flame, and she fed it twigs and sticks, and finally the squaw wood.

Joyously she dug in the kit for the cotton sack of parched corn, filled her little pot with river water and started the corn to boiling. As she waited, she cleared away the debris from a bedding place, gathered wood, and examined everything in her kit. Peter, who didn't want her to go, who loved her and wanted to marry her, had made it possible. She wouldn't forget.

She awoke to the howling of wolves, eerie and wicked in the blackness. They were close! Too close. She lay in her cocoon of blankets and canvas, afraid that at any instant they'd burst through the junipers and leap at her throat. One howled from a distant knob; another nearby in the river bottoms. She heard the yap of pups, glorying to be alive and stalking prey. She shifted about, wanting her only weapon, a knife. It would be small comfort against any wolf, but she had nothing else. Then she spotted the solemn orange glow of a last coal in her fire, and knew at once she had succor after all. She slid out of her bedroll, feeling the icy night bite her neck and arms, and groped for a few twigs, which she found easily in the detritus. These she settled over the coal and blew until a tiny flame sprang up. A few minutes later she enjoyed a cheery blaze, as if that would shield her from the designs of the wolf that were so evil they could not bear the light. Animals that murdered other animals usually did it in the night to hide their wickedness from the eyes of God.

The wolf howls ebbed, but she could not sleep. She

pulled her blanket about her and sat at the fire, peering into its mystical light as if it were an altar. She realized that her fears had been those of a white woman. The Indian within her didn't fear this place or the creatures around it. A Pikuni would have enjoyed the music of the wolf brothers and wolf sisters. A Pikuni would enjoy this place; it was home as much as all the other places upon the breast of earth mother were home. When white people penetrated the wilderness, they felt its terror and emptiness. They felt out of control, strangers in a strange land. Not until they mapped would they know where they were; not until they built settlements, homes and farms and churches and stores, would they find comfort. Not until they drove away the wolves and bears and buffalo, and scratched the earth with their plows, would they call it home.

But this was home. Her people didn't need maps. They wandered everywhere, always at home. They read the creeks and grasses and ridges and mountains as the whites read maps. They wandered the empty wastes, and found them filled with life and joy. She didn't know where she was going—the wilderness stretched some infinity into the night in all directions—and yet she needed no road. She would find her people, even if they were tiny specks upon a landscape that stretched beyond the imagination.

She knew then that she wasn't afraid and wouldn't be again. Tomorrow she would walk all alone across an aching emptiness, and it wouldn't trouble her. All of it was her home; the home of her mother's people. She touched the cold earth at her side, feeling something kindred in it. Whites possessed a few square yards of it and felt themselves unwelcome in the rest; her mother's people possessed it all and felt welcome everywhere. Wherever they wandered they owned the land, and whatever they found they possessed.

Her mind turned back to St. Louis, and the convent, and the sisters who lived in poverty and gave themselves to holiness. Sister Thomasita, the catechist, had been cheerful and loving; Sister Ignacia, the one who taught them sewing and cooking, had been dour toward the mountain children.

The mixed-blood children were there on sufferance, considered uneducable and inferior by the sisters and priests—except for Thomasita, who made doctrine somehow jolly and the faith somehow warm and noble.

How afraid they would all be here! Marie laughed softly. She knew exactly how they'd feel, the wild, frightened prayers they would recite to preserve them from unknown terrors; the sobbing confessions, the pleas for succor against—mother earth, and Napi, the Old Man, and Sun and his wife Moon, and their boy-child, Morning Star. She laughed gaily, peering into the lovely face of Moon, half hidden this night. The last of her fears left her, and in the quiet of the night the last of her white men's ways left her as well. When dawn came, she would be a Pikuni woman, not some mixed-blood creature torn this way and that. Gaiety infused her. She stood and stretched, feeling her kinship with the junipers and the stars, and the spirits of the trees and rocks and creatures.

She lifted her hands upward until the tips of her fingers touched the universe. "Noks-sto-mo-au," she said. You are my kin. She wondered how she remembered the Siksika words.

She knew exactly what had been transacted, and wondered how she would look in the morning. Would anything of Charles de Paris, of the sisters, of St. Louis, and even of Fort Benton, remain in her face? She would look into the Teton and see. Then she curled up in her robes and dreamed of buffalo, ee-nau-ah, growing fewer and fewer, until the tail of the last buffalo disappeared and first light awakened her. She saw Morning Star in the east, greeting Sun, his father.

All that day she traced the Teton westward, the trail as plain as a city street. She clambered up a bluff now and then to examine her backtrail. But no one followed. She didn't expect anyone to. Back at Fort Benton they would say, Let her see her mother. She'll be back when winter cold and starvation teach her what life in the village is really like! She hoped only that Peter wouldn't be in trouble for outfitting her.

The high-button women's shoes tortured her, encasing her feet like the convent imprisoned her heart. The leather soles protected her, but the uppers bit and wounded and finally blistered her, until each step tormented her. She dug out the Blackfoot moccasins Peter had supplied, and found them too large. They were summer moccasins made of a single piece of soft leather, folded on the inside and seamed around the outside for a foot larger than hers. Still she wore them in camp, a relief from her black shoes.

She supplemented the parched corn with berries and roots. The ok-kun-okin, or sarvisberries, were gone, along with the pukkeep, or chokecherries. But she found lots of miss-is-a-misoi, or buffalo berry, that she could boil, and sometimes the wild turnip, elk food or mass, that made a kind of potato dish. Vaguely she remembered walking along beside O-toch-koki as she gathered these gifts of nature.

The weather held, but the nights turned icy, and she found her gear frosted each dawn. But the sky had never seemed more cobalt or the air more transparent. With each day the cottonwoods yellowed, but the time for leaves to fall hadn't come. Each walk took her closer to her people, and her anticipation grew keen. One afternoon she spied the Rocky Mountains, a blue ridge along the western horizons, the sawtooth peaks already white. After that they became a looming presence, the western wall of all the lands of the Blackfeet.

Through the long walks she saw no fresh sign of people, but now she resolved to look closely, because this was where Blackfoot bands wandered, living along creeks, sheltering through winters in cottonwood timber under high bluffs that cut the wind. For two days more she followed the twisting Teton closer to the mountains, often detouring around chasms and canyons where the river sliced through giant upheavals. Then, intuitively, she decided to abandon the river and turn north, trusting in mountain-fed streams rushing east to supply her with water.

Now, at last, she would have to ford the Teton. She found a wide, gravelly place with rills flowing around boulders. The bottom couldn't lie very deep. She peered about shyly and undressed, shivering in the chill air. She bundled everything into her canvas poncho, anchored it on her stick, and stepped naked into the stream. The icy snowmelt bit her feet. She gasped at the thunder of cold that laced her feet and ankles, but pushed outward, gasping, wobbling, her footing insecure on the slippery gravel. She reached the main channel and dropped off a ledge, the water boiling over her thighs, so cold that it burnt. But that was the worst of it. From there the underwater grade lifted her out, and soon she stood on the north bank, shivering. She dressed swiftly and wrapped a blanket about her even though the day was mild and Medicine Elk, the Wind Maker, wasn't torturing her. Now that her path would take her across drainages instead of along them, there'd be many more fords ahead.

For two days she walked north, seeing no sign of human life but rejoicing even so because she walked the land of the Pikuni, a land of rolling hills, rushing clear creeks, vast shortgrass prairies, and always the shepherding wall of mountains to the west, their presence a benediction upon the land they watered.

Her parched corn gave out, but she survived on buffalo berries and roots, which filled her even if they didn't nourish her well. She feared she might never find her people, and might starve or die in a sudden blizzard sent by the Cold Maker who lived high in the crags of the mountains to the northwest.

But then she found the travois tracks that demarked the passage of a large village. She followed them into the north, more easterly than she had been traveling, rejoicing at this sign of the People. The next day she forded a goodly stream she thought might be Badger Creek and climbed a long ridge. Just before a cold purple dusk, she beheld a village ahead, the lodges glowing from the fires within, each an amber cone against an indigo sky, the sight so beautiful and welcoming that her soul soared like an eagle. A full moon painted the village in pastels, and she could see the darkness of the horse herd, the silver of smoke drifting from the vents, the poles of countless lodges pricking the early stars, and beyond, the somber black ridge of the Rockies.

And even as she stood on the ridge absorbing a sight so sweet she could not fathom her own feelings, she saw horsemen approach at a trot, and knew the village police, the Mad Dog Society, had seen her.

She awaited them calmly, joyous that her journey was coming to an end, that Es-to-nea-pesta, Maker of Storms, had not molested her and she was safe. Maybe this was her mother's band!

There came to her a song out of her childhood, and she sang it as she rejoiced:

"I fly high in the air.
My medicine is very strong.
The wind is my medicine.

"The buffalo is my medicine.
He is very strong medicine.
The trees are my medicine.
When I am among them I walk around my
own medicine."

They reined their ponies around her and stared, their hands not far from their war clubs and lances. They didn't look at all friendly, and suddenly she feared for her life.

Chapter Thirteen

For as long as he could, Peter avoided Charles de Paris, dreading to own up to what he had done for Marie Therese. He worked furiously, staying away from the post as much as he could, often arriving just in time for supper and to collapse in his bunk.

But the inevitable moment came anyway.

"Monsieur Kipp, a word with you."

The assistant trader had caught Peter in the robe warehouse where he was stacking bales. Peter nodded reluctantly.

"Ah, monsieur, you make yourself invisible, but at last we meet. It's said that you provisioned my daughter. Indeed, on the company books is a credit for fifty-seven dollars, for various things. And the ledger date, monsieur, is the very day my daughter left."

Peter nodded miserably. "She asked for help and I gave it."

De Paris didn't seem angry, and that relieved Peter slightly.

"Half a year's wage, monsieur."

"She is my friend."

"It would seem so! Is there perhaps more to it?"

Peter didn't know what to say for a moment. "She's the best friend I ever had. She's—like me. You know. We talked a lot on the boat."

"Talked and dreamed, I imagine," de Paris said. "She would have gone anyway, you know; with or without your comforts. It's a blessing that she had blankets and fire steel and a knife and parched corn. Ah, oui, she would have gone with nothing."

"Sir, she asked, and I knew I had to."

"I'm not blaming you, monsieur. No, not at all. From the moment she came here I saw it in her—the yearning, the questions about her mother, Meadowlark, the wandering among all the Pieds Noirs who came to the post. Ah, I wasn't blind!"

"Well, I did it, and I suppose I should apologize."

"Ah, monsieur, there's no need. Maybe she'll come back, maybe not." He shrugged. "Really, sir, I came to repay you. You've done me a favor, protecting my daughter. I will pay the company and remove your debt from the ledger."

"No, please! It was a gift! Please let it be my gift!"

De Paris eyed him, faintly amused. "I fear I've given offense. I want to repay . . . ah, if you wish, we will call it a gift. A big gift for one so poor."

"That's what I want it to be! Maybe it's the only thing I'll ever be able to give her!"

"I am honored, monsieur, that you think so highly of my daughter. May your wishes be granted."

"They won't be, but I'll keep trying."

De Paris peered into the silent yard, as if seeing other yards inside of other posts. "Meadowlark. Even now, my young friend, she is music to me. She came to me bright and wild and happy, beautiful in the loveliest fashion of her people, eager to be a trader's wife, eh? Ah, I loved, I loved, just as you do. But after a few years, why, this Frenchman—and all the quiet days inside a fur post no longer appealed to her; the wild rambling of her people did. She left—with Marie Therese."

Peter felt that the assistant trader wanted to say a lot more, but instead he saw only a shrug, Gallic resignation.

"We build our little lives out of nothing. A love of an Indian maiden who consented to be mine—for a while. And you, young man—a love for a mixed-breed like yourself, who didn't treat you badly—who is even farther away from you than Meadowlark is from me. Eh?"

"Someday, sir. Times change—maybe I'll have something more to give her in a few years and she'll come to me."

The trader didn't respond to that. "We grasp dreams, but they are like chaff in the wind, monsieur. I'm in your debt, and I admire you."

"Me? Admire me?"

"You're the scandal of the post, Monsieur Kipp. The other engagés, they grumble because you make them look so lazy! Be careful not to offend."

"I have to get ahead!"

"For Marie Therese?"

"Yes, sir."

"Maybe it's best to live for reality—not dreams, eh?"

But Peter knew he never would. He'd find a way to win her, even if it took a long time.

De Paris wandered back to the trading room, and Peter felt a certain relief. He'd avoided this moment for weeks, but it turned out much better than he'd feared.

As fall surrendered to winter and the nights grew endless, Peter awaited her return. He studied the surrounding bottoms in the dull gray light, wanting to see a small form wrapped in a bold blue blanket walking home. He took to cutting wood on the Teton so that he might discover her en route home, but he never did. She had vanished from his life, as swiftly as the meadowlarks had fled south.

He worked frenetically, driven by some demon he didn't know, dreaming of getting ahead. He took to repairing things without being asked. One day he rebuilt a broken hayrack in the horse pen; another day he made a new bench for the dining hall. He cut and hauled so much firewood and stacked it in the post in so many places that even Alec Culbertson, chief of all operations on the Missouri, took notice.

"Peter, we've never been so comfortably ahead of the cold," he said. "You're a splendid help, lad."

"I'd like to assume responsibilities, sir. Any time you think I'm ready."

"Ambitious, are you?"

"I need to get ahead, sir."

Culbertson nodded.

In January the bottom fell out of the weather. Temperatures plunged to forty below, and no chinook came to melt away the heavy snows of December. They had always counted on the magical chinooks of the northern prairies, those warm westerly breezes out of the Pacific, to unthaw their world, give them a few days of respite and even warmth, when men could wander about in shirtsleeves and animals could race and play before another arctic blast rolled in.

Without the chinooks, the Blackfeet stayed away, and the post did a poor business. Only the most desperate tribesmen braved the brutal cold and drifts to buy something necessary, such as powder and lead, or blankets. Peter listened to the talk, and knew the factors feared that the Piegans might be trading elsewhere, maybe at Hudson's Bay posts in Canada.

Then, from someone in command, came the word: This year they'd send trading wagons out. If the tribesmen wouldn't come in, the Benton traders would go out to them. Each of three wagons would be stuffed with trade goods, small qualities but of wide variety, and whatever provisions could be crammed in for the traders. If all went well, the wagons would soon be emptied of trade goods and filled with prime winter robes, thick and furry and warm. It'd be a hard life for the traders, who would have little shelter and a lot of misery.

Malcolm Clarke, the post's factor, summoned Peter one afternoon so cold that his hands numbed just crossing the yard.

"I'm sending wagons out," the factor said without preliminary. "You want to go with one? It's mean, hard work."

"Yes, sir!"

"You'll be the mule, you know. Fetch firewood, make camp, take care of horses—if there's no grass, you'll end up peeling cottonwood bark for them. Hunt if you can. Freeze all the time."

"I want to, sir."

"You won't do any trading, but maybe you can learn a little about it—maybe learn some Blackfoot too."

"I want to get ahead."

"So we've noticed, Kipp. All right. I'm sending you out with Charles de Paris in the morning. You'll outfit today and leave tomorrow. Head up the Marias to Willow Round. I'm sending Picotte up to Milk River Crossing the La Roux up to the Sweetgrass Hills—maybe he can find some Bloods up there. There's soddies and livestock pens at Willow Round and Milk River."

"To Willow Round? With Monsieur de Paris?"

Charles frowned. "Something wrong with that?"

"No! Perhaps we can find Marie Therese!"

Clarke smiled. "That never occurred to me."

They rolled north in a subzero dawn, with frost whitening the long hair of the six scrawny drays, and every breath of man and beast a cloud. But the earth was hard as granite and the rivers capped with ice, and they made good time. In some places arctic winds scoured the snow away; in others it lay in great barrier ridges that the horses had to buck and plunge through. Peter exhausted himself at each camp, chopping through river ice to water the horses, gathering wood, picketing when possible, or hobbling horses when nothing could be driven into the frozen earth. Peter never stopped being cold, even with a good blaze jabbing heat into an open-sided shelter.

He and Marie's father didn't talk much; there seemed too much to do, and a lot that neither wanted to say. And yet a bond grew between them, unspoken, undeclared. It rose from the thing they shared, a yearning to find Marie Therese—de Paris's only child, and Peter's only love.

"She won't come," Peter said one day while de Paris was handling the lines.

"Then we will visit her, mon ami. Love, it is going, not coming sometimes."

Love meant going, not coming. The thought struck

Peter dumb, as if he'd been poleaxed. He'd always thought of her coming to him, coming back, always coming. And now the Frenchman was saying we'll go to her, visit her, let her see our love.

"What's at Willow Round?"

"A trading camp—beside the river on a meadow. Sheltered in willow bottoms, set up for winter."

"How far will we be from the Piegans?"

"Ah, ami, why do you think the fur company builds the little outposts there, eh? Clarke and Culbertson and your pére—they know where to get robes, eh?"

They raced toward her on their wild ponies, their lances lowered, their war whoops frightful. Marie Therese cringed. She had no place to flee. Were they not Siksika? One on a brown and white paint led the charge, and when he drew near, he threw the feather-decked lance. It bolted straight at her. She wrenched aside just as it bit into the earth a foot ahead. The young man raced by, laughing.

Trembling, Marie Therese cried out. "Siksika!" she said. She dropped her bundle and grabbed the lance, just as half a dozen more crowded in, bowling her over with their frantic ponies. "I'm Siksika!" she cried, tumbling in the earth. She peered out into young faces, boys in their teens, hawkish and bloodthirsty.

"She's Absaroka!" said one.

"Maybe Assiniboin!"

"No, she's a Shoshone dog!"

She understood their Siksika tongue but couldn't summon up the words from her childhood. One slid off his crazed pony and snatched her bundle, while another retrieved the lance and the rest pushed their wild little mounts right into her huddled form.

"Siksika!" she screamed.

They paused.

"She doesn't wear the clothing of the People!"

"We've never seen this Siksika!"

She realized these Mad Dogs were all young ones, full of boldness and bravado, full of dreams of coups and honors and war; youths playing men's roles, imitating the gallantry of the warriors of her people. On some other occasion she would have been proud of them.

She clambered to her feet, angry. "Siksika!" she yelled, in a tone that crackled with rage.

An older man pushed a larger horse through the Mad Dogs. This one had a notched eagle feather tucked into a hair knot at the nape of his neck, stern eyes, and a visible scorn for all mortals etched deep into his umber face.

"Is this how you treat a guest?" she cried.

He snarled something at the young men. "I am Neno Kyio, Bear Chief, a chief of the Mad Dog Society," he said. "What name have you?"

Marie Therese avoided that. "I am looking for O-toch-koki, wife of Sinopah. She is my mother."

"What is your name?"

"Marie Therese de Paris."

"I know of no such woman."

"My father is a trader. My mother is of the Ich-poch-semo, Grease Melters. But she is with the Lone Eaters, whose chief is Siyeh, Mad Wolf."

They all consulted, speaking faster than she could understand. Then the older one nodded. "Come," he said.

She retrieved her stick and bundle and walked down a long grade to the village, escorted by all the raucous youths, mocking her and pointing at her shoes. They took her among the glowing lodges and past an empty one stained yellow, with buffalo galloping around its side, the bottom a black polka-dot band, the symbol of dusty stars. She recognized the Yellow Buffalo Lodge, one of the sacred lodges of the Blackfeet. They stopped before one of the bigger lodges. Everywhere, drying buffalo meat hung from racks.

"Oki!" Come in, said someone within.

She let the Mad Dog leader precede her, and entered into an exquisitely furnished interior where a tall man stood beside two wives.

"I am Stock-stchi, Bear Child, chief of the Black Patched Moccasins. You are here for what purpose?"

She explained again, searching for words.

He studied her a long time, suspicions crawling over his face. Finally he told her that the Lone Eaters were in the next drainage west for the great fall hunt, and he would send her there with an escort.

"It is true that Kit Fox has the Meadowlark who fled the trader," he said.

"Thank you," she said in English, knowing it meant nothing. Then she remembered her bundle outside, backed out the lodge door and found the little sack of brown sugar in it. This she gave him. He nodded, dismissing her.

Her reception had been less than warm. They saw only the French in her, and missed their own blood. Was there no home on earth for a mixed-blood?

Seven young Mad Dogs escorted her over a broad windy divide, through a silver-frosted night, their raillery and mocking a substitute for the war honors they had yet to earn. She knew she was the butt of much of it, but they spoke too fast and furtively for her.

She stopped on the ridge. "When you have killed an Absaroka or a Cree, then you will have the right to make fun of me," she said slowly.

"We will give you the Cree medicine, Ito-wa-mami-wa-natsi," he said. The others laughed and smirked. She wondered what it meant.

From there she beheld the camp of the Lone Eaters, the camp of her mother! It glimmered in the bright autumnal moonlight, its lodges glowing orange cones, the whole aspect joyous beyond anything she'd experienced. She'd come home.

They descended the long slope, were met by this camp's Mad Dogs, and after a lot of whispers and talk, the new police warriors escorted her into the village while the young rascals retreated. These warriors were older and harder, and eyed her with eyes measuring her scalp. She ignored them and walked toward the glowing circle of light, a city of the Blackfeet, each street lit by the gas lamp of a beautiful cowhide lodge.

They took her through whirling dogs, wood smoke,

and redolent manure dropped by buffalo runners tied to the lodges, straight to a lodge at the far end. They didn't even pause at the taller one of the chief near the center of the village. Her heart ached. What if her mother wouldn't recognize her? So many years! What if they sent her away—would a breed girl be welcome here? What if her stepfather didn't want her? Why had she come so far, instead of waiting at the fort to meet her mother?

They stopped before a handsome moon-gilded lodge, with weasels running around its sides and the familiar polka-dot "dusty stars" on the black hand at its base. A fire flickered within, the cottonwood smoke ebbed from the wind ears above. Her mother's home. Would it be her home too?

A Mad Dog scratched softly. The door flap parted, pouring light out upon her, and she beheld her mother there.

"A woman from the traders has come," said the Mad Dog Society leader. Meadowlark looked puzzled, and peered into the whited night at Marie Therese. Then, as recognition lit her eyes, she cried out. "Marie Therese! Eeyah!"

For a long frozen moment Marie couldn't speak. Her mother looked beautiful in that warm firelight, but so much older, and somehow strange . . . more—Indian. How strange. She'd barely perceived of her mother as *Indian*.

"Oki!" Come in!

The Mad Dogs faded away, and Marie Therese stepped into the lodge of Sinopah and felt afraid. This moment terrified her. They might turn her out into the cold, drive her away. She beheld another woman, younger, sitting close by. They all wore plain buckskins, much splattered with dark shining stains Marie knew were those of butchery. They'd spent the day cutting and processing buffalo.

"Ah!" cried Meadowlark. She peered at Marie, studying her daughter, exclaiming at her shoes, pinching Marie's rich blue blanket and finally running a finger over Marie's golden cheeks, which were shaped by her mother's bones.

Then, swiftly, Meadowlark rattled out words, slapping down like hail, explaining to Sinopah and the young woman, pointing at Marie.

Marie peered shyly at the man of this lodge, finding him gaunt and graying, his face sharp, his black eyes proud and suspicious, his hair in two braids that fell over his buckskin shirt. He wore an eagle-bone whistle suspended from a thong around his neck.

"You have come for a visit, Marie Therese?"

"To stay!"

"You have turned away from the napikwan?"

"I want to live here!"

Something shadowy slid into her mother. "Will he come? Will he punish us?"

"No. He told me he loves you."

Meadowlark sighed. "I could not live among the napikwan. But you—they sent you down the Big River to the many-houses and taught you. You won't stay here with the Pikuni."

"I will if you'll let me."

At last Meadowlark remembered they were all strangers. "This is Sinopah, my husband. And this is his younger wife, Isto-ko-pence, Tears in Her Eyes."

Without asking Marie, Meadowlark dipped a horn ladle into an iron pot filled with buffalo tongue and sarvisberry stew, and filled a wooden bowl, which she handed to her daughter.

"Tell us your story, and we will think about it," said Sinopah. "Perhaps I will talk to a medicine man tomorrow, and the elders."

Chapter Fourteen

Siksika words bloomed like daisies in Marie Therese's soul, and soon her mind was brightly carpeted with them, each springing from seed that had lain dormant through all the arid winters of her youth in St. Louis. Until she reached eight years, the Blackfoot tongue had been her tongue, with a smattering of French and English besides. Now it grew in her as camp life stirred the childhood memories.

Even as the tongue returned, she began to befriend the strangers in her mother's lodge. Soon she was spinning long stories about napikwan—white man—St. Louis, and the sisters who taught so many mountain children. But it wasn't the past that absorbed her, it was the new life she hungered for. She pestered her mother about the meanings of things; the prayers and rituals of the buffalo hunt; the morning devotions of the Pikuni; the roles of men and women, parents and grandparents.

Then one cold morning Sinopah changed her life. "You must have a Pikuni name. This other name, Marie, it signifies nothing. You are without a spirit helper. I will take you to a great medicine man of our people, Natosin Nepe-e, Brings Down the Sun. Sun Giver we call him. Bring a gift!"

Marie had so few possessions, she wondered what she could spare, and decided at last upon the hatchet she'd used on the trail. Then Kit Fox solemnly walked with her through the camp, past women and children who still peeked furtively at her, sensing someone not quite Pikuni—someone without a name. Her mother's husband left her before a small tattered lodge at the eastern edge of the village. She scratched softly as she had learned to do, and presently an old man peered out. He seemed to be wrapped in poverty, wearing the plainest buckskins with no adornment at all. But his piercing eyes seemed adorned with something finer than possessions. He peered at her kindly, and invited her in.

"You have come for a name," he said.

"I would like a Pikuni name, Grandfather."

She wondered how he knew. He circled the fire and the altar behind it and settled himself at the rear of the lodge. She presented the hatchet, and he nodded, as if the hatchet meant nothing itself, but her gift meant something. Sun Giver closed his eyes a moment, and she studied his seamed face and gray hair, which hung in two braids. She saw no evil in it, no downturn of lips or scorn lines or the pursed mouth of pride, and felt that she had come to someone with mysterious and beautiful powers.

He extracted a long medicine pipe with a red pipestone bowl from the soft pouch, tamped tobacco into it, and lit it with a tiny brand from the hearth fire. He puffed contentedly, and then blew four puffs of smoke toward the sky, and four more toward the earth. He didn't hand the pipe to her, but serenely smoked the whole charge and knocked out the dottle. Then he dropped a twist of braided coarse sweetgrass upon the hearth. It ignited, lifting a pearly smoke that filled the lodge, perfuming it like a priest's incense.

"A Siksika name," he said. "Are you Siksika?"

"Yes, Grandfather."

"What part of you is Siksika?"

"My heart."

He nodded. "I have heard that the napikwan virgins taught you all the secrets of those people."

"Not much more than O-toch-koki would have taught

me, Grandfather. But I learned to read and write and do numbers."

"You are a gift to us, then. We will need someone who can do these things so we can know about the napikwan."

"I was called here by something within me, Grandfather."

"Yes, yes. I have seen that. It's good."

"I understand the napikwan, and I'll give my understanding to the people."

He stared into the coals, as if reading mysteries in them. "You're destined to see great things happen, things wrought by napikwan. You'll wish you never knew their ways. Your heart will quake with the word you will bring to the Siksika. Your tears will spring from all that you learned from the virgins in St. Louis. You will not like the future, but you will be solaced by all that you do."

Fear clutched her. "Grandfather, the black robe, DeSmet—he told me the same thing."

Brings Down the Sun nodded. "He is a good man."

"I don't want those burdens. I just want to live among the Pikuni. Take them away!"

"They will be thrust upon you, Marie Therese. You will be like the napikwan virgins. Many of our young men will play the love flute outside your lodge, but you will not hear it. Others will give you the Cree medicine, but it will not have the usual effect."

"Cree medicine?"

He laughed. "Love medicine . . . a powerful potion—put a little on the birch-bark image of a girl, a drop right upon the heart, and she will not be able to resist! But you will. You are destined for greater things than marriage."

So the young Mad Dogs were making jokes about love potions when they escorted her here. "The sisters taught me to resist such things," she announced primly.

Brings Down the Sun laughed softly. "You'll be the greatest catch—and no one will catch you!"

"Grandfather, is it forbidden for a woman to seek a vision, a spirit helper?"

"Not at all, Marie Therese. Any Siksika may seek a

spirit helper. Anytime you wish, purify yourself with sweetgrass, take no water or food, and go to a high place and wait. Sometimes it takes only a day and a night. Many times it takes four days and nights, and a questing person becomes so weak he is close to death. Sometimes a vision does not come, and that's a great disappointment."

"I will do it soon."

He nodded. "I knew you would. You will have great medicine, great power."

"How do you know?"

"My spirit helper is the golden eagle. He sings to me."

"Will you give me a name?"

"What name do you wish?"

"That is for you to say, Grandfather."

"Then I must choose for you. Let me see now."

He laid another twist of sweetgrass on the coals, and smoke plumed out, bathing both of them. Then he rocked quietly, sometimes singing a song that echoed softly against the wall of some distant canyon of the soul—eagle songs, soaring and diving songs of his own composition.

"I will give you a name," he said.

She found the moment strangely stirring, like the great sacrament of the Mass back in St. Louis.

"Natoya-niskim," he said. "Sacred Buffalo Stone. You see, you were wearing your name all the while you were away. Natoya-niskim is stronger than the napikwan cross medicine."

"Sacred Buffalo Stone. I am honored, Grandfather."

He smiled. "I will chop lots of wood now!"

She knew he was dismissing her. She was Natoya-niskim—no longer Marie Therese, but Sacred Buffalo Stone. She clutched the amber amulet that dangled on her breast. Natoya-niskim . . . how odd it seemed, vaguely disappointing. She wished she had been named for something beautiful.

She backed out of the lodge door into the blinding autumnal sun and drew her thick blanket about her. This very night she would begin her vision quest, but first she must return to her mother and stepfather and proclaim herself.

She walked through a brisk October afternoon, drawing the stares of villagers as usual. Everywhere the women were processing meat or scraping fresh hides staked to the earth, gossiping as they drew their buffalo leg bone and metal fleshers across the underside of hides, scraping away the white inner tissue and fat before tanning the hide with brains. The whole village seemed to rejoice in the success of the fall hunt. Sun and Napi had been kind.

She found Meadowlark and Tears in Her Eyes slicing meat and hanging it on racks, but Sinopah had ridden off for more buffalo along with most of the men.

"I am named Natoya-niskim."

"Ah!" Pleasure lit Meadowlark's eyes. "It's a beautiful name, and you should be proud. Why, you're named for the medicine stone at your breast. The one I gave you so long ago." Her mother's face was wreathed with happiness.

"It's a beautiful name, with much medicine given to it," said Tears in Her Eyes.

"When Kit Fox returns, we shall have it announced to the village," said her mother. "Meanwhile, Natoya-niskim, come inside. I have a naming gift for you."

The woman who had been Marie Therese followed her mother into the somber brown light of the lodge. There her mother handed her exquisite winter moccasins, calf high, lined with rabbit fur, with sturdy buffalo rawhide soles.

"Oh! Mother! How did you do all this and hide it from me?"

Meadowlark laughed, pleased by her daughter's joy. Natoya-niskim slid them on, rejoicing at their soft, perfect fit. She gazed at her white woman's shoes, knew she would never wear the clothing of her father's people again, and silently set them aside. She would give them away as fast as she could.

"Tonight we will have a feast for you!"

"Oh, Mother, I'd love to—but I can't. Tonight I begin my quest for a spirit helper."

"Tonight? Must it be tonight? It's going to be cold."

"Yes, tonight. I am called, and I must go."

"What will I tell Kit Fox?"

Natoya, once Marie, turned solemn. "Tell him, and tell the others in the village, that if I receive my vision, and a spirit of the living creatures has mercy upon me, I'll come down from the hilltops a Pikuni. Only then will I be of the People. And only then will I know what I am to give to my people."

She settled herself on a high ridge a short walk from her village, a rocky private place guarded by junipers. At dusk she stood and faced the dying sun.

"All the creatures of the world, hear me, O hear one who beseeches you. Flying creatures hear me; land-walking creatures hear me; creatures that crawl and creatures that burrow underground hear me; bring your wisdom and strength to me so that I may serve my people."

With that she settled to the cold earth again and drew her blue blanket tightly about her. She smelled snow in the air, and knew the weather would soon grow cold and damp and harsh, and perhaps Es-to-nea-pesta, Maker of Storms and Blizzards, would seek her out for her effrontery. She emptied her mind of everything and sought to wait calmly, but already she hungered and thirsted, and her white blood begged for nourishment. She would need to be more Pikuni, she thought.

The Seven Brothers in the north sky vanished early in the night and she beheld a deepening blackness that snuffed out the stars until she could see none, and could see nowhere at all, not even her numbing hands. What sort of vision quest was this, that a small Pikuni woman would be tortured by cold and wind? The sleet came, stinging her face, collecting on her blanket and dampening it, and riding down her hair to the nape of her neck. She felt her feet numb; even her new winter moccasins would not keep the Cold Maker out. She sat and endured, feeling her body heat ebb from her, leaving her limbs and arms numb and her face frosted and biting. She knew this storm, in the Month When the Geese Fly South, would not be as cold as the storms to come. She didn't know how long she could last, or what a ruin of her dreams it would be if she fled, like a white woman, to warmth. So she waited, licking sleet from her lips, emptying her soul for the spirit to come.

She stood to limber her numbing legs, and sat again, while the ground grayed around her. She could tell snowy ground from barren ground, but she could see no more. She wondered if she was really Marie Therese, a napikwan woman, and not able to endure through to the end.

"I am Natoya-niskim," she said to the Storm Maker.

A blast of crystalline snow lanced her face.

"Hurry to me!" she cried.

Then it turned warm, and she felt no snow though the blizzard raged about her, murderous and mocking. She saw the beautiful white buffalo cow standing before her, gazing upon her with moist brown eyes. She had never seen a buffalo so perfectly formed, so sleek and proud, nor had she ever seen the sacred white buffalo, as rare as rainbows. Her spirit helper! The white buffalo cow kneeled before her and bid her to climb on, and then took her for a grand ride through herds of thousands of buffalo, galloping freely through the great white blizzard. But gradually the other buffalo slid away, fewer and fewer, and only White Buffalo Cow remained.

Then the white buffalo cow flew over the proud villages of the Siksika, rich and powerful and warm, each with thousands of ponies. She saw happy people everywhere, warriors returning to camp painted black for victory, the scalps of enemies dangling from their lances. Then the white buffalo cow flew over more villages, these poorer, the people sick and haggard. She saw the young men slip away with robes to trade with white men in wagons. Then White Buffalo Cow showed her villages of the dead and dying, with only a few Siksika left, huddled miserably close to fires because they lacked blankets and robes.

Then a soldier dressed in a blue uniform rose up and shot the white buffalo cow, which shuddered and collapsed, leaking blood from her mouth. Natoya-niskim sighed and slid off the back of her spirit helper.

It was cold again, and dark, and the darkness stretched to infinity and she could find no light anywhere, or hope.

"Thank you for coming to me, White Buffalo Cow," she said.

She knew everything to know about herself, her purposes and her future, and she found no light anywhere. She stood stiffly, numbed to the marrow, and left the ridge, steering more by instinct than by vision, while the winds whipped her.

She groped through a village in which every lodge looked alike, seeking the small one at the periphery where she had to go first, even before going to the lodge of Sinopah. It took her a long time, stumbling over racks of drying meat, tripping over a picket line, her hands and face red and raw, and her toes torturing her.

She scratched softly on the lodge flap of the old medicine man, Natosin Nepe-e, Brings Down the Sun.

Miraculously the flap parted at once.

"Oki," he said, and she plunged into a darkness not much warmer than what lay outside.

He threw tinder upon the coals and blew softly, and a tiny cold flame lit the lodge. The old man wore exactly what he wore by day. He motioned her to sit while he added sticks and fanned the little fire until at last a grudging heat reached her.

Then he pulled his buffalo robe around him and seated himself across the altar and the fire from her.

"You have been visited, and you have come to tell me," he said.

"A white buffalo cow."

He sucked in air and fussed with his robe.

"I'm glad she came soon; I feared I would die, or surrender like a napikwan woman."

"Tell me everything."

She did, reciting it step by step as he studied her with his piercing eyes. After she had finished, he thought about it, gazing into the little blaze.

"And so you know your death."

She nodded bleakly.

"And you have seen what is to become of the Pikuni."

She nodded again.

"You have the saddest task ever given to a person. Not since Napi created us has any person been given a task so sad. Have you the courage to do it?"

"I haven't, but White Buffalo Cow will give it."

"That is a good answer."

"Shall I tell my vision to the people when the sun rises?"

"Yes, all of it."

"Then they'll know."

He shook his head. "They will be told and not know. What happened after the soldier shot the white buffalo cow?"

"The cold and night came back."

"There was no light? You did not see a calf beside the white buffalo cow?"

"No."

He sat quietly, shaking his head, and then he wept. Tears slid down his seamed cheeks and dropped into his robe. Finally he fingered them away and smiled. "I will not live to see it," he said. "Now you must go to your mother's lodge and rest. Soon you will carry on your shoulders the weight of the world."

He was dismissing her. She rose, spraying melted snow from her blanket, and slid into the night.

"It is a good hatchet," he said behind her.

It had grown lighter. A full moon was shining above the mantle of snow clouds.

She found her lodge only because snow had slid off its sides, baring the running weasels. Her mother and Tears in Her Eyes and Father barely stirred as she entered. Gratefully she crawled into her appointed space near the door, the place of the least and lowest in the lodge, and drew up her other blanket and a buffalo robe as well, and tried to warm up. But the warmth didn't come and she shivered under her robes, thinking that the sun and warmth and fire would never come. Perhaps they never would.

She awakened to a radiant fire and odd stares, and she knew they were wondering if the half-napikwan girl had fled the storm instead of enduring through to her vision.

"I'll tell you. My spirit helper is White Buffalo Cow, and she came to me. I rode her."

Relief filled the lodge. Her mother smiled.

"Let us hear of it," said Sinopah.

She told them the entire vision, and they agreed it was especially powerful. Later that morning she described her vision to the village elders and headmen and medicine men, and they listened happily, hearing a rare and holy story. A daughter of the village had been visited by the sacred white buffalo herself, and it made her a sacred woman, a medicine woman of great repute at once. The medicine men nodded respectfully.

Soon she had told her story to others, and messengers had carried her vision to the Black Patched Moccasins and the Small Robes and the Grease Melters, the other bands that had joined in this fall hunt.

In the space of a few days she had become a revered medicine woman, to whom they would all listen closely. Now she was Pikuni. Some of the boys played love flutes outside her lodge, but she ignored them. Other boys tried to capture her and throw a blanket over the pair of them and court her boldly with roving hands under the blanket, but she slid away. Still others tried the Cree medicine upon her image, sure to capture the pretty one, but she ignored them, her soul preparing itself for what was to come. After a while the boys gave up, chased after more pliant girls, and left her alone. Her mothers and stepfather chided her for that.

Each morning she walked to a hilltop and prayed to Sun, and Napi, and White Buffalo Cow, for help with what was to come, and through the time of preparation her spirit changed. The last of the napikwan vanished from her; even from her body. She wore a plain doeskin dress, as shapeless and uninviting as she could make it, like the dark dress of the sisters in St. Louis, and for the same purpose. With the arrival of the Moon When the Buffalo Calves Are Black, she felt ready to teach the Pikuni people about their doom.

Chapter Fifteen

For a while the little outpost on Willow Round did no business at all, but Charles de Paris didn't seem to mind.

"Mon ami, they'll come in after the fall hunt, and after they've made their winter camps," he told Peter. "About December—they call it the Moon of the First Chinook."

"I want to learn how to trade," Peter said.

"Learn the language. That's where it all begins for anyone wanting to trade with the Indians."

"I know a little Blackfoot. Marie Therese taught me some words on the boat."

"Ah, she remembered them from her childhood. You'll need more than those."

"I'll learn them if you'll let me watch."

"There'll be time if you make time, oui?"

Peter nodded. Ever since they arrived and swept out the two-room sod-roofed building, he'd been so busy he hardly had time to think. He had to chop firewood to feed the ever-hungry fireplace, care for the horses, peel cottonwood bark for their emergency feed, shelve all the trade goods in the front room, and hunt when he could. Later, de Paris explained, they'd trade for a buffalo carcass or two as well as robes, and the frozen meat would fill their bellies all winter.

"When will they come in?"

"Oh, when the fall hunt is over and the hides are prime. When the women have had a chance to tan them. After the hunt the Piegans scatter to their winter camps. Mostly along the Marias, the Two Medicine, the Teton—anyplace where there's shelter from wind, lots of cottonwoods for fuel and horse feed, water and game."

"Will . . . Mrs. de Paris come in?"

"Ah! You have strange notions, young man. She's not my wife now. Not for many years. But I suppose you wish to see Marie Therese, eh? I don't miss the look in your eyes."

"I dream of it."

He shrugged. "Maybe, maybe not, eh? We have no word. Is her maman with the Grease Melters or the Lone Eaters—or maybe with the Bloods in Canada?"

Peter felt crestfallen. Here he was in the heart of the Blackfoot country. Marie Therese could be wintering a few miles away and he might never see her.

In the evenings, toasting their front sides before the fire, they became friends. Charles de Paris smoked a clay pipe while Peter pestered him for Blackfoot words.

"You're not like the other Creoles," Peter said once.

The trader had turned solemn. "No, I'm not one of the Louisiana French, if that's what you mean. Not a French-Canadian either. I'm a refugee from France. It's not safe for me there. The assassins of the revolution guillotined my grandparents, tracked my parents down here in the New World and killed them. I must stay apart until the last convulsion in France."

"But surely the Creoles here know—"

De Paris shrugged. "One must go on," he said dourly.

"How did you meet Meadowlark?"

"Ah, you are a nosy *garçon*." He gazed into the darkness of the smoky room, as if seeing distant things. "Her band came to trade at Fort MacKenzie. I saw her. She was belle—beautiful, my young friend. The Blackfeet are the most handsome of all the tribes of America. Tall, slim, proud, well-formed, refined features, eh? There she was, O-toch-koki, Meadowlark, daughter of a headman, bright-eyed, her smile as joyous as the song of the yellow-breasted bird. She wore festival clothing—they sometimes do for trading—and hers made her ravishing. Ah, ravishing!"

"I mean, ah, how do you propose to an Indian girl?"

The trader laughed. "You mean, how do you propose to Marie Therese, eh? You speak her tongue. You tell her the things you'd tell a white girl. She's beautiful. She has dancing eyes. You want her forever and a day. If she wants you, she'll let you know. Then you must seek out her parents, and if you're a Blackfoot boy, you'll leave a gift horse and other things before the girl's lodge, and if the gifts are taken in and the horse accepted, why—you've made a match!"

"I wish I had a horse."

"Ah, mon ami, I didn't give a horse. I am a trader, and I made many gifts, eh? A good rifle and powder and lead. Blankets. A kettle, an ax, a knife, and an awl."

"Then what happened?"

"Then I had a wife! They brought her to me dressed in wedding finery, velvety fringed buckskin, calf-high moccasins beaded brightly. Her black hair had been braided, and her face glowed. Ah, such a people, the Pieds Noirs! The women are more beautiful than all the courtesans of France! She was shy and afraid—marrying a white man, eh?" He sighed. "She was always afraid—like a free, wild bird in a willow cage—and the trading posts were never home to her."

A strange foreboding filled Peter. Maybe the daughter would be like her mother, and all his hope would be dashed.

About when the weather turned harsh, small parties of Blackfeet drifting in from nearby villages began to trade, all of them bearing prime robes. The hunt had been good. Knots of Blackfeet appeared on horseback, sometimes in the middle of ground blizzards or storms, and deposited thick, glossy robes on the crude counter. De Paris spread them out, examining them for grade and flaws, and then traded for vermilion, kettles, knives, axes, bars of lead, waxy packets of gunpowder, percussion caps, thick blankets, and sometimes even a trade rifle. Peter clerked, scratching each transaction into a logbook, toting robes away, leaping to the shelves to get the trade goods that de Paris requested. Peter's days alternated from frenzied clerking to utter boredom while the occasional blizzard raged, or temperatures plummeted so low that no one would travel. But the work never ceased. No matter how brutal the weather, horses needed care; water and wood had to be gotten; robes had to be carefully folded and stacked in a corner of the soddy. Peter's restless soul wouldn't let him waste a moment, so he added amenities such as hewn wood and rawhide chairs, a table, bunks, and better shelter for the horses, while Charles de Paris observed him pensively.

"You're mad for *travail,* mon ami."

"I have to get ahead!"

The trade goods dwindled swiftly, while the mountain of prime robes grew, and de Paris speculated that they'd sell out by the end of January, well ahead of their planned stay. By the end of the year, they knew who their neighbors were. The Small Robes and Black Patched Moccasins were on the Marias; the Lone Eaters on Two Medicine River; the Buffalo Dungs on Badger Creek.

Then, in the Moon When the Buffalo Calves are Black, the Lone Eaters came. Almost fifty of them, rising out of a whirling ground blizzard, tying starved and miserable ponies to the rail in front. Only a few could jam into the trading room, and Peter could see the rest erecting a storm lodge outside, or traipsing into the cottonwoods to peel the inner bark for their gaunt ponies. Even in the trading room their breaths raised steam and the snow caking their garments didn't melt. He yearned to see the face of one he loved, but these were mostly warriors, wrapped in robes and blankets, wearing heavy caps of rabbit or other fur.

He did his clerk's dance, fetching axes and hanks of beads and bolts of trade cloth, and making his numb fingers record each transaction in the logbook.

From Sinopah, Lone Eaters, six prime robes, three

split; to same, 1 lb sugar, three twist tobacco, three yd flannel, 1 pk vermilion, 1 lb powder & 3 lb St Louis lead.

Even as he wrote, de Paris was measuring the red flannel the mountain way, a yard being from fingertips to chin. The trader had short arms and the Piegans were getting no bargain.

Peter froze. Worming through the crowd toward Sinopah were three women, one of them a striking girl in a bold blue blanket.

"Marie Therese!"

De Paris looked up sharply. Marie exclaimed. So did the older one with her, a woman whose gentle features seemed as familiar as Marie Therese's, though Peter had never seen her before.

"Peter! It's you!"

"O-toch-koki!" said the trader in a voice filled with joy and pain.

A dozen Piegans stared and then began whispering. In moments the room was bedlam, with people talking, gesticulating, laughing. Peter couldn't understand the Siksika, or the excited exchange between de Paris and his former wife, or the amusement of the warriors. But he could talk to Marie Therese, who worked her way to the split-log counter.

"I was hoping, I was hoping!" Peter cried.

"It is good to see you, Peter. You are a clerk now?"

"Yes!"

"You are very busy."

"Yes! No! Marie Therese—"

"I am Natoya-niskim now."

"But—"

"The name was given to me by a medicine man, Brings Down the Sun. Now I am Sacred Buffalo Stone."

"But Marie—you're mixed-blood. Like me! You're white too."

"Oh, Peter. I'm not."

He looked sharply at her, seeing something odd: except for her deep gray eyes, he saw not the slightest trace of her father's blood in her. She'd been transformed somehow. She wore Siksika clothing, but that wasn't it; her expression had been transformed. The cast of her face was proud, smoldering, strong, and somehow shocking. To see her was to know she'd slid forever beyond his hopes—but not beyond his aching love.

"Peter, *garçon*. We must make the trading. I've invited Sinopah's family to eat with us after we're done trading. *Vite! Vite, mon ami.*"

He did, while Marie Therese smiled from across a chasm.

She had scarcely ever seen her parents together. They conversed in the Siksika tongue beside the snapping fire, along with Sinopah and Tears in Her Eyes. Her father seemed grave and intense and courteous, as if the knowledge that her mother had abandoned him remained a barrier to intimacy. Her mother seemed more at ease, chattering aimlessly about the hunt, about a war party that had brought back Absaroka ponies and scalps, and about the Cold Maker.

Peter couldn't really understand, though he grasped an occasional fragment. So she pulled him aside and addressed him in English. The young man looked at her with such adoration that she felt pangs of regret. But she could not change a thing, nor be the wife he wanted her to be. She knew she had to convey that to him once and for all, and to help him understand her mission and its sacredness.

"I guess you'll be visiting your ma for the winter, then," he said.

"More than the winter."

"I guess you'll get tired of living in tents sooner or later."

"They're more comfortable than this cold room, Peter."

"I could give you better. I'm working hard for us both. I'll have a business of my own someday. Maybe I'll be an opposition trader. We'll have a big house, like the ones in St. Louis, and woodstoves, and real beds. Everything! It's for you, Marie."

"Natoya-niskim."

"You're a mixed-blood like me. You'll always be Marie Therese, and nothing you do will ever change it. That's how you were christened."

"Sacred Buffalo Stone, Peter." She said it stubbornly. This thing between them had begun on the boat near St. Louis, and now it loomed large. Still, her heart reached out to him. "Peter? Listen. A great medicine man, Brings Down the Sun, gave me my name. And then I had a vision."

"A vision? Like a vision quest? I thought that's for boys."

"It's for those who seek it. Peter"—she spoke urgently, wanting him to understand—"I was given a vision the first night. Not just a vision, not just a spirit helper, but . . ." She didn't know how to tell him the rest. He'd scoff.

"Hoodoo, Marie. There's the real world, steamboats and railroads, and science, and that's all."

"The white buffalo cow came—she's sacred to the Siksika. She came and I rode her and she showed—she's not just my helper. She gave me something I have to do. She showed me . . . what will happen to the Pikuni."

"And what'll happen, Marie?"

"Will you listen, or will you just scoff at me?"

"I'm not scoffing. I just don't think you can see the future, and it's superstition."

"I will do what I was shown," she whispered. "All my life."

"You're only sixteen!"

"It's not too young. We marry at sixteen sometimes. But I'll never marry, Peter. I'll be like the sisters in St. Louis."

"Marie! All because of a hunger dream?"

She nodded. "The white buffalo cow became my friend. I saw her and loved her, and she loved me."

"But I love you!"

"I know, Peter." She reached for his hand and held it. "Whatever I do, I want you to be my friend. I'll always need you. You'll be the only friend I have among the napikwan."

"You sound like you're going to send the Blackfeet to war against whites."

She shook her head. "No. But I'll show my people how to keep our ways as long as we can. I'll keep the treaty-makers from cheating us. I'll show them that when the napikwan come to make peace treaties—it's the beginning of the end for us. And when the soldiers and settlers come, our end is coming. And when the buffalo are gone, we will be gone too."

"Aw, that's doomsday stuff. You'll get a reservation, the Blackfoot homelands, just like the rest."

"Peter, don't you believe in visions, in prophets?"

He stared uncomfortably at her.

"I saw the last days of my people, when the tail of the last buffalo went away. I saw—" She decided not to tell him she saw a soldier shoot the white buffalo cow.

He seemed angry. His face had flushed. "I don't see any white people coming here. And if they do, it'll just be nicer. Stores and things. The chiefs and headmen, they won't believe you anyway."

"I've told my vision—but only Brings Down the Sun believes all of it. To the rest of them, I'm a mixed-blood."

"You're just gonna cause trouble."

"Peter? Be my friend. Always be my friend. Please?"

"You'll probably marry some warrior."

"The white buffalo cow had no calf, Peter."

That didn't mollify him, and she stopped trying to explain her mission or make anything easier for him. It seemed so useless. In the space of a few months, she'd crossed into a world that he would never share or understand, and there was nothing she could do to help him or comfort him. She turned toward the idle talk of her French father and Siksika mother while Peter sulked, excluded by a tongue he didn't know.

O-toch-koki urged her to tell of her naming and vision to Charles de Paris, and she did, in the Siksika tongue. She didn't think her European father would understand either, but when she had told everything, concealing nothing, she found him sympathetic.

"My petite chérie," he said, "I regret that so great a burden is placed on such small shoulders. May your vision be a blessing to your mother's people."

"You know what it's like to see something so terrible?"

De Paris sighed. "My parents were born into a world that was destroyed, and they were destroyed along with it. I wonder what the new world will be like? I wonder what the Siksika will do or become after the buffalo are gone?"

Sinopah said, "Ee-nau-ah will come back to feed us. After the napikwan go away."

Natoya-niskim sighed. Those of the Pikuni who had never been to St. Louis, or seen Independence, or stopped at Fort Leavenworth, would never grasp what she knew. The napikwan would not go away, not ever. Her nation would die. Maybe some of her people would live, but her nation would vanish. It made her ache within. Some inexpressible sadness attended her thoughts about her proud people. Not even Sun, or Napi, Old Man, would shield them. Not even the Beaver Bundle, the greatest medicine of her people. Her nation would wither away like grass in a drought. It would never rain again upon her people, but only upon the white men. No people in all the plains were more proud, but nothing would remain but burial bundles in trees. She held more sorrow within her than any young woman of sixteen should, or could.

They bided the night at the fur post, and she felt Peter's presence nearby, hot and restless and filled with a man's pain and need. He didn't sleep. She felt his gaze. She could not comfort him. When Sun returned, the trader gave Sinopah a twist of tobacco, gave Meadowlark and Tears in Her Eyes each a waxed packet of vermilion, and gave Marie Therese a heavy ring with a small flower incised in its polished stone.

"Chérie, this is a fleur-de-lis, the lily," he said. "It is me, it is you." It glowed magically in the dawn light.

"I will cherish it, Papa." She undid the thong that held her buffalo amulet and added the ring to her necklace.

Then he helped them saddle their horses. The others of her people had gone back to her village. This would be a grim day; the wind would numb her toes and fingers and make her cheeks burn. The blinding glare would draw tears from her eyes, which would freeze to her face.

She bestowed the gift of a hug upon Peter, who seemed so dejected he barely could speak.

"Will I ever see you again, Marie Therese?"

"Yes, Peter. From time to time."

"I love you. I'm going to live all alone—I don't want anyone. You're the only one, all mixed like me."

"Peter . . someday I'm going to need you. Need you so much you'll be my only hope. Will you remember, and help me—and my people?"

He nodded.

"When the napikwan—the white men—come I'll call on you."

Peter seemed to choke back some thought, and nodded. "I'll always be around, I guess. I'm not going anywhere. If any white men treat you bad, they'll answer to me."

"Not me alone! The People! Would you be the friend of all of the Siksika? When we are shot and killed and starved and herded like animals, will you be our friend?"

He nodded. "You sure got dark ideas, Marie—"

"No, Peter—like your prophets, the ones in your bible—I've been shown what is to come."

She hugged him and left him standing there, his breath pluming the air. They climbed into icy saddles and rode west. She took one last look at him, knowing the foreverness of the gulf between them. He was crying.

Part Two

THE SEIZERS

Chapter Sixteen

1853

The seasons slid by one by one, and the Lone Eaters band wandered as it always had over country the Siksika called their home. Nothing changed. In the winters they huddled beneath a protective bluff near water, and endured. In the spring they rejoiced at the power of Sun, and the young men grew restless to ride away and steal ponies from the Absaroka. Summers brought the annual Sun dance, when all the Siksika gathered in a vast camp and rejoiced. With the autumns came buffalo hunting and robe dressing and preparations for the time of the Cold Maker.

Natoya-niskim drifted through these unchanging cycles, which seemed as eternal as the earth itself. She barely had contacts with whites at the fur posts, and at times almost forgot her St. Louis life. She spent many of her free moments in the lodge of Brings Down the Sun, absorbing the tales of her people, learning all the things she had missed during her long sojourn away from them. Eventually she knew more of the sacred ritual and belief of the Siksika than most of the people her age, perhaps because she wanted to know it and didn't take it for granted. She had no close friends and didn't want any. Even the most aggressive of the youths finally ceased courting.

She had become a woman apart. The whole nation eventually learned of her vision and her medicine, but no one sought her help or counsel. Her medicine wasn't wanted. Who would listen to a girl of sixteen or seventeen? Neither did she see the white buffalo cow again, though sometimes in her puzzlement she climbed to a lonely place and asked for assurance from her spirit helper. So distant did her first great vision become that she began to doubt that the white buffalo cow had ever come to her or shown her what the future would be for herself and her people. But even in the midst of her doubts, she knew, she *knew*, that she had been set aside and given a sacred mission. The white buffalo cow would return to her—someday.

She absorbed the sweet, indolent rhythms of the Siksika life. Her people roamed, hunted, made war and married; they celebrated the first thunder of spring with the opening of the medicine pipe bundle, listened to the great ceremony of the Beaver medicine, gathered for the joyous reunion of the Sun dance, and mourned those who departed for the Sand Hills. No white men invaded their country other than a few traders, and no one worried about them. She heard nothing of great events far away that might signal change. Even the wagon traffic along the Platte River road, far south, changed nothing in their life. Who cared if the napikwan rolled across the prairies on their way to the land beside the great western seas?

Her people thought all these ways were eternal, and their children and children's children would hunt the buffalo and roam the high plains beside the benevolent Backbone, as they called the Rockies, just as they always had. Buffalo were plentiful; giant herds grazed vast pathways through the luxuriant shortgrass, multiplying each year, an eternal commissary for as long as Sun gave his light.

Her mind turned, now and then, to the memory of St. Louis and those restless, masterless men who lived there and dreamed of land and gold and pelts and great herds of cattle, and a world where no Indians lived. Perhaps it would never happen. But to think it was to know, sadly, that someday things would begin to change for her proud people. She grasped something about the future that eluded all the others.

The young warriors returned from their summer forays with ponies and blue-black scalps, and her heart rejoiced. No nation was half so powerful as the Siksika! Beyond the beyond the Salish and Absarokas quaked; the Shoshones fled in terror; the Blue Paint people lived in dread; the Lying People and Cutthroats, Cree and Assiniboin, kept their respectful distance; and even the mighty Hair Partners, the Lakota, avoided the armed power of the Siksika. They were lords of all the world, even the lands of the Grandmother to the north, and the lands of the Great Father to the east.

Natoya-niskim did not shirk her duties. She patiently fleshed hides and pounded buffalo brains into them. She gathered the berries in season, made waterproof winter moccasins from the smoke-blackened tops of old lodge skins, dug roots and camass bulbs, cared for the children of her neighbors, and gathered squaw wood for fires. When the village moved, she helped lower the heavy lodge cover, or raise it over the naked lodgepoles, using a long lifting pole. Sometimes in the deeps of the night she heard soft sounds and knew that Sinopah was lying with her mother or with Tears in Her Eyes.

Oncc in a while a strange boy from another band would try her at the Sun dance or during the fall hunt, but she always squirmed free, though she herself didn't know why she did. The youths in her own band, like A-po-at-sis-ipo, Looking for Smoke, or See-pis-to-komi, Screaming Owl, eyed her constantly but knew she had been set aside by her vision. Once when Screaming Owl had drunk white men's spirits he had attacked her. She'd writhed free, but the pain and humiliation had been terrible. It happened to nearly all Siksika girls, and none of the people made much of it unless the girl got pregnant. The boys bragged and laughed; the girls smiled. But Marie Therese—odd how she thought of her other name when it came to this—felt wounded by it right to the marrow of her bones even though Screaming Owl had been thwarted. She would never again speak to him!

She had not seen Peter again, but sometimes word of him came to her ears, when one or another of her people visited Fort Benton. He was a trader now, they said. He could speak the Siksika tongue fairly well—they could understand him, anyway. He had risen swiftly in the company, vaulting ahead of the other engagés. He wore old-man clothes now; a black frock coat that signified he was a great one of the Chouteau company. Sometimes she thought of him and the yearning in his eyes. She felt glad she didn't see him, because she sometimes yearned for him too, especially after Screaming Owl had wrestled her into the grasses beyond the creek where no one would hear her scream.

The band lingered through the summer of 1853 on Two Medicine River, where game abounded. Many Siksika didn't like some places up the river, where the water ran between arid bluffs. That was where the spirits of ancestors who didn't go up the Wolf Trail to the Sand Hills lurked to torment the living. Some said the river took its name from the two piskuns, buffalo jumps, on it, where the ancient ones stampeded buffalo over the cliffs. Others said it was named for two great medicine lodges that had been found on it, sacred places. But wherever the name had come from, Natoya-niskim found the mysterious river tugging at her spirits in ways she couldn't fathom.

One day that summer she packed a small bag of necessaries and told Meadowlark she would be found somewhere up the Two Medicine. Then she walked up the brooding river, piercing through arid canyons and gloomy wastes until she found a happy bottom on the south bank of the river, laughing with cottonwoods and willows, glowing within the arms of steep dark bluffs. She could not see the arrogant blue Backbone to the west, where the Two Medicine rose cold in sweet alpine valleys, nor could she see the limitless buffalo lands above the brooding bluffs. Something within bid her to stop. Now and forever more this would be her spirit-renewing place. Each summer before the Sun dance she would come to this sun-washed bottom. Here she would commune; here she would listen; here White Buffalo Cow would meet her. Maybe the spirits of the dead would speak to her too. The time of growing up was over, and now her mission to the Pikuni would begin.

She built a small fire and tossed sweetgrass on it, bathing her gaunt body in its fragrant smoke. She added sagebrush, letting the smoke permeate her doeskin dress. She lifted her hands and prayed to Napi, Old Man; to Sun and Moon and their child, Morning Star. And lastly she addressed her spirit counselor.

"White Buffalo Cow, hear me now. My time has come. I am called here. This place, on the Two Medicine River, near the buffalo piskuns, is my sacred place ever more. I will wait for you here; I will not leave here until I have heard you."

White Buffalo Cow didn't come and seemed in no hurry to come, so Natoya-niskim waited patiently, becoming one with the wind and the river, waiting through four days and three nights. Then on the fourth, when she was starved and thirsty, her spirit helper came. White Buffalo Cow's presence filled Natoya-niskim with joy. But that night she rode the buffalo into the sky and beheld bluecoat seizers marching from the east; others coming up the Missouri River on the fur company steamer; and still more marching from the west, stopping at Owen's Fort in the Bitterroot, and then proceeding to Fort Benton. Seizers! And with them were Alec Culbertson, the top man for the fur company, and his Blood wife Natawista, a Blackfoot like Natoya-niskim, and other white men in black suits.

Times were changing at last, and her heart ached. From now on her people would die bit by bit, and they would be caged—first in a giant cage, then a smaller one, and finally in one so small no one could breathe or eat. And after that—no one would feed the caged people. White Buffalo Cow returned her gently to her embers on the Two Medicine and vanished, leaving her in a strange euphoria laced with foreboding. Morning Star, the beautiful child, glowed in the east, heralding the arrival of his father.

The next morning she had a lone visitor.

Imitaikoan, Little Dog, drew his pony to a halt before the young and handsome girl who had been given the great powers by White Buffalo Cow. In the camp of the Lone Eaters her mother, O-toch-koki, had told him where he might find her, and he had ridden alone. He wore the plainest buckskin dress, and displayed none of his ensigns of office or war honors, for this was a spiritual journey and he wished to be merely a supplicant.

Even so, she knew him instantly. What young woman of the Pikuni wouldn't? He was the head chief of the Pikuni, the chief above chiefs of that great arm of the Blackfoot nation. He also led the Black Patched Moccasins band, which even now was camped not far down the Marias River.

He slid off his horse, a fine dappled gray gotten from napikwan traders, taller and better formed than the wild ponies of the tribes.

"Grandmother," he said, a term of great respect, even bestowed upon a bold-eyed young woman not yet twenty. "I have brought you a small present."

He untied a scarlet and black Hudson's Bay blanket and laid it at her feet.

She stared at it, and at him, some anguish in her face. And then it dissolved. "Yes, you have come. I should have known you would. Last night I was visited by my spirit helper—the first time since I returned to the Pikuni."

That first occasion, the vision of White Buffalo Cow, had been carefully recited from one lodge fire to another, one band to another, until its exact nature was known not just to the Piegans, but also the Bloods and Blackfeet proper. Some had dismissed the visitation as a young girl's foolishness. Here and there an old shaman nodded. When Little Dog had been told of it by his own shamans, he had walked into a cold night and wept.

"I have come to sit at your feet and learn what fate

will be ours," he said. "I was told of your first visit from White Buffalo Cow, and I knew you had been picked, a sacred vessel to bring us through ice and fire."

"Oh, my chief, I'm nothing. It's not I who count. I only know what is given me. I'm—humbled by your presence here."

"If the blanket isn't enough—"

"Oh!" She picked it up and stroked the luxurious carded wool, a sign that she welcomed the gift. "I—No one has ever come to me," she said. "You're the first. I'm so honored. . . ."

He tied his horse to a cottonwood and settled into the lush grass. This private place appealed to him. She had come to some sacred spot on the Two Medicine where she could rendezvous with her spirit helper. Great and terrible things would issue from this place.

"Now I will smoke and honor the four winds. Then I will seek your knowledge, Natoya-niskim—what White Buffalo Cow has shown you, and how you understand it. And also, I wish to learn everything you know about the napikwan from your time in the place of many houses."

He extracted his pipe and tobacco and built a fire, using a brand from her little fire to ignite his charge. He honored the four winds, earth and sky, puffing quietly while the disconcerted young woman composed herself. He understood perfectly; a head chief of the Pikuni, who was indeed the second chief of all the Blackfeet, with only Lame Bull above him, would scarcely heed the voice of a slender maiden.

But now he would. Now, after he had word from the head of the fur company, Alec Culbertson, that the bluecoat seizers were coming and wished to talk with all the chiefs of the Siksika, as well as those of neighboring tribes. The man in charge, Culbertson told him, was Governor Isaac Stevens, en route to the new Territory of Washington, with instructions to meet with the leaders of the Blackfeet and begin a treaty-making process. Young governor Stevens, a soldier trained at West Point, wished to talk with the chiefs at Fort Benton in late summer.

Meet with the chiefs . . . Little Dog had listened to Alec Culbertson as if listening to the doom of his people. He could not forestall a meeting with the soldiers, but he could seek wisdom. Hastily he had sought out the girl who had received the vision of these times, the gray-eyed beauty that no boy could claim.

"It is the beginning of the end," she said softly. "I learned that from her last night."

"Tell me the visions, Natoya-niskim."

She did, beginning with her vision quest after she had come up the river from St. Louis and sought out her mother. She described the ride on the white buffalo cow, the tenderness of its eyes, the race through the buffalo herds, the swift disappearance of the herds as one by one buffalo vanished, the great sadness of that. She depicted the dwindling villages, and described her ride through a snowstorm—a winter time—and the shot of the blue-clad seizer, and the death of White Buffalo Cow, with no calf beside her.

"And tell me now what vision came to you last night."

"The white buffalo cow took me on a ride again, and this time I saw seizers coming from the east, and some from the west, and some coming up the river on the boat. They were coming to make a cage for us. It will be a big cage at first, but then it will be smaller and smaller, until we are pressed together and can't breathe. Then the napikwan will let us die."

Little Dog stood and walked restlessly, while the girl sat cross-legged at her post, her head bowed with burdens too heavy for a young woman to bear. Then he sat down again.

"How do you know this?"

"I have seen a vision."

"Do you understand the vision truly?"

She nodded.

"Why have you received the vision? Is there something you must tell us, the Siksika? Have you come only to warn us—or to give us wise counsel?"

"The only words I can give you, Grandfather, is what I have seen of the white men in St. Louis."

"Nothing from White Buffalo Cow?"

She shook her head and told him of a world filled with houses and farms, cities with so many whites they seemed numberless . . buildings where rifles were manufactured by the hundreds, and other buildings where the whites made all their amazing things—truly an amazing people! She told him of the rough frontiersmen who cared only for themselves, cruel and willful, so unlike Siksika warriors who cared always for their people. These white men would shoot Indians like squirrels, and when they came, no Siksika life would be safe. They would drink spirits in grog shops and then desecrate the world.

But in the midst of these were people of better character, men like Father DeSmet; women like the sisters who had taught her; men as fair and kind as any. But these were fewer. It was as if the whites had a grand religion with beautiful ideals, which they ignored, and this made them mean and crazy and dangerous. She'd seen the seizers at Fort Leavenworth, many hundred of them, all trained to kill. They were coming now.

"My chief, there's no way to resist them. We'll all be slaughtered if we do. We can only be friends, and when they take our good things away from us, we must smile and nod. Otherwise we'll die."

"We'll survive if we don't resist?"

"I don't know. I've received no vision."

He digested all this for a while. "Always we've been as free as an eagle, to soar where we wished and hunt where we wanted, and to raid for ponies, and show them the strength of the Siksika! I've done it! Tell me, Natoyaniskim, what the leaders should do."

"It's not for me to say, Grandfather."

"Tell me what you think."

She seemed frightened, and he waited patiently. But at last she ventured an idea. "I would be sure not to fight them or kill them—soldiers or the others. But I would give nothing away. When they come to make a treaty, they will talk about peace—peace with whites, peace with other tribes. That will hide what they really want. They wish to put the Siksika onto little patches of ground and open up the rest for white men."

He nodded, dreading her wisdom.

"I would resist but not fight—delay meetings, ask for many things. Give in a little, but don't make war for it will mean the doom of the women and children. Grandfather, now we'll step backward, one step and another, but we must be pushed. When we aren't pushed, we must step forward, or stand still."

"Will we all die anyway?"

"I don't know!"

"Maybe it's best to fight to the death. If the nation dies, then we all must die!"

"Oh, don't say that!"

He shrugged. "Maybe we should learn the ways of the Old Man People, the napikwan. They're clever and powerful, and their time has come. They must increase and we must decrease. Maybe we should learn of their God and what's in the Black Book, and be like them."

"No! No!"

Her outburst surprised him. "Natoya-niskim, I'll heed your wisdom. We'll step backward when we're pushed. But I'll try to learn the ways of these people. Maybe I'll have a farm and raise crops like the earth-lodge people on the Big River. Maybe I'll eat the white men's cattle."

"We must always be Siksika!"

"We may not have the choice. Natoya-niskim, when White Buffalo Cow returns to you, tell me everything. Send for me. For the sake of your people, let me know."

"I will."

He thanked her and rode away, filled with foreboding about his people. Something she had said troubled him. White Buffalo Cow had showed her seizers coming from the west! Alec Culbertson had said nothing about that. If seizers did come from the west, he decided, he would know that her visions, and White Buffalo Cow's spirit, were true.

Chapter Seventeen

Early in the moon When Leaves Turn Yellow a runner with a spare horse came to the Lone Eaters seeking Natoya-niskim. The Lone Eaters sent him to the Two Medicine River, Matoki Okas, where she had lingered into the fall. He found her there.

"Haiya, haiya! Medicine woman, I have been sent by Little Dog," the runner said. "He would like you to go to Fort Benton at once. The napikwan have asked that all the Pikuni chiefs gather there for some talks. A great one among them, named Isaac Stevens, has arrived with many seizers."

"I will go," she said. "But what does Chief Little Dog want of me?"

"You have received the vision—you'll give the chiefs wisdom. And you'll translate. The napikwan have good translators—Alexander Culbertson and your father—but the chiefs want one of our own."

"Won't Natawista Culbertson—Medicine Snake Woman—be there? She knows the napikwan."

"Yes. She has helped her husband bring our chiefs to the meeting. No one likes this meeting."

"Where is Little Dog?"

"At the Cyprus Hills, along with some of the seizers, gathering the chiefs."

"Have my chiefs left?"

"The Lone Eaters? They've gone. You must hurry to catch up. The chiefs are worried. They remember your vision."

"Has this man Stevens come to make a treaty with us?"

"We don't know. He sent a message to the bands, along with tobacco and gifts. He said he was on his way to the western seas, and wanted to tell us of the fatherly feeling toward us of the Ka-ach-sino, Great Grandfather, in the east. He tells us to come to Fort Benton; and to stay at peace with our neighbors."

She sighed, knowing that peace had other meanings for the white men. "And who are you?"

"O-tak-kai, Yellow Mink, of the Buffalo Dung people. I am a Kisapa, a Hair Parter."

"You've come a long way and have carried your message faithfully, O-tak-kai. Tell my chief I will go to Fort Benton as fast as this mare will carry me."

He nodded and rode eastward. She gathered her simple possessions and took off, wrapped in her new scarlet blanket against the sharp chills of the nights.

It was not long before September dark, but she didn't hesitate to start at that hour. She would ride through the nights for warmth, pausing only to let her mare rest and eat. She struck south toward the Teton River, Ikinitskatah, which would take her to Fort Benton. It would take her two days to reach the river; two or three more to reach the post. She would live on almost nothing, having little need of food. White Buffalo Cow always seemed to provide for her: buffalo berries, chokecherries, roots. She never lacked.

She rode alone across a broken land, but didn't feel alone at all. White men called it wilderness, but for her it was home. Her world brimmed with four-legged creatures, flying creatures, crawling creatures, and the Above Spirits. When her horse tired, she dismounted and let it graze while she walked a creek bank in search of berries. She felt more at home trekking across the breast of earth mother than she ever had within the walls of Fort Benton.

She reached the fur post mid-afternoon of the fifth day, and was not surprised to see a company of bluecoats camped nearby, their canvas tents staked in orderly rows. She wondered whether to stay with the Siksika or with her father. She saw many lodges around the post, but she chose to visit Charles de Paris. As she steered her mare through the open double gates into the rectangular yard, she rode into the stare of a red-haired young man in a black frock coat.

"Peter!"

"Marie Therese!" He rushed to her, unbelieving. "It's you! . . . Have you come home?"

"Peter, have my chiefs come?"

"No, not yet. Any time now, they tell us. Little Dog, the rest of the chiefs, and Governor Stevens and his party. But Marie Therese, what are you doing—"

"I will stay with my father," she said, steering the pony across the yard.

"You've come to stay!"

"I've come to help my people."

"You'll stay; I know you will. Winter's coming."

She smiled. Peter would always be Peter. "Help me with the horse and we'll talk in a minute." A talk with Peter would be delightful, and would let her practice her rusty English.

"Your pa's at the trading window. He can't get loose, but I'll tell him—"

"Oh, Peter, there's no hurry."

He led her mare to a small pen in a corner of the redolent yard, and then carried her small kit into Charles de Paris's quarters.

"Now, Peter, tell me who those seizers—soldiers—are and why they're here."

"Those are from Washington Territory. They came a few days ago, under a lieutenant, Rufus Saxton. They're gonna take the governor over the mountains to Washington Territory."

Seizers from the west. "This meeting—it's just soldiers passing through?" she asked hopefully.

"No, bigger stuff than that, Marie Therese. Governor Stevens, he's got a commission from Congress to study a northern railroad route, and he's going to put together a peace treaty with the Blackfeet and the rest so a railroad can be built."

"A treaty? With us, Peter?"

"Yeah, with your ma's people. You can't hardly run a railroad through wild Injuns. Not right away. Soon as Congress says. Stevens is a West Pointer. He fought in the Mex War."

A railroad. The napikwan would pour in. She grieved.

"I'll put this stuff in the alcove," he said, leaving her parfleche on the pallet she had used for a bed when she lived there. Her father's bachelor quarters were exactly as she remembered.

She peered at Peter Kipp, seeing a serious young man in black clothes. "You've changed," she said.

"Well, I'm coming on twenty and I'm a clerk. Pretty soon I'll be a trader. Soon as I master the court language—that's the trading tongue. I'm getting the hang of some Cree and Crow too. After that, nothing'll stop me . . . Marie Therese."

"I'm Natoya-niskim."

"Sacred Buffalo Stone. Uh, it don't sound like you."

He stared at her. "You've changed some yourself," he said, a faint edge in his voice.

"Yes, Peter. The teaching sisters in St. Louis—I didn't like them very much. But now I know they're like me. We're—set apart."

He eyed her unhappily. "What're you doing here?"

"I've had another vision from White Buffalo Cow about the fate of my people."

"You come here because you've had some old dream?"

"A vision, Peter. It's important to all the Siksika."

He laughed shortly. "Aw, Marie Therese, that stuff—"

"I was asked to come by Little Dog. To advise the chiefs."

"A dream's not gonna change the world."

Peter would never grasp that it wasn't a dream; it didn't come in her sleep; and it had given her a terrible insight into the future of the Blackfeet. "I'll translate. Sometimes napikwan—white men's words conceal other things."

"You mean you're gonna stir them up to resist. That'd just stop progress."

She shook her head. "I can't stop what is destined. I can help them prepare themselves for change—and maybe keep them from fighting."

"Well, you'd better. The Blackfeet don't like this none. We heard Mrs. Culbertson, she had to stop a fracas and calm 'em down. Over to Fort Union they—the Blackfeet—saw soldiers and got plum ornery until she told them to cut it out."

"Peter—you don't know how it is to be Indian—Siksika—and see soldiers with rifles. When I rode past the soldiers outside, I felt—more afraid than I ever was in my life."

"It's you that don't understand, Marie Therese. They're gonna stop wars and horse-stealing and make this a safe place. A good place. The Blackfeet'll get a nice chunk of land and live good on it, as long as they don't get to messing with others, white or red."

They assessed each other edgily, aware that the years had pulled them further apart. She saw pain in his eyes.

"Peter?"

"Aw, Marie Therese—"

"Let's tell my father I'm here."

Wordlessly he led her to the trading room beside the front gates.

Peter Kipp admired the soldiers. They'd pitched their tents in orderly rows west of Fort Benton, a display of white men's power that had its effect on the surrounding tribesmen. These riflemen had marched clear from Minnesota with Governor Stevens and various civilians including a naturalist, Dr. George Suckley, a topographer, John Lambert, and artist, John Mix Stanley, studying a northern railroad route for Congress. Other troops and engineers had come up the Missouri on the steamer, and still another contingent had crossed the Rockies from the new Washington Territory to rendezvous right here in the heart of the Blackfoot Nation. Change was in the air!

A buzzing excitement had built up at Fort Benton as

more and more of the parties drifted in. Stevens and a contingent of soldiers had arrived September first. Alec and Natawista Culbertson, along with two dozen chiefs and headmen, came in later, escorted by a contingent of soldiers. Other Blackfoot chiefs, summoned by runners with the traditional diplomatic gift of tobacco, were straggling in from the various bands. Within the post the important men of the fur company and the army, along with engineers and other civilians, had billeted in all available quarters.

Even though Peter wore the black frock coat of a clerk, he was excluded from the company of officers and executives. He spent his time among the engagés and clerks, as he always had. But he was bursting to participate in the forthcoming great events, and pondered ways to make a name for himself. He could, after all, read and write well, so he could take minutes; he knew his arithmetic too. He could speak passable Blackfoot, and knew some Crow and Cree. In two years his relentless ambition and industry had carried him far up the ladder. But he was required to spend his hours manning the trade room, often with Charles de Paris, while all the excitement whirled by without him.

Still . . . there was Marie Therese. She seemed as out of place in this hubbub as he, and sometimes she slid into the trading room just to be with Peter or her father. Their talk hadn't gone well: He just couldn't make her see that all this—the arrival of the white men, a forthcoming treaty, settlement, a railroad—was the most delightful prospect imaginable. It would open up these new lands, the way the rest of the nation was opening up.

She had just shaken her head sadly and said that her Siksika nation would wither away, and she with it. That exasperated him; as a mixed-blood, she could choose a better life any time she wanted . . . a life with Peter Kipp.

The Blackfoot chiefs and headmen had been offered quarters also, but seemed uncomfortable there, except for Little Dog, who appeared completely at ease among whites. They were mostly Piegans and Bloods. The Northern Blackfeet weren't well represented, but didn't need to be because they lived in Canada. Solemnly the chiefs peered into the fort's rooms, studying the warehouse, the robe press, the kitchen and barracks, the bastions at opposite corners, the storage rooms. They were curious about white men and plainly worried about what Governor Stevens would tell them.

Peter caught glimpses of the governor, and admired what he saw. The diminutive soldier limped because of a Mexican War foot wound, but that didn't diminish his stature or authority. He seemed restless, eager to be off to Washington Territory, where he intended to impose the firm hand of federal power on the restless tribes and pacify the area.

Finally, when no more chiefs were expected, Stevens decided to wait only two more days and hold his conference on September 21.

That's when Peter saw his chance: He waylaid the governor in the yard after a supper, at a moment when the governor was with his aide, Lieutenant James Doty, a son of the Wisconsin governor.

"Sir? May I have a word?"

Stevens paused, assessing the young fur company employee in the black suit, his cold, perceptive eyes lingering long on Peter's freckled, tawny half-blood flesh, kinked red hair, and prominent cheekbones. "Yes, I suppose. What've you in mind?"

"I'd like to clerk, sir. I'm Peter Kipp, James Kipp's son. I know Blackfoot; I keep the post journal. I thought I could make myself useful during your parley tomorrow by making a good record."

"We have our clerks, Kipp."

"I can translate."

"Why, we have several."

"I know the chiefs, sir. I can identify them as they speak—help your clerks."

"We're well-staffed, Kipp," said Lieutenant Doty, not unkindly.

"Look, Kipp," Stevens said. "Our clerks are highly trained and literate. They wouldn't have . . . mixed loyalties. They are honorable white gentlemen." He smiled. "We couldn't be sure of your entries—ah, unless we knew you better."

A swift hard sickness engulfed Peter. He had forgotten, in the cocoon of the fur post, how it was for a breed. "I'm as able as any of them, and more familiar with the chiefs!" he cried.

But they'd already abandoned him.

"I'm *Mister* Kipp!" he said to their backs.

He walked numbly toward Charles de Paris's quarters, needing Marie Therese, but didn't find her there. He poked through Fort Benton, hungry for her, and finally found her away from the stockade, sitting cross-legged among some Blackfeet that had come to trade.

"You're the only person in the world like me, Marie Therese. I need you bad."

She registered that, troubled. "Peter—come be one of us."

"I've no Siksika blood."

"My stepfather will adopt you."

Among the tribes, that would seal it. But he couldn't. He knew she and her kind were the past. It'd be like stopping progress. Why, why was she drawn to the past? Why did she believe in hoodoos and visions? They were separated by a wall of belief more than anything else. He took her hand and held it, loving her more than ever.

The next morning Governor Stevens convened the conference in the engagés' dining hall, the only room large enough for it. Peter wormed his way in, though he wasn't invited and should have been in the trading room along with de Paris. He settled unobserved in a corner behind the soldiers and white civilians. He saw only two women: Natawista Culbertson, sitting beside Alec and Governor Stevens; and Marie Therese, a small dark wraith huddled across the room behind the Blackfoot chiefs and headmen.

The Blackfeet looked grand in their ceremonial clothing. Little Dog wore an elkskin shirt dyed yellow and blue, elegantly beaded; Chief Low Horn wore a bear-claw necklace and a fringed shirt.

In his opening address, Stevens asked for peace: "Your Great Father has sent me to bear a message to you and all his other children. He desires that you should be under his protection, and partake equally with the Crows and Assiniboins of his bounty. Live in peace with all the neighboring Indians, protect all the whites passing through your country, and the Great Father will be your friend."

It seemed to Peter the talk of a schoolmaster addressing first graders. In their souls the white men thought Indians were little better than children. Peter had tasted some of that gall in St. Louis.

Low Horn responded for the assembled chiefs. They were all peaceful, he said, but they couldn't control the young men seeking war honors to impress the maidens or win status.

Stevens nodded absently, uninterested in details. He would return in a year, he continued, to make a treaty between the Blackfeet and the whites. He'd give them a permanent home and many gifts, for as long as the Blackfeet children of the Great Father were good and remained at peace with their neighbors and whites.

In a dusky corner Little Dog whispered with Marie Therese, and then the Piegan chief stood: "We are already at peace with traders and white men and don't need a treaty with them. We don't want this. The white men are our friends, as all the traders know. But if we must have a treaty, we want it to give the Siksika a home forever, from the great Backbone to the Elk River—the Yellowstone—on the south; to the lands of the Assiniboin to the east. And to give the Siksika the right forever to hunt in the country of the Three Forks of the Missouri. And to prevent the passage across their lands of anyone if they choose."

Peter had no trouble translating, but he listened closely as Alexander Culbertson translated for Stevens. For there was contention.

Stevens listened intently. "You will have a home, though it may not be just that," he said. "Meanwhile the Blackfeet children of the Great Father must remain peaceful, especially toward white men passing through."

Peter watched Marie Therese translate quietly across the gloomy room, and then Little Dog spoke again.

"How long will such a treaty last? We've heard what happens to treaties white men make with other tribes. As soon as white men want the land, the treaty is no good anymore."

"It'll last as long as the Blackfeet are peaceful and don't war on white men," Stevens said evenly. "You must be good."

"Haiya! My friends the white men teach us many things. We will learn how to farm and plant in live in peace," said Little Dog.

"That's what the Great Father wants to hear, my friend Little Dog. We'll provide you with a farm and teach you the ways of peace. Be sure now that the Blackfeet don't make war."

It ended on that note. Stevens's aides distributed good knives and blankets to the chiefs and headmen, along with twists of tobacco. Marie Therese stood somberly in the far corner, her face registering the conference without a trace of joy.

Outside, Stevens's army escort stood ready to travel west, and the governor made haste to be off, looking highly pleased. He paused only to shake a few hands, and then his column of soldiers marched up the Missouri under guidons and to the tune of a trumpet, with a fanfare intended to impress red men. Lieutenant Doty remained, assigned to the fur post for a year to prepare for the great treaty conference.

Later, Peter found Marie Therese still in the gloomy dining hall, sitting as if pinioned there.

"Let's go somewhere," he said. "It's too dark in here."

"Please leave me alone, Peter."

"Aw, Marie Therese—this conference was good! The whites are giving the Blackfeet a home—forever. And everything. All they gotta do is stop fighting. Even a school so you can be like them—us."

But Natoya-niskim stared back, something terrible burning in her eyes.

Chapter Eighteen

1855

Nothing less than the future of the Blackfoot nation was being debated there on the open meadow beside a cottonwood grove. Natoya-niskim listened gravely, knowing she had done what she could—and had failed. She had reached her twentieth year and possessed a strange solemn aura that still brought her suitors among the bold youths of the Pikuni. But she had quietly turned their suits aside. She still had a sacred mission.

This autumn of the great treaty council with the napikwan, she had spent many days at her refuge on the Two Medicine preparing herself. She'd fasted and waited, but White Buffalo Cow hadn't come; she had been given no vision. In anguish, the young Dreaming Woman had doubted; had wondered whether the understandings she had been given were nothing but a chimera. This was her time of testing, and she feared she had displeased Old Man, Napi, or perhaps Sun himself. Then the runner had come, as she knew he would: Go to Fort Benton for the great council with Governor Stevens; the chiefs need you. She had gone at once.

There, at the American Fur Company post on the Missouri River, which her Siksika called Big River, the assembled chiefs of the Blackfoot nation had waited through the

Moon of the First Frost, September, along with the compact governor, his aide Lieutenant Doty, the enormously heavy Alfred Cumming, superintendent of Indian Affairs at St. Louis, and other white men, including bewhiskered Major A. C. Hatch, who was to become the tribe's first Indian agent, or ninnana. A throng of Blackfeet and Gros Ventres and Flatheads camped there as well.

She had spent many of those sunny fall days with Peter Kipp, who had become a top trader for the American Fur Company, alternating in the trading room with her father. He had reached his early twenties and seemed to be the soul of confident young manhood, his Indian blood somehow less and less visible because his soul had become that of a white man. But they still shared the bond that had been forged on the *St. Ange*; they were mixed-breeds in a world that rejected them. He loved her as deeply as ever, and she, in return, offered an ethereal love stripped of all desire.

"I'm still waiting for you, Marie Therese," he had said. "I'll always wait for you, and someday you'll come." This time his declaration seemed less soulful.

Word had come that the riverboat bearing the government's annuity goods, to be distributed upon the signing of the treaty, had been delayed, and the impatient white men had decided to head downriver to meet the keelboat earlier.

And so she found herself sitting outside the rings of chiefs at a great council on the north bank of the Missouri a hundred or so miles east of Fort Benton, opposite the confluence of the Judith River, in the Moon of Falling Leaves. Watching quietly from a distance were three thousand men, women, and children from every tribe in the Northwest.

There, the twenty-seven chiefs of the Blackfeet confederation quietly sought her medicine wisdom, and she sat with them shyly, a single young woman in the midst of the great ones. She could only tell them that White Buffalo Cow had not visited her this time; she had no sacred vision to impart. But she would say something to them anyway, drawn from her own medicine-wisdom: Don't make a treaty with the napikwan; don't sign; don't accept the annuity goods. Be friendly, promise peace, and stay free. Never had the Blackfeet been so powerful, so proud, so rich. Since the meeting in 1853, war parties of young men, fearing that the seizers would put a halt to their raids, had streamed out of the Blackfoot nation, terrorizing the Blue Paint People, the Lying People, the Hair Parters, and all the rest, taking scalps and ponies, and letting the whole world know of the imperial power of the Siksika people.

She had gazed proudly upon the great ones of her nation, absolute lords of a land larger than most European nations, tall and dignified and wise. But she had feared they would cave in, especially when they saw the boatload of beautiful napikwan things intended to bribe them.

"We have listened to your wisdom, Natoya-niskim, and we will take heed and consider these things carefully," Lame Bull had said. "But the napikwan put great pressure on us, and we must listen to them too."

She'd known even then that there would be a treaty, even as she had witnessed in the vision many years before. She had given them what she could; the rest was beyond her control. A nation's fate lay in the meadow grass.

Now they sat debating it; the white chiefs and seven interpreters in a canvas-covered arbor beneath the cottonwoods; the Blackfoot chiefs sitting cross-legged in semicirucular rows, the great ones in the first row, the lesser ones in succeeding rows. And here also were the chiefs of the enemies of her people, from the western and eastern tribes, numbering almost as many as the Blackfeet.

She had no quarrel with the Blackfoot territory defined in the treaty, and neither did the chiefs: It ran from the spine of the Rockies eastward to Assiniboin country, and from the Canadian border south to the Musselshell, a country four hundred miles by two hundred. In addition, there would be common hunting grounds, shared with the western tribes, in the mountain great valleys to the southwest, especially around the three forks of the Big River, the Missouri. All of that was traditional Blackfoot territory. Nothing was taken away—but was it the white man's to give?

"We want to establish you on farms," Governor

Stevens said at the opening. "We want you to have cattle and raise crops. We want your children to be taught, and we want you to send word to your Great Father, through us, where you want your farms to be and what schools and mills and shops you want.

"You know," he added, "that the buffalo will not continue forever—get farms and cattle in time."

As if the Siksika knew what he was talking about, she thought. Mills and shops and farms! No good Blackfoot would want to be like the miserable Dirt Lodge People, the Mandans, anchored to their earthen mounds along the Big River, raising a few squash and some corn, forever at the mercy of the Hair Parters. Every Siksika male would consider such labor demeaning, and not even starvation, after the last buffalo was gone, would drive them to it! It just went to show that the napikwan didn't know anything about the Blackfeet.

In a mellifluent voice, Superintendent Cumming read the treaty, article by article, while the translators conveyed its meaning. Two of the articles disturbed Natoya-niskim. One proposed that the Blackfeet would agree to roads of any kind, telegraph lines, military posts, Indian agency buildings, and missions; and that navigation on any stream or lake would be open to any United States citizen. Another asserted that United States citizens would be free to live in, and pass through, Blackfoot lands unmolested.

"They give the Siksika land and then take it away!" she whispered to a warrior sitting before her. "White men can settle in our country and we can't send them away! The chiefs should not sign this treaty!"

She listened patiently to the rest of it, knowing that it would add nothing. The Blackfeet would agree to live in perpetual peace. They would receive annuities, useful goods totaling $20,000 annually; and another $15,000 would be spent each year on agency business, such as schooling the children, teaching the agricultural arts, and building the agency cattle herd.

The chiefs listened patiently to the translators, understanding only a little of it. But they did understand peace and territory. The chiefs of the western tribes objected that they could no longer hunt buffalo on the plains reserved to the Blackfeet, but Lame Bull, head chief of the Piegans, pointed out that this was the design of white men, not Blackfeet.

"It is not our plan that these things are going on," Lame Bull said. "It is not we who speak. It is the white chiefs. We intend to do whatever the government tells us."

Seen From Afar, head chief of the Bloods, didn't think much of the peace provision. "I wish to say that as far as we old men are concerned, we want peace . . . but I am afraid that we cannot stop our young men. The Crows are not here to smoke the pipe with us, and I am afraid our young men will not be persuaded that they ought not to go to war against the Crows."

Natoya-niskim thought that was understatement.

"Tell your young men that your Great Father wishes all his children to live in peace," Cumming warned. "If you do not live in peace, and continue to go to war, he will be mad with his children; ashamed of his children. He will not send you blankets and provisions, coffee and tobacco. Tell your young men to take wives and live happily in their own lodges. . . ."

The schoolmasterish tone didn't escape Natoya-niskim. "Don't sign it!" she hissed. "Don't take these things—they're bribes!"

Lame Bull stared coldly at her, his message plain: Don't interfere in men's business. The woman who had once been celebrated as the prophetess of the whole tribe shrank under the great chief's withering rebuke.

But at last an agreement was hammered out between the Blackfeet and the government, and the other tribes. The white men signed first. Then Lieutenant Doty scratched the name of each Blackfoot chief at the bottom of the treaty. He left a space and then wrote, *His mark*. One by one the leaders of the four branches of the Blackfoot nation, North and South Piegans, Bloods, and Blackfeet proper, rose to scratch their X in the blank space after his name, where the lieutenant pointed.

She watched old Lame Bull rise and sign. He above all had argued for the treaty with the napikwan. He was chief of the Hard Top Knots Band, and head chief of the Pikuni; his authority would move the others. He was followed by Little Dog of the Black Patched Moccasins, and second among the Pikuni; Big Snake, of the Small Brittle Fat Band; Middle Sitter of the Don't Laughs; Mountain Chief, Low Horn, Little Gray Head, The Skunk, The Bad Head, and Spotted Calf, all for the Pikuni. For the Kainah, Seen From Afar, the greatest chief of all the Blackfeet and leader of the Fish Eaters Band, signed; then Calf Shirt of the Quarrelers Band, followed by The Father of All Children, Bull's Back Fat, Heavy Shield, Sun Calf, The Feather, White Eagle, and some minor chiefs. For the northern Siksika, Three Bulls, Old Kootenai, Pow-ah-que, and Rabbit Runner. Twenty-seven X's on a parchment had snared the Siksika nation forever.

Then eight chiefs of the Gros Ventres scratched the treaty, and twenty-seven chiefs from the western tribes, including the Salish, Pend d'Oreille, and Nez Perce.

The whole Blackfoot federation had committed itself, like a bride at the altar . . . but what was she marrying?

Numbly, Natoya-niskim watched the white men lead the chiefs to the mountain of goods. Not a chief or a headman or a warrior around her shared her sense of foreboding. All they cared about was whether this would curtail war and keep them from raiding the Crows and Assiniboins.

Then the chiefs and headmen received the white men's booty: blankets, gaudy cotton fabrics, and various staples such as coffee, flour, and sugar. After that the throng lined up to receive the largesse handed out by napikwan soldiers. Of these things the Indians knew little. They cherished the cotton bags more than the contents. They tossed the flour into the air and boiled masses of rice into an inedible mess. They poured sugar into the Missouri, and joyously tasted the sweetened water. But the tobacco twists they understood, and snugged them safely into their parfleches.

Sacred Buffalo Stone watched it all impassively, not

trying to rescue the flour as it sailed like a ground blizzard when the gamboling Blackfeet played with it. She watched enough food to feed the Blackfeet for months vanish into the grasses—but it was napikwan food, and its fate seemed fitting to her. What was flour compared to the tongue of a buffalo? Perhaps the great ones would learn something about the gifts of the napikwan.

Natoya-niskim rode westward in a great column led by many of the chiefs and headmen after the council. They would ride together a few days and then separate, the members of each band returning to their camps. There, the chiefs would gather those who had remained in the villages and tell them about the agreement with the napikwan and other tribes. She doubted that the chiefs would accurately convey the meanings of the sixteen complex articles, and that much would be lost. Their memories could not contain so many provisions.

She felt empty. All the talk of peace and boundaries and the affairs of nations seemed distant and vague. More real to her was the surly rhythm of her misbegotten mare, and the bared fangs of the Cold Maker. They traversed grassy hills laced with ponderosa and cedar, plowing through clear autumnal days. Nothing seemed different. She rode alone, staying carefully to the rear of the parade, well behind the great ones of the Siksika nation, followed only by the Mad Dog Society warriors who were protecting them all. She kept herself small and invisible among these lordly leaders and all those who had come to the council.

But she was not forgotten. The second afternoon she received word from ahead; the chiefs wished to consult with her. She heeled her rebellious mare forward and drew up beside Lame Bull when he beckoned her. On her other side rode Little Dog. She wondered what the two greatest chiefs of the Pikuni could possibly want of her.

"We've made a fine agreement with the napikwan chiefs," old Lame Bull said without preamble. "We have all our lands and gave up nothing, except maybe a little to the south. And we have it forever, guaranteed by the talking signs. What do you think of that?"

"Nothing is forever, my chief."

"Well, then, consider this: I asked the new agent, our ninnana, what would come to us each year from the Great Father. He told me we would have many rifles, powder, lead, kettles and skillets, knives, cloth, awls, blankets, and a lot more—enough for every Pikuni, Kainah, and Siksika. Now, that's a good thing. No longer must we depend on the greedy traders for these things. All we have to do is go get them."

"And keep the young warriors from fighting," she said.

"Oh, yes. I heard the father, Cumming, say that. But they always say that. Nothing is changed, and we have mountains of goods coming each year. We made a good bargain."

"My chief," she said, "the robe traders have never brought soldiers or settlers or the wires that send messages. They use our trails and do not make roads. They do not force us to change our lives or tell us to learn to tear up the earth mother and plant seeds."

"Ah! That is true, Natoya-niskim. But these things won't happen. It's all talk. The napikwan are few, but we are many."

"I've been to the east, to places where they have many houses—and they aren't few. They are many times more than all of us."

Lame Bull laughed easily. "So they say."

"See?" said Little Dog, waving his hand at the empty hills. "It is just the same as it was. And now the napikwan agree that it's ours. And, Natoya-niskim, the napikwan have good things, and we can learn from them. They promised to teach us their secrets, and then we'll have their medicine."

She could not convey to them what she knew of white men, so she held her peace, riding quietly into a biting wind that sliced under her scarlet blanket.

"It is on our minds, Sacred Buffalo Stone, that your vision is gone. White Buffalo Cow didn't come to you with a picture of the future. White Buffalo Cow didn't speak to us through you, to tell us not to make this agreement with the white chiefs. Haiya! Is it not so?"

This was the real reason they had asked her forward, she knew. They had concluded her medicine vision was false. She saw no reason to say anything.

"It's so," Little Dog said. "You were only a girl when you said White Buffalo Cow came to you; and the vision came to you after your first night instead of the usual four days of fasting and prayer. We understand how this is: This would be what a young woman who is half napikwan would see and hear, and tell the Siksika nation."

She froze. At no time since she returned to her mother and the Pikuni had anyone made anything of her mixed blood. No Siksika scorned her for it—unlike white people. But here it was. She nodded bleakly.

"It was a false vision, we think," Little Dog continued kindly. "Now you've grown, and become a true Pikuni. Surely you will find your true spirit helper if you seek one."

"My chief, I know what I saw, and I told it to you truly."

"Why, we don't doubt that you saw it. We think perhaps it wasn't given you by White Buffalo Cow, but by the Beneath Ones. You've been a holy one among us, and we all admire your dedication. But now you should find a strong young man, and give the people more children. You are a comely woman, tall and strong, and the young men will vie for you if you let them."

Rejected.

"Thank you for your counsel," she said.

Lame Bull nodded kindly, dismissing her. She reined her mare to a halt and let the headmen slide by, singly and in knots, an appraising look on their faces as they scrutinized her. And then the shamans, warriors, and women, many of them toting what was left of the napikwan gifts. Somehow they all knew. She had come to the meeting grounds a high Dreaming Woman of the Siksika; she was returning to the Lone Eaters, to Meadowlark and Sinopah and her almost-mother, Tears in Her Eyes, a misguided girl who had twisted the nation.

She thought of Peter Kipp, and wondered whether to veer off toward Fort Benton to see the one person she loved who was a mixed-breed, like herself. A rush of tenderness slid through the empty chambers of her heart. They were already north of the fort, and she would have to decide at once who she was.

Part Three

GOLD

Chapter Nineteen

1865

Peter Kipp knew better than to drink. He couldn't hold spirits. They made him either crazy or stupid or both. He knew better than to wander into the grog shops along the levee too. They wouldn't let a breed into most places, and in the dives where they let him drink, there were always bearded ruffians waiting to pick the scab.

But sometimes he had to, the saloons and hurdy-gurdies were the only places to recruit teamsters, or at least men who could drive an ox or handle a team, when he needed extra help. He could work anyone who wanted work, but most of the pilgrims off the riverboats headed straight toward the goldfields, pausing in Fort Benton only long enough to outfit themselves for the long walk to Bannack or Virginia City or Last Chance Gulch. These days, the hot spot was Confederate Gulch, where, they said, a man could pan enough gold in an hour to keep himself in booze and vittles for a week.

When news of strikes at Salmon River, Gold Creek, and Grasshopper Creek had reached the outside early in the 1860s, the argonauts flooded up from Salt Lake and spread through the mountains of Idaho. But that meant a long overland trip out the Platte Road. The Missouri offered a faster and more comfortable way. A gold seeker could buy a ticket in St. Louis and arrive at Fort Benton, head of navigation on the Missouri, a few weeks later, and hike the rest of the way to the diggings.

And they'd come. Fort Benton boasted a long levee, with saloons, mercantiles, blacksmiths, and claptrap hotels shouldering the waterfront from the old American Fur Company fort on the east to the huge warehouse of Carroll and Steell, the big freighting outfit upriver a mile, with thousands of oxen and mules, and hundreds of freight wagons, all feverishly hauling goods to the goldfields. In 1864 there had been only six saloons; now Fort Benton was a hell-raising city.

Peter Kipp had a more modest outfit, but it still required tough men, ones who wouldn't ditch the wagons and mules and oxen when they arrived at the goldfields. He employed a few Creoles, but he always needed more. To make a crew he had to plunge into one of the dark, jerrybuilt log and canvas outfits, buy a shot of red-eye, and talk to men with names like Keno Bill and Buckskin Bob and Whiskey Brown. Peter's red hair didn't hide his mixed blood much, and they listened skeptically, sometimes spitting a brown gob at his boots.

"Look, breed, soon's the red niggers got shut outta hyar, the better," said one named Spring Heel Jack. "I do mah part." He dug into his greasy canvas coat and dropped a curled scalp on the plank bar. Its blue-black hair advertised its original owner. "Gimme a double," Spring Heel Jack demanded.

Peter stared. Indian scalps were legal tender at any saloon in Fort Benton. Nausea crept up his throat, and he left, raucous laughter echoing behind him. He should get used to it: Flamboyant Sheriff Hamilton was offering twenty-five bucks for any Indian scalp, and boasting that he'd solve the Indian problem all by himself.

Outside, the evening air smelled cleaner. Down on the levee a man was yellowing the Missouri; knots of other men meandered from one lamplit dive to the next. He heard shots, but he was always hearing shots. Mostly it meant a drunk was exterminating lamps. Sometimes it meant they were exterminating Blackfeet. Last winter someone had shot a Piegan and stuffed him through a hole in the ice off the levee, but his feet hadn't followed and the Injun's legs stuck upward until the ice melted.

On this cold June evening two riverboats, the *Deer Lodge* and the *Twilight*, were tied at the riverbank. It had been a low-water year, and not many of the dozen boats racing up the Missouri had made it this far. The shallow-draft *Deer Lodge* had been doing a fat trade shuttling passengers and freight from the boats that hadn't made the distance. The riverboats would float downriver traveling light: nothing but passengers and gold heading for the states. Their presence here, not far below the Canadian border, had been the marvel of the West. To reach this point they'd battled the Missouri for almost 2,500 river miles; scraping over sandbars, dodging submerged boulders and snags, wrestling rapids, chewing up firewood, ducking hostile Sioux, and gathering game along the banks to feed the mobs of passengers. A traveler could come here by water from New Orleans, about 3,500 river miles away. But not much farther. Upstream a bit, the great falls of the Missouri stopped river traffic.

A man with a freight outfit could coin money. Which Peter Kipp was trying, with some small success, to do. Freight had been piled at Cow Island, 120 miles east, waiting for any outfit that would take it to Benton. And the dunnage heaped on the levee came to more than Carroll and Steell, or the Diamond R, could haul to the gold camps.

Peter avoided McNulty's Saloon, knowing it'd be worth his life to go in there, and settled instead on the Buffalo Head, where old-time fur traders often gathered. Old Arnaud Leveque, a relic of the fur-trading days, poured libations there, giving customers a choice of rotgut or redeye, drawn from the same keg.

"Ah! Monsieur Kipp!" Leveque said, dribbling some tawny stuff into a tin cup. "You are looking for teamsters."

Peter nodded, not sipping the stuff because he already felt dizzy and crazy. "I've got four wagons going to Cow

Island, and two to Confederate Gulch; oxen to Cow Island, mules and horses going west."

He peered through the wall of pipe smoke at the denizens, who were playing euchre with greasy cards at several hand-hewn tables. Some he knew. Most were former engagés of American Fur, who left when Charles Chouteau came upriver that spring and sold out to a new outfit, the Northwest Company. The Chouteaus, suspected of being southern sympathizers in the war, had lost their trading license.

They'd all heard him, and he waited patiently at the adzed plank bar while they thought about it. These were old friends, men who didn't mind working for a breed.

"Hey, Kipp, what're you giving, eh?"

"A dollar a day, chow, and a dram each night." That was more than double their engagé wages of $150 per year.

"T'ain't enough, not with the red devils fixing to kill us."

"What'll you do it for?"

The man shrugged. "Five a day, eh?"

"That would break me."

The big, bushy-bearded man laughed. "A war club or rifle bullet, monsieur, would break me!"

That met with appreciative laughter. The Blackfeet had begun a guerrilla war. A few months earlier the Bloods had killed ten woodcutters building the town of Ophir at the confluence of the Marias River a few miles east. There'd been random killings of teamsters. White men had retaliated by killing any Indian who dared to come to the Blackfoot agency in Fort Benton, often in cold blood. In May a pair of Benton loafers, Henry Bostwick and Joe Spearson, had been sitting in front of the Indian agency when four Bloods showed up boasting of scalps they'd taken. The pair shot the four Bloods and dumped them into the Missouri. The Blackfeet were enraged by this invasion of their treaty lands. Every grog shop and outfitter in town was there illegally.

"Two a day—high as I can go and not be skinned," Peter replied.

"Two dollars to be scalped and skinned meself. Well, mon ami, I think I'll just go to Cow Island and fill my pockets with your gold."

"Be at my yard at dawn. We're taking robes east; bringing back dunnage from the *General Grant*. Anyone else? I need six more. Four for the Confederate Gulch run."

"I'll go for the hell of it, Kipp," said old Picotte. "Woowee!"

"You're crazy. Dem drunk Bloods—I get the itches just walkin' down Front Street!" said another old-timer.

"Wall, you're all a bunch of cowards. I'm a-goin,'" said a fellow Peter didn't know. "For two a day."

"You can handle oxen or a team?"

"Sonny boy, since before a squaw birthed you."

"All right, be at my yard."

He got his men. He preferred former engagés. They weren't gold-crazy, they worked hard, knew the country, and above all knew the Blackfeet and were often on friendly terms with some of them.

But one could never know. The whiskey traders had wrecked everything, sneaking out with wagons full of whiskey, meeting up with wild young Piegans or Bloods, tapping a keg and starting a debauch that turned the Indians crazy-drunk—and cleaned them out of every robe and pelt they had. The Blackfeet called them "sneaking drink givers." Older men watched sadly, helplessly, as the crazed young Indians drank themselves to a stupor, traded away everything they had, and then went raiding to recover what they'd lost. The law, such as it was, posed no problems for whiskey traders, and didn't even dent the traffic. Whiskey had always been illegal in Indian country, but now it flooded in, every boat bringing hundreds of barrels—which ultimately enflamed and degraded and impoverished the proud Blackfeet.

"All right, then, we'll leave at dawn. I'm with the Cow Island outfit; La Rue's captain of the Confederate Gulch outfit."

Some wouldn't show up and he'd be shorthanded—but he always managed. Somehow he'd kept his little half-breed operation going, in spite of the giants like the Diamond R, and all the rest. He'd started it in '63. The Civil War had wrecked the fur trade, with both sides commandeering boats and cargoes, and threatening to kill the pilots and masters. That year, no boats reached Benton because of the war and low water. And that year, when the Blackfeet didn't get their annunities, their feelings about whites turned sour. Peter had known it was time to get out, and with his hefty savings he'd bought wagons and oxen from the failing La Barge company upriver from American Fur.

Peter slid into an eerie dark caused by a clouding sky, making his way back to the old fur post, where he rented the trader's apartment once occupied by de Paris. He hadn't gotten fifty yards when three shadowy figures loomed out of the gloom and jumped him. He felt himself being wrestled into the dust and cow manure, fought hard even as three sets of arms pinioned him. His shoulder hit hard ground. Rough hands poked and probed and found the leather bag of gold dust—the currency of Fort Benton.

"Got it," muttered one whiskey breath.

"That'll teach 'im. Hey, breed, don't you go gettin' airs. Don't you go mixin' with white men."

Peter said nothing. He'd learned that long ago. These three were from McNulty's, the dive he'd avoided. They were probably wolfers, a mean species armed with strychnine they gave to wolves, buffalo—and even Blackfeet. Wolf pelts sold for plenty and were also legal tender anywhere. Blackfeet pelts went for even more. They rose, laughing, and booted him hard. He grabbed a boot and hung on, toppling its owner, who cursed roundly as he fell.

"Get him good. Ain't got respect for white men!" yelled another.

They hammered him. He ducked and dodged and landed some of his own, but six fists and six boots outmatched his two. They never stopped laughing, even as a blur and then oblivion overtook Peter.

Later he scraped his aching body off the cold earth. A light rain was chilling him right to the gut. He stood dizzily, feeling nausea crawl up his gullet, and limped back to the old post, hoping one or another of its new owners, Hubbell or Hawley, would let him in. He figured his red hair had saved him from a scalping.

Fort Benton wasn't home anymore.

Peter ignored the stares of the old Creoles driving his oxen east. What had happened to him was none of their damned business; nothing ever to talk about to white men. He'd seen his other outfit off, three jerkline outfits in the hands of some good mule skinners. That would be the profitable trip, at a dollar a pound to Confederate Gulch. This one to Cow Island would cost shippers two-bits a pound, a rate they considered ruinous. But it was a rate that enabled Peter to stay barely ahead of loss. Keeping almost a hundred oxen and mules fed, and wagons repaired, ate money. He employed a dozen men, mostly breeds, just cutting prairie hay in places where the Diamond R and the rest hadn't got to first.

The trip took nine days each way. The new road was so crude that oxen and wagons regularly plunged over cliffs. It had been born of low-water desperation: Boats had unloaded their dunnage in 1864 on the island off Cow Creek, a safe haven from raiding Indians. With wagons and a flatboat, the cargo had reached Fort Benton safely. This year the water was still lower and the opportunity even better for freighters.

Peter whipped along the lead yoke of oxen, growling at the slavering beasts in time-honored fashion, while behind him his Creoles kept their outfits moving. They did well to make twelve miles a day in that hilly country. There'd been bad trouble with the Piegans, who saw the road as a chance to plunder. Peter always stayed within a few steps of his good Henry rifle, the first fast-loader in the area. But most of the Creoles weren't armed; a lifetime with the fur company had left them nothing.

He cursed his bruises; they shot pain through him with every step, but the only thing was to go on, never stop, show the white men what Peter Kipp was made of. For three days he and his men followed the Missouri toward its north bend, and then they cut along the southern flank of the Bear Paw Mountains in a beeline toward Cow Creek. At dawn of the fourth day they ran into trouble.

They awoke to find about forty Piegans grinning at them, rifles pointed and arrows nocked. Young men mostly, looking as murderous as any lot of savages ever did. Peter reached for his Henry, lying beside his bedroll, but it was anchored under a moccasined foot.

A Piegan laughed and lifted a tin canteen of something—booze, it seemed. All of them looked to be drunk or nearly so.

The Creoles sat in their bedrolls, looking scared. In the old trading days a meeting like this would have been the occasion for joy, songs, stories, and some gift-giving. Now it was the occasion for murder.

"Sit down and have some coffee with us," Peter said in his trader's Blackfoot.

They laughed. Some of them poked around in the wagons, obviously disappointed to find only buffalo robes in them. A little whiskey might have eased the situation, but he hadn't a drop.

"I know some of you from the old days," Peter said. "At the trading window."

A half-truth. He hardly knew any of these young ones. A few years ago he could name every Piegan, and most of the Bloods. But that was in a different world. He began to sweat. He had nothing to give them, and they'd kill the whole outfit because of it.

"Look, who are you? I'm Peter Kipp. You know me. I've been trading with you for years. My father's your friend James Kipp."

One giggled.

Peter wondered if these were Gros Ventres. They weren't responding to his Blackfoot words.

"Peterkipp, Peterkipp." An older one sitting a bay pony said it. He seemed as drunk as the rest, weaving and grinning. He wore the traditional breechclout and leggins, unlike the younger ones in ready-made white men's shirts.

And the old one still braided his graying hair, unlike the young ones who wore their hair loose.

"Sinopah."

"Ah, yes, I am Sinopah! What a bad Siksika I am, Peterkipp." The old Piegan kneed his pony forward. A wave of his hand drove the younger warriors back a step, and Peter sat up, carefully not touching his Henry. The Piegans lowered their weapons. There'd be no blood shed this time.

"Sinopah! I haven't seen you in many winters. It is good to see you!" Peter said in Blackfoot.

The teamsters watched warily, understanding only a little of the tongue.

"These are bad days for the Pikuni, Peterkipp. The napikwan have come."

"We can make coffee for you, Sinopah!"

"Ah! Coffee! It tastes bad. Everything the napikwan gives us is bad. Last night the Sneaking Drink Givers found us, and now you see how we are."

"I'd gladly shoot every Sneaking Drink Giver, Sinopah."

The old Piegan laughed. "There are too many. They come in wagons, with barrels of whiskey—bad stuff, bad, bad. They see us, and pour some, and then we are all crazy, and next thing they have our robes and anything else they can steal. Sometimes they make us so sick we die! Then they take our scalps."

"Strychnine," muttered Peter. Some of the whiskey traders dosed their rotgut with a little strychnine to make the Indians crazier. Sometimes the little dose was too much. No lawman could ever catch up with them, in all those endless prairies and wastes.

"Who were they?" Peter asked sharply.

Sinopah shrugged. "Men with yellow beards and evil eyes and two revolvers at their waists, with a wagon drawn by two mules. Who knows?"

"You should report them, Sinopah."

"Ha! It's worth your life to go to the nannana in Fort Benton."

"Tell the Pikuni I will feed them and give them coffee to make them well again."

Sinopah shook his head. "They don't want coffee—they want whiskey. And yellow metal for guns, and napikwan scalps."

Peter stood restlessly. "Sinopah, tell me about Meadowlark, O-toch-koki, and—"

"The one you speak of has gone to the Sand Hills, Peterkipp. Two winters ago."

Meadowlark dead. "I am sorry. Tell me about Natoya-niskim."

"Ah, you still have eyes for her. She shares my lodge, with Tears in Her Eyes and our little girl. Natoya-niskim is very strange. Now she is seeing visions from White Buffalo Cow again, but no one believes her this time."

"I want to see her. Will you tell her that?"

He shrugged.

"Where are the Lone Eaters, Sinopah?"

"The Lone Eaters. We are fewer now—so many dead. On the Two Medicine, Peterkipp. The Heavy Runner is our chief now. A great friend of the napikwan, when the Sneaking Drink Givers don't come."

"Is she still beautiful—Sacred Buffalo Stone?"

Sinopah laughed. "Every Pikuni and Kainah boy and man has tried to take her. She will never have a man, including you, Peterkipp."

"Is she happy?"

Sinopah sighed. "Her medicine is very bad. She tells the young men not to drink spirits. She tells the old to endure and learn how to live without buffalo meat and eat flour and rice. She tells the elders to prepare for worse, but her words are like mosquitoes. No one in the band pays any heed, and they walk away when she comes."

"But is she happy? Is her life good?"

Sinopah shrugged. "Yes, Peterkipp. She says she is doing what she was given to do—save her people. No Pikuni is happier."

Chapter Twenty

Natoya-niskim did not like the looks of the whiskey traders who rode into the camp of the Lone Eaters that evening. They arrived at dusk, driving a rattle-trap covered wagon drawn by two span of mules, and steered boldly through the throng toward the chief's lodge at the center of the camp.

She followed, knowing what would transpire and feeling saddened by it. The white men reined to a halt before The Heavy Runner's large lodge and peered about cheerfully, their mouths distended into a crooked grin, their unblinking eyes measuring and recording the wealth of their hosts.

"We don't speak Blackfeet none," said one. "Anyone in this outfit speak American?"

She chose to say nothing, not wanting to help them.

One turned to the other. "Well, Reubin, these red niggers don't talk. Guess we'll just show 'em."

The one called Reubin, a black-bearded fellow with a slouch hat, turned around and lifted a small cask from within the covered wagon, and a tin cup. These he held for all to see.

"Sneaking Drink Givers!" said a warrior beside Natoya-niskim. "Haiya! We will have a party!"

"This here's good honest-Injun whiskey, pure corn spirits, guaranteed to pickle any red Injun with one whiff," said the one. "We'll fry your brains, shoot the red bejabbers through you, make you crazy as loons. I'm Monk, and that there's Reubin, and we're gonna give away a drink absolutely free—just git yerself a bowl or a cup and we'll pour out the joy juice, men, wimmin, children, it don't matter. First one's on the house, and we'll all have us the biggest, meanest shebang in the whole Blackfoot country."

He wheezed cheerfully. Even as he stood there orating to deaf ears, his partner filled a tin cup and proffered it to the chief. The Heavy Runner took it, grinning.

"Now, after this here sampler, we'll get us down to business, ladies and gents. We'll do us some robe and pelt tradin'. One cup for one robe. One cup for two wolf pelts. One cup for three elk hides or four deer hides. Owweee, we're all gonna have fun!"

While Monk was declaiming, Reubin was poking around in the wagon, pulling out pelts. He held up a buffalo robe and a cup; then two wolf pelts and the cup; then three elk hides and the cup, making the point clear to the whole throng.

How different this was from the old days, Natoyaniskim thought. Then, the fur traders waited to be invited; they smoked a pipe with the chief first, receiving the peace and friendship of the village. They weren't eager—the way these men were eager—and respected the cherished ways of the people. Soon the debauch would begin, and before the night was over, many lodges would be stripped of every robe and pelt, even those that wrapped them when they slept. It had been this way for several years now, and the village had grown poor, the lodges tattered, and the young people sullen.

Old Natosin Nepe-e, Brings Down the Sun, approached her, looking stern. He alone among the Siksika had always believed in her vision, and had continued to instruct her in the ways of the People. He'd grown frail but his authority remained. A wave of his hand would hush them all, and a command from this great medicine-giver would be heeded.

"What are the Sneaking Drink Givers saying?" he whispered.

She told him.

"They must leave this village. They come to destroy us and ruin our young men! I will ask you to translate for me."

He stepped out to the wagon, a dignified man in unadorned buckskin, his hair braided. His authority sprang from something unfathomable and pure in his nature. He raised a hand, interrupting Monk's spiel.

"We will not listen to the Sneaking Drink Givers!" he began in the Siksika tongue. Behind him, Monk spat tobacco. "We will not shame ourselves. We will not trade robes and pelts for a moment of craziness. We have grown poor. Our lodges have few robes. Our young men steal away to the drink givers, and do not hunt the buffalo or bring us game to eat. Now, we will be strong. We will not let these filthy napikwan destroy us! You, The Heavy Runner, shall give the example. Pour the drink into the ground. I have spoken."

Reluctantly the chief turned his cup over, and the amber fluid dribbled into the clay.

A great silence filled the twilight. Even those who lusted for the spirits stood stonily.

"Here now, old man, you can't keep a good buck down. Have yourself a cup on the house!"

Instead, Brings Down the Sun turned to Natoyaniskim. "Tell them in their tongue they must leave right now and keep on going. Our Mad Dogs will follow them out."

She turned toward Monk: "You are instructed by the elders to leave at once. The village police will follow you to make sure you do. Never return."

Monk noticed her for the first time, his gaze raking her tall, lithe form. "Well, an English-speaking squaw! Ain't you the pretty one. Never saw the likes in a squaw. Have ye a cup, and we'll just have us a party. Cup or two and we'll have us a little special fun. You like ribbons and foofaraw?"

"Get out."

Brings Down the Sun waved at the Mad Dogs, and several armed warriors moved in, their trade rifles at the ready.

"Well, Reubin, looks like they don't want a party. Least for the moment! Maybe tomorrah. Guess I'll remember the old boy, and the squaw. Yessir, there's a pair to remember."

The two settled in the seat, and Monk hawed the mules. Slowly the wagon rattled into the dusk, followed by the village police. A number of the young men looked unhappy.

The old shaman addressed them curtly: "You will shame us all with your drinking. As long as I live, there will be no Sneaking Drink Givers here. Go to your lodges. Live in holiness!"

Silently the Lone Eaters returned to their lodges to begin the evening meal. A slender peace had returned. Natosin Nepe-e, the Sun Giver, walked to his small lodge at the edge of the village, followed by the gazes of a hundred people, and vanished inside. They all knew he would be praying all night, burning sweetgrass, supplicating Sun and Napi and the sky spirits.

The next morning, Natoya-niskim awoke to screams. She threw her robe aside and raced into the dawn toward a place where women were keening. She pushed through to a cottonwood and beheld Brings Down the Sun hanging from a limb, his head twisted, his tongue jutting out the side of his mouth, his old brown hands tied behind him. A white man's hemp noose suspended him.

Natosin Nepe-e! The greatest shaman and medicine-giver of all the Siksika people! Her one true friend! She stared, sickened, unable to endure the sight. Nausea crept up her throat and she turned away, afraid to look any longer. Two of the powerful village police, Seco-mo-muck-on and Emonissi, raced to the tree, shouting for help. Gently they herded the wailing women away, cut down the old man and sliced the terrible rope from his neck. Natoya-niskim fled to Sinopah's lodge and drew her robe around her, awash with grief.

That afternoon, the whiskey traders boldly rode back into camp, a smirk on their bearded faces, and new many-shots Henry rifles across their laps.

"Well now, ladies and gents, we'll have us a fandango, a blowout, a wild rootin'-tootin' soiree!" Reubin announced. "Go get your robes and line up for the joy juice!"

No one moved. The village elders stared. The Heavy Runner stood.

"Hey now, ol' Heavy Runner. You some friend of white men or you some hostile red nigger, eh? We got us a little gift for the big old chief."

Monk handed The Heavy Runner a tin cup of rotgut. "Drink up, you old fart. Open the ball."

Leadenly, Natoya-niskim watched the chief drink and grin.

"Well now, you're a real peace chief after all. Frienda white men. For you, old pal, booze's on the house."

"My chief, don't do that," she whispered to him.

The Heavy Runner sipped and smiled. "We'll have a party, Natoya-niskim. A good time."

"Wall, there's that gray-eyed squaw that talks English. You got some old Creole's blood in ye? You sure are pretty, sweetheart," said Monk. "I'll fix you up a little special drinkee."

She turned away. Behind her laughing villagers raced to their lodges for robes and pelts. Women abandoned their supper-making. Warriors erupted from lodges with furs in hand, and traded them all for bowls and dishes of diluted rotgut.

She clambered into her dark lodge, listening to the whoops and laughter outside. Soon it would turn into craziness, yelling and shooting, bloodcurdling war cries, knife fights, brawls, giggles, vomit, groaning, matings, and finally stupor. She had seen it all. In the morning the traders would roll away with nearly every robe in the village; even some lodge covers. A thirteen-skin lodge cover would net two drinks. One with seventeen lodge skins would buy three watered drinks.

She closed her ears to it and lay in the blackness, grieving her friend and mentor Brings Down the Sun, a man set aside and holy, like Father DeSmet; a man who had never failed to believe the vision of the white buffalo cow, even after Natoya-niskim herself doubted and finally disbelieved.

She lay quietly, hearing the ruin of the Lone Eaters. It'd take many moons of hard labor to rebuild their stores, and even then they'd be poorer than before.

She heard the whisper of the door flap. A sour smell assaulted her, and she froze. A bulk loomed over her, breath rasping. One of the Sneaking Drink Givers!

"Ah, now, gotcha, squaw. You're some pretty squaw, never did see one so tall. I'm gonna have me a pretty Blackfoot lady—"

She dove at him, clawing fiercely, her nails scratching into his beard. Frantically she tried to edge around him, reach the lodge door and safety, but he caught her easily, giggling, coughing up whiskey phlegm, wheezing as his hands pawed at her skirt.

"Gimme a fight, eh? That makes 'er more fun!"

He threw her down while she kicked and kneed. He laughed and pressed down on her, pinioning her under two hundred pounds of hard muscle. She screamed, only to hear her desperation blend in with the whooping and howling and madness in the brutal night.

Then, suddenly, he whoofed out air, shuddered, and sank upon her, a dead weight. She felt something dripping.

"Natoya-niskim, I have protected you."

Sinopah!

He pulled the whiskey trader away and blew on embers of the lodge fire until a small flame curled up. She stared, aghast, at the sight of Monk with a war ax cleaving his skull.

Dead!

"Sinopah! Sinopah!"

Her stepfather grunted. He wasn't sober, but he wasn't

crazy drunk either. He lifted the dead Monk and dragged him into the night. Terrified, she arranged her skirts and followed, passing by Lone Eaters lying on the good earth, stupefied, laughing, copulating. Sinopah carried the dead trader to the wagon, where Reubin was cheerfully counting robes by the light of a lantern. Sinopah dropped the dead man over the robes. A span of mules sidestepped.

Reubin paused, slowly registering what lay before him. "Why, you red niggers kilt old Monk!" He studied the hatched buried in Monk's skull. "Bygod, kilt him!"

"He tried to rape me," she said.

"Rape, hey, squaw, there's no such thing as rapin' a squaw."

"You heard me."

Reubin sighed, studying her, memorizing her every feature. "I ain't gonna forget you, squaw. I ain't gonna forget. You'll taste some white man's justice soon as I catch up with ye."

"Get out!"

"I believe I will," he said.

A few minutes later the Sneaking Drink Giver drove away with a wagon full of robes and one white man's body. A few hours later drunken and hung over Lone Eaters dismantled their camp and fled in terror. Except for Natoyaniskim.

The tall, sad-faced woman who had spent her childhood in a St. Louis convent watched her people reel away, the village scarcely packed on the travois, the children wailing. That was what the Siksika had become. Her sanctuary on the Two Medicine River lay a day's walk upstream, and she would be there well before dusk. She started out, taking nothing but a small knife, because she needed nothing, and padded along the familiar lodge trail beside the mysterious river where spirits danced.

She had done that for years, spending time apart from the Lone Eaters, especially in the Moon of High Water, and the Moon of Flowers. There, in the protected bottom she had made her spirit lodge, she lived simply, always finding enough food—roots and sarvisberries, chokecherries, and prairie turnips. After her mother had taken the Wolf Trail to the Sand Hills, Natoya-niskim had spent more time on the Two Medicine, feeling less welcome in the lodge of Sinopah and Isto-ko-pence, who didn't quite understand her calling, her cloistered life.

After the Treaty of 1855—Lame Bull's treaty, her people called it—life had continued as it always had. At the time of the first thunder in the spring, they gathered for the Opening of Beaver Bundle. In midsummer they gathered for the Sun Dance; and in the fall they gathered for the great buffalo hunts. In between, the warriors spread terror among the Crows and Assiniboin, ignoring the treaty. The villages grew fat with captured horses, parfleches of pemmican, and curly robes that would buy them anything the traders offered.

It had all seemed the same to them, but not to the woman who had once been Marie Therese de Paris. In 1859 a party of prospectors had panned every creek up the east side of the Rockies to Canada and found no color. The Siksika carefully left them alone. Soon enough they had left. Now and then companies of soldiers had arrived on the riverboats and marched westward to Washington Territory. But they had not stayed, and the elders had nodded and said nothing had changed. Never had the young medicine woman, the Dreamer, Natoya-niskim, been less heeded. The young men mocked her and asked what Sacred Buffalo Cow was telling her those days.

Then, with the civil war in the east, everything had changed at once. Men escaping army duty flooded up the river and began prospecting every mountain creek for gold. Ruffians, cardsharks, and boomers followed, erecting shantyvilles in the goldfields. The war interrupted the robe trade: traders had nothing on their shelves and could pay little for peltries. And in 1863 the Blackfoot treaty annuities didn't arrive, enraging the people. It had all turned into war—hit-or-miss, sporadic, but deadly.

She reached her familiar river-bottom flat before dusk and discovered its peace at once. This had been her refuge, the place where a woman of her calling could bring down the spirits and receive instruction from them. She found a whole slope filled with pach-op-it-skinni, wild potato, and with her digging stick freed a few to boil for supper. Soon the ok-kun-okin, sarvisberry, would be ripe. She never lacked.

In the twilight, after her simple meal, she prepared herself for grieving. She wished to say good-bye to Brings Down the Sun, and remember his wisdom and his steadfast faith in her vision and medicine power. After that, perhaps, she would meditate into the night, keeping a vigil with the Above Spirits, and listen to their wisdom. It had been over a decade since White Buffalo Cow had visited her, and the memories had decayed to doubt. But she still believed in her mission. She knew she must steel herself for the worst sort of struggle: one she could never win. She wondered whether she might rally the Siksika to victory, like the woman the sisters had read about, Jeanne d'Arc. The Frenchwoman had heard the voice of God, inspired armies on behalf of the dauphin, triumphed, only to lose everything and be burned at the stake for heresy. Natoya-niskim loved that story, and drew inspiration from the French saint.

She sat cross-legged facing west, where the memory of the sun lingered as a blue band at the brow of the cliff. It wasn't hard to bring the old man to mind and hear his reedy voice. She immersed herself in his presence, remembering that he had believed her; he understood the fate of the Siksika, and had spun out his last years in sadness.

"Oh, Grandfather!" she cried. "I'll always remember you. May you have a joyous life when you reach the Sand Hills!"

But the spirit person she was addressing did not look like the old shaman. She beheld the form of a white buffalo, which grew more and more distinct, until she found herself in the presence of White Buffalo Cow once again. But how the spirit guide had changed. Now White Buffalo Cow bore arrows in her flanks, and from each wound blood gouted. Her eyes were troubled, even frantic, and she tossed her horns angrily.

"Ride me, Natoya-niskim," said the spirit.

"White Buffalo Cow!"

"Hurry, for my blood runs out of me."

Natoya found herself on the back of her spirit counselor, flying over the darkened world. She beheld blue and gray armies spilling blood in the east; white men swarming into the land of the Siksika; boisterous gold camps teeming with ruffians and murderers; men building railroad tracks; and everywhere, blue armies marching. Then she beheld a great noose made of hemp rope, the very noose that had killed Brings Down the Sun, but now it was spread into a gigantic loop that traced the borders of the Blackfoot nation. Then something yanked the noose and it shrank, and the people were confined to half the land they had before, with everything gone below Ikinitskatah, the Teton River. She saw the Sneaking Drink Givers rolling north, building a post named Whoop-up across the medicine line in the Grandmother Land, where wild Siksika could drink themselves mad and kill each other. Then White Buffalo Cow settled gently to earth, and Natoya-niskim thought surely the vision had ended, but it hadn't.

There was something else. The spirit cow, weary from its flight, panting from its wounds, walked to the lodges of the people who had never touched the bad water, and died before them, giving the remnant of the Siksika her own meat.

Speechless, Natoya-niskim peered into the night, but White Buffalo Cow had vanished. She sat alone in darkness, her mind reeling from all that she'd experienced.

"You have shown me the way at last," she breathed into the close darkness.

She would have to struggle without hope of victory. The Blackfoot nation would be lost—but she would nurture a remnant, giving up herself that others might survive. The night was the darkest she had ever known.

Chapter Twenty-one

There'd never been such a throng in the Benton bottoms. All the southern Piegans had come in; most of the Bloods, and even more of the northern Piegans and Blackfeet proper, from Canada. No one knew how many, but the number had to be somewhere between four and five thousand.

It had all been Gad Upson's doing. These degenerate savages, as he called his charges, had become unmanageable lately, killing white men, interfering with commerce. It was time for a new treaty. So, with the consent of his superiors in the Bureau of Indian Affairs, he'd called in the chiefs and presented them with a new treaty. The Blackfeet would cede about half their tribal lands and common hunting grounds to white men. In exchange, the chiefs would each get $250 a year, and the tribe would get $50,000 a year in annuities over twenty years.

The hundred or so denizens of Fort Benton felt pretty smug about this November powwow. Old Upson was getting a quarter of Montana Territory in exchange for some trifles. He'd bribed a few chiefs. And the new treaty would stop the troubles too. Once this thing was signed, the savages would have to stay north of the Teton River, well away from Benton and its bustling commerce, and well north of the roads out to the goldfields.

Peter Kipp didn't like it and didn't agree with the merchants. The Blackfoot agency would still be in Fort Benton, and any Indian wanting to see the ninnana, or agent, would risk his life coming into town. Sourly, Peter avoided the smug newcomers, the ones who'd never befriended the Indians as all the fur traders had, and turned his back on the whole business.

That blustery morning, he donned his mackinaw and wended his way into the great encampment, past brightly decorated lodges, children and lazy dogs, past dark-haired women feeding out pemmican because there wasn't a stick of firewood within a dozen miles. They knew him, and he knew them. He knew every Piegan family, and many of the Bloods, and most of the older people by name. They'd all come to his trading window many times.

"Grandmother, where are the Lone Eaters?" he asked a wrinkled old woman stealing warmth from the pale sun.

"Why, my son, I don't know. You are looking for your sweetheart."

He grinned. His love for Marie Therese had compassed the winters and decades. Eventually he found his way to the Lone Eaters, who were camped on the western extremity of the great gathering, and there he inquired about Natoya-niskim.

"Haiya, Mr. Kipp. She didn't come with us. She disapproves of this," a gray old warrior, Menepoka, told him. "She's not alone."

That disheartened Peter. "She's on the Two Medicine?"

"No, she's at our village on the Marias."

"How is she, Menepoka? What does she do?"

"She says her medicine has returned, Peterkipp. She spends her time with the young men."

That stabbed straight through Peter's heart. "The young men?"

"Yes. She is beautiful, Peterkipp, filled with a spirit that no fire can quench."

Peter sighed. After all these years, he'd lost her at last.

"Yes," Menepoka continued, "she gives them heart. She teaches them the old ways. She gives them a vow: they swear never to touch the firewater and live a pure life. Now that's a good thing. She gives them strength for the future. The rest of us—we go to the Sneaking Drink Givers and become bad. Oh, it is fun to be bad! But then the black-footed people suffer."

"Is she happy?"

"Never happier. All the years she waited for White Buffalo Cow to return, she wasn't sure of herself. Her only friend was the one who went to the Sand Hills."

"Brings Down the Sun is dead?"

"The one you speak of has gone up the Wolf Trail, yes, to the Sand Hills. The Sneaking Drink Givers killed him."

Menepoka hesitated, uncertain about saying what was on his mind, and Peter waited. "I should not tell a napikwan this—but, ah, you are a mixed-blood, not all napikwan. She fights the Sneaking Drink Givers. The young men in her circle destroyed many casks of whiskey with their hatchets! It was a good thing too. But now the Sneaking Drink Givers are wary, and they shoot any Siksika that comes close. They guard the barrels all the time. Her young men can't do that anymore—and live."

She was resisting. What a sad, hopeless business it was, Peter thought. Like commanding the tides to stop. Still, it made her happy, and that made him happy.

"Menepoka, when you see her, tell her Peter Kipp loves her and wishes her well. Tell her I'm well, and have a wagon business with many mules and oxen."

The old man grinned. "The message is always the same, Peterkipp. She will smile. And I will see the sadness in her eyes when she smiles."

"Thank you, Grandfather," Peter said, feeling somehow desolated by the story of a tall, beautiful, powerless woman trying to snatch a few infants from the jaws of Moloch.

Peter wandered back to the levee, where the treaty talks were winding up. There, old Little Dog, now the head chief of the Piegans, was orating.

"We are pleased with what we have heard here today,"

the handsome chief said. "The land here belongs to us, we were raised upon it; we are glad to give a portion of it to the United States, for we get something for it."

You don't get anything for your thousands of acres, Peter thought dourly. Little Dog had always tried to steer his people toward white men's ways. He had even farmed on Sun River awhile.

Grinning, Major Upson signed the parchment with a flourish, followed by the territorial governor, Thomas Meagher. And one by one the chiefs scratched their mark on the document, duly witnessed by clerks.

"It shore makes the hair prickle on my scalp," said a teamster to Peter.

"What does?"

"Them redskins—they's four, five thousand on this bottom. Maybe a hunnert of us white men, and half of them cowardly northerners too. Them skins, they took a mind to it, they could butcher the whole lot of us in about five minutes."

They could at that, Peter thought. Many of the younger warriors and headmen sat sullenly in their blankets, disapproving of the diplomacy of the elders. There'd been guerrilla war and death for months, and one treaty wasn't going to sweeten their bitterness.

The signing done, Upson delivered a benediction, but it sounded like a requiem to Peter. The damned agent was burying the Blackfeet, piece by piece. He'd treated them badly, and part of the troubles had been the result of his disdain. Peter thought it was a miracle the whole Blackfoot nation hadn't exploded and killed every white man in the territory. Little Dog's diplomacy had kept it from happening—and made the chief some enemies among his own people.

Peter spotted some of the town's businessmen and joined them.

"It's enough to make a man nervous," said George Steell. "All them devils within hatchet-reach of us."

"Yeah, I've been thinking that too," Colonel Broadwater said. "Maybe we can show them a little white men's medicine. You got any ideas?"

"Yup," said Joe Healy. He pointed at a Diamond R freight train standing in front of I. G. Baker's store. The rear mule, a sleepy-eyed old beast dozing in the weak sun, carried a brass four-pound mountain howitzer on its pack-saddle, the barrel poking rearward. It was being used to protect the pack train from the selfsame Indians who crowded the Fort Benton bottom.

"Ah!" exclaimed Broadwater.

Peter knew at once what the medicine would be.

"All right, Kipp. You can speak the tongue. You tell 'em we're going to treat 'em to a little white man's medicine. Tell 'em they're going to see mighty big hocus-pocus."

Annoyed, Peter declined. But other clerks and translators raced off to tell the Blackfeet they'd see a great show. Within minutes the whole throng of Blackfeet arrived at the levee, while the mule was detached from the freight outfit and led to the waterfront. Young Beidler, out of Virginia City, volunteered to perform the honors. He loaded the little cannon with a charge of powder and grapeshot. Then he cut a time fuse and stuffed it into the touchhole. Then he turned the sleepy mule so that the barrel pointed across the wide Missouri.

"All right now, here's some white men's medicine," someone cried. With that, Beidler scratched a lucifer and lit the time fuse. It hissed. The mule turned its head to see what the hissing was all about, swinging the bore around. The mule decided he didn't like that hissing at all, and began circling, while the bore of the cannon scythed the crowd. White men and red alike ran for cover, or flattened themselves to mother earth. The mule, annoyed now, began bucking, and the bore aimed at sky and ground and every point in between. Peter dove into the Missouri, followed by Colonel Broadwater, Joe Healy, Mose Solomon, and Matt Carroll. The last thing in Peter's eye before he went under was the sight of Hi Upham and Bill Hamilton trying to throw up a breastwork with their sheath knives.

The excited mule whirled, and now the Blackfeet fled

for the cliffs, scattering blankets; or dropped to the ground like tenpins. Then it blew. The grapeshot wiped out the painted buffalo head sign that advertised the Northwest Company store at Old Fort Benton, sending wood shivering to earth. The recoil threw the old mule into the river, where it sank like a stone under the cannon, sending up a stream of bubbles.

Peter stood up, dripping water, and glared at Broadwater, Healy, and Solomon, who were also emerging from their underwater lairs. The Blackfoot agent, Gad Upson, stood up, brushed manure off his britches and smiled.

"Kipp, if you tell anyone I got wet, you'll get no more freight contracts from me," Broadwater said solemnly.

"I won't tell a soul, Colonel."

"I won't either," said Solomon.

"I might confess it," said Hamilton. "A few years from now."

They clambered out of the river and stood dripping on the levee. The Blackfeet drifted toward their lodges to break camp.

The fun was over, Peter thought.

That winter, gold was discovered in the Sun River valley, and five hundred prospectors rushed into the area. Only there was no gold. It had been one of those mad rumors that uproot mining camps. The stubborn prospectors continued to hunt for the legendary gold until winter trapped them. Then they built hovels and starved. Many would have died, but for that faithful friend of white men, Little Dog, who hunted antelope and gave the meat to the prospectors.

The white men didn't return the favor. When four Piegan warriors stopped to beg food at a Sun River cabin, the prospectors shot one and hanged three. After that, the guerrilla war was on again, with redoubled fury. The Piegans, under Bull's Head, burned the Sun River farm and slaughtered stock and a herder at the Jesuit mission on the Sun River.

Peter watched it all unfold with a sense of helplessness. His shipping business had survived in spite of the competition of the big outfits. In the spring, when the upriver cargo arrived, he'd have more contracts than he could handle. He paced his apartment restlessly the early months of 1866, feeling inchoate needs and bursts of anger. And more than anything else, a deepening loneliness. He was a man alone, set apart by race. He was accepted—to a degree—only because he'd become a white man in all but his blood. Only among the many Creoles living in town, former engagés of American Fur, was Peter wholly accepted.

He'd established himself, built a business—but one thing was lacking. He despaired of ever winning Marie Therese, but his love never faltered. She would be too old for children now, but all he wanted was her beautiful self in the house he would give her. The news he had of her, arriving in bits and pieces, was always of a hauntingly beautiful and spiritually luminous woman who had given herself to her people. Bleakly he considered his prospects. No white woman would even consider him, and there were almost none in the territory anyway. His hope of love lay with another breed—or with an Indian woman. No Indian condemned him for his white man's blood. Of these choices, a mixed-breed woman well schooled in white men's ways seemed best to him—but he knew of none who were still single. And anyway, there was only Marie Therese . . . always.

One overcast, blustery day he loaded a packhorse with supplies and then saddled his fastest horse, a tough dun mustang that never quit. He turned the company work over to La Rue for a spell and rode north, not really knowing why he rode. There were things a man did sometimes that required no reasons. He quartered into a raw north wind that sliced under his mackinaw and down his neck and made the travel a lot colder. Except for occasional berms of snow piled up by the scouring wind, the prairie lay clean, and he made good progress.

What if she wouldn't want to see him? Why was he going to her? As much to win her as to free himself from her so he could marry another, he told himself. But that was just the patter of his mind, not a serious reason. . . . Maybe it was serious. A man needed a woman's love; maybe a woman needed a man's love. Somewhere, perhaps back in St. Louis, he had read a Greek myth: Once, long ago, human beings were androgynous, without sex. But they angered Zeus, who punished them by splitting them in two, male and female. And forever more, man and woman wandered the earth looking for their other half.

White men's mythology . . . was it so different from the beliefs of the tribes? He noted wagon tracks stretching northward, whiskey traders not even bothering to conceal their passage. The truc murderers of the Blackfeet. He paid no attention, steering northwest toward the Two Medicine, where the Lone Eaters were sheltering this winter.

He paid no attention until he heard a rifle shot—and felt his good dun horse slowly cave in under him. Angrily, he slid out of the stirrups and sprang aside as the saddler collapsed and sighed, gouting blood from a dollar-sized hole in his chest. The next shot blew Peter's hat off. He crabbed behind the dun and tried to pull his rifle from its sheath, but couldn't. Four white men emerged over a gentle ridge, spaced in a great arc. They closed on him, their rifles at the ready. He saw, on the hazy horizon, a wagon, and wished he'd been more attentive. He knew he was a dead man.

They'd shoot him if he didn't stand. Slowly he raised his arms and waited. Then he unfolded himself and stood. It was one of the hardest things he'd ever done. They closed, grinning, their rifles ready. Then four ruffians surrounded him, peering at him curiously from squinty eyes, their faces hidden behind unkempt beards, their lips slashes of amusement.

"Who be ye?" said one in a gravelly voice.

"Peter Kipp."

The man spat, a great brown gob of chaw landing at Peter's boots. "Never heard of ye." He studied Peter, recognition building. "You some breed," he said.

"I was a trader at Fort Benton."

"Were ye now! Takin' up robes and handin' out rifles and shot—Injun lovers."

Peter feared to say any more. The reply would be a bullet.

"Ye be followin' us."

"Not knowingly. I'm on my way—west."

"Ye be followin' us. Pull out yer pockets. Let's see the badge."

Peter slowly pulled out his pockets, setting a jackknife on the ground, and then a steel and flint. He slowly unbuttoned his mackinaw, feeling the slice of wind into his flannel shirt. No badge.

"Maybe you are, and maybe you ain't. Guess we won't take chances, though." The squinty man lifted his rifle.

"Wait," Peter yelled. "Everyone in Fort Benton knows me. Every Creole, everyone else. They know where I'm going. And they'll see what you'll—leave behind. You'll stretch a rope soon enough."

The man wheezed, his laughter like an accordion whine. "What law?" he laughed again. "Creoles. Them Frenchies are so dumb they sweat for old Chouteau for a hunnert fifty a year."

"Where are you from?"

The question surprised the man. "Missoura, boy. Sesech, if it means something to ye. The handle is Chop-ear, 'cause that's what I do to Yanks."

"You in the fur business?"

The squinty one wheezed out laughter again, like a man long at stool.

"I hear the Black Patched Moccasins killed a lot of buffalo this fall. They'll have robes."

"Where'd you hear that?"

Peter shrugged.

"Where they be?"

"On the Marias near Willow Round." That was all true. Peter hoped it would save his life.

It did. One wheezed, then another. All four guffawed. Peter sensed it was where they were heading, and he'd said the one thing that drew a frail veil of words between his flesh and lead bullets.

"You killed my horse. How'm I going to travel?"

Chop-ear nodded to one of the others. That one headed for Peter's packhorse, ripped open the pack, and studied the contents. He poked into shirt pockets and did not find the badge he was looking for. The man gave up, and spat.

"Well, breed, looks like you gotta walk and lead the critter," said Chop-ear. "If you're up to it. Most niggers ain't."

That was what Peter was waiting for.

"Let 'im be," said another. "I don't like risks."

They stole some roasted coffee beans, yanked out his good Henry and kept it, found a box of metallic cartridges, and left him there. He watched them vanish over the ridge, and then buttoned up his mackinaw. The cold was killing him. He loaded up his packhorse and walked west, keeping the wind at his side and putting distance between himself and the Sneaking Drink Givers. He wished there was some way to kill them before they killed a nation.

Chapter Twenty-two

Peter fled through the day and into an arctic night, afraid the whiskey runners would change their minds. Darkness didn't stop him: He stumbled and pawed westward, and didn't rest until a cold moon rose not long before dawn. He made camp in a naked woods, fearful of lighting the fire he needed badly.

A cup of camp tea balmed his nerves, and he dozed fitfully until the grudging winter dawn nagged him out of his bedroll. He had expected trouble from the bitter Blackfeet; he'd scarcely imagined that he would stumble upon whiskey runners ready to murder him on the spot. He left the iced-over Teton River and struck north toward the Two Medicine, feeling somewhat better as he trudged through the stark loneliness of the wintry plains.

Three days later he struck the mysterious river and intuitively cut eastward where the bottoms were broader and timbered. He raised a village the next morning, when the sun hung low and glazed, and rode into a layer of smoke. No one stirred. He judged the temperature to be not much above zero. On days like this, the Mad Dogs rarely patrolled. Off in the cottonwoods some blanketed women hacked at dead limbs. He paused, studying the drifted-in lodges, each leaking smoke from its peak. He could tell a village by the lodge paintings. The Lone Eaters had a Sun Lodge, a ceremonial tepee that was not lived in. He looked among the cones for the blue lodge with yellow suns painted around its middle, and a band of fallen stars, like polka dots, at its base. He saw it far off, near the timber—the Lone Eaters . . . Marie Therese.

Joyously he plunged ahead, ignoring his numb toes and fingers, and headed for the larger lodge to pay his respects to The Heavy Runner. No one stirred; no town crier announced his presence. Visitors weren't expected in such cold. Something about the village disturbed him. The lodges looked shabby. In better times the worn, smoke-blackened tops would have been turned into fine winter moccasins that would repel water. The whiskey trade had done its work, he thought bitterly.

He scratched softly on the lodge door. It parted and a seamed face appeared.

"I'm Peter Kipp, Grandmother. I have come to see The Heavy Runner."

A moment later someone pulled the flap, and Peter stepped into a wall of warmth and redolence. This was a crowded lodge, with an elderly couple and three women, as well as The Heavy Runner, sprawled on pallets around its periphery.

"Haiya, Peter Kipp," said the chief, waving Peter in. Peter stepped around the smoky lodge fire, past the altar, and settled himself in the place of honor beside the burly chief.

"I've brought you this," Peter said, handing the traditional plug of tobacco to The Heavy Runner.

The younger women set an iron pot of something over the fire, while the children huddled shyly in their robes and stared at their unexpected guest.

Unhurriedly the chief plucked a soft pipe bag hanging from a lodgepole and extracted a long pipe with a bowl of red catlinite. Leisurely he tamped some of Peter's tobacco into it. Peter would have to wait. The preoccupation of plains Indians in midwinter was to make every diversion last as long as possible. But eventually The Heavy Runner sucked a fire into life, blew four puffs toward mother earth and four more toward the sky spirits.

"You have come without a horse to ride," the chief said.

"It was shot by Sneaking Drink Givers," Peter replied, using the Blackfoot term. "They almost shot me."

The chief frowned. "Where were they going?"

"To the Marias."

The chief frowned. "They are bad. They come here and I cannot stop my young men. And many of my old men. I can't stop myself sometimes." He smiled ruefully. "It makes us crazy."

"The white chiefs can't stop them either. They're destroying your people."

"Maybe not. Maybe Natoya-niskim will stop it. You've come to see her."

"Yes."

"She has a sun spirit. We talk many times."

"What does she say?"

He sighed. "She says that no matter how bad the napikwan are, we must not fight them because that will make things worse. She tells me things about the napikwan villages far away in the east. She says there are so many they are more than buffalo, but it's hard to imagine. There aren't many here. Still, she has been there and she is a holy one who speaks truly. I will do as she asks. For as long as I am chief, I will befriend the napikwan, though many times I have wanted to fight them. Maybe then we'll survive."

"Your thoughts are heavy, my friend. Things have changed."

The chief looked sharply at Peter. "You have some news?'"

"Only that the killing continues. The treaty made things worse."

The Heavy Runner grunted, and knocked the dottle from his pipe. "My young warriors are angry. They want to fight. At the same time, they squander their robes—and everything else—for a drink from the Sneaking Drink Givers. They're lazy and soft and don't hunt. They're rebellious and won't listen to the elders. They would make very bad warriors now."

The chief stared moodily into the fire. "If Natoyaniskim weren't here, I'd fight. We'd all fight. Bull's Head led his Kainah to the Sun River farm and burnt it. That was good, but I'd start with the Sneaking Drink Givers. I'd kill them all. I'd bash the kegs with my war ax. Why don't the napikwan chiefs do something? Are they so helpless?"

"It's out of control. Hundreds of barrels arrive on every boat for the miners. It's against the law, but the army can't stop the flood—and the miners demand it."

"The miners are drunks! We're strong and many; they're few. We could clean them out! They've violated Lame Bull's treaty. They've killed us. We want revenge!" He stared at Peter. "You've been down the Big River to the many-houses. Is it true what she says? That they are more than the buffalo?"

Peter nodded. "They are many times more. And they have—magic—metal bridges across rivers, houses on top of other houses, railroads—fire wagons on wheels, like the riverboats—and that's just the beginning."

The Heavy Runner sighed. "It's hard to believe, but it is so. She says it and you say it—and others who have been there. I would like to see it. There is no choice, is there? Whatever happens to us we must endure—and never fight back."

"Little Dog wants the Siksika to learn the ways of the napikwan. Send the children to school. Learn to plow and plant. He has tried to farm. That's a choice."

"Little Dog!" The Heavy Runner grunted. "Maybe Little Dog is right. At least the napikwan like him. He can walk around Fort Benton and not be shot. We can't even see the nannana because it isn't safe to go there. They shoot us right in front of the agency. Let me tell you, Peter Kipp, there are many Piegans who don't like Little Dog and think he has betrayed his people."

Peter shrugged. "Would you do anything different?"

It was a question The Heavy Runner couldn't or wouldn't answer. "And what is your news?" he asked. "No longer are you at the trading window talking to your Siksika friends. No longer is American Fur at Fort Benton. I hear you are a freighter with many oxen and mules and wagons."

"I am doing well."

"Taking supplies to the miners who dig for yellow metal on Blackfoot land."

Peter had no answer.

"It was better in the old days. Just a few napikwan came, and they had good things to trade. They respected us and our ways. They married our daughters. Now . . ." His voice drifted off. A sadness crept into the chief's face. "Will you be going back to Fort Benton soon?"

Peter nodded.

"I have a message to send to the nannana, Upson. Tell the agent that The Heavy Runner is a peace chief. Tell him that I'll always be a friend of the napikwan. Tell him that it's hard to keep my young men under control because they are angry—and because the Sneaking Drink Givers corrupt them. Tell him that I want the Sneaking Drink Givers stopped."

"I'll tell him that, Grandfather. And I'll tell him about my brush with them coming here."

"Will you make Upson understand I am a peace chief? The Lone Eaters are friendly to the napikwan?"

"I will say it and make sure he understands."

"Then it will be better for the Lone Eaters," the chief said. "Now you will want to see Natoya-niskim. She is awaiting you."

"Does she know I'm here?"

The chief grinned for the first time that wintry morning. "She knows. You cannot hide much in a village. Sinopah's lodge is beside the river. It is painted with running weasels—his medicine."

Peter rose and worked his way past quiet, pensive wives, sons, and daughters toward the lodge door.

"Peter Kipp," the chief said, staying him at the door flap. "Natoya-niskim is not the woman you remember."

* * *

Peter found Marie Therese in Sinopah's lodge.

"Peter! Oh, Peter!" she exclaimed, her face wreathed in surprise and joy.

"I came for a visit," he said. "Where's Sinopah? And Tears in Her Eyes?"

"Sinopah's playing the bone game with his friends. Tears in Her Eyes has gone to gossip. She does that all winter."

"We can talk English then."

"Yes, it is good for me to talk English. Oh, I am glad you came! I want to talk about so many things."

She motioned him toward the place of honor and settled herself across from him. She seemed different, and yet she was still the tall, slender woman he'd known. She had reached her middle years now, and the creases had begun to feather her face.

"You are staring at me."

"Yes. You're beautiful, Marie Therese."

She smiled wryly, her father's smile, and he realized what was different. In her middle years she'd become more like her father. Her other blood would not be denied. Now she possessed the slender, clean lines of de Paris's face, his brow and gray eyes. It astonished him. All these years she had seemed more and more Indian, and he'd thought her white blood had been submerged forever.

"Others have noticed it too, Peter. I am more and more like my napikwan father. Have you word of him for me?"

"No. He left Fort Benton four years ago. We think he returned to France. He said only one thing, something about the revolution being over and the assassins dead at last."

"It's sad that I know almost nothing about him, Peter. He told me so little—but I know that his family was very important once."

"The nobility, I guess. Marie Therese, you never came to Fort Benton. You never saw him."

"I have enemies, Peter. There are napikwan—white men—who would kill me."

Peter guessed why, but he thought he'd let her say it, if she chose.

"The whiskey traders—they haven't dared to kill me in my village. When they come, they look at me and I can see their thoughts. But they will not kill me in front of the People. My time has not come. I walk up to them and tell them to leave. But they don't. And many want them to stay so that they can drink and be crazy."

"I guess they'd be here all the time—but for you."

She smiled. "They do better in other bands. I have many here. I wish I had more Pikuni of the other villages."

"You're in danger, Marie Therese."

She nodded. "My time has not yet come, though."

"You believe that stuff."

"I know when my time will come." She said it somberly, fear in her voice. "I don't want it to come."

"Well, that's what I'm here to talk about. Marie Therese, how many years has it been? Since 'fifty-one? I've never stopped loving you. You're the only one for me. Us two—we got both bloods. We could make a good life. You're young still. We got a lot of time—"

She reached across to touch his hand, smiling. "Sometimes I think you're right, Peter. But it can't be. I'm the same as always."

"Maybe you're gonna break two hearts instead of one."

"Ah, Peter. I do love you so, but in a different way."

That felt like a knife sliding into his ribs, though she meant it to be an expression of her devotion.

"I guess you're fighting a losing battle, just like I am. I just thought a couple of mixed-bloods, we might find some corner of the world that'd be safe for people that aren't wanted much. I guess a lot of the Pikuni think you're not one of them."

"It's true."

"There's only us! Let's find a little place where we can make a little paradise."

A gust of icy wind rattled the lodge and drove smoke back upon them. Marie Therese stepped outside and adjusted the wind ears. Peter waited, noting that this lodge, too, had been stripped of most of its robes and pelts. Sinopah had no doubt traded them for whiskey. She returned carrying firewood, and added sticks to the small, bright blaze.

"Peter, I'm glad you came. I've been needing you."

"Not in the way I'd like you to need me!"

She laughed softly. "Being loved by you is beautiful."

"I can give you a future! There's no future here!"

She turned solemn instantly, pondering her words. "Each day I fight a losing battle, Peter. Soon the Siksika nation will be no more. This village is better than some. Some bands—they're almost destroyed by the whiskey. I save a few. I talk to them. They make the sacred pledge to Napi, and to Sun, never to drink, and to follow the old ways. A few lives is all! But for every one I help, twenty are lost. Oh, Peter—do you know how hard it is to fight on, with no hope? No victory? I do it, though. I have grown strong doing it."

"That's what I'm saying! I can rescue you! Give you a good life, you and me and—and our own children. Bring some children into the world and make them the future, Marie Therese."

She shook her head, a faint, sad smile illumining her face, her gray eyes knowing something that Peter didn't know. "Peter—would you help me? The time has come. I think the spirits brought you here now—for me. . . ."

Peter nodded uncertainly.

"Fight them for us! The whiskey traders and the wolfers. And all the rest too. But especially the whiskey traders. It's illegal; they can't sell whiskey to the People—but they do. Tell the sheriff or the nannana, Upson. Tell the army. The army used to stop all the boats and inspect them, remember? Tell them what's happening to the People!"

"Marie Therese, you don't know—"

"Yes I know. The sheriff's in the whiskey trade himself . . . and no one cares. But I want you to do what you can. Destroy the kegs! That's what we did—for a while. My friends—the one that follow the old ways, they destroyed many kegs. But the Sneaking Drink Givers have their own spies. They found out who was doing it and—killed some of us. Now it's very hard. We can't even get close to the whiskey—they guard it, and shoot!"

"So I found out."

"But you can help. You can tell the nannana to write letters to Washington. We need soldiers to stop it. Stop the wolfers too. They kill everything: They poison a buffalo carcass to kill our dogs, and the eagles—and even our men. They give poisoned meat to our young men and scalp them. Peter—is it true that a Blackfoot scalp is like money in Fort Benton?"

"Yes."

She didn't respond. She sat staring at him, a terrible sadness flooding her face until he could not look at her.

"I try to remember the sisters in St. Louis, and not hate white people," she said at last. "Is it true that all the white miners—all of them—want to take our land away and destroy us?"

Peter nodded.

"We have no one, Peter. This Gad Upson, he says we are degenerate savages. He is supposed to be our protector, our friend, our voice in Washington City. But we never see him, and now he's taken half our land from us for a bribe or two. We see him laughing; we hear him joking. Peter, we have no one. Only you."

Peter expelled a sudden breath. She was asking him to be the protector of her people—he, a mixed-breed.

"Do you know what you're asking, Marie Therese?"

She nodded. "You're a mixed-blood. They will say you're not to be listened to. But you're all we have."

"I'm not all you have! You can learn to farm, like Little Dog! You can stop warring! You can go to school and learn what white men know! You can give up the old ways and accept progress!" Some wild anger boiled through him.

But tears were sliding down her eyes. "Not until the last buffalo is dead will any Blackfoot man do that. It's beneath them. They can't be taught that; they'll die rather than learn those things. You know that, Peter."

"They could herd cows if they won't plow."

She laughed bitterly. "They're hunters. And *warriors*!"

He hadn't come to bring her to tears, but to propose; to offer once again a different life, a life with hope. He watched as she wept silently, the tears leaking from her gray eyes and sliding down her cheeks. Was there no hope in all the universe? He stood, edged toward the door flap, avoiding the altar and fire, and came around to her side, the women's side, and sat next to her. He drew her into his arms. She didn't resist. He held her closely, his hands gentle and respectful, conveying his love. She buried her face in his chest, and he felt the wetness of her tears pierce to his heart. He held her and she wept, and the bitter wind rattled the lodge of Sinopah.

Chapter Twenty-three

Gad Upson frowned at Peter from behind his pine desk, his cigar jabbing from his pursed lips like a gun barrel.

"I don't have much time, Kipp."

Actually, Peter knew, the Indian agent had all the time in the world, and usually consumed it with his cronies at any of the saloons along the levee. "I want to talk about something—in confidence."

Upson ran a thin hand over his bald head. "I suppose you want to be enrolled. You got a Piegan ma?"

"No, I'm half Salish. I want to talk to you about the law being broken all the time."

Upson extracted the cigar from his teeth and tapped ash to the plank floor. "Talk to Hamilton. He's the sheriff."

"Federal law."

"He's the U.S. Marshal too."

"Law involving the Indians."

"Look, Kipp, they hardly know what the law is. They can't read or write."

"I'm talking about white whiskey traders. I've been visiting . . . a friend. The traders are destroying the tribes. No one even slows them down."

"The Blackfeet are destroying themselves, Kipp. No one's forcing them to drink. All they have to do is say no."

"They are!"

Upson laughed easily. "I'll make note of your concern, Kipp."

"You could ask the army to enforce the law and stop this—this murder. That's what it is."

"It'd put Fort Benton out of business!" Upson quipped. "Including you."

"Maybe Fort Benton should go out of business!"

Upson paused, shifted his slimy cigar to the other side of his mouth. "Well, yes, a breed would say that."

"I was shot at and nearly killed by whiskey traders. They killed my horse. They had barrels of the stuff, and shot anyone who even came close, like I did. They'll peddle that rotgut to some band or another, take all their robes and pelts. The Piegans'll all get drunk and crazy and mean. They'll kill each other—that's what spirits do to them. Even the women—they get drunk and sell themselves for a cup. Mr. Upson, it's destroying them. You've got to stop it."

"How, Kipp? Wave my magic wand? Let's face it, you can't keep the booze from redskins that want it. They're gonna get it. If not from us, then from Hudson's Bay up north."

"You can try. You can ask the army to destroy the wagons and stocks."

Upson laughed. "You think anyone in the territory's gonna stand for pouring whiskey into the ground? It ain't popular. I can walk into any saloon or inn on Front Street and three quarters of the men in it are selling booze to the Blackfeet. And if they ever got word that you're trying to shut down the profits—well . . ."

They'd kill him. That's what Upson was saying. Everyone in Fort Benton except some of the Creoles from the old post was getting rich at the game.

Upson pulled a fingernail file from his desk and began honing his nails. "Look, Kipp, you're a breed, so maybe you can figure it out. They're degenerates, savages, wild as Mongols. You can't civilize that type. They'll all drink themselves into the ground sooner or later, and let's hope sooner. No one can stop 'em because they love to go crazy, get so drunk they turn into animals. That's what they are—animals.

"Remember, Kipp—they don't have to touch a drop. It's all choice. They want it bad, they trade anything—lodges, wives, skins, daughters, you name it. They'll trade it. They ain't white men, Kipp. They're gonna die out, and then we can have some progress in this territory—settle it, run in cattle, build it up. I'm here to keep the lid on the kettle."

"There's some that won't touch a drop. Some who'd break every barrel if they could. There's some that remember the old ways."

"Who? Gimme names."

"There's Natoya—" Peter stopped abruptly. Upson had a pencil in hand.

"Yeah her, the virgin bitch that never comes in here. She's the one stirring them to war. I keep hearing about her. I oughta git her. Ship her down to the Nations. I may have to send Hamilton after her. Who else?"

"Lots," Peter said sullenly, a wariness crawling through him. "You're here to uphold the law! See to their interests and defend them!"

Upson laughed. "Kipp, Kipp. You damned breed. You get outta here before you get your red ass in more trouble."

So that's how it was. Peter left the leering agent and hunted down William T. Hamilton, expatriate Briton, innkeeper, sheriff, U.S. Marshal, mountain man, braggart, and ladies' man. The Indian agent had been bad; Hamilton would probably be worse. Hamilton had made himself famous in half the saloons in the territory by reciting his motto: *Never scalp an Indian in front of a lady.*

But Peter wasn't going to let that stop him. He found the marshal in his log establishment, which doubled as a restaurant and butcher shop, waxing his luxurious mustache to catch the eye of the one or two respectable women in town who might dine at his eatery that evening.

"I want to talk to you about the Blackfeet," Peter said. "I've been to see Gad Upson."

"He don't know which end of an Indian eats."

"They're being hurt by the whiskey traders. I've just been out there. They come right into the villages now. The Blackfeet can defend themselves against a lot of things—but not whiskey traders."

"You're talking about the entire population of Fort Benton, boy."

"You're the federal marshal."

"That's what the badge says."

"Look, Hamilton, I was attacked by four of them. They shot my horse out from under me, almost killed me. They hunted through everything to see if I had a badge."

"Good thing you didn't!"

"I have good descriptions of all four. The one that did the talking, he was—"

"You're taking your life in your hands, kid."

"—He had a full beard, a skinny frame, a droopy eye, and called himself—"

"Chop-ear. Yeah, he tole me all about it. He comes askin' if you was a deppity a couple of days ago. He done real good this trip. They made twenty-seven thousand profit on a five hundred dollar investment."

"Why didn't you arrest him? Uphold the law?"

"Chop-ear? He ain't but one of about seventy, Kipp. What's a man to do?"

"Enforce the law!"

"Who says I'm not? Indian gets drunk around here, I kick him outta town. Indian shoots a white man, we hang him."

"What about white men that kill Indians?"

"You gonna find me a jury that'll convict? Hell, they'll give the man a medal. I could pinch 'em, but it's no use."

"I'll write the Commissioner of Indian Affairs."

"Ah, Kipp. You'll wreck the fun. My advice is to keep your nose clean. No one much likes a breed messing around with stuff like that. It's like you ain't for progress."

There it was again. Peter knew he'd never get used to it. It was a fact of life, and not worth getting mad about. He'd been mad often enough; now it didn't matter.

"Yeah, well, I wanted to report a crime," he said. "Against me. Your friend Chop-ear owes me a good horse."

"Sure, Kipp."

Peter retreated to the cold street of a place that he hardly recognized anymore. He knew of no one he could trust; not even the Creoles. Some of them were trading the whiskey too. The Blackfeet didn't have a friend in Fort Benton. Wearily he let himself into the old fur post and licked his wounds in the gloom of his apartment there. He wanted to help Marie Therese but didn't know how, and he knew no help would ever come from the white men of Fort Benton.

The next morning Peter walked out to his freight yard east of the old fort. Even in the slack spring season he did that to check on wagons and stock, and make sure La Rue was manning the place. A raw March wind shoved him along. When the June zephyrs arrived, so would the riverboats, and he'd be up to his eyeballs in freight contracts for the next six months.

He saw La Rue standing glumly at the big yard gate, his collar up against the gale. Something looked odd. Closer up, Peter found himself staring at a dead mule, suspended by a noose of heavy manila hawser from the gate beam. His stomach heaved. The mule dangled in the breeze, its neck broken, its mouth in a rictus. LaRue nodded, saying nothing, his expression grim.

The mule was Peter's and had been taken from within. It would have required the strength of half a dozen men to draw it up. A little warning party, then. Probably half the businessmen of Fort Benton. The symbolism didn't escape Peter either. A mule—a cross between a horse and a jackass—had been selected. A half-breed. Peter felt gorge rise and swallowed it back. It could be him swinging there.

"Da big outfits, Diamond R, dey don't like no small fry competing," said La Rue.

"Not mixed-bloods anyway," Peter muttered.

"You done something?"

"Yeah, I complained about the whiskey trade."

"Oh, dat. It ain't so different from the old days when Chouteau done it."

"It's different, Jacques. No fur trader ever wanted to clean out the tribes, kill 'em off and take the land."

La Rue shrugged. "You shouldn't a done dat."

Anger flared through Peter, but he said nothing. He stomped into the yard to find what else was amiss. It all looked vulnerable to him. Wooden freight wagons and carts waiting to be burned; livestock that could be easily driven away. A rough warehouse awaiting a torch—as soon as it was full of someone else's property. All of it a mixed-breed's business, which was the same as saying a business not protected by the sheriff. Bleakly he counted mules and oxen and horses, studied wagons for sabotage, and found nothing. Only a warning, then. He sighed, feeling the bite of March wind.

Who'd done it? Men he talked to every day, like Hubbell and Hawley, his landlords and operators of North West Fur? Broadwater? I. G. Baker? Matt Carroll or George Steell? Bill Hamilton himself? Or their wage men? It didn't matter. It'd be all over Fort Benton now, and the ones who hadn't done it were all wishing they had—enjoying the joke on the breed.

Peter slumped into his corral fence, back to the wind, knowing he could lose all this if he even filed a complaint with Sheriff Hamilton. They'd all be waiting for it, and would finish the job—and maybe him—next time around. There'd be no second chances for a mixed-breed, not in this new world. In the old fur-trading days a mixed-breed could rise as far as his abilities would take him, valued precisely because his blood helped the commerce between traders and Indians. But now . . . Peter was coming to a decision. He'd be a white man; more white than any of his tormentors.

By late May four riverboats had clawed up the Missouri and unloaded over eight hundred tons of merchandise on the levee at Fort Benton. The *St. John, Deer Lodge, Cora,* and *Waverly* were the first in, but they brought word that an incredible fifty boats were bound for the High Missouri that summer with cargoes for the ravenous mining camps. Mountains of dunnage choked the Fort Benton levee, and Peter's little freight outfit was offered more work than it could handle. Day by day he saw his Creole teamsters off to Helena, Virginia City, and other burgeoning camps, and saw them return bearing heavily armed miners, gold, pelts, and luggage, all heading back to the States. Even at thirteen cents a pound, the competitive rate, Peter was coining money.

Almost overnight Fort Benton had exploded into a wild river town, where armed miners carrying tens of thousands of dollars of nuggets and dust sopped up whiskey alongside thugs, footpads, tarts, informants, sharpers, gamblers, wolfers, and whiskey runners. Several hundred barrels of booze rolled in on the boats, with thousands more en route, turning Fort Benton into an open-air saloon where any sly loafer could set up a plank on stumps and pour joy juice for the parched mobs. Savvy freight outfits entrusted the barrels to teetotaling Mormon teamsters to keep the "leakage" under control.

Peter paid his faithful Creoles well, posted them day and night at his yard with fowling pieces, and avoided trouble. He loved the business as well as any white man, and began planning a brick home back from the levee—whenever he could capture some masons and carpenters more interested in their trades than in easy wealth.

He'd learned his lesson in March. From that day on he'd quietly let it be known he was all for progress; for containing the pesky Blackfeet; for opening up the country. He'd said it in the saloons before the mocking eye of white men, and he'd come to believe it too. He always had believed it, ever since he'd seen St. Louis. It was only when he encountered Marie Therese that any doubts assailed him. He'd be a white man—as much as white men let him be one of themselves.

By the time the mobs of May had exploded on Fort Benton, he'd simply forgotten the Blackfeet. Few came to town except Little Dog now and then; none visited their nannana at Council House, the agency building on Front Street. Those who did slip in came to the rear doors of saloons to make an exchange of some sort: something, anything, for a cup of watered rotgut. And then they slid away, quiet, invisible, and drunk. Peter rarely even saw them, but his teamsters did. The Piegans watched the rolling wagons go by, stood around Sun River Crossing sullenly studying the armed freighters, waiting for their chances. Teamsters who didn't stick with their outfit vanished.

Peter lost two of his Creoles and grieved. Jean Gallant and Hector Briand had gone on a binge in Helena, only to be murdered and scalped by miners who thought the Creoles were redskins, and taking black-haired scalps was doing the world a favor. Somberly his Creoles continued with him, wary, careful, and making top dollar. Big dark Frenchmen, often quarter-bloods, weren't popular in the camps, or in Benton either, and it didn't matter that many of the Creoles had grown up in that country and knew it better than the parvenus ever would.

One morning after he'd come to an agreement with I. G. Baker to haul flour, coffee beans, and tins of tomatoes to Confederate Gulch, he discovered Little Dog and some Piegans leading a dozen horses toward the Blackfoot agency. Little Dog's flashy son, The Fringe, had several in tow.

"Ah! Kipp! It is good to see a face I know!" the chief said.

"What're you doing here?"

"These are horses the Pikuni have stolen. I am a friend of the white man and I'm returning them. That was the agreement, yes?"

"You're bringing in horses?" It amazed Peter.

"I made my mark on the treaty. I will keep my word." Little Dog's dignity somehow affected Peter deeply. Alone among his people, he tried to befriend whites and keep the peace. He, more than any other chief, had an inkling of the future.

"Well, Upson's gone down the river. But they got an acting agent named Upham."

"Very well, I'll take the horses to him."

A crowd of spectators, many of whom had scarcely seen an Indian, crowded around the Piegans, openly deriding them.

But Little Dog, now the head chief of the Piegans, ignored them. "Peterkipp, when will the annuities come? My people are very eager for them, and we have no word."

"Well, ah, I hear that treaty was never ratified. I mean, Little Dog, the Senate—the headmen back in Washington—they have to approve it; it ain't a treaty yet until they say so."

Little Dog stared at Peter, disbelieving. "You say that no annuities come up the river?"

Peter shrugged helplessly. "It's not a treaty yet."

"But we gave white men the land. I put my mark on the paper."

"It's still your land, Little Dog. Blackfeet still got all the land down to the Musselshell."

Little Dog stared around him, noting the mobs. "You may say so," he said slowly, "but I think not. We have gotten nothing for it."

Peter felt acute embarrassment, while Little Dog translated to the Piegans.

"I will keep the honor of the Pikuni," Little Dog said slowly, heading for the agency with the stolen horses.

Peter felt bad again; he did whenever he was reminded of what the bustling white world and its commerce were doing to the Blackfeet—and Marie Therese.

That turned out to be the last time Peter laid eyes on Little Dog, the one chief who had tried to befriend whites. That very evening word came in from woodcutters up on the Teton. Little Dog had been murdered by his own Piegans three miles north of Fort Benton. The Piegans, sullen about not getting annuities, had bought whiskey before leaving town, gotten drunk, started a brawl with Little Dog and The Fringe, and ended stabbing and shooting the head chief and his son. A great man had died because he kept to his word and tried to make peace with the unpeaceful white men.

Peter listened somberly, and wondered if the Blackfoot war that had been on everyone's mind for years had begun.

Chapter Twenty-four

1868

Natoya-niskim could barely make herself look at the spectacle before her, but she forced herself to. There, in the cold light of dawn, dangled three bodies from a simple scaffold. She knew each one, though not well. They were from Mountain Chief's band. A note had been pinned to one: *This is a good Indian.*

They had been here many days; long enough for her to hear of the horror. The news had raced from band to band, inflaming the warriors, angering chiefs. This hadn't been the first of such murders, but it had hurt the most. These had been murdered in front of the Council House, not for any deed they had done, but because the Crow Indians had killed two sheepherders. These three were decomposing now, and soon the white men would cut them down and throw them into the Missouri.

Fort Benton lay quiet in the dawn light. She had chosen this hour because it was safest. Few Blackfeet ventured to Fort Benton now because it was no longer safe, especially when the shipping season started in May, and mobs of white men disembarked from the riverboats. But this was April. She didn't recognize anything about the place except the old fort where her father had traded for so many years. Peter lived somewhere here, but she didn't know where.

It was true, then. More Piegans had been murdered, and from Mountain Chief's band too. The powerful old chief hated white men; now he would hate them more. Upon the death of Little Dog, Mountain Chief had become head chief of the Piegans, and things had changed. Like the others, he had stopped short of war, but he had quietly approved when his young men gathered into war parties and struck here and there, harassing traffic on the Helena Road, roaming far to the south to raid white travelers on the Bozeman Trail. But as much as Mountain Chief hated the whites, he was dependent on them for weapons, powder and lead, knives, and all the rest, and those realities had checked his instinct to begin an all-out war to drive white men away forever.

She drew her blanket tight against the morning chill and padded down Front Street, looking for the Council House, the Blackfoot agency where she would find George Wright, the new agent. She'd heard good things about Wright. Maybe this one would be better than the corrupt Indian-haters that had come and gone, year after year. Maybe this one hated the whiskey traders . . . maybe this one cared.

She found the log place easily enough and knocked, wondering if anyone would be up at this hour. She was admitted at once by a half-blood clerk. He addressed her in the Siksika tongue, saying, "I'll get the nannana."

Moments later she found herself in the agent's office, before a jut-jawed, balding, kind-eyed white man. The clerk stood beside him to translate.

"What may I do for you, daughter?" Wright asked.

"I am not your daughter," she replied in English.

The agent was surprised. "You can speak English? We won't need a translator then," he said. He nodded to the half-blood, who withdrew. "Now then, who are you and what may I do for you?"

"I am—Sacred Buffalo Stone, of The Heavy Runner's people, a Piegan."

He stared at her. "You're more than a Piegan."

"My father was a trader for American Fur."

Wright nodded. "Then you're the one we've heard about for so long but have never seen. You're Peter Kipp's friend,

Marie Therese de Paris. Let's see. The reports of my predecessors say that a mysterious breed woman, who never comes to Fort Benton, encourages the Piegans to live according to their traditions, to avoid spirits, and to avoid war with white men. The whiskey traders complain about you."

Natoya-niskim said nothing.

"This is most fortunate," Wright said. "We've much to talk about."

"The whiskey traders are killing the People," she said. "Hundreds have died—some from drinking too much, some from poisoning. Many from fights, because spirits make our people crazy. Are you going to stop it?"

"I've good news for you, Marie Therese. We're stopping it. We've had several arrested, and they'll be tried shortly. And we will be licensing only two traders for the Blackfeet—Northwest Fur, and I. G. Baker and Company. All the rest will be illegal, giving us a basis to prosecute—"

"They will come anyway. They always do."

Wright paused. She liked the look in his face. "Since the Civil War ended, we've been able to get a few troops here. The ones at Fort Shaw are all needed to patrol the Helena-Benton Road against—your Piegans. But the Thirteenth Infantry up at Camp Cooke . . . I think you can count on some help."

"If your seizers—army—would stop the whiskey traders first, they wouldn't need to patrol the road."

Wright shrugged amiably. "You're right, of course. But the army bends to the clamor of citizens. They want the road patrolled."

She loosened her blanket in the warmth of the room, letting her long hair fall loose. "I have come because the People want justice. What are the white men going to do about the murders of three innocent Blackfoot men? It's a test with us. If you arrest them, we'll know that you are just, and we will have hope. If you don't—no one can hold the young men back."

Wright sighed, running a hand over his bald head. "Miss de Paris, I've consulted with the U.S. Marshal. He says yes, we could arrest the murderers. They're right here in Benton and known to us. But it'd be an exercise in futility. No white jury would convict them."

"Then there'll be war."

"Miss de Paris, I don't know how to make miracles. There're two classes of people here—those who think every Indian should be exterminated, and those who think they should be Christianized and penned up. The latter view—which I partly share—is held by only a handful. There's not a white man in the Far West who thinks the Indians should stay the same. Does any miner in Montana object to what the whiskey traders are doing? Does any newspaper editor object? No, Miss de Paris. They applaud. I could show you the newspapers—"

"I know what they say. I will go to my people now and tell them that white men will not punish the murder of Indians."

She turned to leave, but he stayed her with a wave of his hand.

"Wait! Your trip here is a godsend for me. I've messages of hope to send to your people."

"I have no hope."

He motioned her to the wooden chair, and she sat reluctantly.

"First, I want you to tell your people that we're doing something about the whiskey trade. Our U.S. Marshal, William Wheeler, is working on it. I am also. Second, I want you to tell them that we're going to have a new treaty. Tell The Heavy Runner. And get the news to Mountain Chief."

She laughed.

"I know, I know," he said. "You could help peace along by explaining something. The Senate didn't ratify the 1865 treaty, so those annuities were never sent. It wasn't a matter of white men lying; it was misunderstanding. Tell them that a treaty isn't effective until the Senate—a body of elders, you might say—approves it. Only then will the annuities come. Would you explain that?"

"I already have. Mountain Chief knows it. What good does it do to tell them? They say if there was no treaty, then Lame Bull's treaty of 1855 is still in effect. The Siksika possess all the land down to the Musselshell; all the land where the mining camps are—that's still our land; the gold is our wealth; this house is on our land. If there was no treaty, Indian agent Wright, make them all go away from our land! That is what your law requires!"

"There's law—and there's reality," he muttered. "There are things no man can help. I sincerely wish I could."

This man was fair, and he cared about the Blackfeet. She wished she could like this man and forgive him, but she couldn't. "I will go now," she said.

"Wait. Cullen—he's the new commissioner in Washington—he wants a new treaty. Wants me to call in the chiefs for a council late in August. Cullen wants the 1865 treaty provisions—your people would cede land south of the Teton, and we'd offer larger annuities."

"Here?"

He nodded.

"Sir, no Siksika would come to Fort Benton now."

He nodded. "Where would they like to meet us?"

"Not here. The Teton River maybe. A few miles from here."

"Tell them to gather on the Teton above here in August, then. Maybe it'll make peace. The new boundary'll be north of here, north of the Helena Road."

"Not as long as the agency is here."

"I've been making plans to move it to the upper Teton River next year—seventy-five miles from here. Your nannana—whoever it may be—will be close to you. And you'll be safe."

"Until the white men want our lands again."

"I don't think that'll happen," he said quietly.

"I have seen it. The cattlemen will come next."

"Your visions of White Buffalo Cow are well known, Miss de Paris."

"Natoya-niskim," she said, rising.

She stepped into the cold sun. Fort Benton hunkered hard and mean along the river, as naked of trees and mercy as the bottom of Hell. She would have hastened away but for

Peter. No Siksika came here now except on agency business. Its merchants still did a great robe trade with the Indians, but not in town: They sent trading wagons out to the villages these days. The old trading room at the fort had become a store for the napikwan.

Warily she walked eastward along the levee toward the old fort where Peter lived. Men were up and about now, opening their stores. Even some saloons had opened. She saw no women and doubted there were any in this ugly line of shacks on the riverfront.

A pair of yawning men approached her, and she angled toward the river to give them a wide berth. These two wore huge beards and slouch hats, flannel shirts and jeans, black high-top boots. She drew her red blanket tighter.

"Hey, lookee here. A squaw!" said one.

"A dusky Injun!" said the other, steering toward her.

"Hey, missy, ain't you pretty! You want a little lovin'?"

She ignored them, wishing she didn't know English.

"Damn murdering Blackfeet. She's probably got her a butcher knife under that blanket."

"She got more'n that! She's plumb pretty. I never did see no dusky squaw the like of her."

They paced beside her now, grinning.

"What do ya think she'll charge?"

"Cuppa booze maybe. Maybe nothing. They like it."

She walked determinedly toward the old post. But then the taller one blocked her path, grinning. She veered, but he sidestepped. She whirled, but the other one blocked her. She pushed through, only to feel a hard hand clamping her arm.

"Hey! You! We're gonna have us some fun!"

She wanted to say something. Instead she shook her head.

"I guess it's too early in the mawning for her, Abel."

"Aw, it ain't. Squaws do it morning, noon, and night."

"Behind Thwing House there's a little shack."

"Yeah, we don't wanna rile up them storekeepers."

"Rile 'em up! They'd stand around and cheer!"

"Come on, you red slut." The shorter one steered her across the street toward a gap between the buildings.

She fought hard now, twisting, tugging. Her blanket fell away.

"Hey, slut—you wanna hang like them others down there?"

From the porches of the stores others watched, doing nothing. Six or eight men stared, amusement creasing their faces. She cried out.

"Whatcha got, a little Blackfoot hellcat?" one shouted.

"She's ripe for some funnin'. Hey, bring me a cup. I'll dose her. She just needs dosing."

The one in front of the saloon laughed and disappeared.

"She shore is pretty for a redskin. Tallest one I ever seen," said a blacksmith. "You git done with her, you send her over to me and I'll nail shoes on 'er."

More hands held her arms, while others probed familiarly about her person. She stopped struggling and stood stock-still, sensing they enjoyed the struggle.

"She's got her some gray eyes. You ever seen that in a savage, Jake?"

"Nope, I never. Look at that face. She's got her a dusky angel face. She'd be one to play with."

The aproned barkeep emerged carrying a tin cup. He carried it to the gathering crowd.

"Ah, Charley, that'll grease the chute!"

"Here, little squaw bitch, you drinkee!"

She shook her head.

"We gotta pour this down ya."

She trembled. She'd never touched a drop. She'd kept her virginity all these years. Fear rose in her, and along with it tears.

"Aw, lookit her! Get that hooch into her, Charley, and she'll sing a different tune. Red sluts love it, but you gotta grease 'em up first."

"Would you speak to white women that way?" she said in English.

They stared, amazed.

"Well, I'll be damned. She speaks English. She musta been some old camp slut somewhere."

"Would you say that about your mothers and sisters?"

"Nope, they ain't red!"

The gentlemen laughed.

"Where'd you git the English, eh? Lyin' with miners?"

"I grew up in St. Louis."

"You mean, some old miner tole you about a big white man's city with lots of houses one night when you was lovin' him up."

"I was educated there by nuns. Many mountain children were."

"This here's an English-speakin' red slut. I never seen the like," said Charley. "Here—drink up!"

"I don't drink."

"All red niggers drink!"

"Pry her jaws open, Charley. We got to dose her."

"Please let me go. I just want to go."

"Let you go! Why, you just got here!"

"I came to see the agent. I'll go now."

"Oh, you'll go all right. We got just the place to go to," said Abel.

She hated herself for weeping, but the tears slid down her cheeks. "Let me go," she whispered.

Charley grabbed her jaw and drew it forward. His grip was harder than iron. He lifted the cup and poured. She gasped, spit, and jerked her head free. They laughed.

"You gotta do better than that, Charley. Here, I'll hold the hellcat's head."

"What's going on here?" A thin, hard man pushed through. He wore a star.

"Jist having some fun, Marshal."

A lawman. "They're raping me," she cried.

The crowd laughed.

"Ain't no such thing as raping a squaw, Marshal."

"Who are you, miss?"

"Natoya-niskim."

"How do you know English?"

"My father was a trader at the fort."

"Let her go," said the marshal. "Fun's over."

"Aw, Marshal, she's just some ol' red slut."

"You heard me." He turned to her. "You'd better get

out. I'm the U.S. Marshal here, William Wheeler. You came to see Wright, I take it?"

She nodded.

"Well, these boys have lost a lot of their friends to your Blackfeet warriors, and it's not healthy for you to be here."

"I would like to see a friend. . . ."

"Who's that?"

"Peter Kipp."

He nodded, and turned to the others. "You hurt her and you'll answer to me for it."

The mob drifted apart, and she plucked her blanket from the manure-laden street.

"It'd be safer if you dressed like a white woman," he said.

She knew she should thank him, but she couldn't. A loathing for all whites boiled through her. She nodded, brushed away tears.

"You probably have another name," he said.

"Marie Therese de Paris."

"I thought so. You get some white woman's duds on, and you won't have trouble."

She fled toward the old fort where she'd spent some of her childhood. She remembered that Peter lived in her father's old apartment. She hastened across the familiar yard, feeling safety under her feet, and banged on the door, hoping he was there. She didn't know where his freight yard was.

He opened to her. "Marie Therese!"

"Oh, Peter!" she cried, and swept into his arms. She felt him enfold her while she wept. She couldn't stop. She sobbed into his shirt and clung to him as if he were life itself.

"Marie Therese—what happened?"

She couldn't say. She hugged him and wept, her sobs convulsing her.

"I think I know," he said darkly.

Chapter Twenty-five

1869

In the Moon of Ripe Berries, Natoya-niskim walked to her retreat on the Two Medicine River and began the four-day fast that she hoped would bring her a new vision from White Buffalo Cow. She dreaded the knowing. On each occasion of a visit, she had reported the vision as exactly as she could to the elders of the Lone Eaters, and they in turn had spread the story to the other bands.

Some Siksika scoffed and said these were the false imaginings of a half-blood. Others, young warriors especially, hated her visions and ignored them: They itched to fight the napikwan, win war honors, and restore the glory of the Siksika people. She knew she had divided the Siksika, and she knew that her visions had kept the chiefs from uniting and waging full-scale war against the invading white men. Her friend Little Dog had been murdered because he had heeded her visions. Oh, how it tormented her that she should be the cause of such division and hatred among her people. And yet she knew she was only a vessel; she revealed the messages of her spirit helper—messages intended for all the Pikuni, Kainah, and Siksika.

All the rest she had done with her life counted for little. She had explained the white men to them, drawing from her years in St. Louis. She'd offered her counsel about whites and their purposes each time her people were called to make a treaty. She'd fought the whiskey traders at the risk of her life. She'd met the Blackfoot agents at Fort Benton and laid the grievances of her people before them. She'd found a few allies among the young men, and these had tried to halt the whiskey trade, stop the drunken brawls that impoverished the People, and to foster the old ways. To do all these things, she'd set aside her own life and lived wholly for the Blackfoot Federation. But that counted for little among the People, and many thought she was simply a half-blooded meddler. Only the great visions she brought them from White Buffalo Cow gave her a voice among the Siksika.

Now, in the familiar cottonwooded flat, she fasted and waited, begging the mercy of Sun, Old Man, and all the Above Ones. On the fourth night, when she had grown so weak she could barely stand, White Buffalo Cow came to her once again. But Natoya-niskim was horrified by the sight before her. Her spirit helper gouted blood from bullet wounds; her head was lowered and her eyes dulled.

Natoya-niskim, I can no longer carry you. This time you must walk beside me. I will show you all things. This is my last visit, and you must take heed and tell the People at once.

Then, White Buffalo Cow led her up the Wolf Trail to the stars, and let her look down upon what was to come. She saw war: Angry young men from all the bands were striking the napikwan everywhere, stealing hundreds of good horses, burning wagons, taking scalps of men and women, killing babies. She saw the warriors return to the band of old Mountain Chief, head of all the Pikuni, there to count coups and receive war honors. The stolen horses they could trade to the Sneaking Drink Givers—it was easier to steal horses and trade them than to kill buffalo and tan the robes. And more satisfying too. At last the Siksika were getting even for all the shame and humiliation, for all the lies and perfidy of the whites.

Slowly White Buffalo Cow lumbered across the darkness until they peered down upon Fort Benton. And there

Natoya-niskim saw white men killing Siksika just because the Indians were there to be killed. Then White Buffalo Cow showed her Helena, where white men were holding meetings and demanding war. Then her spirit guide showed her Fort Ellis, near Bozeman City, and Natoya-niskim beheld three columns of bluecoated cavalry riding north toward Fort Shaw. And from there cavalry and mounted infantry rode out in the middle of the Moon When the Buffalo Calves are Black, through brutal cold, their breaths steaming.

Then White Buffalo Cow showed her a tragic thing: the villages of the Siksika bound by snow and cold, while within the lodges men, women, and children died of white-scabs disease, the white men's smallpox, once again. One by one they died, until a quarter of the people were swept away, just as in the past. But that was not the end. She saw the bluecoats creep up on a stricken village one dawn and then attack it while it still slept, killing almost everyone, burning it, and driving the few survivors into the bitter cold, homeless. The dead were old men, women, and children; the able-bodied men were all out hunting because the stricken village was starving. She saw them ride back with fresh buffalo meat—only to discover their wives and children shot, their lodges burnt.

And then White Buffalo Cow died. After that Natoya-niskim saw only darkness.

Natoya-niskim wept.

When dawn came she rose, giddy from her long fast, and fed herself with sarvisberries. It was a bright summer day, but without light or warmth. She sat numbly, knowing that this vision, more intense and terrible than any she'd known, dealt with the immediate future. For the Blackfeet, the hour had come.

Her Lone Eaters were summering far to the west, high up in the Backbone on Two Medicine Lake, where they were cutting fresh lodgepoles and hunting elk. She wondered whether to go there. From the beginning her office had been to reveal the visions given her by White Buffalo Cow. Nothing else mattered, not even her efforts to pluck a few from the Sneaking Drink Givers and inspire them to follow the old ways. All the Siksika knew that the visions of the Dreaming Woman were important.

She gathered her strength that day, sipping broth, boiling roots, praying to Sun and Old Man for strength. In the morning she would begin a long journey. The vision must be told to the elders and chiefs without delay. She dreaded going to Mountain Chief with her vision. He hated white men, gathered the young men to his camp and encouraged their raiding. Were it not for her visions, Mountain Chief would have unified the Siksika and started a great war to the death. He loathed her and her messages even more than he despised white men.

Still, she would do what she had to. His camp was on the Teton, close to the new Blackfoot agency. The head chief liked to harass the new agent, army lieutenant W. A. Pease, about the lack of annuities and the thousand, thousand white men's lies. His camp was also close to the roads of the white men, where the angry young men could steal horses and take scalps. The next morning she struck southward toward the Teton, dreading to enter the camp of the head chief and describe her vision to those angry men. She dreaded especially the abuse she'd receive from Owl Child, a caldron of hatred and brutality who had murdered both Siksika and white men and had threatened to murder her.

She walked numbly through two days, and found Mountain Chief's camp the following evening, greatly swollen with all the war makers of the Siksika nation. Even as she approached, an angry phalanx of wolves, or camp guards, surrounded her as if she were a prisoner and escorted her into the seething place.

As she approached Mountain Chief's huge lodge, she discovered a council in progress. There, in a circle, were the war chiefs of her people, and the most chilling of warriors, including Owl Child, Star, Crow Top, Bear Chief, Under Bull, Red Horn, White Man's Dog, Bull's Head, and Black Weasel. She approached through twilight and stood quietly among the throngs of Siksika.

They were talking of war to avenge white men's murders. Natoya-niskim listened quietly, eventually learning that at Fort Benton a few days earlier, white men had caught and executed four Pikuni who had gone there to trade. All were from Mountain Chief's band, including the chief's own brother. She knew the others, too: Heavy Charging in the Brush, Bear Child, Rock Old Man. This had been done, it was said, to avenge the deaths of two white cattle herders. But, as everyone in the council knew, no Siksika had killed any herders.

A great heaviness filled her; so heavy she could barely stand up. The thing she had been shown by White Buffalo Cow had happened even as she had seen in her vision; death would follow swiftly.

She listened to the language of war. She heard the bitterness of her people, their hatred of the napikwan, their shame and frustration because the Sneaking Drink Givers corrupted young and old and impoverished the whole nation. She heard the music of death, and the song turned her soul brittle and sere.

"The Dreamer observes us," said Mountain Chief. He had seen her all along, standing in the evening shadows. "You have come to tell us something. Have you a new vision from White Buffalo Cow to share with the Pikuni?"

"Yes."

"We will all listen now. I will listen, though your visions are false. They please only the fat soft chiefs who are afraid of napikwan. I have never been afraid."

The headmen in the circle eyed her coldly, the war lust painting their faces.

"What can a half-napikwan woman tell us?" asked Red Horn. "She doesn't belong here, and we shouldn't listen."

"Maybe she should die for leading the Blackfoot nation astray," said Owl Child. "Let us not listen to one who divides the People. I will tell her what I will do: I will spill her guts upon the earth, and slice off her ears and cut out her tongue if she speaks lies to us again."

Dread filled her. "My life doesn't matter. I must tell

you. I am here to tell you what my spirit helper wishes the Siksika to know about the future."

"Speak," said Mountain Chief. "And after that I will decide what to do with you."

The medicine dreamer was careful not to step into the circle of the elders and war chiefs. She stood near Mountain Chief and addressed them quietly.

"I will tell you what White Buffalo Cow showed me, and then I will leave," she said. "I want only to pass on to you what I have received."

Mountain Chief hated her so much, he could barely stand to be near her. His impulse was to leap at her and strangle her and put a stop to the destruction of the Siksika. For more winters than he could remember, she had been thwarting his plans to rid the Siksika nation of the napikwan.

He listened dourly as she described the mortally wounded white buffalo cow showing her the very murders at Fort Benton that this gathering of war leaders intended to revenge.

"I saw also the murder of a napikwan rancher, Four Bears, and after that a great clamor of the napikwan in their cities. I was taken to Fort Ellis, and there I beheld columns of horse soldiers riding away in the winter. They were riding to Fort Shaw, and preparing to strike the Siksika people . . ."

Mountain Chief listened attentively. If there was any truth in this, at last there'd be war. He wanted it. His warriors had more many-shoots guns than the bluecoats; he could drive them from the country. How he despised the napikwan, with their fish-belly flesh and their lies! Only last summer he and his son had gone to many-houses, Fort Benton, to complain to the nannana about napikwan living upon treaty lands of the Siksika—and there on the streets the loafers had spit on them, called them savages and threatened to murder them. The insult still burned in the breast of Mountain Chief. He would avenge it—he would burn many-houses to the ground.

"White Buffalo Cow took me to a winter camp of the

people. It was very cold; the people were starving. The young men no longer hunted the buffalo because they loved to steal horses from the napikwan and trade them for whiskey from the Sneaking Drink Givers. I saw the white-scabs disease upon the Siksika people, and I heard the groaning of the sick—men, women, children, groaning and dying in the lodges, just as before. I saw the spirits of the people who died of white scabs walking up the Wolf Trail, and they numbered a quarter of all the Pikuni."

This struck terror in the breast of Mountain Chief. Twice had the white men's smallpox swept through the Siksika, carrying off a third. But maybe Natoya-niskim was lying; maybe this vision was like all the rest, from the Under-Earth Spirits rather than Sun or Napi, or the Above Ones.

"Then I was shown the same scene that I received eighteen winters ago when I was given my first vision. I saw the seizers spring upon a Pikuni winter village at dawn. It was very cold, and the snow was thick. They shot into the lodges and killed everyone, mostly women and children and old men. They killed those who were sick with white-scabs disease." She paused. "And then White Buffalo Cow, pouring blood from many wounds, died. After that I saw only darkness."

There it was again, the terrible vision this half-napikwan woman had presented to them so long ago; the vision that had turned some of the chiefs, like Little Dog, into peace chiefs and advocates of good relations with the napikwan. How he despised them! This very thing had kept the Siksika from uniting and driving away the napikwan when they were few and vulnerable. Now they were many, and the task would be much harder—especially because the nation wasn't united. Not even the lies and insults of the white men, the cheaters, the Sneaking Drink Givers, could move The Heavy Runner or Big Lake to war!

"I will go now," she said. "I have told the people what I saw."

"Not yet," said Mountain Chief. "How did you receive this vision—if it is a vision?"

"After four days of fasting, on the Two Medicine River."

"It is a false vision that keeps the Pikuni from defending themselves. You are half napikwan, and a stranger in our midst. Because of you, the Siksika people are driven like dogs to their own doom." He turned to the council. "I, Mountain Chief, will tell you to ignore these bad words. It is time to strike the white men, steal their horses, take scalps, avenge ourselves."

Natoya-niskim remained silent, standing gravely in the thickening darkness.

"I despise them. They are killing our buffalo and taking our land. I am an old man, too old to fight, or I would lead you myself. But I know the napikwan. They are cowards. If any young men want to raid them, they go to war with the blessing of Mountain Chief."

The medicine-vision woman turned to leave. But Owl Child sprang up and caught her arm. Hatred burned hot in this young warrior, and the murder lust filled him. He was so violent toward the napikwan and any Siksika who opposed war, that he had been banished from other bands. Only Mountain Chief would tolerate him.

"I am going," she cried.

But he dragged her into the center of the circle, close to the council fire, where all eyes would see what was to happen. He unsheathed his belt knife, yanked her toward him and pressed the keen edge to her throat.

Mountain Chief was sure Owl Child was going to murder Natoya-niskim before the very eyes of the elders.

"You have divided the Siksika!" Owl Child snarled. "You must die. You are half napikwan!"

Natoya-niskim stopped struggling and froze, her eyes revealing her terror. It pleased Mountain Chief to see terror in the eyes of the false prophet.

Something cruel and insatiable filled the face of Owl Child; a joy in killing. "One who kills the Siksika nation must die, slowly. Now I will kill you bit by bit and send your pieces back to The Heavy Runner!"

He slid his glinting knife across her throat, leaving a

hairline cut that oozed blood. She stood silently, tears sliding down her cheeks.

That galvanized Mountain Chief. "Stop," he barked. He didn't care about the false-vision woman, but he cared about the other chiefs. If he let this happen in his village—it would tear the Siksika people to bits.

Owl Child whirled and sprang at the chief, knife in hand. But Red Horn tripped him, and Owl Child tumbled to the earth.

Mountain Chief watched Owl Child warily, as one watches a great cat lashing its tail. But Owl Child sat on the grass, exuding a heat and menace that touched all those in the council circle.

"No vision giver will die in my village. It is bad for the People, bad for this village. He who kills her must die."

Slowly, defiantly, Owl Child slid the knife back into its belt sheath and stood, looking no less deadly.

"Go!" he said to Natoya-niskim. "No more false visions. You are divided by two bloods, and untrue to the People. You should be exiled. You belong with the napikwan, not with us. If I hear of you giving us one more vision, I will see your death. I am the head chief of the Pikuni, and I will make sure you never weaken the Siksika again."

She stood, tear-streaked, her throat still oozing blood. "There will be no more visions, Grandfather," she said. "I have received the last one, and have done all that was given for me to do. Now I must wait—for what is to come."

With that she left the council circle and fled into the night. He heard the soft footsteps of her mare, and then she was gone.

Mountain Chief stared at the war chiefs and warriors in the circle, who were all locked into their private thoughts. Some of them, he knew, were appalled at the treatment of the beautiful, strong woman who had surrendered her entire life to the well-being of the Siksika people. She had fought the Sneaking Drink Givers, counseled the headmen about the ways of the napikwan, shared the visions accorded to her—and asked utterly nothing in return, not even esteem or honor.

Fear seized Mountain Chief. What if all her visions were true? If so, then he had offended the Above Ones and sealed his own doom, and the death of his nation.

Part Four
WINTER

Chapter Twenty-six

Peter Kipp often wondered these days whether his freighting business would survive. Competition from the big outfits, like the Diamond R and Kirkendall, had driven the price down to two cents a pound for the Helena Run. His small company took a loss on every pound it delivered at that rate. But he hung on stubbornly. There were always some good months when the boats unloaded mountains of dunnage on the levee, and Helena or Virginia City merchants wanted goods fast. He kept on, carrying small loads to odd places, cutting back his Creole teamsters, and often driving a wagon himself to save wages.

He had a good load this time; eight wagons filled with hotel furniture for The Miner, a fancy hostelry rising in Helena. The dry August weather held, and the road was hard. Cavalry from Fort Shaw patrolled it, and travel was relatively safe even though the post was undermanned. He and his Creoles passed Sun River and continued on up the Missouri, turning off at Prickly Pear Creek and the road to Helena. At the confluence of Wolf Creek, a squad of cavalrymen stopped the freighters.

"Trouble ahead, gents," said a sergeant. "Them Blackfeet are at it again. Raidin' and horse-stealin' everywhere. There's a bunch, maybe twenty-five or so, murdered Malcolm Clarke and injured his boy Horace last night."

"Malcolm Clarke!" Peter exclaimed.

"The same."

Peter couldn't believe it. The chief factor at Fort Benton had left the fur trade and settled on Wolf Creek, a stage stop on the road to Helena. He had been married for years to Kakokima, Cutting Off Head Woman, and had several half-Blackfoot children. The Blackfeet called him Four Bears, and he had been a friend to them all through all his trading years at Fort Benton. Around Helena they considered him one of the great pioneers and settlers of the territory. Dead! Killed by Blackfeet!

"He was my friend. We'll go there to hclp."

"Naw, army's not letting anyone in. You jist stay on the road and keep your rifles to hand."

"But—" Peter objected. He knew they wouldn't let him see his friends. "You know who did it?"

"Yeah, the chillun, they recognized that outfit. From Mountain Chief's bunch. Son of Mountain Chief was the one shot Horace. Owl Child, meanest buck Injun around, he kilt Clarke. Bunch more. Lieutenant's gitting the story. Clarke's kids, they're saying Star and Crow Top was in on it."

Peter was mystified. "You got any notion why?"

"Owl Child, he was revenging himself for something. Kind of a family affair, since he was the wife's cousin. Owl Child, he got crosswise of old Clarke somehow last time he visited."

"Will the boy live?"

"Yeah, I guess. That's what they say. Kipp, we'll escort you a piece. Maybe five miles or so. You can make a run to Helena from there."

Somberly Peter started his jerkline outfit toward Helena, twenty-five miles distant, while his teamsters cracked the whips behind him. Beside and behind them ten mounted infantry walked their horses. Peter was grateful for the protection.

In spite of the army patrols, this had been a bad year, Peter thought. The Blackfeet had stolen about a thousand horses and mules, and scores of people had been murdered and scalped, mostly by Mountain Chief's young rebels, but also by other bands of angry Bloods.

The freighters pulled into the mountain-girded mining camp the next day without further trouble, and whipped their mules up Last Chance Gulch toward The Miner, rising close to the Chinese quarter. The placer miners, with their gold pans, had departed for newer strikes, but hard-rock miners were extracting gold, silver, and lead from shafts in the area. The place seemed frantic compared to the bucolic calm of Fort Benton.

And afire with outrage.

"You come past Clarke's?" a miner in brogans shouted.

Peter nodded.

"You see savages?"

"No, we had an escort."

"Only thing to do with them Blackfeet is wipe 'em off the face of the earth so decent people can live!"

"Time to git up the militia! A few companies'd clean 'em out forever!" exclaimed another.

Peter unloaded mattresses, bedsteads, stuffed chairs, armoires, vanities, dining tables, dining chairs, wash stands, chamber pots, and brass hardware that afternoon. Then he headed for mercantiles and saloons, looking for return freight for Benton. Sometimes he found a little, but most often he returned empty.

"Even if I had Fort Benton freight, I wouldn't send it," said Hiram Edgerly, a hardware man. "Savages'd destroy it. Say, Kipp, we got to do something about this, once and for all. I say if the army doesn't, we should do it ourselves. Put 'em on reservations? Not for them murderers. I say wipe 'em out, every man, woman, and child. Stop the breeding—nits make lice."

Peter kept his silence while the man glared suspiciously at him.

"I suppose you breeds think different," he said slowly. "Maybe I'll try the Diamond R next time."

There it was again. Peter swallowed and backed out of

the drafty store. Out on the busy gulch, he ran into a news butcher hawking the *Montana Post*, a Virginia City paper.

"Hey, mister, read about the massacre. Read about the outrage!" the boy hollered.

Peter paid his two cents, stared at the flamboyant headlines, then read the story:

> How long, how long will the blood of innocent murdered men cry out against a policy more cowardly and disgraceful than ever dishonored a nation, ancient or modern? How long will the butchery of good citizens by these bloody fiends invoke the curses of western people upon a government that wantonly fails to protect its citizens from a savage foe?
>
> The causes of war will continue while the larger game lasts, unless sooner the Indians learn their inferiority and submit to their destinies.
>
> As for this reservation business, it can never be a success until the tribes are reduced to a mere handful of decrepit and diseased creatures each.

Peter caromed around the inflamed city, finding the darkest emotions in the human breast suddenly unbridled, feeling murder in the air and naked hatred oozing from the street. The *Helena Weekly Herald* announced a state of war: "The pleasant and innocent amusement of butchering and scalping the pale-faces is believed by some likely soon to begin in good earnest."

The paper appealed to the territory's new Indian commissioner, General Alfred Sully, for action: "We are well satisfied that with a force of four or five regiments armed and equipped in accordance with General Sully's mode of Indian warfare, he would soon put an end to these outrages, and give the red devils a whipping that would last for all time to come."

Peter fled the city in fear of his life, knowing that half-Indian blood was all that a lynch mob needed. He and his Creoles joined a Kirkendall train for mutual protection and made it back to Fort Benton without incident. The sunny hours on the road, listening to the jangle of mule harness, seemed peaceful enough, but Peter felt himself being torn to bits. He snapped at his own men, sulked through the nights, and swallowed back a seething hatred of everyone around him.

At Fort Benton he fled to his rooms as soon as his wagons and stock were cared for and his Creoles paid. He slammed the door on the ruthless sun and paced the floor, as taut as a drawn bow. He hated his savage blood, his inferior, barbaric Salish Indian blood. He dreaded white men who stared at him with knowing eyes, reading his bad blood in his flesh and bones.

And yet, he was who he was. He couldn't help having an Indian mother. He was half Indian, and he couldn't deny that side of himself. It seemed wrong to despise his own blood or deny his own roots. He had friends in every band of the Blackfeet. In his trading days he'd visited every village, known every family and traveled to every outlying post owned by the fur company. He'd seen every chief and headman come to the trading windows; laughed and exchanged gifts, and joked through long winter nights with them. They were his friends; they seemed a kinder and prouder people than the whites he'd known.

For every white man who'd been murdered in this undeclared war, probably ten Blackfeet had been casually slaughtered. But Indians didn't count, and no one kept a tally. Only in the lodges did the tormented Blackfeet nurse memories of fathers and sons and wives and mothers butchered by the scalp hunters, wolfers, whiskey traders, saloon keepers, miners, and cattle herders who thought nothing of shooting or hanging any Indian, innocent or not.

He could not resolve his anguish or blot out half of himself. But he could do something; from the moment in Helena when he had realized that white men wanted to exterminate every Blackfoot Indian, he had feared for Marie Therese.

He knew the Blackfeet. They would continue through the summer, unsuspecting. They would regard Owl Child's murder of Four Bears a family matter, not a cause for war. He had to find Marie Therese and warn her. Tomorrow he would saddle up and ride toward the Two Medicine—he would betray his own white sympathies and blood. That night he lay in his bed and wept.

Natoya-niskim fled to her camp on the Two Medicine and wrapped herself in her loneliness. She'd been rejected and rebuked by the head chief of the Pikuni, and by many others. Her visions had been called false, her loyalties questioned, her life's mission scorned. She'd become an outcast. Nothing she had done in her whole life mattered to the chiefs and headmen. She'd sacrificed everything she might have had for the asking—a husband, children, acceptance, comfort—because something within her had led her to a life of abstention and sacrifice and private surrender. But it had all come to nothing.

She retreated into a haze of meditation, sorrow, and the drudgery of keeping camp and finding food. For the first time doubt pierced her. Had she thrown her life away? What good was her life? What had been given or received? If her visions depicted the inevitable fate of the Siksika, what good did it do to describe them to the People? What good was any sort of prophecy, anyway? If something was bound to happen, what difference did it make if people knew about it or didn't know about it?

For the first time since she had returned from St. Louis, she thought about the religion of her father. What good were those prophets? They too had been given visions of the future; the calamities that would be visited upon their people.

And then she knew: Those who listened and heard sometimes reformed themselves, even though their nation suffered. A glimpse of the inevitable might stir the hearts of those who could see and hear.

She knew at once that not all had been lost. Some of her people had listened and were listening still. Little Dog had listened and had made a serious effort to transform the Piegans. Even now her Lone Eaters' chief, The Heavy Runner, was listening to her. He didn't like the napikwan any more than the rest, but he saw the shape of things to come, thanks to her visions. He would not fight the seizers, no matter what the provocations. Perhaps the visions from White Buffalo Cow had not been meant for the whole nation, but for those with eyes and ears.

She remembered what Father DeSmet had told her on the *St. Ange,* long ago. "You're a child of destiny, set for the fall of nations," he'd told her. A captive of God, a priest and messenger of God, he'd said. One who'd be rejected by her people; one who'd see the destruction of her world.

She remembered it all and marveled at it now. Everything the Jesuit had said was coming to pass. It troubled her: How could he call her a captive of God? She was a Siksika! She tried to put the priest out of mind, but couldn't. She reached to her breast to find the small silver crucifix she'd worn in St. Louis—but it was long gone. Only her sacred buffalo stone, and her father's gold ring, were suspended there now. Angrily she swept the tendrils of Christianity from her mind, only to find them creeping back in again. Had she thrown away everything that was good in the universe?

Disconsolately she wandered into the cottonwood groves, snapping squaw wood from the shaggy trunks. That's when she discovered a rider approaching along the river. She stood quietly, well-hidden by the forest, and watched. The rider was a white man. He reined his horse and peered around uncertainly.

"Marie Therese?" he called.

"Peter!"

Joyously she threw her armload of wood aside and ran to him as he dismounted. He caught her and crushed her close, his arms a tight prison.

"Peter, oh, Peter," she whispered into his shirt.

"I found you!" he murmured in her ear.

She was filled with questions, but they could wait. They held each other a long time and then she led him to her camp.

"You're more beautiful that ever," he said gravely.

She felt a schoolgirl shyness. Before her was a mature man, hard and lean, his gaze radiating a mixture of pain and confidence, his expression tender. "You've done well, Peter?"

"I did at first—until the big outfits crowded me. Now I'm just hanging on."

"What are you going to do?"

He grinned. "There's always something. I might ask the same of you."

She felt flustered and could not answer. "You came all this way for a reason."

"Yes. There's trouble, Marie Therese."

"Natoya-niskim."

That evoked a grimace. "Malcolm Clarke's dead, his boy wounded. It was Owl Child and some others did it. The settlers—they're screaming for war, and they'll have it, I think."

"I know."

That startled him.

"I have been shown things I don't want to see."

"Marie—Natoya-niskim—there's danger. You don't know how riled up they are; they're ready to kill—"

"I know."

"It's too big—it can't be stopped now. It's—It's going to be terrible."

"Not as bad as the smallpox, Peter."

He looked puzzled. "Has it—you mean it's come again?"

"Not yet."

He stood and paced, studying the early evening light above the bluffs. She watched him, filled with knowing. At last he sat down beside her again and took her hand in his hard one.

"I've always loved you. I don't know how or why. It just came to me on the *St. Ange,* long ago. I've loved your beauty—I've never seen a woman more beautiful. I've loved your spirit. I've never seen such depths of wisdom, and kindness, and . . . caring. I've loved your dedication to something larger than yourself. I've loved you because you're a mixed-blood and we have something to share. I've loved you—for reasons beyond reason, because it rose in me and grew. Now it owns me, this love of you, Marie Therese. I'd give you anything; I'd work forever for you; I'll love you forever and a day; I'll love you beyond death, when we are souls. There's never been another, in all these years. Only you . . . I guess you know where this is leading."

Anguish built in her, feelings so deep they reached the bottom of her heart and hurt there. She nodded.

"I'd like to care for you all my days. Now, at long last, would you marry me?"

The pain burst within her and she could only weep. He stared into her tear-streaked face, dismayed.

"I didn't mean to hurt you. My God, I only wanted—"

"Oh, Peter, I love you too."

"Then let's marry! I can take you from here. To safety. We can escape!"

She couldn't respond. Something caught in her throat and burned there, something beyond words. He caught her and held her, and she felt at peace in the circle of his arms.

"I'm not much," he whispered. "I'm just some fur trader's bastard child, plucked up by the Kipps. I'm just some breed caught between two hating worlds."

"No, Peter! You're the most courageous man I know! Nothing got you down! Nothing was too hard for you to overcome!"

"But my best isn't good enough for you."

She sobbed then, unable to help him, wanting him to know that she wasn't worthy of so great a love from so fine a man. But at last she released him. "I am the one not worthy, Peter. I don't deserve you. I don't know how to tell you."

He sighed. "You don't have to tell me. You're one of those few who've been called for some great purpose. You've never had a choice."

Her tears started again, sliding from her gray eyes down her cheeks. She could not heal his anguish. "If I had a choice, Peter, it'd be you. Only you, forever."

She couldn't look at him; she couldn't endure to see what was to be seen in his face. But she felt his resignation and his deepening calm. When at last she could meet his eyes again, she found them warm, and a smile on his face, incongruous with his own tears.

"I was thinking about Father DeSmet today," she said. "He told me long ago, on the boat, that I was a prisoner of God, a priest and messenger to my people; and that I would see the fall of nations. Oh, Peter, I want to be with you more than anything. . . . Could you free yourself now? Could you find someone else? You're young still—any woman would want you!"

"No white woman." He smiled ruefully. "I'll try, Marie Therese. I'll find someone. It would honor you if I did, I think."

"Please—please try. If only to release me."

His face lit up in the dusk. "I brought some chow," he said.

They ate in the lavender twilight, enjoying the utter serenity of the hour. The birds sang their evening songs, the moon crawled over the eastern hills, the balmy zephyrs seduced their troubles away, and she could not imagine that beyond, somewhere, men hated, and plotted murder.

He stayed that night, the first they had ever spent alone together. He kept a careful distance, spread his bedroll out and pulled it over him, tactiturn and stern. She understood every thought and feeling within him, and felt the same wild yearnings within herself, so strong and unbearable that several times in the sweet and anguished night she threw her blanket aside and started to go to him. But she didn't.

When dawn came he gave her a whole saddlebag of white men's foods, tins of things she could scarcely name. But he could not speak. His eyes were beautiful; she beheld a man.

Impulsively she drew the thong of her necklace over her head and handed it to him. Dangling from it were the sacred buffalo stone and her father's ring.

"But Marie Therese—you can't. You're giving me yourself."

"Yes! That is the natoya-niskim, the sacred buffalo stone. And my father's ring!"

"I—I can't—this is, this is *you*!"

"I want you to have me."

"What are you saying? My God, Marie Therese!"

"Remember me with these."

Chapter Twenty-seven

There'd be nothing to do this short, dark winter day except to feed the stock. It was so cold, Peter knew he'd be quick about it. The thermometer hovered well below zero, and there'd be no freighting until the weather moderated. Peter didn't have any contracts anyway.

The knock surprised him. He opened to James Bradley, the young lieutenant commanding a company garrisoned in the old fur post. The army had taken over the post in July, ousted Peter and Northwest Fur, and moved in. Peter had found rooms in Bill Hamilton's log inn. He wasn't welcome at Thwing House, which was too uppity for breeds.

"Mr. Kipp, your presence is requested at the fort, sir," said Bradley. The lieutenant was wrapped in a buffalo greatcoat and buffalo cap.

That surprised Peter. "Not another party, I hope. New Years was enough."

Bradley grinned. "No, sir, it's not that. You'll know in a bit."

Peter bundled into his own greatcoat and braved the bitter gusts that had emptied Front Street of all life. He and the lieutenant hurried to the old adobe post, passed a sentry at its ancient gates, and raced toward what, in better days, had once been the home of Alec Culbertson. He could not imagine why the army desired his presence on this tenth day of January.

Upon being ushered in, he found himself in the presence of more brass than he'd ever seen before. A glance at epaulets informed him he faced three generals and a lieutenant, as well as Bradley. He knew two of the generals: Alfred Sully, famed Indian fighter and now the superintendent of Indian Affairs for Montana Territory; the other the patrician son of a French baron, General Regis de Trobriand, commander of Fort Shaw. The third, a major general, he didn't know. The other lieutenant was the current agent for the Blackfeet, W. A. Pease, stationed on the Teton River at the new agency.

Peter grasped something of what these officers were about even before an aide carted away his greatcoat.

Bradley made the introduction: "This is the man I told you about, Peter Kipp, son of James Kipp, one of the principals of the old Chouteau company. You'll find that he's the perfect man for the job. Peter, you probably know of General de Trobriand and General Sully. The major general is James Hardie, sent out here on a fact-finding mission by General Sheridan. And of course you've met Lieutenant Pease."

War.

De Trobriand took the initiative. "Mr. Kipp, before we proceed further, may we have your pledge of absolute confidence? We don't want a word of what we'll tell you made public. You'll understand in a moment."

"If you're about to make war on the Blackfeet, sir, I'm not your man. I'll leave at once and say nothing." Peter turned to leave, but Hardie stayed him.

"Hold up, Kipp. We think you're the man. And the reason we think it is that you have steadfastly fought the whiskey traders."

A war upon the whiskey traders?

"I'll keep your confidence, sir."

"Very well. We'd consider the disclosure of any of what you hear today to be a grave matter, Mr. Kipp. It'd ruin a great deal of planning. I'm sure you understand." Hardie's steady stare missed nothing.

Peter nodded reluctantly. He wondered what he was getting into.

"General Sheridan sent me out here from his Chicago headquarters for the Department of the Missouri, to examine conflicting reports about the Blackfeet. Some reports asserted that the territory's engulfed in war and the Blackfeet are all hostile; other reports said the matter was greatly exaggerated, that most of the chiefs are friendly, and that a few renegades are responsible for all the troubles.

"I've reported to him that the truth lies somewhere in the middle. We've been preparing a military action that falls far short of all-out war, but is intended to curb the young troublemakers. In short, a careful, surgical strike against just one band, that of Mountain Chief. The rest we'll leave alone. They're friendly."

Peter listened quietly, anticipating what would be asked of him. "That makes sense, sir. I know almost every Blackfoot family—at least the Piegans. They are friendly. The real trouble lies with the whiskey traders."

"You've put your finger on it, Kipp," said Sully. "If we had the men, the general would go after them. They're the ones that inflame the young warriors. The citizens of Montana lost a thousand horses to the Blackfeet last year—most of those horses simply bought a cup or two of rotgut from the whiskey peddlers. But there's little we can do—the postwar army's down to bones."

"Fifty-six lives," de Trobriand added. "Don't forget the fifty-six men, women, and children, butchered and scalped—including Malcolm Clarke. William Wheeler's grand jury brought indictments of Clarke's killers—Owl Child, Eagle's Rib, Black Bear, Bear Chief, Black Weasel, and the rest. Sully has them. He and Lieutenant Pease have tried—in vain—to persuade the chiefs to turn in the killers, or their bodies, and restore the stolen stock.

"We're back from a meeting with the chiefs at the agency. We invited them all to talks on New Year's Day, but only four showed up—The Heavy Runner, Big Lake, and Little Wolf of the Piegans, and Gray Eyes of the Bloods. The rest, we found out, were too drunk to come in. Drunk!

"We informed them that the Piegans would have to bring in Clarke's killers and the stolen stock in two weeks—or face war. We have no hope at all that it'll happen—but we had to try. The Heavy Runner, in particular, affirmed his friendship, and we gave him a paper testifying to that."

"We want those murderers," Sully said. "They're all in Mountain Chief's bunch. We've had a stroke of luck. Most of the Piegans have been up in Canada beyond our reach until a few days ago. But we've intelligence now that they've come south for the winter. They're setting up along the Marias, from the Big Bend almost down to here."

"Are you familiar with General Sheridan's approach to Indian war, Mr. Kipp? I might add, General Sully's also," Hardie asked, amending his question.

"Winter campaigns?"

"Yes, Kipp—winter. Strike them when they don't expect it. When their ponies are weak. When they're in their lodges. It worked at Washita. The lieutenant general is mighty proud of that one, and proud of Custer. Surprise is the key—and that requires secrecy. If word of the army's plans reached the ears of the whiskey traders, our quarry would flee to Canada. So far, not one civilian in the territory is privy to this. You're the first."

"What General Hardie's saying, Mr. Kipp, is that we've made inquiries about you," said de Trobriand. "Mr. Culbertson commended you highly. You've, ah, proved your loyalty over and over. You've been out trading in every Piegan and Blood village. You know the Piegans better than any . . . white man alive. Others know the Piegans also—but they're tied up with the whiskey trade. We can't trust them, but we can put our chips on you. Tell me, how would a scout know one village from another?"

Scouting for the army. Peter knew at once he would accept. He *had* to accept. He had to steer them away from Marie Therese's people. "Why, sir, they paint their lodges.

It's easy, once you know the lodges. Also, sir, they have spirit lodges, such as the sacred buffalo lodge, painted yellow. No one lives in it, but it is owned by the Black Patched Moccasins.

"Now old Mountain Chief, he's a rich man, with lots of wives. He's got a big lodge, maybe twenty-five hides. It's the biggest lodge around, blue with black ravens painted on it, and fallen stars around its base. I can tell any village if I can look at it for a minute or two, sir."

"You can positively identify his village?" asked Hardie.

"Yes, sir." Peter refused to wilt under that stern gaze. He wanted this task desperately.

"We don't want mistakes. It'd ruin the President's Indian policy if we hit the friendlies. We've got Ely Parker to deal with, and all the Quaker bleeding hearts."

"I have good friends in all the bands, sir. The last thing I'd want is to hurt innocent people." *Like Marie Therese.*

"Well, they're not so innocent, Kipp," said Sully. "Stolen stock's scattered through all the villages. But we're pursuing a moderate policy. We don't want to spill a drop more blood than we have to for the sake of peace. It's my task as Indian commissioner to look after these people. We do want to punish Mountain Chief's rabble. Just last month they raided west of here, stole more stock, killed some people. We have to stop it."

"I'll scout for you, sir."

De Trobriand smiled. "Very good. This is going to be a surgical strike. I've ordered Colonel Baker—Eugene Baker—up from Fort Ellis with two squadrons of cavalry. We'll supplement with mounted infantry and foot soldiers. He's on his way to Fort Shaw right now.

"Your immediate task will be to locate Mountain Chief's village. We want positive identification. You know the old chief; go in and talk to him. By the time you get there, Sully's two-week ultimatum will be up. You can tell him that; tell him the army wants Clarke's killers and stolen stock."

"You're talking about his son, sir. He won't bring in Bear's Rib."

"We know that, Mr. Kipp. Your task is to locate his village—it's somewhere up in the Big Bend of the Marias—and talk to the man. Make sure he's there. And identify any other villages in the area. You can talk to any of the chiefs. We want you to find out where every Piegan band is wintering."

"I'll leave in the morning, General. It's not far. I'll be back in three or four days—if the weather permits. If it gets much colder, I may have to hole up for a while."

"Yes, yes, of course. But hurry, Mr. Kipp. When you get back, you'll scout for Colonel Baker. His column will leave at once. You take him right to that village, and that'll be it."

"Count on me, sir."

"Oh, Kipp, the army pays thirty dollars for scouting."

"It's not for the money, sir."

Nena-es-toko, Mountain Chief, marveled at the power of the Cold Maker. Even though his five wives kept a bright fire burning in his great lodge, the cold stole in past the lodge cover and inner lining. He and his women and children buried themselves in buffalo robes and blankets and endured. The door flap parted and Ekitowaki, his youngest and prettiest, clambered in with another load of wood. Sis-tse, Bird, his sits-beside-him wife, immediately placed three sticks on the dwindling blaze. They all waited patiently for heat. Outside, Es-to-nea-pesta, Maker of Storms and Blizzards, was howling down upon them again. Twice this winter he had visited. Once, Ma-kai-peye, the blizzard, had swept over the lodges.

Mountain Chief was in a bad mood. He usually was. Age made him hurt, especially in the winter. But this season worry beset him and would not go away. Every village of the Pikuni suffered from the white-scabs disease, and his people were dying, two or three a day, endlessly. Twice before the white-scabs disease, brought by napikwan on the fireboats, struck his people, killing a quarter or a third. And now there was weeping and suffering in the lodges. How he hated the napikwan!

But that was not the only thing that burdened his mind. As much as he hated the medicine seer, Natoyaniskim, he grudgingly admitted that she had spoken truly; White Buffalo Cow had warned the people that the white-scabs disease would strike them this winter. And more . . . The seizers would strike in the snow. It made him restless and afraid and murderous. He itched to drive every one of them from the land of the People. Maybe in the spring. But now he could barely live through each day without fearing the bluecoats. Why had Sun abandoned his people?

They heard the polite scratching on the lodge door that signified a guest, and he wondered who had braved the Cold Maker's terrors to come calling in the lavender twilight. Sis-tse admitted a napikwan bundled up in a buffalo greatcoat and buffalo cap, his face hidden by a woollen scarf. The man shed snow and exuded steam as he stood inside the enormous lodge. Then he pulled his scarf loose.

Peter Kipp!

Mountain Chief grunted, and motioned the former fur company trader to the place of honor. The head chief of the Pikuni knew he would not like this visit a bit. He didn't mind Kipp, even if the former trader had the blood of the napikwan in his veins, and the blood of those cowards, the Salish. Kipp had made himself a napikwan, but he'd done the People no harm.

Kipp undid his greatcoat and settled into the robes. He dug into a pocket and handed a twist of tobacco to Mountain Chief, the traditional symbol of friendship—and diplomacy. The chief took it and reached for his pipe.

"Peterkipp," he said. "It is a strange day to be traveling, when the Cold Maker roars and all sensible people keep to their lodges. Something important bring you here."

"Yes," said Kipp.

"We will smoke," said Mountain Chief. That was the way of the People. Important things required thought and time. And in the winter, when there was so little to do, they helped pass the long dark hours. Leisurely he tamped Kipp's tobacco into his pipe and lit it, and handed it to Kipp, who sucked on it and passed it back. Thus they smoked until the charge of tobacco had burnt down to nothing. Mountain Chief's wives listened silently, bundled in their robes and blankets.

"I've been sent by the seizers," said Kipp at last, in excellent Blackfoot. "They want those who killed Four Bears, and all the horses that have been stolen from the napikwan. They want them right now. Fourteen days ago they met at the agency with The Heavy Runner, Big Lake, Little Wolf, and Gray Eyes, and said they must have Owl Child, Eagle's Rib, Bear Child, Bear Chief, and Black Weasel in this much time—or there'd be trouble."

"So it was told to me," Mountain Chief said. This meeting would be a sour one. Peter Kipp antagonized him. "I refused to go. I would not dignify the meeting with my presence. This is a private matter. Four Bears insulted Owl Child many times. Owl Child told me that Four Bears tried to steal his wife. He was a great one of the napikwan, but was a bad man. Tell the seizers who sent you this is a family matter—not a cause to kill and insult more Pikuni."

"They don't see it that way. I'm to tell you that your time is up. Return the stolen horses at once, and bring in the wanted men or their bodies—Owl Child especially. Half of the Pikuni hate him—more than the napikwan do."

Mountain Chief laughed harshly. "Yes, he is a bad one. But he's not here. He's not anywhere. He glides through the night, stopping here and there. None of the ones you speak of are in this village."

"Then there will be trouble."

Mountain Chief stood and peered through the smoke hole into a night so cold the stars looked like chips of ice. "I don't think so," he said. But it was bravado. The vision sent to the people from White Buffalo Cow disturbed him. "No one stirs when the Cold Maker roars like this. Tell the seizers my people are dying of the white-scabs disease."

"I will tell them," Kipp said. "And now I've told you what they want, and brought their warning to you."

"It is all I can do to keep the young men from sweeping away the napikwan. They're angry and ashamed. It is not their fault; it's the fault of the Sneaking Drink Givers. The whiskey sellers come and destroy the dignity of the young men. And when the young men have no more robes, they steal horses to buy more bad water. Tell the seizers to keep the Sneaking Drink Givers away from the treaty lands of the people."

"I'll tell them, Nena-es-toko," Kipp said.

"If I were a young man, I'd go fight too. The napikwan have insulted me and my son in many-houses. They shoot us in the streets. They make treaties and don't keep them. Here in this village are many would would like to drive them away forever."

"Nena-es-toko, the peace chiefs don't feel that way."

"Maybe they feel that way and are afraid to say it to napikwan. They're like grandmothers."

"I stopped at the villages of Little Wolf and Big Lake on my way here. Where are the others?"

"We are all on Kaiyi Isisakta."

"The Marias . . . I wish to go to The Heavy Runner's camp."

"Ah, I forgot him. The Lone Eaters are on the Matoki Okas, the Two Medicine." He smiled sarcastically. "You want to go talk with the friendly Pikuni."

A strange composure settled across Kipp's features. "That's what the others say also. The Heavy Runner heard there were some buffalo there."

"Peterkipp, the Lone Eaters are in bad shape. White-scabs disease kills many of them. They starve because their young men go to steal horses to trade to the Sneaking Drink Givers rather than hunt for food. All the old and weak of the Pikuni have gone to The Heavy Runner." He paused. "The strong, the proud young men, they have nothing to do with that band."

"That is what the other chiefs told me," Kipp said. "They all say that I can find The Heavy Runner at the mouth of the Two Medicine River." The mixed-blood sighed softly, keeping his thoughts to himself. "Where are the Kainah?"

"Far up this river—many days to the west."

"What of the northern Siksika?"

"All north of the white men's medicine line."

"That's where you were until a few days ago."

Something stirred in Mountain Chief. This man, sent by the seizers, kept asking too many questions. He grunted, signifying he would say no more.

Kipp left the next dawn, saying he would tell the seizer chiefs at Fort Shaw that, according to Mountain Chief, none of the men they wanted were there. The old chief watched him ride away in a brutal dawn when ice crystals reddened the sun.

He let the mixed-blood spy ride for half a morning and then sent word out to his village: That very day, in spite of the cold, they would move their camp from this cursed place.

Chapter Twenty-eight

Each day three or four of the Lone Eater people died. And everywhere through the village, one could hear the groans of the sick, and the wailing of children. The white-scabs disease moved from lodge to lodge, torturing and finally murdering the Pikuni one by one. Natoyaniskim grieved. She did not catch the terrible disease, perhaps because of the French blood of her father. Napikwan suffered from smallpox, but not as terribly as the Indians, who rarely survived it.

The village was beset by other troubles too. It was on the brink of starvation. The bitter young men hadn't bothered to hunt buffalo, but had joined the raids on the napikwan ranches to steal horses to trade for whiskey. The parfleches, usually stuffed with the good things given to the black-footed people by Sun, were almost empty. There wasn't enough jerky or pemmican or buffalo backfat in the whole village to last more than a few days.

Nor was that the worst of it. The thirty-seven lodges of the Lone Eaters were filled with the old and infirm and sick, refugees from other bands that had disintegrated under the evil of the white-scabs disease. Over 350 Pikuni crowded the lodges of the Lone Eaters. The Heavy Runner had taken his people south from Canada, heading toward the agency on the Teton River, believing that the Great Father, Ka-ach-sino, would look after his Pikuni children. Indeed, when General Sully sent word to The Heavy Runner that he should come in, the chief hastened eagerly, certain that the Great Father would supply the starving people with meat and blankets. Instead, he listened to Sully and the new agent, Pease, complain about Owl Child and stolen horses. The Heavy Runner had returned to his starving, sick people empty-handed.

Now they camped at the mouth of the Two Medicine River because The Heavy Runner had heard there were a few buffalo bulls in the area that might feed his hungry people. But the hunters had found none, and the village would have to move again. If it could.

Natoya-niskim wiped the fevered brow of Tears in Her Eyes, Isto-ko-pence, her almost-mother, who was gravely ill and hurting so much she groaned. Sinopah's lodge had become the haven of seven others, the old and sick from other villages, huddled around its cold perimeter waiting for the healthy—Sinopah or Natoya-niskim—to care for them and feed them. But she could do almost nothing except make a thin soup from the last of the jerky. The buffalo backfat, succulent seasoning stripped from the backbone of the sacred ee-nau-ah, black horns, was all gone.

She was too harried to think much about the vision she had been given by White Buffalo Cow, but in her few private moments, gathering squaw wood from the timbered flats of the river, it came back to her in violent rushes of memory and stole through her heart. That was where she encountered Sinopah, who was stripping cottonwood bark to feed to their emaciated ponies.

"The Heavy Runner has told us we must move again," he said. "We'll leave at dawn. Many more will die this trip, with the Cold Maker so powerful."

He looked tired, she thought. "No game?"

"Not even a rabbit. But there are buffalo near the Big Bend of Kaiyi Isisakta. That's where the others are gone. The Grease Melters and Black Patched Moccasins are there, and below them, the Small Robes and Buffalo Dung and the Don't Laughs. If we must all die, we'll die beside the other Pikuni. It's up to you and me to move them all."

She wiped frost from her eyebrows. "Tears in Her Eyes will die."

He sighed, as helpless as she. "We will do what The Heavy Runner wishes. He has taken good care of the Lone Eater people."

The next dawn, in the red ice-haze of a brutal day, every able-bodied man, woman, and child among the Lone Eaters caught the winter-gaunted ponies, attached the travois, wrapped the sick and infirm in the few robes and blankets they still possessed and anchored them to the travois, and then lowered the lodges. It took a long time, with so few able to help. But before noon the stricken village slogged its weary way eastward, down the Marias River, through drifts and cold. Sun didn't smile, and supplied them with no game before sliding into the southwestern horizon in mid-afternoon. On that first day, seven died, and were tied into cottonwood trees to begin their spirit journey up the Wolf Trail to the Sand Hills.

The next day was a little better. The hunters brought in two mule deer, and this precious food was carefully apportioned so that everyone in every lodge had a bite or two of meat. That night, too, they camped in a place where the snow had blown clear and the ponies could graze on the tan grasses poking through. But it had turned colder, and the lodge fires didn't warm those who had no robes. These were many, because the young men had traded most of the robes in the village to the Sneaking Drink Givers.

Tears in Her Eyes survived, and Natoya-niskim spooned venison into her between her terrible moments of delirium.

"Soon I will go to the Sand Hills," she whispered. "I have always loved you and believed you, Natoya-niskim. You have brought honor to our lodge."

Natoya-niskim turned her face to hide her tears, but she could not hide them in a lodge filled with ten staring people.

The next day it turned bitter. The Cold Maker would

have no mercy on the Pikuni. But they pushed eastward in the gale, consoled only by the fact that the bitter wind was on their backs. It drove them far down the Marias River to its great bend, for to stop or to even slow down was to die. And there, miraculously, was an abandoned campsite, in good cottonwood forest, protected from the vicious winds by high bluffs, with plenty of wood for fires and cottonwood bark for the ponies. And even smoothed and readied lodge floors that would spare the exhausted Lone Eaters a lot of hard work.

"We will stay here," Sinopah told her. "We are close to the People now, and the hunting has been good. The Heavy Runner has chosen this blessed place. May Sun have pity on us now, and heal us."

"We lost twelve more, Sinopah. Grandmothers and grandfathers, all frozen this day as they rode the travois. And we've left a trail of blood behind us. The cold has bitten the feet of the People until they bleed in their moccasins."

Sinopah shook his head, but never stopped the ceaseless toil. Before the blackness enfolded this village once again, he would need to take care of the ponies, raise the lodge, help his stepdaughter gather wood—and hunt.

"The hunters—did they find anything?"

"Not this day, Natoya-niskim."

It disheartened her.

"Tomorrow, every man and boy in the village will hunt from dawn to dusk," he added, trying to console her.

"Tomorrow another ten will be dead," she said.

"We'll send runners also. The People are close, and they will bring us food."

But the next day the Cold Maker redoubled his cruelty, and no Pikuni could step outside a lodge for more than a few minutes. The cold slapped and bit, and the north wind stung like wasps. Natoya-niskim knew that at Fort Benton the mercury thermometer outside the trading room would show thirty or forty degrees below zero. Within their fragile lodges the stricken Lone Eaters fed wood to the fires and endured. A few hardy young men chopped holes in the river ice for the horses, peeled green cottonwood bark for fodder, and then fled to the warmth of the lodge fires.

Within her lodge, Natoya-niskim boiled sage-leaf tea to settle the stomachs of the old and sick, fed cottonwood sticks to the fire and ignored the cramping hunger in her stomach. She pushed the terrible vision from White Buffalo Cow out of mind because she couldn't endure the knowledge within her. When the weak sun reached its low zenith, she braved the stinging cold long enough to hunt a few roots and frozen berries. From the banks of the river she gathered a handful of buffalo berries. From the slopes behind the village she plucked nits-ik-opa, squaw root, an edible vegetable that was known to heal sore throats and inflammation. She found a little mais-ton-ata, crow root, and chopped the roots free from the frozen clay. Its tea would help the old ones cope with stomachaches and swellings.

But mostly she starved. One brutal night, a grandmother of her lodge, Feather Woman, slid away on her journey to the Sand Hills. Sinopah carried her out to the cottonwoods and tied her on a limb, numbed to the bone by that task. Natoya-niskim grieved, and pleaded with Sun and Old Man to release the stricken village from their anger. A nameless terror had bloomed in her, something dark and barely hidden and unknowable, something that turned day into night and made her search the bluffs anxiously.

The terrible cold imprisoned them for six days, and then it warmed a little.

"The Heavy Runner has said that every able-bodied man and boy will go on a great hunt tomorrow," Sinopah told her. "We've heard from the other villages, and we know where the buffalo are. This was Mountain Chief's camp, but he left it a few days ago. There are many buffalo a day's walk away."

"Oh, Sinopah! Buffalo! That's the first good news in many days," she said.

Colonel Eugene Baker eyed the half-breed scout with some amusement. The red-haired fellow seemed all too eager to please. He'd just ridden into Fort Shaw, and now he was reporting to General de Trobriand and several senior officers. Kipp, the name was; a bastard child of the fur-trading days. A son of James Kipp, the Chouteau company man. He knew his Piegans, and that would help.

"You positively located the camp of Mountain Chief?" de Trobriand was asking.

"Yes, sir. It's at the big bend of the Marias, about five miles below Medicine Creek, near Blackrobe Butte. It's the northernmost of the Piegan villages. They're all down from Canada, as far as I could tell."

"How do you know it was Mountain Chief's village—I mean, apart from the lodge paintings?"

"I went in and talked to him, sir."

The thought of that breed, Kipp, spilling all the beans to Mountain Chief, riled Baker. "What did you say to him, Kipp?"

"I said I'd been sent by the army to tell him there'd be trouble if he didn't bring in Owl Child and the rest—and the stolen stock. He said Owl Child wasn't in the village. I told him there'd be trouble. He railed against the whites. That was it. I left and doubled back here as fast as I could."

"He doesn't have an inkling of an impending attack?"

"Not an inkling sir—and not from me. But he's heard, ah, a certain medicine prophecy describing just such a thing."

Baker laughed. Medicine prophecy. A breed would put some credence in it.

De Trobriand seemed pleased. "All right, Kipp. That was good work. You'll accompany Colonel Baker as scout and lead him to that village."

"Mountain Chief's the only hostile chief, sir. The others I talked to—"

"Yes, yes, Kipp. We know." The general turned to Baker. "Eugene, you may take the field. I'll read your orders, so all may know them. First, the lieutenant general wired this yesterday: '*If the lives and property of citizens of Montana can best be protected by striking Mountain*

Chief's band of Piegans, I want them struck. Tell Baker to strike them hard. *Lieutenant General Philip H. Sheridan.*' "

"Hard," said Baker. Old Phil had learned how to do it in the Washita campaign. That was Custer's victory. Now it'd be the turn of Major and Brevet Colonel Eugene M. Baker.

"Now I'll read my own field orders, Colonel, so that all your command may hear.

> "Fort Shaw, January sixteen. You will proceed with your command, without any more delay than may be required by the present condition of the weather, to chastise that portion of the Indian tribe of Piegans which, under Mountain Chief or his sons, committed the greater part of the depredations of last summer and last month in this district.
>
> "The band of Mountain Chief is now encamped on the Marias River, at a place called the Big Bend, and can easily be singled out from the other bands of Piegans, two of which should be left unmolested, as they have uniformly remained friendly, viz., the bands of The Heavy Runner and Big Lake . . . "

De Trobriand droned on, something old-womanish in his tone, about leaving the Bloods alone and protecting the nearby trading post of Northwest Fur during the operations. Baker listened politely. De Trobriand and Sully were a pair, all right. Sheridan had to yank Sully out of the Washita because the man wouldn't act, and turned him into an Indian commissioner for this territory, while de Trobriand had been so cautious that the entire population of Montana wanted him ousted. Baker grinned. Sheridan knew the man for the job.

"All right, then, Colonel. You may leave when ready. I should remind you that frostbite, as Napoleon discovered, is more dangerous to armies than combat." He handed the order to Baker.

"Yes, sir," said Baker, much amused.

He was as ready as he could be. Over three hundred horses had been shod by the farriers. He had wagonloads of bagged oats for the horses. Two wagonloads of Sibley tents and sheet-iron stoves if the weather got bad. Spare gloves for every man; spare tack and harness, and all the rest.

"Kipp," he said. "We'll be leaving at five in the morning. You'll take us well clear of Fort Benton and the whiskey traders. We'll go just as fast and far as the column will move. Movement is a great remedy for frostbite, and helps preserve surprise. If you need rations or anything else, see the quartermaster."

"I have my own gear, sir. I've been traveling to trading outposts in the winter for many years."

"Very well, Kipp. We'll have us some redskins for breakfast."

Kipp winced, as Baker knew he would. Breeds amused him. Timid old generals did too.

But they didn't leave in the morning. The temperature stood at forty-five below that dark hour, too cold even for well-dressed troops. For a week the savage winter imprisoned his column at Fort Shaw, but at last the worst of it abated and the temperature climbed grudgingly to a little above zero. That was good enough.

He led his column out of Fort Shaw in the icy dark of the next morning, with the temperature at twenty below. His troops didn't look like an army column at all in their ankle-length buffalo greatcoats, otter caps, woolen face masks, and heavy gloves too thick to permit a finger into the trigger guard of their rifles. There wasn't a blue uniform in sight, which suited Colonel Baker fine. The more camouflage, the better. And in any case, old Mountain Chief's band would get to see some blue. Or maybe they wouldn't. He hoped to wipe out the whole lot before they knew what hit them.

He stood to one side, watching his column depart in the somber light of a few lanterns. He commanded 350 men, including Companies F, G, H, and L of the Second

Cavalry, men he had brought from Fort Ellis; fifty-five mounted infantry and seventy-five foot soldiers of the Thirteenth Infantry, some of them green postwar recruits. He had, in addition to Kipp, Malcolm Clarke's son Horace, recovered from his wounds, and determined to see justice done. The young man could help identify Clarke's killers—for the summary justice that Baker intended to mete out. This was the Regular Army at its best. The date was Friday, the twenty-first day of January, 1870; the estimated distance eighty to ninety miles, a two-day trip if he pushed them hard and snow didn't slow them. That would poise them for a dawn attack on Sunday, the twenty-third.

Kipp led them straight northeast, and they camped that night on the Teton, only twenty miles from Fort Benton. By the next night they had reached the Marias, and hid themselves in a coulee west of the Big Bend. Colonel Baker felt uncommonly cheerful. It had gone without a hitch. He'd dismounted his men frequently to stir their blood, and so far no one had reported frostbite.

Long before dawn on Sunday, Baker ordered his command to switch to light marching order, deployed his foot soldiers to guard the large pack train, and crawled through the blackness with his cavalry and mounted infantry toward their rendezvous with Mountain Chief. The night air was vicious, even to men in greatcoats and face masks. The scout, Kipp, rode silently beside Baker, his thoughts masked.

Baker had learned how easy it was to taunt him. "You know where to find these red niggers?"

Kipp muttered something.

"This is gonna be fun, Kipp."

"It's time to be quiet now, sir."

Baker took the hint. A word to his lieutenants hushed the column, which plodded softly through light snow toward a starlit bluff that descended to the Marias.

"Hold them back, sir," said Kipp.

A minute later Baker and Kipp peered over the lip of a steep incline to a murky village wrapped in sour wood smoke below.

"Good, Kipp. All right. We'll wait to dawn."

They eased back to the column and he gave his instructions: There'd be no bugle call. At the wave of his hand, they'd descend the bluff and shoot into lodges. Immediately beforehand his men were to doff their greatcoats and gloves and see to their arms. The blue uniforms would help prevent mistakes. The mounted infantry were to dismount and leave their horses to the holders. They would follow the cavalry.

A gray dawn seeped into the wintry wilderness, and Baker could pick out the black latticework of the cottonwoods, the white patches of snow, the mostly frozen iron-gray river. And the lodges, in the murk of smoke and ice-haze.

"That it, Kipp?"

"No sir! Wrong village!" Kipp whispered. "That's not Mountain Chief! That's The Heavy Runner!"

"Looks like Mountain Chief to me, Kipp." Baker grinned.

"It's not sir! I know! Something's happened. They—"

"Shhhh, Kipp."

"Sir," the scout said with an odd desperation. "Those are friendlies. I know the lodges; I know—"

"One buncha Piegans good as another, Kipp."

"No!" Kipp cried. "No, no! Your orders—"

"Shhh!" Baker eyed the breed with amusement. You never knew what got into the head of a half-redskin. The man was about to blow the surprise. He burrowed under his greatcoat, extracted his Colt revolver and aimed it at Kipp's chest. "Kipp, if you warn them, you're dead."

Peter Kipp stared, horrified, into the bore of Baker's revolver. "But sir . . . " Tears oozed from the man's eyes and froze on his cheeks.

Never trust a breed, Baker thought. He nodded to his sergeant major, Paddy Gavin, who lowered his carbine and aimed it squarely at the scout.

"All right, Kipp. Paddy's gonna hold you here for a bit," Baker said. "You can cry up here."

He waved to his command. All down the line men

shed their greatcoats and gloves. The cavalry drew their icy carbines from sheaths and readied themselves for war. The cavalry mounted. The infantry stood ready, rifles in hand.

Baker brought his arm down sharply, a move duplicated by Lieutenant Doane of the cavalry and Captain Higbee commanding the infantry, and without a bugle note sounding, the blue line raced down the grassy slope and began firing into the slumbering lodges. Baker let them roll, grinned at Gavin, nodded to his bugler, and left the crazy scout behind.

Chapter Twenty-nine

Stricken, Peter stared at a sight too terrible to bear. The troops were attacking The Heavy Runner—attacking Marie Therese! Dumbly, he watched cavalry shoot into lodges, sweep through the village and wheel around for another pass, while infantry trotted in, blowing holes in the hide covers. He saw The Heavy Runner peer from his lodge, duck back inside, and emerge a moment later holding his friendship paper high in front of him. Bravely the chief walked into the open, waving his emblem, yelling, "Friend, friend," one of the few English words he knew.

Then he collapsed, a bloom of red upon his chest, and tumbled head first into the snow. His friendship paper fluttered into the snow, white on white, invisible to all eyes. Everywhere, cavalry troopers rode freely among the lodges. Sharpshooters paused, aimed carefully at the binding cord that held the lodgepoles together, and blew the cords apart. One by one lodges collapsed as their bindings severed. The poles landed akimbo on the lodge fires and caught; the inhabitants of each lodge, trapped by the sturdy stakes that pinioned the lodge to the frozen ground, screamed, choked, burned, and died.

There was no resistance. He saw not a single warrior fighting back. The cavalry rode freely among the silent lodges, firing into them at will, and then the infantry swarmed in, shooting the lodge covers to ribbons. The screams of women and children rose up to Peter. He heard women singing their death songs. He saw a little girl stagger among the lodges, wailing, until a bullet felled her. She writhed on the snow for a moment, turning it red, and then lay still.

Now the soldiers gathered around each lodge, firing mercilessly through the hide and then cutting through it with their knives, while the screams of the dying rent the dawn. One young woman burst from a lodge clutching her infant to her breast; she and the baby bloomed red, and she collapsed.

"Well, laddie, I think I'll go join the party," said Gavin. "Slow now, open your coat and hand me your piece."

Numbly, Peter unbuttoned his heavy mackinaw and slid his revolver out. He handed it butt first to the smiling sergeant major.

"Have a good cry, laddie," the sergeant said, spurring his black horse down the slope.

Peter watched him go; watched Baker sitting calmly near The Heavy Runner's lodge, surrounded by aides and his trumpeter, directing operations. Watched the soldiers massacre Piegans, topple lodges, kill ponies, all unmolested. No one fought back. There was scarcely an able-bodied warrior in the village. It was war on women.

Marie Therese! The thought of her galvanized him. His dumb horror had paralyzed him. He spurred his horse down the rough slope, bouncing hard, heading for Sinopah's lodge far to the right, his heart in his throat. The lodge still stood. He whipped past laughing troops, leapt off his mount just as blue-clad infantrymen closed.

"Don't!" he screamed.

They paused, puzzled.

He plunged in and saw her sprawled on the earth, blood leaking from her mouth.

"Peter!" she cried. She gasped and wept, her breath coming in short, desperate spasms. She'd been shot. A bullet had pierced her back and exited through her right breast.

"Marie Therese!" he cried, plunging down to her, lifting her head to his lap. "Oh, oh, God . . ."

"Peter . . . don't let me die. . . ." she gasped.

"I won't, I won't!"

She panted, sobbing, tears mingling with her blood.

"Don't die, don't die, I love you!" he cried.

He heard infantrymen pull aside the door flap. "Leave me be!" he screamed.

"What good was my life?" she gasped. "What good was it?"

Peter wept.

"Outta the way, Kipp," said Captain Higbee behind him.

"Leave her be!" he screamed.

A terrible blow sent him reeling; the butt of a rifle along his skull. Pain exploded in him. Dizzily he clambered to his hands and knees, fighting the rush of darkness. He heard a shot, violent in the enclosed lodge, and more; each like a cannon discharging in his eardrums.

"Never mind, Kipp," said someone.

He found himself alone, with bullets whipping through the lodge like hornets. His doubled vision cleared and he stared into Marie Therese's gray eyes, which returned his gaze sightlessly. A terrible hole had replaced her mouth. He stared helplessly at the woman he loved, dead on the lodge floor, her blood soaking the earth. Around the lodge lay the bodies of the rest, including Tears in Her Eyes, dead of a bullet wound to her chest. White scabs covered her face.

Numbly he crawled out of the lodge, hoping for the bullet that would send him to wherever Marie Therese's soul was going. But no one fired. Around him soldiers were finishing off the rest.

"Watch out, they got the pox. Don't touch nothing," one shouted.

"I seen the scabs. Git your gloves on. This whole outfit was sick," said another. "Just like Baker to give us the pox."

The smoke of a dozen burning lodges eddied through

the ruined village, the smell of scorched leather and frying flesh offensive to the nostril.

Stupidly Peter stood and then wandered aimlessly while soldiers entered each of the lodges still standing, shot the living and then collapsed the lodge over its lodge fire until great columns of black, foul smoke lifted into the midnight sun. He saw no warriors except a few covered with white scabs, sprawled lifeless in their bloody blankets. Everywhere he saw women and children slumbering in their own blood, often clutching each other in their final terror.

An old man clambered slowly out of a lodge, lifted a rifle and shot a trooper off his horse. Moments later the old man sank into the snow, his body leaking blood from a dozen wounds.

For some unfathomable reason some of the women and children survived, and these the troopers herded into The Heavy Runner's lodge and another next to it. Their wailing scraped mercilessly through Peter's aching brain. Death songs. None of them believed she'd live through the day. He knew most of them: So-at-saki, O-tak-kai, Emonissi, Ips-e-nikki . . . the living dead, their brown faces stained with horror. It was the end of their world. Only the Wolf Trail and the Sand Hills stood before them.

"You having yourself a good cry, Kipp?" asked Colonel Baker, a wry smirk building in his lean, weathered face.

"Marie Therese is dead."

"Some squaw you fancy, eh?"

"I met her on the boat. Coming from St. Louis."

"Some breed, I guess."

"Her and me . . ." He couldn't say the rest.

"Fortunes of war, Kipp."

"This is—was The Heavy Runner's—"

"Yeah, yeah. I saw the old boy's paper. Want to find us another? Lots more down the river a piece, I understand."

"There weren't any warriors here. You've killed women and children. All friends."

"Oh, I don't know about that, Kipp. Lots of warriors in the lodges. They killed a trooper."

"They're out hunting, I think. There's no food in the parfleches."

"You see Owl Child, Kipp? Or the rest of those devils? Mountain Chief got away."

Peter shook his head mutely.

Systematically the troopers heaped the possessions and comforts of the whole village into huge bonfires, whose licking orange flames ate the Lone Eaters. It took them all the morning.

At last Baker ordered his columns to mount.

"What're you gonna do with them prisoners?" asked Gavin.

"Let 'em loose, Paddy. Hand out some hardtack."

"They'll die in the cold!" cried Peter. "They haven't food, they haven't blankets!"

"Tough on 'em, isn't it?" Baker asked.

"What's the count?" asked Lieutenant Doane.

"Oh, who cares? Maybe a hundred twenty warriors, fifty women, and a few nits. We're releasing maybe a hundred. That sound about right?"

The lieutenant grinned, saying nothing.

Peter listened solemnly. There had not been even twenty adult men in this village, and those were infirm or bedridden with the pox. He had walked through the ruins counting the dead, and they numbered over two hundred.

"It's a great victory, sir," said Gavin.

"The Piegans won't forget it."

"You didn't get Owl Child," said Horace Clarke. "Or the rest. You killed a friend."

"Well, Horace, they'll get the message," Baker said. "We got Red Horn. He was on the wanted list."

"Yeah, but I wanted Owl Child. I wanted him all for myself."

"Like I say, kid, they'll get the message."

"Column's mounted and ready, sir," said a lieutenant.

"All right. Come along, Kipp. You'll take us back and I'll report our victory to old de Trobriand at Fort Shaw."

"The people of Montana, they're gonna be cheering, Colonel," said Gavin. "You'll git yourself a hero's parade."

"It's a dirty business," said Baker. "They don't know war."

One mean March day Peter opened his door to find the Blackfoot agent, Lieutenant William Pease, seeking him. That meant talking about the Marias River again, which Peter hated. Curtly, he admitted the man. He scarcely knew Pease, and had no relish for talking with anyone connected with the United States Army.

The slender young officer settled himself uncomfortably in a horsehair settee and stared earnestly at Peter. "I'm sorry to bother you, Mr. Kipp. I was hoping I might talk."

"Well, be about it."

"You lost the woman you loved."

"Little good it does to lament it now," Peter replied harshly, knowing the lieutenant was only seeking common ground.

"I—I wished to talk about things that don't appear in the sensational press," Pease said.

Peter listened. All he'd seen in the Helena papers reaching Fort Benton was lies, lies, and more lies. The whole territory was celebrating. De Trobriand was crowing about Baker, about success, about striking the malefactors. But unfortunately, the general was saying, Mountain Chief and his worst henchmen had somehow escaped. The citizens of the territory had eaten it up, and were busily advocating a second brevet promotion for Baker, savior of Montana.

"I'm tired of army lies," Peter said, deliberately being as insulting as he could. He was tired of white men.

"That's what I've come to talk to you about, Mr. Kipp. Army lies. Would you listen? I want to tell you what's been happening that hasn't been publicized in the inflammatory press."

Peter nodded.

"Perhaps I should begin by telling you I've been relieved of my duties as Blackfoot agent. To put it bluntly, my army career's over before it began. But I'm getting ahead of my story."

Peter nodded, wondering what this earnest young man wanted of him.

"There are terrible discrepancies between what the army is saying publicly and what my Piegans are telling me," the lieutenant continued. "Colonel Baker and the general are saying that a hundred seventy-three were killed, including a hundred twenty able men and fifty-three women and children. About a hundred forty women and children were captured and released.

"But, Mr. Kipp, that isn't what my Piegans have told me. They've come in to the agency—the surviving men, some of the women, and several from the bands that took in the homeless. They were pox-stricken. Every able-bodied man was out hunting, Mr. Kipp. They were on the brink of starving. I wrote General Sully that of the hundred seventy-three, only thirty-three were men, and of those, only fifteen were young or warrior-aged men; ninety were women; fifty were children."

"What good does it do?" Peter asked. "What do you want of me?"

"I'm coming to that. General Sully, sir, is an honorable man. An old Indian fighter he may be, but in his office as the territorial Indian superintendent, he at once forwarded the real figures to the army—and to the Indian Bureau in Washington City. That's what started the uproar back there. I've been branded a liar and told that since I wasn't at the battle, I don't know what I'm talking about." He paused, a rueful smile forming on his serious face. "When you upset the generals, sir—Hardie, Sheridan, and the general of the army himself—Sherman—your career is doomed."

"I'm sorry."

"Don't be. I believe my Piegans. They were talking about their loved ones. They had nothing to hide. As for my career, sir, it is nothing compared to my honor. That, Mr. Kipp, is intact."

"You haven't stated why you're here."

Pease sighed. "There exists in my mind the need for corroboration. I've talked to over twenty survivors and a dozen others who've heard the story. But I need to hear it from someone who is not a Piegan and not an army man. That leaves you and Horace Clarke."

"I don't want to make statements."

"I'm not asking for a public statement, Mr. Kipp. Look—I know you lost a certain woman named Natoya-niskim there. My informants told me you wept as she died. I know she was their prophet. For her sake, would you tell me what happened? Privately? I need that, you see. For my own assurance."

"I don't even want to talk about it. Every day since then I've tried desperately to drive what I saw out of my mind. But it keeps coming back. Lieutenant . . . maybe if I stop bottling it up I can live with it better."

"If you wish, it'll remain private, sir, though I'd like permission to tell General Sully."

Peter came to a decision. "Go ahead. It won't bring Marie Therese back to life."

"Who?"

"Marie Therese de Paris. Natoya-niskim was the daughter of a trader. The death count was over two hundred women and children, and a few old men, or men sick with the pox. I tried to count and couldn't because some of the bodies were under burning lodge covers. The soldiers pulled down the lodges that weren't burning and dragged them to big bonfires, so I could see most of it. There were almost no bodies out in the snow. They'd shot into all the lodges and then cut into the leather sides with knives and finished off the rest. They entered the lodges where the women were weeping and clutching their babies, and shot them. Shot them one by one, ignoring the tears.

"A hundred twenty warriors—what a laugh. If there'd been a hundred twenty in the village, would the army have gotten only one casualty—a soldier shot by an old man after the village was taken? It's all lies. A hundred twenty warriors would have grabbed their rifles and fought back like hornets."

Pease nodded. "What about the captives?"

"There were some. God knows why. They were herded into two lodges, The Heavy Runner's and one next to it. You can't get a hundred forty captives into two lodges. I'd say there were less then twenty women, and about the same number of children."

"The press is jubilating. The bad Indians were all killed off, the guilty ones."

Peter shook his head. "The army killed its friends. Mountain Chief and the wanted men didn't escape—they weren't in the village in the first place. Of the fifteen they wanted, only Red Horn was there, and they got him."

"Didn't you identify the village correctly?"

"Colonel Baker had me held at gunpoint when I told him it was The Heavy Runner's village. He was afraid I'd spoil his surprise. He said one Indian's as good as another."

"I've talked to Horace Clarke, Mr. Kipp. The young man's very angry. He went along to identify the killers of his father, and the one who wounded him—Mountain Chief's son. But of course they weren't in that village. He says the army struck a good friend, The Heavy Runner—and he says Baker was drunk. Was he?"

"No, I don't think so. Not drunk. But the man was amused at the murder of women and children. That smile—while women wept and begged for life and held their infants up to the soldiers, hoping the soldiers would spare them—told me all that I want to know about him."

"Thank you, Mr. Kipp."

"Don't thank me."

"Would you put it in writing?"

"Maybe. Sometime."

Pease stood. "I won't take more of your time. I believed the Indians and I stuck my neck out. Now I have your corroboration. It wasn't in vain." He frowned. "I wonder what I'll do next. Or whether I can survive the damage to my reputation. They're calling me a member of the Indian Ring—an army term for people who enrich themselves in the Indian Bureau. My name may be stained, sir, but not my honor—or my soul."

"I'm glad your soul is unstained."

Lieutenant Pease turned, chagrined. "I'm sorry. I've been thinking about my honor. That could hardly be more—insensitive. You've been thinking about a massacre. Please forgive me."

"It doesn't matter," Peter relented. "You did what you could, and I'm glad you've exposed their lies."

"They call it a great victory, Mr. Kipp. They're jubilating in Helena and Virginia City. Why, Baker and de Trobriand can hardly keep up with all the balls and dinners and parties. They're pushing for an additional brevet for Baker."

"But he disobeyed orders!"

"When you're celebrating a great victory, Mr. Kipp, that's a trifle. Sherman is going to petition congress for Baker's brevet promotion."

"It doesn't matter," said Peter.

Chapter Thirty

One robust April day when the sun was pummeling the last patches of snow into the ground and the earth felt soft beneath Peter's feet, he saddled a horse. Then he saddled a packhorse, adding to his usual camp gear two items: a thick pine headboard and a spade.

He had wrestled long with the wording on that headboard when he was making it at the smithy in his freight yard. He had wanted to burn *Marie Therese de Paris* into the wood with his red-hot iron rod, but surrendered in the end to the name she choose: *Natoya-niskim.* He had carefully penciled it at the top of the board and burned it deep. Then the dates, 1836–1870. And then the answer to her dying question, What good was my life? *A martyr for her people,* he had penciled, and then burned in. After that he had varnished it several times. He wanted it to last awhile—at least as long as his own memory lasted.

He rode north into a glorious spring day, when puffball clouds scudded close to the plains and coy warmth wrestled with the retreating cold. He wondered what he would find on the Marias, and hoped he could cope with the grisly sights he was sure to see. But he had a task to do, and he would do it, even if he did it on all fours, after vomiting up everything in his stomach.

He rode into the ruin of The Heavy Runner's village late that afternoon, grateful for the softer light and spring grasses that hid the worst of it from his eyes. Predators had been at work, and he saw not decaying bodies, but bones scattered everywhere, ribs, femurs, fingers, pelvises, and skulls—with black hair still attached. Wolves and coyotes, eagles, hawks, crows, magpies, skunks, badgers, and a dozen other creatures with sharp beaks and teeth had cleaned away everything edible. He was grateful not to recognize anything or anyone.

The lodges hadn't burned well, and mounds of charred leather that had once been people's homes and trunks and clothes still remained, moldering, with snow caught in creases. It was hard now to locate Sinopah's lodge. Everything looked different in winter light, with light snow on the ground. He had no lodge-cover paintings to guide him now. But after a bitter search, he narrowed the possibilities down, and finally selected one lodge with a scatter of skulls and bones.

Some of them were hers. He stared, swallowing down his sickness. Was that skull hers, or that of Tears in Her Eyes? And which were the bones of the rest, the people they'd taken in? He would never know. Maybe he could bury them all. He dismounted and stared about him. The campsite was glorious in its spring dress. The budding cottonwood leaves were a lacy lime green; the grasses bright and tender; the river dancing and sparkling. It would be a good place for the bones of Marie Therese to spend their eternity. He hoped her soul had gone to wherever she wanted it to go—perhaps the Sand Hills, the barrens far to the north where the Blackfeet believed spirits went—if they were successful.

He found a parfleche he knew was hers. He picked up the soggy leather, recognizing the dyed design. Nothing was in it, and it had been chewed by tiny teeth. This was Sinopah's lodge, then. He would bury all the bones, hers and the rest.

He jabbed his spade into the cold, moist clay and set to work, gradually cutting a trench down three feet, wrestling with roots and rocks. Then, gently, he picked up human bones with his gloved hands and carried them to his trench and laid them to rest. Some of them were hers. He lifted a thong necklace from his neck and lowered it into the hole. From the shadowed earth her father's gold ring and her buffalo amulet, the natoya-niskim, glimmered up at him. He would give these back too. He added the parfleche and the last debris from Sinopah's lodge, and shoveled the yellow clay over the bones.

At the head of the grave he planted his headboard. Then he tamped earth around it and added rock from the bluffs, building a mound that would keep it from falling over for many years. The varnished headboard shone bravely in the setting sun, out of place there.

Peter wasn't any good at prayers, but he pulled off his felt hat and stood, thanking whoever and whatever lord of the universe for her, for her beauty of mind and body, for her friendship and her love. And for her sacrificed and selfless life.

Insensately he grew aware, in the deepening lavender, that he was not alone. His pulse leapt and he feared murder. A Blackfoot man had padded close and stared alongside him.

Sinopah!

Sinopah was weeping.

The old man slid a hand over Peter's shoulder and silently stared at the shadowed grave.

"You have honored the one you loved and the one who was my wife," he said, carefully avoiding the names of the dead.

"Yes. I gave her back her ring and amulet."

"What do the signs say?"

"They say, Natoya-niskim. Then the napikwan dates, 1836–1870. Then it says she sacrificed her life for her people."

"That is a good thing."

"I wanted to answer her dying question. She asked what good her life was."

"She was a holy woman."

"I planned to make camp well away from here, Sinopah. Come join me."

"I will. It is not good to spend the night here. The bad spirits will fly."

They rode upriver a mile or so and made camp on lush spring grass beside the laughing Marias. They ate silently from the tinned food Peter had packed. Peter was glad to keep the fire going; it chased away the evils lurking just beyond their camp.

"We found buffalo," Sinopah said. "All of us. The Cold Maker roared, but we didn't mind. The buffalo were standing in a drift and couldn't move fast. We shot six—enough for all for a few days. At last, Napi and Sun heard our prayers! We butchered and then we rode back to our village, happy to bring food to the poor and the sick. We'd all suffered.

"But there was no village. Only the dead, and all our possessions still burning in great heaps. Our joy turned into tears and cries of disbelief. We wandered about, seeing our wives and babies, our children and old men, sprawled in their own blood! I went to my lodge—but there was no lodge. It lay burning in the great heap. I saw the one who was my woman, and the one who was the vision giver, lying dead. And the others we were caring for. All dead. And everywhere in the snow, the tracks of seizer boots and iron-shod horses.

"Why did they do this? The Heavy Runner was their friend, and he had a friendship paper. We found the paper lying in the snow, its black marks smeared. Our chief lay on his stomach, shot through the chest. Why did they do this, Peterkipp?"

"Because Owl Child shot Four Bears—that's what they said. But mostly because they wanted to kill Pikuni."

Sinopah shook his head. "I will never understand it." He stared sharply at Peter. "It is said that you led the seizers."

Peter doubted he could ever explain. "They wanted me to take them to Owl Child and some of those—in Mountain Chief's village. I told them this was not the village—but I could not stop them."

"Ah. I believe you. Many a Siksika would like to kill Owl Child. He is a murderer of many of us too. And Mountain Chief—he let the young warriors run. But most of the chiefs wanted only peace. Now they are frightened, and many have fled across the medicine line to the protection of the northern napikwan. They are afraid to come here."

"The grandmother's napikwan will treat you just as badly."

Sinopah stood, slowly, peering into the stars. It had turned chill. "The time of the Siksika is over," he said. "We were a brave and great people. Now is the time of the napikwan. They have great magic. We didn't know about guns and powder and steel knives. Those of us who survive the white-scabs disease must change and be very quiet. If we cause them trouble, they will come again and kill our babies and women."

Peter had nothing to add or subtract from that.

Sinopah left in the morning. He had come to see the place of the dying, and now he had seen it. He was living with a cousin among the Grease Melters, who were hunting buffalo near the Cypress Hills.

"I will never come to that place again. It is cursed," he said. "Neither will I go to many-houses. And never will I go to the agency or talk to the nannana again."

Peter shook his head. "I'll never see you again, Sinopah, but I won't forget. You were like a father to me. And you gave a home to the woman I loved, all these years."

"I am your Pikuni father. Maybe we'll meet in the Sand Hills, eh?"

Peter watched the wiry man ride up the north bluffs and vanish into the sky.

He stood alone, caught between past and future, his blood divided. The April morning was achingly sweet. Zephyrs toyed with the supple grasses and teased his red hair. The smells rising from the moist earth filled his nostrils. The astringent smell of the new-leafed sagebrush slid on the breeze. Life stirred, as it always stirred. Soon the silent blue void would be alive to the songs of meadowlarks and the laughter of crows.

Life would give him nothing else. This lonely wilderness was his only world.

Afterword

The central characters in this novel are fictional, but their story is set against real events. Most of the background characters are real. In the scenes leading up to the Baker massacre, and in the story of the massacre itself, I have substituted the fictional character Peter Kipp for the real Joe Kipp, half-Mandan son of James Kipp of the American Fur Company. Because I needed to meld the stories of my central characters with the actual events surrounding the Baker massacre, I have digressed from the historical record in minor ways.

RICHARD S. WHEELER
March 12, 1992